The Forget-Me-Not Summer

Katie Flynn has lived for many years in the north-west. A compulsive writer, she started with short stories and articles and many of her early stories were broadcast on Radio Merseyside. She decided to write her Liverpool series after hearing the reminiscences of family members about life in the city in the early years of the twentieth century. For many years she has had to cope with ME, but has continued to write. She also writes as Judith Saxton.

Katie Flynn

The Forget-Me-Not Summer

arrow books

Published by Arrow Books 2013

10

Copyright © Katie Flynn 2013

Katie Flynn has asserted her right under the Copyright, Designs
and Patents Act, 1988, to be identified as the author of this work.

First published in Great Britain in 2013 by Century

Arrow Books
The Random House Group Limited
20 Vauxhall Bridge Road, London, SW1V 2SA

www.randomhousebooks.co.uk

Addresses for companies within The Random House Group Limited can be found at:
www.randomhouse.co.uk/offices.htm

The Random House Group Limited Reg. No. 954009

A CIP catalogue record for this book
is available from the British Library

Typeset in 11/13.5pt Palatino by Palimpsest Book Production Limited,
Falkirk, Stirlingshire

Penguin Random House is committed to a sustainable future for
our business, our readers and our planet. This book is made from
Forest Stewardship Council® certified paper.

Printed and bound in Great Britain by Clays Ltd, Elcograf S.p.A.

For Barbara Turnbull who has been a good friend and has run the Clwyd Support for M.E. Group so enthusiastically for so long.

My thanks go to my niece, Heather Cross (nee Hague), for drawing my attention to Liverpool's connection to the slave trade. Thank you, Heather.

Note to the reader

Dear Reader,

Long ago, when my niece, Heather Hague, was about twelve, she was taken by her school to an exhibition regarding the slave trade in Liverpool during the eighteenth century. After visiting the exhibition, their teacher took them to the Goree Piazza to see the bucket fountain, which intrigued Heather so much that she told me about both visits in great detail.

For some reason I had not, until then, heard of the Liverpool connection with the 'black birders', as slave traders were called, but when I myself visited the Goree Piazza, I was tremendously impressed by the sculpture which was there then; a most dramatic and intriguing memorial to those men and women, stolen from their own lands, who were brought to this country, auctioned like animals, and worked out the rest of their lives in miserable slavery.

And when I began to think about the plot of *The Forget-Me-Not Summer*, I remembered what Heather had told me and found it the perfect solution for a problem which had haunted me. The mystery of Arabella is never quite solved, but that long ago connection between what goes on in any port and a missing woman began to take shape in my mind. In the thirties, white slave traders were feared in all the English ports and *The Forget-Me-Not Summer* takes place in the thirties and forties, so the story seemed credible and, whilst my heroine, Miranda, searched for her mother, I hoped devoutly that I should find out what had happened to her before the story ended, for, as is so often the case, my characters tell me what is going to happen rather than vice versa.

You cannot see the exhibition of slavery now, and neither can you see the magnificent sculpture of slaves in the Goree Piazza, bearing buckets which tilt as they fill so that the water runs constantly down, progressing from bucket to bucket, in a fascinating and indeed beautiful way, because some councillor or official decided that the splash of water into buckets reminded him of toilets flushing (how odd!!), so he had the sculpture removed, which is sad.

But I still remember the bucket sculpture and my niece's contribution to this particular story with gratitude. Have I got you hooked??

All best wishes,

Katie Flynn

Chapter One

1937

Miranda Lovage was dragged up from fathoms deep in sleep by some unexpected sound. Groggily she sat up on her elbow and peered about the room, suddenly aware that her heart was fluttering. An only child, she shared her room with no one, had it all to herself, but night noises had never previously worried her. Indeed, she seldom heard them, for she usually went to bed late, at the same time as her mother, and slept as soon as her head touched the pillow, continuing to do so until roused by her mother's call up the stairs, or even a hand on her shoulder.

But then Miranda remembered the row which had raged between herself and Arabella – she always called her mother Arabella – earlier that evening. Now that she thought about it, she realised that it had started because she had been telling Arabella that her teachers thought she stood a good chance of getting her School Certificate, perhaps even going to university. She had come home from the Rankin Academy both excited and delighted, and had been horrified when Arabella had said, flatly, that university was out of the question. 'I've done my best to get you a decent education, living in a good neighbourhood and seeing that you were always nicely turned out, with everything the other girls have, even though I've been on my own ever since your father died,' she had said. 'Well, Miranda, I've been meaning to tell you that I've reached the end of my tether. I simply can't afford to go on paying your school fees indefinitely, so I'm afraid that next term you'll have to start at an ordinary council school.' She had wagged a reproving finger when Miranda began to protest. 'Don't try to bully me, Miranda. Just remember you are still a child and have to do as I tell you. Next year you will be at the same school as your cousin Beth . . .'

She would have gone on to explain more fully but Miranda had not been listening. She had been too busy trying to shout her mother down, saying that she had no intention of changing schools, that Arabella must jolly well find the money for the fees from somewhere; she had even suggested that her mother might do 'a real job' instead of hanging round the theatre taking every tuppenny-ha'penny part she was offered.

Arabella had waited until Miranda had run out of breath and had then replied, with a cold finality which had frightened her daughter. 'Miranda, in case you have not noticed, we are in the middle of a depression. I admit my wages from the Madison Players are small, but I'm sure that one day I'll get the sort of parts I deserve and then money will not be so tight. As it is, the only means I have of continuing our present way of life is by what I think of as clipping both our wings. You will go to a council school until you are old enough to work on your own account, and we'll move into a house in one of the courts and take a lodger – two, if necessary – because the rent of this house is crippling me, honest to God, queen. The only alternative is to marry Mr Gervase, that fellow who haunts the stage door . . .'

'A stage-door Johnny?' Miranda had been both scornful and incredulous. 'But you laugh at them, say they've never got two pennies to rub together . . . isn't Mr Gervase that little weaselly one with a bush of grey hair? You scoffed at him, you know you did! You said he ought to be a monk because he had a built-in tonsure. You can't mean to marry him!'

'He's rich,' Arabella had said simply. 'During the week he lives in a service flat. Oh, Miranda, it's the height of luxury. He gets his breakfasts and the most wonderful dinners as part of his rent, and the flat is kept clean as well. And then he's got a mansion in the Lake District – I've always loved the Lakes – and he says that if I marry him, we'll live there whenever I haven't got an important part at the theatre.'

'But you told me ages ago that if you got an important part at the theatre we'd be in clover . . .' Miranda had begun, only to be immediately interrupted.

'Don't rub it in. It was sheer prejudice which got Maria the part of Lady Macbeth instead of me,' Arabella had said hotly. 'So now you jolly well choose, Miranda Lovage: a pauper's existence on our own or a life of pampered luxury with Gervase. And since it would be me who had to put up with him day *and* night, I don't see why you should even be asked which you would prefer.' She had looked sideways at her daughter through her thick, curling, blonde lashes. 'I've told him that *if* I agree to marry him it will be what you might call a marriage of convenience. I shall have my own room, and though we shall share a name I will be like a – a sister to him. Or a housekeeper. Do you understand, Miranda? He is offering me a way out of my difficulties and

3

expecting nothing in return, save for the duties a house-keeper would perform. Of course he hopes I will become truly fond of him as time goes by, but . . .'

But Miranda had heard enough. 'Just because you aren't a good enough actress to earn a decent salary, that doesn't mean I have to suffer,' she had shouted, but even as she did so she realised her own helplessness. Until she was old enough to earn her own living, she really had no choice. Her father had died some years previously, and she knew of no living relative save for her Aunt Vi, her mother's half-sister, and Aunt Vi's daughter Beth, both of whom disliked Arabella and her offspring and would, Miranda knew, be more likely to gloat over the Lovages' misfortune than to offer help.

So when Arabella had said: 'Oh, darling, if I'd got Lady Macbeth . . . or if you'd agreed to my joining that repertory company last year, when I was offered a place – only you didn't want to move up to Scarborough – then we would have managed somehow, but as it is . . .'

She had held out her arms as she spoke and Miranda had hesitated, then heaved a sigh and gone stiffly into her mother's embrace, saying: 'But do try to think of a way out, Arabella. Surely there must be something you could do so I wouldn't have to change schools and houses and everything. I'll think as well, and perhaps between us . . .'

'My dearest little Miranda, do you not realise that I've been racking my brains for a solution ever since the Madison Players gave Lady Macbeth to Maria? Things have got to change. The rent for this house has gone up again; your school fees are downright ridiculous – even the uniform . . . but it's no good talking. It's either marry

4

Mr Gervase or change our whole way of life, and I do think Mr G's offer is extremely generous. However, we'll both sleep on it and tomorrow we'll talk about it again.'

So now Miranda, finding herself abruptly awake, remembered the quarrel and thought it was a miracle that she had ever managed to get to sleep at all. Indeed, it had taken her quite a while to drop off, but having done so she had slept so deeply that for a moment she wondered what on earth could have woken her, apart from a trumpet call, or a brigade of guards marching through the bedroom and exhorting her to get up at once. But judging by the dim light coming from between the curtains, it was still the middle of the night. So what had woken her? Miranda lay down again, but sleep would not come. Suppose her mother had been so upset by the quarrel that she had failed to lock the door, and burglars had entered the house? The Lovages lived in Sycamore Avenue, near Prince's Park, for Arabella Lovage believed appearances were important, and if a thief did ransack their home it would be a major expense. Worse, even, than the increase in the rent and school fees, to say nothing of the smart uniform.

Miranda took a deep breath, slid out of bed and crossed to the window. They were having a hot summer so the casement was up and the night air, warm and scented, came pleasantly into the room. She peered up and down the street, examining their neat little garden and those of the neighbours on either side, but saw no sign of any living soul except for a cat which appeared on the pavement opposite and made its way down the hill, no doubt on some nefarious business of its own.

Miranda squatted on the comfortable bench beneath

5

the open window trying to guess what had disturbed her. Suddenly it came to her. It must have been the front door closing; she guessed that Arabella, to calm her nerves and forget their quarrel, had decided to take a walk before coming up to bed. Miranda knew she sometimes did this and was reassured by the thought. But perhaps she really ought to go downstairs and make sure that Arabella was all right, and had locked the door against night-time intruders.

But the annoyance she had felt over her mother's arbitrary decision to take her away from her school or present her with Gervase as a stepfather still rankled. Arabella had no right to change their whole way of life without consulting her. Well, all right, she had consulted her, but it wasn't much of a consultation! Live in penury or accept that ugly old man as a stepfather. Drowsily, she decided that there was no need to investigate. If her mother needed a period for quiet reflection and had chosen to go walking in the middle of the night, that was her affair. Miranda got off the bench and returned to her bed, suddenly conscious of chilled feet and the flimsiness of her white cotton nightie. She cuddled down, pulling the sheet up round her ears, and this time, as her body warmed into a delicious glow, she slept.

Afterwards, she could never decide at what moment her life had truly changed. Had it been when she heard the sound which had woken her from her deep and peaceful sleep? Or had it been next morning, when nobody woke her, and she was left to wash in the tiny bathroom on her own and to struggle into her clothes whilst her heart beat a wild tattoo, for when she had put her head round her mother's door there was no one there and Arabella did not answer Miranda's shout. Galloping down the stairs, she had burst into the kitchen expecting to see her mother turn from the stove with a smile and apologise for not waking her even as she spooned creamy porridge into two small earthenware bowls, before exhorting her daughter to eat her breakfast whilst it was hot.

But the kitchen was empty, nobody stood by the table, the curtains were still drawn across the windows and when Miranda ran to the back door, to check that her mother was not in the garden, it was unlocked.

Miranda stood in the cold kitchen and big tears welled up in her eyes. Arabella must have gone for a walk, and something must have happened to her! Suppose she had fallen, or been attacked by some wicked person intent upon stealing her fine gold chain with the locket, or her thin little wedding ring, who had then left her unconscious in the gutter? Suddenly, their quarrel seemed of no significance; what mattered now was the whereabouts of her beautiful, talented mother. That she was beautiful had never been in question and now Miranda told herself, loyally, that only jealousy and spite had prevented Arabella's talent from carrying her to the very top of her profession.

Miranda burst out of the house and looked wildly up and down the street. What should she do? She must go to the neighbours, get help, contact the police. She knew she should do one or all of these things, but she was, after all, only thirteen, and had never had to take a decision without consulting an adult in her life. So she returned to the kitchen and simply sat down at the table, put her head on her folded arms and began to weep in earnest.

When someone knocked on the back door she flew across to it, wrenching it open and almost falling into the arms of the girl standing there. 'Miranda! What on earth's the matter? You don't look as though you're ready for school; aren't you well?'

Miranda stared at her friend, who often called for her so that they might walk to school together. 'Oh, Louise, it's you. I thought it was my mother . . . oh, Lou, I heard something in the night which woke me up, and when I came down for breakfast this morning, Arabella had gone.'

'I 'spect she ran out of milk or bread or something and has gone down to the shops to buy some more,' Louise said cheerfully. 'Why are you in such a taking? But for God's sake make your own breakfast or we'll be late for school.'

'But there's no note; if my mother means to go anywhere she always leaves me a note,' Miranda said, but she was insensibly cheered by the other girl's easy acceptance of the situation. Perhaps Louise was right and her mother had simply slipped out to buy milk; there was a delivery every morning but sometimes it came too late for breakfast. Hastily, Miranda went to the pantry, and her hopeful heart dropped into her neat button shoes once more; there was a good three quarters of a loaf and a whole pint of milk left, besides all the usual things: porridge oats, butter, jam and a couple of the little milk rolls she always took to school for elevenses.

Turning, she saw that her practical friend had filled the kettle, put it on the stove and lit the gas, and was looking at her expectantly. Then Louise seized the loaf from its place on the shelf and cut two rather chunky

8

slices, buttered them briskly, and pushed them and the jam pot across to her friend. 'Come along, Miranda,' she said impatiently, 'we've not got all day. Your mam will be back in time to get your tea. Did she take the key with her? We don't want to lock her out.' Miranda crossed the room and checked the hiding place: no key. She returned to the kitchen, went across to where her school blazer hung on its peg, and checked again. Her key was in the pocket. She said as much to Louise who nodded with satisfaction. 'There you are then!' she said triumphantly. 'Your mam realised she needed something from the shops, unlocked the back door, tucked the key in her jacket pocket, and went off. That means that when we leave – do eat up, Miranda, or we'll be late for class – we can lock the back door and know we're not shutting her out.'

Miranda stared doubtfully at her friend's bright, self-confident face. Louise was almost a year older than she and far more worldly wise. She must be right; her own abrupt awakening in the night must have had an innocent cause. Miranda finished her breakfast and tidied round quickly so that her mother would not have to do so on her return, for during the quarrel the previous evening Arabella had claimed, with justice, that her daughter never helped in the house, made her own bed or offered to do the messages. When she sees the nice tidy kitchen she'll know she misjudged me, Miranda told herself defiantly. And I'll make our tea just as soon as I get home from school; that'll show her!

'Come on, slowcoach,' Louise said, helping herself to a round of bread and butter and shoving it into her mouth rather less than delicately. 'Here's your blazer.'

'Thanks,' Miranda said, shrugging it on and locking the back door carefully behind them. 'What's our first subject, Lou? Oh, *not* French! I didn't learn that poem last night – Mum and I had a bit of a disagreement – but if you'll hear me when we're on the tram I'll get it lodged in my brain somehow, before Mamselle asks awkward questions.'

When Miranda returned home from school later that day, however, it was to find a deputation from the theatre awaiting her outside the house in Sycamore Avenue. The manager, Tom Fox, Miss Briggs the wardrobe mistress, Lynette Rich, who was a member of the chorus, and Alex Gordon, the theatre's leading man, had all come along. They wanted to know if Arabella was ill because there had been a matinée performance that day and she had neither arrived at the theatre nor sent a message to say she was unwell. Miranda nearly fainted, but fortunately Louise was with her and between the two of them they explained the little they knew.

Arabella's colleagues gazed at one another before saying that the police must be informed and ordering Miranda to unlock the door so that they could search the house to see if there were any clues as to why on earth their bit-part player and assistant stage manager should suddenly disappear. Only the wardrobe mistress seemed to realise that this was a body blow for Arabella's daughter. 'You can't stay here tonight, chuck,' she said kindly. 'Not all by yourself, at any rate. Got any aunties, have you? You could move in with 'em for a few days, just till your mam turns up again, which she's bound to do.'

'I dunno,' Miranda said doubtfully. 'I've got an aunt and a cousin that live up Old Swan, but I don't know them very well. Couldn't I – couldn't I stay here, if Lou's mum will let her stay with me? My mother can't have gone far. Oh, I wonder . . . does anyone know where Mr Gervase lives? She – she was talking about marrying him, though I can't believe she'd really do it. But she might have gone to his house to talk things over, I suppose.'

'She could have gone anywhere, lighting out without a word to a soul,' Alex Gordon said irritably, and Miranda saw the wardrobe mistress give him an angry look and flap a hand to shut him up. Alex, however, was clearly more annoyed than worried. 'Typical of a bloody woman to bugger off without a word to anyone. Arabella's got a contract, the same as the rest of us, but if she's prepared to let us down in mid-run . . .' He turned angrily to Miranda. 'Do you mean that stage-door Johnny? He's got a service flat in the city centre. I went there once, so I'll nip round and hear what he has to say. If she really means to marry him, though . . . to let us down without a word . . .'

Now it was the manager's turn to scowl at Alex. 'She's never let us down before, and I see no reason why you should think the worst,' he said angrily. 'Just you mind your tongue, Alex Gordon, or it'll be you searching for a company prepared to take you on, because you can say goodbye to the Madison Players.'

The man muttered something like 'That'll be your loss' but said no more, and Lynette Rich cut in before more acid comments could be exchanged. 'I'll go to the flat, find out what Mr Gervase knows,' she said. 'If Arabella's not there and he can't help us, I suppose I'd better take

Miranda up to her aunt's house, since she can't possibly stay here alone, though I'm sure Arabella will be home before dark. I'll pack a bag with the kid's night things and that and leave a note for Arabella, explaining what we've done.' She turned to Miranda and gave her a reassuring smile. 'Your mam will be home tomorrow, sure as check,' she said. 'I'm rare fond of Arabella, 'cos I've known her these past six years, and to my knowledge she's never done a mean thing or let anyone down before.' She glared at Alex, then held out a hand to Miranda. 'Come and help me pack a bag with a few bits and pieces to last you till your mam gets home.' She turned to the rest of the players. 'You'll do the necessary? I'm sure Arabella will be back tomorrow, but just in case, the scuffers ought to be told, and the neighbours . . .' She glanced uneasily at Miranda. 'Now don't you worry, chuck, it's just a precaution, like.'

So saying, she led the way into the house and let Miranda take her up to her bedroom where the two of them packed a bag with rather more clothing than Miranda thought necessary, but, as her new friend pointed out, you could never tell what you might need until you needed it. As they crossed the room, Miranda took one last look around her and suddenly realised that she was saying farewell to her own little room, for a while at least. She would have to share not only her cousin's bedroom, but maybe her bed as well, and she knew that her aunt despised her half-sister's feckless ways. But then Beth and Aunt Vi were not beautiful or talented, Miranda reassured herself; they were just ordinary, as she was. Nevertheless she lingered in the bedroom doorway and, on impulse, ran back into the room and snatched the beautiful old-fashioned looking-glass, with its gilt cherubs and swags of gilded fruit, from its hook on the wall. She loved that little mirror and told herself that it would be safer with her than in an empty house. She tucked it into the top of the bag she and Lynette had packed and set off, leaving the only home she had ever known behind her.

Though she did not know it, she would never again sleep in that cosy little bed, or bask in the solitude of her lovely room. In fact, her life would never be the same again.

For the first few weeks of her sojourn in Jamaica Close, Miranda was so unhappy and so bewildered that nothing seemed real. Arabella neither returned nor got in touch, and Mr Gervase had been as puzzled – and upset – as Miranda herself. She felt as though she were enclosed in a glass case, through which she could see people and movement, but could make no sense of what was said. She had terrifying dreams in which she saw Arabella's body floating in the dock, or cast up by the roadside after a fatal accident. She began to see her mother – or someone very like her – in the street and would run in pursuit, sometimes even following a woman on to a tram or a train, only to realise, with sickening disappointment, that this was yet another stranger whose resemblance to Arabella was so slight that she wondered how she could possibly have made such a mistake.

Things simply grew worse when Mr Gervase, saying ruefully that he had always known Arabella was too good for him, left the city, whilst the police stopped being comforting and simply said that she must remain with her aunt in the little house in Jamaica Close until such time as her mother chose to return. To her horror, the contents of the house in Sycamore Avenue had to be sold, as Arabella had owed a month's rent, and now Miranda was dependent on Aunt Vi if she needed so much as a tram fare.

But she continued her search. Desperate, she asked everyone in the Avenue if they had seen Arabella that fateful night, and very soon it was commonly accepted, as Mr Gervase had clearly believed, that she had gone off with some man. This cruel slander was backed up when word got around that a handsome young acrobat, working at a larger and more prestigious theatre in the city, had disappeared on the same day as Arabella. Perhaps it was this that persuaded the police, and the Madison Players, to say that they had done all they could, although they advised Miranda to keep on asking around. However, it was soon clear to her that Arabella's disappearance was something of a nine-day wonder, and the nine days were up.

Because she was living in a nightmare, the attitudes of her aunt and cousin did not bother her at first, but gradually it was borne in upon her that her mother's half-sister had cared nothing for the younger woman. She began to realise that Aunt Vi and Beth actually resented her, hard though she tried to be useful, and her unhappiness was so intense that she would have run away, save that she had nowhere to run. She would simply have to endure until she was old enough to leave Jamaica Close. Then she would concentrate on searching for her mother, because she was sure she had a better chance of finding Arabella once she was able to leave her aunt's malignant influence. She knew Aunt Vi did not believe her half-sister would ever return.

Perhaps because Aunt Vi was much older than Arabella, the two women had not really known one another very well. Arabella had taken Miranda to see her aunt and her cousin Beth in Jamaica Close perhaps twice a year, once at Christmas and once in summer, but had never attempted any sort of friendship. She had explained to Miranda that their mother had been a gentle soul, but that her first husband had been totally different from her second. Vi's father had been a warehouseman and a bully, and Arabella had confided in her daughter that when he was killed in an industrial accident her gran must have heaved a sigh of relief. 'She couldn't stand up to him; she wasn't that sort of person,' she had said. 'But despite the life he had led her, your gran – my mum – was still a very pretty woman. Then John Saunders fell in love with her and they got wed; I was their only child and your aunt thought I was spoiled rotten.' She had sighed. 'Compared to the way Vi had been brought up, I guess I was. The thing is, though, it didn't make for a happy relationship between her and myself, so I wasn't sorry when she got married and moved away.'

The young Miranda had nodded her comprehension. She had seen the spiteful glances cast at her mother when they met her aunt, had heard the muttered comments, indicating that Vi thought Arabella was what she called toffee-nosed, too big for her boots, and considered herself above ordinary folk.

And so she might, because she *was* better than other folks, the young Miranda had thought rebelliously.

Arabella was not just pretty, she was very beautiful. She had a great mass of curly white-gold hair, skin like cream and the most enormous pair of blue eyes, the very colour of the forget-me-not flowers she loved. And those eyes were framed by curling blonde lashes whilst her eyebrows, two slender arcs, were blonde as well.

Aunt Vi, on the other hand, was short and squat, with sandy hair and a round, harsh face, for she took after her father, whereas Arabella's looks seemed to have come from their mother. Miranda would have loved to look like that too, but in fact she did not. To be sure, Arabella often congratulated her on her colouring; her hair was what her mother called Plantagenet gold, but kids in the street called carrot, or ginger. 'When you're older, it will darken to a beautiful deep auburn,' Arabella had been fond of saying. 'You're going to be a real little beauty one of these days; you'll knock me into a cocked hat, so you will.'

But Miranda had no desire to knock anyone into anything. She had no urge to be an actress, though she admired her mother tremendously, and was proud of her. However, it was one thing to be proud of someone, and quite another to wish to emulate them. Miranda's own ambitions were far less exotic. She wanted to be a writer of books and had already hidden away in her bedroom cupboard a number of wonderfully imaginative fairy stories. To be sure, these stories were often connected with the theatre – perhaps one day she would turn them into plays – but wherever her writing ended up, it was her secret hope for the future.

Now, though, nothing was important but to find Arabella and escape from the horrors of life in Jamaica

Close, for after the first few days, during which Aunt Vi and Beth had pretended anxiety for her mother and affection for herself, they began to show their true colours. They had disliked Arabella and now they disliked her daughter, besides resenting her presence in the dirty, neglected little house. She was forced to sleep in a creaking and smelly brass bedstead with her cousin Beth, who was a year older than she, though they were now in the same class at the council school, for Beth was slow-witted and Miranda was bright. The pair of them did not have the bed to themselves, however; fat Aunt Vi took up more than her fair share of the thin horsehair mattress – she kept promising to buy another bed, since she had sold Miranda's beloved mirror, but so far had failed to do so – and grumbled every night that her bleedin' sister might have taken her horrible brat with her when she ran off. Miranda tried to ignore such jibes, but when she had nightmares she soon learned to slip out of bed and go down to the kitchen, for if her cries woke her aunt she would speedily find herself being soundly slapped, whilst her aunt shouted that she was a selfish little bitch to disturb folk who had been good enough to take her in.

Another threat was that she would be sent to an orphanage, but Miranda thought that as long as she was useful she need not fear such a fate. Beth was lazy and spoilt, encouraged by her mother never to do her share around the house, and very soon Miranda got all the nastiest jobs. So when her aunt pretended her young half-sister had dumped her child and gone off just to annoy them, Miranda said nothing, deciding that the remark was too stupid to even merit a reply.

The members of the cast at the theatre had done their best to persuade the police, and anyone else who was interested, that Arabella Lovage was not the sort of woman to simply walk out on her colleagues and friends and particularly not on her daughter. But unfortunately the police had felt it incumbent upon them to visit Aunt Vi and had gained a very different picture of the missing woman there.

'She'll ha' gone orf with that young feller she's been seein', the acrobat, you mark my words,' her aunt had assured everyone. 'Oh aye, a right lightskirt, our Arabella.'

For a few moments anger had driven Miranda out of her glass case, and she had shouted at her aunt that this was a wicked falsehood. The Players had agreed that they were sure their fellow actor had had nothing to do with any young man, save Gervase, who could scarcely be described as young. It was he who had discovered that the rival company's acrobat had also gone missing, leaving his lodgings and the variety show on the very day that Arabella had disappeared.

Furious, Miranda had assured anyone who would listen that her mother would never have left her to go off with a man, but though she knew, with utter certainty, that her mother would never have willingly deserted her, she stopped repeating her conviction. She felt life was stacked against her, that the harder she tried, the less convincing she became. So she retreated into her glass case and simply waited.

After the first month of bewildered misery, Miranda had stopped expecting the door to open and her mother to reappear. She had forced herself to face up to the fact that something had happened to keep Arabella from her, and when spiteful remarks were made by Aunt Vi, indicating that Arabella had deliberately landed her with her unwanted daughter, she simply folded her lips tightly and said nothing. What, after all, was the point? She and the cast at the theatre had tried hard enough, heaven knew, to make the authorities take Arabella Lovage's case seriously, but with little success. The police had gone over the house with a fine-tooth comb, searching for any clue as to Arabella's disappearance or evidence of foul play; there had been none. They had asked Miranda if any clothing was missing, but she could not say. Arabella's wardrobe bulged with garments; for all her daughter knew, she might have taken away a dozen outfits without Miranda's being any the wiser. In fact, she could not even remember what her mother had been wearing that last evening.

Only one small indication, several weeks after Arabella's disappearance, caused people to raise their brows and become a little less certain that she had gone of her own free will. One dark night, Miranda was woken from a deep slumber by someone shaking her shoulder and speaking to her in a rough, kindly voice.

'What's up, me love? Good thing it's a fine night, but if you asks me them clouds up there mean business.' The hand on her shoulder gave a little squeeze. 'Lost your way to the privy, queen? My goodness, I know it's not as cold as last night, but you've got bare feet and the road's awful rough, and there was you walkin' down the middle of the carriageway as though you'd never heard of cars, trams or buses . . .'

Miranda, completely bewildered, opened sleep-drugged eyes and stared about her. In the bright moonlight everything looked very different; the shadows black as pitch, the moonlight dazzlingly white. She looked down at her feet and saw that they were indeed bare, as well as very dusty and dirty. Then her eyes travelled up her white cotton nightie and across to the man bending over her. He was a policeman, quite young, and his expression was puzzled. 'Where's you come from, chuck? I don't know as I reckernise you. How did you get here?'

Miranda's brows knitted; how had she come here? Where was here, anyhow? She shook her head. 'I dunno,' she mumbled. 'Where am I? It doesn't look much like Jamaica Close to me.'

The policeman hissed in his breath. 'Jamaica Close?' he said incredulously. 'Is that where you come from, queen?' He stood back and Miranda looked up into his face properly for the first time. It was a young face, and pleasant; a trustworthy face, she decided. But he was giving her shoulder another gentle shake and repeating his question: 'Have you come from Jamaica Close?'

Miranda looked wildly about her, but could recognise nothing. Reluctantly, she nodded. 'I suppose I must have walked from there to wherever we are now,' she said slowly, 'only I must have done it in my sleep because I don't remember anything. I guess I was searching for my mother; she's disappeared. Only I know she's still alive somewhere and needing me.'

The policeman stared, then nodded slowly. 'Oh aye, you'll be Arabella Lovage's daughter. Well, you won't find her here, my love, so I guess I'd best take you back home again. You live up the Avenue, don't you?'

Miranda heaved a sigh, realising suddenly that she

was terribly tired and wanted nothing more than her bed. Even a miserable little four inches of mattress, which was all she managed to get at Aunt Vi's house, would be preferable to standing in the cold moonlight whilst she tried to explain to a total stranger why she no longer lived up the Avenue.

But explain she must, of course, and managed to do so in a few quick words. The scuffer pulled a doubtful face. 'That's well off my beat, chuck, so perhaps the best thing will be for the pair of us to walk back to the station. The sarge is a good bloke; he'll get you a cup of tea and see that someone – probably me – takes you home. I reckon there'll be a fine ol' to-do in Jamaica Close when they find you're missing.'

They carried out the policeman's suggestion, and as he had assumed he was told to accompany Miranda back to her aunt's house. First, though, because of the chill of the night, he wrapped her in a blanket and sat her on the saddle of his bicycle so that she was pushed home in some style, and for the first time in many weeks she felt that somebody cared what became of her.

They reached the house to find the back door standing open, but it soon became clear that she had not been missed. The policeman, who told her his name was Harry, was rather shocked and wanted to wake the household, but Miranda begged him not to do so and he complied, though only after she had promised to come to the station the next day to discuss what had happened. 'For we can't have young ladies wanderin' barefoot in the streets, clad only in a nightgown,' he told her. 'I'm on duty tomorrow from three in the afternoon so you'd best come to the station around four o'clock; I'll see you there.'

Miranda slipped into the house, closed the door behind her and went up to bed. Beth moaned that her feet were cold, but then fell immediately asleep once more and made no comment when the family awoke the following day.

Miranda, usually the most eager of pupils, sagged off school and went straight to the theatre, because she wanted at least one member of the cast to hear about her weird experience, a desire that was fully justified by the excitement her story engendered.

'If you walks in your sleep, ducks, then it's quite likely your mam did as well,' Miss Briggs informed her. 'Runs in families that does, sleepwalkin' I mean. In times of stress some folk can go miles; I've heard of women catchin' trams or buses – trains, even – when they's sound asleep and should be in their beds. If your mam was loose on the streets, someone could ha' took advantage.' She gave Miranda a jubilant hug. 'Mebbe we're gettin' somewhere at last. Wharra lucky thing it were a scuffer what found you. He'll know full well you didn't make nothin' up and mebbe they'll start searchin' for Arabella all over again. Oh, if your mam's e'er to be found we'll find her, don't you fret.'

But the days turned into weeks, and the weeks into months, and both dreams and nightmares grew rarer. The picture of Arabella which Miranda kept inside her head never faded, but Miranda's pretty clothes grew jaded and dirty whilst hope gradually receded, though it never disappeared altogether.

Harry, the policeman, became a friend and Miranda knew it was he who was responsible for notices which appeared around the city asking for information as to the whereabouts of Arabella Lovage, the beautiful actress who had charmed the citizens of Liverpool whenever she appeared on the stage. The cast, too, clubbed together to pay for notices in the papers, begging anyone with information as to Arabella's whereabouts to come forward. They might have enquired also for the young acrobat, but since it seemed he had left the theatre under a slight cloud, and Miranda objected vociferously to any linking of her mother's name with his, they did not. Gradually, Miranda began to accept the terrible change in her circumstances until it was almost as though she had had two lives. The first one, a life of pleasure and luxury, was gone for ever; the second one, of penury and neglect, had come to stay, at least until she could claw her way out of the hateful pit into which she had been dragged.

There had been many advantages to the life she had lived in Sycamore Avenue, and very few indeed to the one she now endured. Her cousin Beth occasionally showed signs of humanity, appearing to want if not friendship at least mutual tolerance, but Miranda ignored such overtures as were offered. She became, almost without knowing it, a sort of Cinderella, a general dogsbody, belonging to no one and therefore ordered about by everyone. She was not even sure that she cared particularly; why should she? She had a strong will, however, and beneath all her outward meekness there gradually blossomed a determination to succeed. She felt she was just marking time, waiting for something wonderful to happen. So she continued to work conscientiously at school, made no objection when her clothes grew shabbier, the food on her plate shrank to the leftovers no one else wanted, and her share of the housework grew heavier and heavier. Once or twice Beth, who wasn't such a bad creature after all, gave her a hand, or put in a word for her; sometimes even stole food for her, but by and large, had she but realised it, Miranda was playing a waiting game. Arabella Lovage, she reminded herself half a dozen times a day, had disliked her half-sister, and would have moved heaven and earth rather than have her daughter live in the dirty, dilapidated house in Jamaica Close. If Arabella could see her daughter now, pale, dirty, always hungry and bitterly overworked, she would tell her miserable half-sister what she thought of her and whisk Miranda off back to the Avenue and the life they had both enjoyed.

But that time had not yet come, and the weeks continued to turn into months until at last it was a whole year, and the hope which had brightened the eyes of the Madison Players grew dim. Then the acrobat returned. He told anyone who was interested that he had got a job with the circus for the remainder of the summer season and then gone on to act in panto – a scene in the giant's kitchen, his ex-colleagues guessed – and had met and married one of the chorus to their mutual pleasure, though this romantic narrative was slightly tempered by the fact that the chorus girl had just announced she would be having a baby before Christmas.

Folk who had been convinced that Arabella had fled with the acrobat had to eat their words, but by now few people thought twice about it. Miranda, who had never believed it anyway, was shocked by her own lack of surprise; why should she be surprised, indeed? But perhaps it was then that little by little Miranda's confidence in her mother's return began to trickle slowly away. She thought afterwards that it bled away, as if from a horrible wound which would not heal, and the worst thing was there was nothing she could do about it. She knew she should fight against the way her aunt treated her, she knew she should tell somebody – Harry, or one of her teachers, or some other responsible adult – but she was too weary. Money was short as the Depression bit deeper and deeper. If you argued about the price of a simple apple in the market the stallholder would throw the Depression in your face. If you chopped kindling, ran messages, or carted heavy buckets of water, where once a few coppers would be pressed into your hand now you were lucky to be given a ha'penny, or maybe a cut off a homemade loaf with a smear of margarine. Yes, times were hard, and if it hadn't been for Steve . . .

Chapter Two

'Lovage! Drat the girl, where's she got to?'

Miranda, who was awaiting her turn to jump into the skipping rope being expertly twirled by two of the older girls who lived in the small cul-de-sac, stood up and headed for the steps of Number Six, upon the top one of which her Aunt Vi stood. She hung back a little, however, for her aunt's expression was vengeful, and even from halfway across the paving Miranda could see her hand preparing for a slap.

'Yes, Aunt?' she said, knowing that it would annoy Aunt Vi if she spoke nicely; her aunt would have preferred impudence so she could strike out with a clear conscience. Not that she would hesitate to hit her niece if the fancy took her, as Miranda knew all too well. Aunt Vi waited for her to get closer, and when she failed to move began to swell with indignation, even her pale sandy hair seeming to stand on end.

'Come *here*, I say,' she shouted, her voice thin with spite. 'Why can't you ever do as you're told, you lazy little madam? There's your poor cousin sick as a cat, smothered in perishin' spots, and instead of givin' me a hand to nurse her, you're off a-pleasurin'. Considerin' it was you give my poor girl the measles . . .'

'She might have caught them off anyone.'

'No; it were bloody well you what passed them on,'

her aunt said aggressively. 'Why, you were still a-scrawpin' and a-scratchin' at the spots when my poor Beth began to feel ill. And now she's been and gone and thrown up all over her bed and the floor, so since it's your bleedin' fault you can just git up them stairs and clean up.' She grinned spitefully as her niece approached the front door, then scowled as the girl looked pointedly at her right hand.

'If you so much as raise your arm you can clear up the mess yourself,' Miranda said bluntly. 'When I was sick and ill you never even brought me a cup of water, but you expect me to wait on Beth. Well, I won't do it if you so much as touch me, and if you try anything else I'll tell the scuffers.'

It would be idle to pretend that the spiteful look left her aunt's face, but she moved to one side and made no attempt to interfere as Miranda squiggled past. Miranda had lately discovered that Vi did not want anything to do with the police, and though mention of Harry's name might not save her from all her aunt's wrath it certainly made Vi think twice before hitting her without reason.

But right now she had work to do and if her aunt had bothered to use her brain she might have realised that Miranda was perfectly willing to clear up the mess. Not only because she shared Beth's bed, but also because she and Beth were getting on slightly better. Whilst Miranda herself had had the measles Beth had brought food up to her occasionally, and had insisted that her cousin should have a share of anything soft that was going. Thanks to Beth, Miranda had kept body and soul together with bread and milk. Now Miranda was actually quite happy to do as much for her cousin, so she went into the kitchen, poured water from the kettle into a bucket, added a scrubbing brush and a bar of strong yellow soap and hurried upstairs. And it was nowhere near as bad as she had feared; the bed seemed to have escaped altogether, and though Beth, lying back on her pillows, was clearly still feeling far from well, it was the work of a moment for Miranda to clean the floor and to grin cheerfully at her cousin. 'Awful, isn't it?' she said. 'The first three days are the worst, but then you begin to realise you ain't goin' to die after all.' She stood the bucket down by the door and sat on the sagging brass bedstead. 'Poor ol' Beth! But at least you'll get all sorts of nice things once you feel a bit better; I had to exist on bread and milk. No wonder I were weak as a kitten and could scarcely climb the stairs.'

Beth sniffed. 'You were lucky to get bread and milk,' she said sullenly. 'Mam wanted to give you bread and water; said milk were too rich . . . well, conny onny was, at any rate. So if it weren't for me sneakin' a spoonful on to your bread and water you'd likely still be in bed and covered in spots.' She pulled a face. 'And aren't you the lucky one? When you had measles it was term time so you missed school, but me, I got 'em on the very first day of the summer holidays.' She glared at her cousin. 'I tell you, you're lucky you even had pobs.'

'You're probably right and I'm real grateful to you,' Miranda said. 'But if you don't mind me sayin' so, Beth, your mam isn't very sensible, is she? When I were ill and couldn't clean or cook or scrub, she had to do all my work whilst you got the messages and prepared the meals. You'd have thought she'd be keen to get me back on me feet, and that would have happened a good deal quicker if I'd had some decent grub now and then.' She sighed. 'Sometimes the smell of scouse comin' up the stairs tempted me to go down and ask for a share – like Oliver Twist, you know – but I guessed I'd only get a clack round the ear and I could do without that.'

She waited, half expecting her cousin to react angrily, for though Beth must know how badly her cousin was treated neither of them ever referred to it aloud. Now, however, Beth gave Miranda a malicious smile. 'Your mam spoiled you when you lived in the Avenue, made sure you got the best of everything going,' she said. 'And my mam gives me the best what's on offer; you can't blame her for that.' Her eyes had been half closed, but now they opened fully and fixed themselves on Miranda's face. 'You're an extra mouth to feed; Mam's always saying so, and neither you nor your perishin' missin' mother contributes a brass farthing to this house. You don't pay any of the rent, nor a penny towards the messages, so don't you grumble about my mam, because you're just a burden, you!'

This was said with such spite that Miranda's eyes rounded. She had always supposed that Beth was jealous of her because she was encouraged to be so by her mother. Aunt Vi knew that Miranda was a good deal cleverer than Beth and found this alone difficult to forgive. But now Beth had made it plain that she resented her cousin on her own account, so to speak. Or perhaps it was just the measles talking? Miranda hoped so, but got off the bed and headed for the door, telling herself that she did not have to stop and listen to her cousin's outpourings. It was true that she did not contribute to the rent of Number Six, but she thought indignantly that on all other counts her cousin was way out. She washed and scrubbed, dusted and tidied, peeled potatoes and prepared vegetables, and sometimes even cooked them, though usually under her aunt's supervision. When she earned a penny or two by running messages or chopping kindling, she was usually forced to hand over the small amount of money she had managed to acquire, whereas Beth got sixpence pocket money each week, and quite often extra pennies so that she might attend the Saturday rush at the Derby cinema, or buy herself a bag of homemade toffee from Kettle's Emporium on the Scotland Road. With her hand on the doorknob, Miranda was about to leave the room when a feeble voice from the bed stopped her for a moment. 'I'm thirsty,' Beth whined. 'I want a drink. Mam went up to the Terrace to get advice on how to look after me and Nurse said I were to have plenty of cool drinks; things like raspberry cordial, or lemonade. Get me both, then I'll choose which to drink.'

The words 'Get 'em yourself' popped into Miranda's head and were hastily stifled; no point in giving her cousin ammunition which she might well hand on to her mother, who would see that Miranda suffered for her sharp tongue. Instead, she pretended she had not heard and went quietly out of the room, shutting the door on Beth's peevish demand that she bring the drinks at once . . . at once, did she hear?

When Miranda entered the kitchen she found her aunt sitting at the table with last night's *Echo* spread out before her and a mug of tea to hand. Miranda contemplated saying nothing about raspberry cordial or lemonade – after all, her aunt had said that she herself intended to be her daughter's principal nurse – but realised that it would be unwise to irritate the older woman any further. Whilst Vi's sudden protective interest in Beth lasted, which would not be for very long, Miranda guessed, she would take offence at any tiny thing, and when Aunt Vi took offence Miranda headed for the hills. She went outside and emptied her bucket down the drain, then walked down to the pump and rinsed it out before returning to the kitchen. 'Beth wants a drink, either raspberry cordial or lemonade,' she said briefly. 'Did you buy 'em when you were out earlier, Aunt Vi? If so, I'll pour some into a jug and take it upstairs . . . unless you would rather do it yourself?'

She had not meant to sound sarcastic, but realised she had done so when her aunt's hard red cheeks began to take on a purplish tinge. Hastily, she went into the pantry and scanned the shelves until she spotted a bottle of raspberry cordial. Pouring some into a jug, she mixed it with water and, making sure first that her aunt's back was turned, took a cautious sip. It was delicious. The nicest thing she had tasted over the past twelve months, she told herself dreamily, heading for the stairs. Lucky, lucky Beth! When I had the measles all I got was water to drink and old copies of the *Echo* to read. Earlier she had seen a big pile of comics beside the bed – *Chicks' Own*, *The Dandy*, *The Beano* and *The Girl's Own Paper* – and had offered to read them to her cousin. Beth, however, clearly thought this a ruse on Miranda's part to get at the comics and had refused loftily. 'You can't read pictures,' she had said. 'And comics is all about pictures, not words. Go off and buy yourself comics if you're so keen on 'em, 'cos you ain't havin' mine.'

Upstairs, balancing jug and glass with some difficulty,

Miranda got the bedroom door open and glanced cautiously across to the bed. Beth was a pretty girl, dark-haired and dark-lashed with large toffee brown eyes and a neat little nose, but today, flopped against her pillows, she looked like nothing so much as a stranded fish. Her skin was so mottled with spots that she could have been an alien from outer space; her curly dark hair, wet with sweat, lay limply on the pillow, and when she opened her eyes to see what her cousin had brought, the lids were so swollen that she could scarcely see from between them. Miranda, having only just recovered from the measles herself, could not help a pang of real pity arrowing through her. Poor Beth! When she felt better she would be given in abundance all the things that Miranda had longed for when she herself was recovering, but right now no one knew better than she how Beth was suffering. Accordingly she set the glass down on the lopsided little bedside table and poured out some of the delicious raspberry cordial. Beth heaved herself up in the bed and picked up the glass. She took a sip, then another, then stood the glass down again. 'Thanks, Miranda,' she whispered. 'It's the nicest drink in the world, but I can't drink it! Oh, how I wish I were well again.' She looked fretfully up at her young cousin. 'Why does it taste so sticky and sweet? I so want to drink it, but if I do . . . if I do . . .'

'Poor old Beth. I felt just the same,' Miranda assured her cousin. 'Just you cuddle down, and try to sleep. When you wake up you'll feel better, honest to God you will. Why, tomorrow morning you'll be eating your breakfast porridge and drinking cups of tea and telling Aunt Vi that you fancy scouse for your dinner.' She smiled with real affection at the other girl. 'You'll be all right; I told you it's only bad for the first three days.'

Beth obeyed, snuggling down into the bed and giving Miranda a sleepy smile. 'You're all right, Miranda Lovage,' she said drowsily. 'I'm sorry I was horrid to you, but I've never felt this ill before. When you come up to bed I'll try some lemonade; perhaps that'll go down easier.'

Miranda did not point out that she would not be coming up to bed for a good many hours, since it was only just eleven o'clock in the morning. In fact, seeing how her cousin tossed and turned, she had already decided to sleep on one of the kitchen chairs that night. After all, she had done so throughout her own attack of the measles, since Aunt Vi had turned her out of the brass bedstead at ten every night and told her not to return to it until breakfast time the next morning. She seemed to think that this might prevent herself and her daughter from catching the infection, but of course time had proved her wrong.

Miranda trod softly downstairs and entered the kitchen, saw that her aunt was snoozing, and let herself out of the front door and back into the sunshine of Jamaica Close. The girls were still twirling the rope and the game was going on just as usual, so Miranda wondered whether to go over and ask to be put in, but decided against it. The measles, and her enforced diet of bread and milk, had made her lethargic, unwilling to exert herself. She had been aware of a great lassitude when she had climbed the stairs the second time, balancing the jug of raspberry cordial and the glass.

Now she decided that since no one else cared what

became of her she would have to start looking after herself, so she strolled slowly along the length of the Close and for the first time it occurred to her that it was a very odd little street indeed. On her left were half a dozen terraced houses, each boasting three steps and a tiny garden plot. Most householders ignored the latter, but some had planted a solitary rose, a handful of marigolds, or a flowering shrub. However, the houses on her right were not terraced but semi-detached; bigger, more substantial. Rumour had it that whilst the even numbers two to ten had to use the common pump against the end wall of the Close, the odd numbers one to nine had piped water, though all the houses had outdoor privies in their back yards. Miranda frowned. She had never seriously considered the Close before, but now it seemed to her that it was downright odd to have such different sorts of houses in one very short street. And perhaps the oddest thing of all was the wall at the very end of Jamaica Close. It must be twenty or twenty-five feet high and blackened by soot, but what was it doing there? Why had they chosen to block off the Close with what looked like the back view of an enormous warehouse or factory? Yet Miranda knew that it could be neither; had there been a building in which people worked so near to Jamaica Close, then surely she would have heard sounds of movement, or people talking when they took their breaks. And the wall was so high! Because of it, the inhabitants of Jamaica Close could not see the setting sun, though its rays poured down on the rest of the area. For the first time, a spark of curiosity raised itself in Miranda's mind. What was the wall there for? Why did no one ever mention what was on the far side of the great mass of bricks which chopped Jamaica Close off short? Had it once been all houses, or all factories for that matter? She could not say, but the imp of curiosity had been roused and would not go away. Useless to ask her aunt, who never answered her questions anyway. But there must be someone who could explain the presence of that enormous wall.

She was standing, hands on hips, gazing up with watering eyes at the topmost line of bricks and wondering what it hid – and, for that matter, why the road should be called Jamaica Close. 'Jamaica's miles and miles away, and all the other roads which run parallel with this one have nice Irish names – Connemara, Dublin, Tallaght, St Patrick's and so on. So why Jamaica? As far as I know it's a tropical island and nothing whatsoever to do with Liverpool.'

'You don't know nothing, gairl.' The voice, cutting across her thoughts, made Miranda jump several inches. She had not realised she had spoken her thoughts aloud, or that anyone was close enough to hear, and, consequently, felt both annoyed and extremely foolish. This, not unnaturally, caused her to turn sharply on the speaker, a boy a year or two older than she, with light brown tufty hair, a great many freckles and, at this moment, a taunting grin.

'Shurrup, you!' she said crossly. 'Trust a feller to stick his bloomin' nose in!'

The boy sniggered. 'If you don't want nobody to answer, then you shouldn't ask questions,' he said. 'What you doin', gal? Ain't you never see'd a wall before? You're the kid what lives at Number Six, ain't you?' He guffawed rudely. 'First time I ever see you without a bag or a basket

35

or without that perishin' Beth Smythe a-grabbin' of your arm and a-tellin' you what to do.' He guffawed again. 'Slipped your leash, have you? Managed to undo your bleedin' collar?'

Miranda glared at him. She knew him by sight, knew he and his parents lived two doors down from her aunt. He was one of a large family of rough, uncouth boys, ranging in age from eighteen or nineteen down to a baby of two or three. Many folk did not approve of the Mickleborough family and this particular sprig, Miranda knew, was reckoned by her aunt – and indeed by Beth – to be a troublemaker of no mean order. On the other hand she knew that she herself was often accused by Aunt Vi of all sorts of crimes which she had most certainly never committed. Could it be the same for this boy? Miranda scowled, chewing her finger. She had not managed to make any friends amongst the children in Jamaica Close, for several reasons. One was that despite the fact that everyone disliked her aunt, despised her meanness, her spite, and her reluctance to help others, they believed her when she told lies about her niece. It seemed strange, but Miranda supposed that grown-ups, even if they didn't like each other, tended to take another adult's word against that of a child.

Then there was Beth. She wasn't all bad, as Miranda acknowledged, but she was an awful whiner, bursting into tears the moment she failed to get her own way and telling the most dreadful fibs to get herself out of trouble and somebody else into it. This naturally made her extremely unpopular.

A sharp poke in the ribs brought Miranda back to the present, and she turned to the boy by her side, eyebrows climbing. 'What business is it of yours if I stare at the wall? And who are you, anyway? I know you're one of the Mickleborough boys – my aunt says you're all horrid – but I don't know which one you are.'

The boy grinned, a flash of white teeth in an exceedingly dirty face. 'I'm Steve, the one me mam calls the turnover. I 'spect you've heard bad things about me, but that's because we used to have a rather mean dad. But now we've gorra nice one – a huge feller what could give you a clout hard enough to send you into next week. Not that he has – clouted me, I mean – but I wouldn't take no chances wi' a feller as big as the church tower. So I'm a reformed character, like.'

Miranda stared at him, eyes rounding. 'I'm like that . . . well, my mam was anyway. She and Aunt Vi had different dads; Aunt Vi's was a right pig, so when he died and Gran married again she chose a gentle, loving feller – John Saunders, that was, who was my mother's father. I never knew my grandparents because they died before I was born, but Aunt Vi blamed my mother for her own hard upbringing. She said my mam was spoiled rotten, never had to raise a finger or contribute anything towards the household expenses, and that's why she blames me for every perishin' thing which goes wrong,' she said, rather breathlessly.

'Well I'm blowed!' Steve remarked. 'It's like my family, too, except that there're more than two of us. I'm the last of the bad 'uns; me little brother Kenny is me step-dad's kid.'

The pair had fallen into step and were strolling along the Close, heading for the main road. 'Wish I had a little brother or sister,' Miranda said sadly. 'Not that I wanted one when Mum and I lived on the Avenue; we had each other and that was all that mattered.'

'Aye, I heard you and your mam were close,' Steve acknowledged. He peered down into her face. 'Things is a bit different now, ain't they? I see'd you runnin' errands, humpin' water, goin' up to the wash house with everyone's dirty clothes . . . and you've got a lot thinner than you were when you first arrived. Reckon they only feed you on odds and ends.'

Miranda thought of the plate which would be put down in front of her at dinner time: a spoonful of gravy, a couple of small spuds, a bit of cabbage if she was lucky, and that would be all the food she'd get until tomorrow's breakfast, unless of course she helped herself and risked being called a thief.

But the boy was looking at her enquiringly, his look half curious, half sympathetic. Miranda gave a rueful smile. 'You're right there; I get what the rest won't eat,' she admitted. She raised her eyebrows, returning look for look. 'You aren't exactly Mr Universe yourself. What did you say your name was?'

'Steve,' her companion said. 'I might be skinny, but I get me fair share of whatever's going; our mam sees to that. And fellers can always pick up fades from the market, or earn a few pennies sellin' chips to housewives.' He looked at her, his own eyebrows rising. 'What's your moniker? I know your cousin's Beth.'

'I'm Miranda Lovage,' Miranda said shortly. By now they had reached the end of Jamaica Close and had emerged on to the pavement, which was thronging with people. Women were shopping, children too. Folk were waiting for trams or buses, whilst others sauntered along peering into shop windows and enjoying the warm sunshine. Miranda would have turned right, chiefly because she expected Steve to turn left, heading for the city centre, but instead he jerked her to a halt.

'What say we pal up a bit, go round together?' he suggested. 'Your cousin's got measles, I've heard, so she won't be out and about for two or three weeks, which means you'll be all on your lonesome unless you join forces wi' me.' He grinned at her and suddenly Miranda realised how lonely she had been, and how much more fun the summer holidays would be if she did as this strange boy suggested.

She turned to face him. They were about the same height – perhaps he was an inch or two the taller – and now she was looking directly into his face she saw that beneath the dirt it wasn't a bad face at all. His hair was mousy brown, his skin only one shade lighter, and he met her regard steadily from a pair of hazel eyes set beneath straight dark brows. But there was something about his eyes . . . Miranda stared harder, then smiled to herself. His eyes tilted up at the corners, giving him a mischievous look; she rather liked it. But her new friend was jerking her arm, expecting a reply to his last remark, so she grinned at him, nodding so vigorously that her bush of long straight carroty hair swung forward like a curtain, momentarily hiding her face. 'That's a grand idea, Steve. We could do all sorts if we could earn a bit of gelt, and two of us ought to be able to earn more than one. The feller who sells carpets from a market stall will always give a kid a few pence to carry a carpet back to a customer's house. I'm not strong enough to do it alone, and Beth wouldn't lower herself, but if you and I offered our services . . .'

Steve grinned delightedly. 'You've got the right idea, pal,' he said exuberantly. 'We'll make a killing while your cousin's laid up . . . but what will happen when she's fit again, eh? I don't fancy being dropped like a hot potato.'

Miranda chuckled. 'Don't worry; at the mere mention of earning a few pence by working for it Beth will come down with a headache, or find some other excuse to let me get on with it alone,' she assured him. 'So what'll we do now?'

'Ever been to Seaforth Sands? It's grand up there on a fine day like this. If we could earn ourselves a few coppers we could stay out there all day. Can you swim?'

'Course not; girls don't,' Miranda said scornfully. 'Besides, where would I learn? I know there's a public baths on Vauxhall Road but they charge you at least sixpence – maybe a shilling – and anyway, you need a bathing costume to swim there.'

'I could learn you. And what's wrong with the Scaldy, anyhow?'

Miranda opened her mouth to make some blighting remark, then changed her mind. Steve was offering friendship, with no strings; the least she could do was to be honest with him. 'I've never heard of the Scaldy, whatever that is,' she admitted. 'I've heard of Seaforth Sands, of course, but I wouldn't have a clue how to get there. You see, when I lived with my mother in the Avenue we hardly ever came into the city, except for shopping and that. Why, I couldn't even find my way to the Pier Head! I've heard other kids talking about playing on the chains of the floating bridge, but I don't even know what that means. You might as well realise, Steve, that all this is strange to me. I know Prince's Park – the boating lake, and the café where they sell you a lemonade and a sticky bun for sixpence – and of course I know the theatre where my mother worked, and most of the Madison Players. But apart from that, I'm a stranger here. Go on, tell me what the Scaldy is.'

Thus challenged, Steve began to explain, then gave up. 'When does your aunt expect you home?' he asked. 'Can you get away for a whole day? If so we'll do the grand tour and I'll show you everything as we go. It'll be easier if you can see what I'm talking about with your own eyes.'

Miranda sniggered. 'I shouldn't be able to see with anybody else's eyes,' she pointed out, and dodged as Steve gave her a friendly punch. 'I can't say when Aunt Vi expects me home but she won't worry, even if I disappear like my mother did. So come on, let's have the grand tour.'

By the end of that momentous day, Miranda felt she was now as familiar with the delights of the city as Steve himself. They had visited the Scaldy, just past Burlington Bridge, so called because that was where the Tate and Lyle sugar manufactory belched out the hot water it no longer needed into the canal. They had watched enviously as boys small and large ran along the towpath and plunged into the steaming water. Miranda had wanted to follow, clad in knickers and vest, but Steve, though he applauded her pluck, had thought it unwise. 'Girls don't swim here,' he had assured her, 'but now you've seen it we'll skip a lecky out to Seaforth Sands. There'll be a deal of folk there, but if you tuck your skirt into your knickers you'll be able to paddle. After that we'll go up to the barracks – sometimes the soldiers will chuck a kid a penny or two to buy tobacco for 'em – and after that . . .'

After that they had a marvellous day. They went down to the floating road, slipped under the chains, and played at mudlarks. They begged a wooden orange box from a friendly greengrocer and took it back to Steve's crowded back yard, where they chopped it into kindling. Miranda divided the pieces into bundles which they sold up and down Scotland Road for threepence each, and with the money earned Steve bought a bag of sticky buns. Miranda had been diffident about following Steve into his mother's kitchen, partly because she was shy and feared a rebuff, and partly because she was frightened of Steve's older brothers, who Aunt Vi was always declaring were dangerously wild and best avoided, but this proved to be yet another of her aunt's spiteful and untruthful comments. Ted, Reg and Joe were easy-going young men, accepting Miranda as their brother's friend, whilst little Kenny, who was just three, clamoured for her to play with him.

Miranda was just thinking how delightfully different Steve's home life was from her own when the back door opened and Mr Mickleborough came in. He was an enormous man, well over six foot tall, with huge hands and feet. Steve had told her that his stepfather was an engine driver and Miranda would have liked to ask him about his work, but Mrs Mickleborough began to lay the table and the older boys disappeared, though Kenny, the baby, rushed to his father, winding soft little arms about Mr Mickleborough's knees and begging for a shoulder ride.

Miranda, all too used to knowing when she was not

wanted, thanked Mrs Mickleborough for her hospitality and headed for the back door. She almost cut Steve in two by trying to shut it just as he was following her outside.

Out in the jigger which ran along the backs of the houses the two stared at one another. 'Isn't he big?' Miranda said rather breathlessly. 'He makes your brothers look quite small. Gosh, I wouldn't like to get a clack from him!'

Steve puffed out his cheeks and whistled. 'You're right there. He's got hands like clam shovels. But he's real good to little Kenny, and Mam says he's gentle as a lamb. Still an' all, I tries to keep me 'ead down, never gives back answers, stays out of the way as much as possible, and do what he says right smartly.' He sighed ruefully. 'He's strict, but he's fair, and much better to our mam than my real dad was, so I reckon I should count me blessings.'

Miranda was looking thoughtful. 'If he's only your step-dad, why do you have the same name?' she asked. 'I thought boys always kept their fathers' names?'

'Oh, me real dad were a right mean old bugger, used to knock Mam about as well as us kids, so when he were killed and Mam married me stepfather she asked us if we'd mind being called Mickleborough too, since she wanted to forget everything to do with our dad. I don't think Reg and Ted were too happy, or even Joe, but I were only a nipper meself and couldn't see as it made any difference, so I said yes at once and the others came round in the end. So now we're the Mickleborough boys – isn't that what your aunt called us?'

By this time the two of them had emerged into Jamaica

Close, and Miranda looked towards Number Six, half expecting her aunt to appear in the doorway shouting for her, but the doorstep was deserted, as indeed was the Close itself. Most families would be either preparing or eating their evening meal, so if she wanted to be fed she would have to go indoors at once and think up some good reason why she had been away all day. She said as much to Steve, who shook his head. 'You've already said they don't care where you go or what you do, unless they need you, and since you also said your aunt was staying at home to look after Beth you don't even have to invent an excuse. All you have to do is look astonished and say if they needed you why didn't they call.'

Miranda sighed. 'It's been the nicest day I've had since Mum disappeared,' she said wistfully. She fished in her pocket, produced her share of the money they had earned, and thrust the pennies into Steve's hand. 'You take care of it; my aunt will only nick it if I take it into Number Six. She'll say I have to pay something towards the rent, or she needs some coal . . . any excuse to take it off me.'

Steve accepted the money and shoved it into the pocket of his ragged kecks. 'Tomorrer, if you get up real early, I'll show you where I cache my gelt,' he said, 'then you can put yours there too and know it'll be safe.' He hesitated, then jerked a thumb at the great wall at the end of the Close. 'Remember we were talking about the wall earlier? Well, now we knows each other pretty well I'll take you round t'other side of that wall tomorrer and tell you something I've not told another soul.'

'Tell me now,' Miranda said eagerly. 'Go on. You've told me so much I might as well know the rest. I was sure there was some mystery about that wall as soon as I began to notice it. Go on, Steve, tell me!'

But though Steve laughed indulgently, he also shook his head. 'No chance,' he said. 'It's like what I told you earlier about the Scaldy; better to see it for yourself than me have to drive myself half crazy trying to explain. Tomorrer is quite soon enough.'

'Oh, but suppose I can't get away?' Miranda wailed. 'Suppose my aunt needs me? She'll only interest herself in Beth for a bit, then she'll expect me to dance attendance twenty-four hours out of the twenty-four. And then you'll be sorry you were so mean.'

But Steve only laughed. 'Maybe I will and maybe I won't,' he said infuriatingly. He seized her shoulders and ran her up the three steps to the front door of Number Six. 'Off you go.' He lowered his voice. 'Don't forget; meet me here tomorrow at six in the morning.'

'Well, I will if I can,' Miranda said. 'My aunt never gets up before eight o'clock, so maybe I'll be lucky.'

She left him, turning to give a little wave as she shut the dirty paint-blistered front door behind her. Then she went down the short hallway and into the kitchen. Her aunt was sitting by the table eating cake, having clearly had her fill of the scouse, potatoes and cabbage Miranda had helped to prepare earlier in the day. She swung her chair round so that she could stare at her niece. 'Where've you been?' she said belligerently. 'I come back after me shopping trip and you was nowhere to be seen. Poor Beth had shouted herself hoarse, but did you appear? Did you hell! All you thought of was your perishin' self.'

Aunt Vi continued to upbraid her as though she had done something really wicked, instead of merely being

45

out of hearing when her aunt had called. As soon as she could make herself heard above the barrage of complaints, accusations and name calling, Miranda took a deep breath and reminded Aunt Vi that it was *she* who was supposed to be looking after her daughter. 'You said *you* were going to nurse Beth; don't you remember?' Staring into her aunt's furious face, she saw recollection dawn there and saw, too, how dangerous it was to be right, especially if it made Aunt Vi wrong. She knew she should have reminded herself that a soft answer turneth away wrath, but it was too late for that now: she had erred and must pay the price.

'Well, since you weren't around when I were dishin' up you can go supperless to bed,' Aunt Vi said, her little eyes gleaming malevolently. 'Now just you go upstairs and see if there's anything Beth wants. If there's nothing you can fetch her, then you can read her the serial story out of *The Girl's Own Paper*.'

Miranda hesitated. She had had a large slice of bread and jam at the Mickleborough house and she and Steve had shared some fades from St John's market and a paper of chips from the chippy in Homer Street, which meant of course that she was not really hungry at all. However, her day with Steve had put fresh courage into her veins and she decided to be bold for once. She pointed to the blackened pan on the stove. 'I prepared that before I went out this morning, and I've had nothing to eat all day,' she said firmly, though untruthfully. 'I've had measles myself, you know, and it's left me quite weak. I'm not running up and down stairs at Beth's beck and call until I've had some supper. And a nice hot cup of tea,' she added defiantly.

Auntie Vi surged to her feet, crossed to the stove and heaved the pan well back. 'You ain't havin' none of this, norrif I have to chuck it out for the perishin' birds,' she said nastily. 'Bread and water's good enough for you; you can help yourself to that if you like.'

Miranda looked at her. She realised that this was the first time she had ever confronted her aunt and that Vi must be wondering what had got into her, but having made a stand she must not back down unless she wanted to live on bread and water. For a moment she contemplated cutting herself a large slice of the cake which her aunt had been devouring when she had entered the kitchen, then changed her mind. She had prepared the scouse, and had looked forward to having at least a helping of the stuff, so she went to the sideboard, took down a tin plate and held it out wordlessly, almost beneath Aunt Vi's nose. Her aunt began to gobble that she should not get a shred of the delicious stew, but Miranda continued to hold the plate and, to her secret astonishment, when their eyes met it was Aunt Vi who lowered hers first. To be sure, she did not ladle any stew on to the tin plate, but turned away, muttering. Miranda heard words like 'forbid' and 'don't you dare' and 'defyin' me in me own house' as her aunt stomped back to her chair, picked up the teapot and poured herself another cup of tea, though her hand trembled so much that tea sprayed out of the spout and puddled on the wooden table.

Miranda could not believe her luck. Never, in her wildest dreams, had she expected it to be Aunt Vi who backed down, but it had happened. She seized the ladle and helped herself to a generous portion, then sat down at the table and began to eat. Halfway through the meal she reached over and cut herself a wedge of bread from the loaf to sop up the last of the gravy, and when she had finished she went across to the sink and put her dirty plate with the others, while Aunt Vi continued to munch cake and stare at her as though she could not believe her eyes.

Miranda gave her aunt a big bright smile and headed for the stairs. 'I don't suppose Beth wants anything now, or she would have shouted,' she said cheerfully. 'However, a bargain is a bargain; I said I wouldn't wait on Beth until I'd had something to eat. Well, now I've had a meal, and a good one, so I think I'm strong enough to get up the stairs and see if there's anything I can do for my cousin.' As she left the kitchen Miranda glanced back at her aunt and had real difficulty in preventing herself from giving a great roar of laughter. Aunt Vi had her hand across her mouth as she shovelled cake into it, and just for a moment she could have modelled for the monkey in the well-known portrayal of *Speak no Evil*. But she managed to contain her mirth until she was well out of hearing.

Upstairs, her cousin was already looking a little less unhappy, though her skin was still scarlet with spots. She had drunk at least one full glass of the raspberry cordial, but the scouse beside it had scarcely been touched. She looked up as her cousin entered the room and indicated the plate of stew with a weary hand. 'Want it?' she asked in a hoarse whisper. 'I can't eat the flamin' stuff; food makes me feel sick.' She sat up on one elbow, peering at Miranda through swollen lids. 'Where's you bin all day? Mam can't make the stairs more'n twice in

48

twenty-four hours, she says, and anyway I wanted *you*. She bought the latest copy of *The Girl's Own Paper* so's you could read me the serial story, but you weren't here.'

Miranda sat down on the bed and pulled the magazine towards her. 'I offered to read to you this morning but you told me comics were pictures and to go and buy me own.'

'So I did,' Beth said feebly. 'But I didn't mean it, you know that, Miranda. And anyway, me mam can't read as well as you. She says her glasses steam up so she misses words out and has hard work to read her shopping list, lerralone a magazine story.' She gave a gusty sigh. 'I told Ma to send you up as soon as you come home.'

'And I told your ma that I needed some food before tackling the stairs again,' Miranda said. 'She let me have a plate of scouse and some bread; I must say it were prime. As for what I've been doing all day, you wouldn't be interested; it was just – just messing around. You know the Mickleborough boys? I know your mum doesn't like them, but they're all right really. One of them – he's called Steve – said he'd take me on a grand tour of the area and he showed me all sorts. Do you know, Beth, there's a huge art gallery quite near the London Road and a marvellous library as well as a museum . . . oh, there's all sorts of things I never dreamed of. While you're laid up I mean to get to know the city as well as he does. Then, when you're better . . .' But Beth's interest in her cousin's doings was already fading.

'Never mind that. Just you do what my mam says and read me my serial story,' Beth commanded. 'If you want to go around with some perishin' rough boy, that's up to you. Oh, and I could do with another drink. Me throat's that sore, even talking hurts.'

Miranda stood up, took the almost empty jug and returned to the kitchen. Presently she was back in the bedroom and sitting down on the bed with the magazine spread out on her knees. 'Ready?' she said brightly. 'Well, Louisa Nettlebed is hot on the trail of the mysterious letter, though it is to be hoped that Phyllis, the heroine, will get to it first. I'll read on from there.'

Miranda enjoyed reading aloud, but was rather chagrined to discover, when she reached the end of the episode, that her cousin had fallen asleep. That meant re-reading the story the next day and she particularly wanted to go off early with Steve. Still, when Aunt Vi came up to bed she told Miranda to sleep in the kitchen, which was all to the good. The clock above the mantel has a very loud tick, and if I pull the curtains back so the early light can come in I'll be ready for the off at six, she told herself.

It was a pearly summer morning when Miranda let herself quietly out of the house. As arranged, Steve was hanging around outside, and he greeted her with a broad grin. 'Ain't it a grand day?' he said. 'I reckon it's too good to waste poundin' the streets and showin' you where I stash me gelt, so I've took some bread and cheese – Mam won't mind – and we can catch the number twenty-two tram out to Fazakerley and then walk to Simonswood, where we can have us dinners and muck about . . .'

'Where's that?' Miranda interrupted. She could feel excitement flooding through her at the thought of another wonderful day with this new – and knowing – friend, though excitement warred with disappointment. Steve had roused her curiosity about the other side of the wall and she longed to see it. However, the prospect of a day in the country was almost enough to cause her to forget what she now thought of as 'the mystery of the wall'. After all, the wall would be there probably for the rest of her life, whereas a day out with Steve could be ruined if rain fell heavily, or her aunt discovered her intention and forbade her to leave the house.

But Steve was staring at her; he looked annoyed. 'What do you mean, where's that?' he said rather truculently. 'Didn't I just tell you? Simonswood's real countryside; there's streams with tiddlers in, ponds for the ducks and geese, orchards full of apples and pears and that . . . oh, everything to make the day real special. But if you don't want to come, of course . . .'

Hastily, Miranda hid her curiosity about the wall and assured him that he was mistaken; she wanted to go to Simonswood very much indeed. As they trotted along to the tram stop, however, she admitted that if she was out for a whole day again there would undoubtedly be reprisals. 'But I don't care,' she added defiantly. 'Mostly I'm in trouble for doing nothing, so it'll be quite a change for my aunt to have a real reason to knock me about.'

'Knock you about? But you're not her kid, and you're a girl . . .' Steve was beginning, but Miranda was saved the necessity of answering as a number twenty-two tram drew up beside them. 'Tell you what,' he said as they settled themselves on one of the slatted seats, 'if your aunt treats you bad, suppose we take back something she'll really like – a sort of bribe, you could say. I know a little old tree what has real early apples; someone told me they're called Beauty of Bath. Suppose we fill our pockets with 'em? You can give your share to your aunt if you think that'll sweeten her.'

Miranda thought this an excellent idea, and when they got off the tram she chatted to Steve quite happily as they strolled along country lanes whose verges were thick with sweet-smelling spires of creamy coloured flowers, and in marshy places with the delicate pale mauve blossoms which Steve told her were called lady's smock.

Once again Miranda had a wonderful time. She accompanied Steve to a farmhouse where they bought a drink of milk, and were told they were welcome to take as many apples as they liked from the little tree down by the gate. After they had eaten their bread and cheese, Miranda was all set to dam a tiny stream so that she might paddle in the pool she meant to create, when Steve astonished her by saying that he felt like a nap.

'You don't,' Miranda said scornfully. 'Naps are for old people. Just you come and help me dam this stream.'

'I'm too tired,' Steve said obstinately. 'I dunno why, but if I don't get some sleep I'll not have the strength to walk back to the tram stop. Ain't you tired, Miranda?' As he spoke he had been taking off his ragged pullover and folding it into a pillow, but even as he lay down upon it and composed himself for sleep, Miranda jerked his faded shirt up and stared at the back thus revealed.

'Oh, Steve, you've been and gone and got the flippin' measles,' she said, her voice vibrant with dismay. 'I thought you'd have been bound to have had them . . . but you've got them now at any rate. No wonder you're so perishin' tired; I reckon I slept for near on three days

52

when I first had them, and Beth's the same. She couldn't even stay awake to listen to me reading her serial story.'

Steve sat up, heaved his shirt up and surveyed his spotty skin with a groan of dismay. 'Oh, hell and damnation, wharra thing to happen right at the start of the summer holidays,' he said. 'I'll try to keep it a secret from me mam, but I doubt it's possible. I say, Miranda, I'm real sorry, but until the spots go I'll be lucky to escape from the house for ten minutes, lerralone ten hours.'

'Well, I suppose we ought to be counting our blessings because we've had two great days,' Miranda said. 'And once you begin to feel better, surely your mam will let you play out? She's an awfully nice woman and I don't suppose she'll want you under her feet for the whole three weeks.'

'We'll see. Mebbe she'll let you come in, 'cos you've already had 'em, and read to me, or just chat,' Steve said, but he didn't sound too hopeful. He grinned up at her and Miranda saw that already spots were beginning to appear amongst the freckles on his cheeks. Soon he would be smothered in the bloomin' things, which meant that he would be unable to fool anyone; one look and he would be driven back to his own home, though Miranda thought this was yet another example of the stupidity of grown-ups. When a measles epidemic struck, the sensible thing would be to let all the kids catch it. Then the next time it happened they would be safe, since she was pretty sure you couldn't catch the measles twice. So Miranda continued her work of damming the stream and paddled contentedly whilst Steve slumbered, though they had to make their way back to the tram stop in good time. Steve pulled his cap well down over his spotty brow and to

53

Miranda's relief no one tried to stop them getting aboard, though once they were back in Jamaica Close Steve got some funny looks from the kids playing on the paving stones.

As she had expected, Miranda was met by a tirade of abuse from Aunt Vi, and a storm of reproaches from Beth, since the first resented having to look after her daughter and the second wanted amusing, and was fed up with her mother's constant complaints. As Steve had predicted, the large bag of apples went some way to placating her aunt, but later in the evening, when Miranda went round to Steve's house, she was told politely but firmly that he was feverish, could see no one and most certainly was not allowed out.

Oh well, I've had two wonderful days and three weeks isn't such a very long time after all, Miranda comforted herself as she pushed two chairs together to form a bed after her aunt had gone upstairs. The maddening thing is that Steve had promised to tell me about the high wall at the end of Jamaica Close, only we both forgot about it when we realised he had got the measles. I wonder when he'll be able to explain just what's mysterious about that wall.

Chapter Three

Despite Miranda's hopes, the three weeks of Steve's incarceration felt more like three months. Beth got better and even more demanding than usual, and though Miranda's show of spirit had confounded her aunt for a little while, Aunt Vi soon began to slip into her old ways. If Miranda tried to defy her, a sly clack round the head would be handed out when she least expected it, making her feel dizzy, and though she persisted in saying she would not work unless she got at least a share of the food on offer this tactic was only partially successful. Sometimes her share seemed to consist of gravy, half a potato and some cabbage, though Beth, when warned that her cousin would not wait upon her unless she was decently fed, saw that Miranda got bread and cheese or a conny-onny sandwich in return for reading anything Beth wanted to hear.

She did manage to see Steve from time to time; once she sneaked into his yard when she had seen him making his way to the privy and the two of them exchanged news. Steve, much to his surprise, found that his mother would not allow his stepfather to so much as enter the little room he shared with Kenny, since the older man had never had the measles. She also bought her son special food, and this was probably as well since Steve got them very badly, and was feverish for a whole week.

To be sure, once that week had passed he made rapid progress and was soon eating hearty meals, playing quiet games with Kenny and occasionally sneaking downstairs to meet Miranda in the cobbled yard at the back of the house, but he was careful to keep these activities undemanding since he had no wish to make himself even more sickly.

When Miranda and Steve met, as they began to do regularly, in the little cobbled courtyard of Number Two, he was eager for any news of Jamaica Close and their various neighbours. Miranda had taken advantage of his absence to spend a good deal of time each day with the Madison Players, who were always good for a bit of gossip, but Steve had never been to the theatre and Miranda soon realised that he was not much interested in her mother's friends.

'When you're better – well, when all the spots have gone – I'll take you with me when I go down after the matinée performance and introduce you to everyone,' Miranda told him. 'You'll like them, honest to God you will, Steve. And then you can hear what they've been doing to try and find my mother; you'd like that, wouldn't you?'

But though Steve agreed that this would be a grand idea, Miranda had the uneasy feeling that he was not much interested either in the theatre or in the disappearance of her mother and she supposed, ruefully, that she could scarcely blame him. A whole year was a long time in anyone's book and even the Madison Players no longer talked as though Arabella would turn up with some believable explanation of where she had been during the past year. Even the sleepwalking incident had been long ago. Several times since then Miranda had woken to find herself halfway down the stairs, tiptoeing barefoot across the cobbled yard or actually in the roadway, but she had never again gone out of sight of Jamaica Close. She had mentioned these episodes to no one but Harry, the policeman who had found her on her very first sleepwalk, and though interested he had not thought it particularly important. 'I've talked about it to me mates, and they say that most folk grow out of it; I reckon you're doing that right now.'

It was unfortunate that as Beth's health improved her temper worsened and she became demanding, fractious and quite spiteful. She had always told tales but now she twisted her remarks to put her cousin in an even worse light, until Miranda was forced to bargain with her. She would refuse to read to Beth or help her with a jigsaw or play draughts unless her cousin would agree to her playing out for at least an hour each day. Beth was well enough to play out herself had she wanted to do so, but on this point at least the cousins were totally different. Miranda thought she would die cooped up in the house, Beth thought she would die if she were forced to breathe fresh air, so arguments were frequent and tempers frayed and grew shorter than ever.

The day came at last, however, when the nurse from Brougham Terrace pronounced Steve free from infection and the next morning the two met outside the front door of Number Six, to gloat over their newly won freedom. 'Mam's give me a few coppers so we won't have to skip a lecky; we can ride like Christians and go all the way out to Seaforth Sands, like we did before I caught the perishin' plague,' Steve said. 'Gawd, I hope I never get

57

the measles again, I'm tellin' you. I scratched, of course – who wouldn't – and when Mam saw me at it, what did she do but trot down to the chemist shop on Great Homer and buy a bottle of pink yuck what the pharmacist told her was good for spots . . .'

Miranda giggled. 'Calamine lotion,' she supplied. 'It's awful, isn't it? When I was six and lived in the Avenue I got chickenpox and my mother dabbed the stuff all over me. It was all right while it was wet – quite cooling, in fact – but when it dried it was awful. Aunt Vi sent me to the chemist to buy a bottle for Beth but I told her how it would be, so we emptied it down the sink and put a tiddy bit of plate powder in the bottle with water and shook it up. Then Beth pretended we'd used it and said it wasn't any good, and when Aunt Vi got a plug of cotton wool and tried to dab it on the spots Beth grabbed the bottle and threw it out of the window. Good thing it was open, because she threw it pretty damn hard, I'm telling you.'

Steve laughed. His skin seemed oddly pale after being shut up indoors for three weeks but otherwise, Miranda considered, he was beginning to look like himself once more. But she vetoed his suggestion that they should go to Seaforth Sands. 'No, I don't want to do that,' she said firmly. 'Before you were taken ill you promised you'd show me the place where you hide your gelt, so I could add mine to it. And you sort of hinted that I'd be surprised when I saw the other side of that great wall at the end of Jamaica Close. I've waited three weeks and never nagged you, but I'm going to nag you now. I want to see the other side of that wall and I want to know where you hide your gelt and where I shall hide mine in future. Why, Steve, if you were to be run over tomorrow I wouldn't be able to inherit your wealth, because I don't know where you keep it.'

Steve laughed. 'I don't mean to get run over tomorrow, nor the next day neither,' he said cheerfully. 'But I know what you mean and I reckon you're right. We'll save Seaforth Sands for another day, and as soon as you've had your breakfast we'll set off for the other side of the wall.'

They agreed to meet outside Number Two in half an hour, and Miranda trotted down the jigger, crossed the courtyard of Number Six and entered the kitchen, where she found Aunt Vi eating porridge whilst Beth sat on a low stool, clutching a fork upon whose prongs was spiked a round of bread. She looked up as Miranda entered the room, and frowned. 'I don't fancy porridge, norreven with brown sugar or golden syrup,' she said crossly. 'I'm havin' toast wi' raspberry jam. What'll you have?'

Miranda knew that this was a rhetorical question. The raspberry jam, her cousin's favourite, was most certainly not on offer so far as she herself was concerned. Not that she minded; porridge with just a sprinkling of brown sugar was her favourite breakfast, and if she helped herself to a full dish it would not matter if she did not come in for the midday meal.

However, when she examined the saucepan there were only about two spoonfuls of porridge left in it, so her hopes of a good filling breakfast were dashed. She put it into her dish, however, then cut herself a round of bread, keeping one hand on it so that no one should filch it whilst she ate her porridge.

A rich smell of burning caused Beth to give a squeak

59

of dismay and throw the cindered slice down on the table, then reach for the slice of bread beneath her cousin's palm. 'Gimme!' she commanded. 'You can have the burned bit.'

'Beth Smythe, you are the most selfish . . .'

Aunt Vi's hand clipped Miranda so hard across the ear that she nearly fell off her chair, making Beth give a muffled snort of laughter. 'Serve you right,' she said tauntingly. 'What's to stop you cutting yourself another slice, if you don't like a bit of burn?' But Aunt Vi was already scuttling pantry wards with the remains of the loaf clutched in her hot and greedy hands, so Miranda jammed the piece of bread into her skirt pocket, ignored her aunt's shout that she was to bleedin' well wash up before she took one step out of the door, and crossed the kitchen.

'No time; I'm meeting a friend,' she called over her shoulder. 'See you later, Beth.' Miranda was sure her aunt would think nothing of pursuing her down the Close, so she decided that loitering outside Number Two was not a good idea and turned right into the main road. Because the summer holidays were now in full swing there were a great many children about, one or two of whom Miranda knew. She stopped and spoke to Jane and Elizabeth Meredith, twins who were in her class at school, and they told her that they had just returned from a wonderful week down on the coast; at Rhyl, in fact. 'Oh, girls, how lucky you are!' Miranda breathed. 'My mother was always promising to take me down to the coast, but somehow she never got round to it.'

She had heard much of the delights of seaside resorts in summer and remembered her mother's description of golden sands, gentle blue seas and the enthusiastic audiences who had attended the shows on the pier. One day, Arabella had assured her daughter, they would go to Rhyl, or Llandudno, or even further afield, but at present she was content to stay with the theatre over the summer, helping with scenery painting, costume repair and other such tasks which were best done when the theatre was empty.

Lizzie was a sweet-tempered girl, but it was her sharp-tongued twin who responded. 'Your mam, your mam!' Jane said contemptuously. 'That were when you were in that posh private school, I suppose? I bet they never knew your mam was on the stage, 'cos that's common that is . . . bein' on the stage, I mean. If she took you to the seaside at all you'd have had your face blacked up and a black curly wig on your horrible head, so's you could earn a few pennies in the black and white minstrel show . . .'

Miranda was interrupted just as she was contemplating handing out a punch on the nose. Someone caught her arm and a voice spoke warningly in her ear. 'Hello-ello-ello? Hangin' round waitin' for me, was you? Gorrany grub? That bleedin' aunt o' yours might hand over a bit of cake or a chunk of bread and cheese. Still, I've got some of each so we shan't starve.'

It was Steve, of course, and as he spoke he had been drawing her away from the twins, giving her arm a warning pinch as he did so. Miranda, who had taken a deep breath, preparing to shout abuse at Jane even as she threw the punch, subsided, though she shook Steve's hand off her arm as they moved away. 'It's all right; it's just that when somebody says something nasty about my mother, I lose my temper,' she said ruefully. She turned to her friend. '*Are* we going to see the other side of the wall, Steve? It's not fair to keep talking about some mystery or other and then making excuses not to go round there.'

They had been walking quite briskly along the pavement, but at this Steve stopped short. 'Look, I told you I've not said a word to anyone else, about either where I stash me gelt or what goes on on t'other side of that there wall. I'm still not sure if I'm doin' the right thing . . .' He heaved a sigh. 'But a promise is a promise, so we turn right here and keep goin' for a bit. Despite what you might think, it's a long way round to reach the other side of that wall and it's no use you askin' me a lot of silly questions 'cos I shan't answer 'em. Chatter away all you like, tell me stories about your mam, but don't ask me no questions about where we're goin' or what we'll do when we get there, gorrit?'

'Yes, all right, if that's the way you want it,' Miranda said rather sulkily. 'But I think you're being awful silly; how can a wall which is so ordinary on the back be mysterious and different on the front? That's what I want to know.'

As Steve had said, it was a long walk to reach the other side of the wall, but when they did so it was just as mysterious and extraordinary as Steve had hinted. The wall which truncated Jamaica Close hid what appeared to be a huge, crumbling mansion of a house; it was only visible over the top of another large wall, and the roof was half missing, telling Miranda that it was now a ruin, though it must have been magnificent years ago. She could see the tops of trees and the staring glassless eyes of windows, but could see no way in. She turned and stared at Steve. 'Are you sure that Jamaica Close is on the other side of that crumbling great house?' she asked uneasily. How did one tell from the only sort of view they could get that Jamaica Close was really so near? For all she knew Steve might have led her for miles, through dozens of tiny streets – well, he had done so – before stopping in front of the only building of sufficient height to own that wall. Miranda looked at the neighbouring buildings, but none of them were houses. There were small and large factories with busy yards full of bicycles in racks, the occasional car, and men strolling to and fro, smoking cigarettes or eating food from grease-proof wrappers, for by now, Miranda guessed, it must be dinner time. Clearly, the reason that no one was interested in the old walled house was because people came here to work and not to live; this was not a family neighbourhood. Whereas in Jamaica Close there were always children playing, mothers shouting to their offspring to run messages or go indoors for a meal, here, Miranda guessed, when the siren sounded for the end of the shift, workers were merely intent upon getting back to their homes and had little or no interest in their surroundings.

She said as much to Steve, who grunted assent. 'The strange thing is that when I'm in Jamaica Close I hardly hear any noise from over here, apart from the hooter which marks the end of the shift; I suppose it's because the wall's so high. And then, of course, grown-ups' voices don't carry in the way ours do. But now that you know what's on this side of the wall, you'll maybe notice sounds which you wouldn't have noticed before.'

Miranda agreed to this, though with reservations. But

then Steve gave her a friendly poke in the ribs. 'What are you thinking?' he asked. 'Don't tell me . . .' he pointed to the slated roof of the mansion so far above their heads, 'you don't believe that Jamaica Close is a stone's throw away. Tell you what, how about if we prove it? No use doing anything now, in broad daylight, but tonight when we're back in the Close and there's no one about I'll get something real brightly coloured and shy it as high as I can, right over the wall and the house as well, if I'm lucky. Then tomorrow we'll come round again, and the proof will be there.'

Miranda sniffed, but gave Steve a reluctant grin. 'All right, all right, I'm sure you've worked it all out and Jamaica Close is just over the wall. And now, how the devil do we get to the house?'

'I suppose you think it's impossible, don't you?' he asked mockingly. 'Like most people, you see what you expect to see, not what is really there. Walk very slowly around this bleedin' great wall and mebbe you'll see a way in and mebbe you won't. I aren't goin' to help you, 'cos this is a sort of test. Go on, start lookin'.'

Forewarned, Miranda began to walk very slowly along the wall. She kept her eyes on the ground, half expecting to find that some animal had dug a tunnel beneath it, but saw nothing. Then she began to examine the brick-work and in a remarkably short space of time, or so her gratified pal assured her, she had found the way in. Perhaps a dozen feet from where she had started looking a mass of ivy hid the uneven brickwork, and had it not been for the sudden tension of the figure beside her Miranda might have passed it by without a second glance, assuming that, in the way of ivy, it had rooted and clung to every crevice in the great wall. But the slight stiffening of Steve's body was enough to make Miranda not only look, but also to put a hand to the gleaming ivy. She prepared to tug, then realised that the ivy was rooted on the far side of the wall and what she beheld was simply a curtain, which, as soon as she moved it away, revealed a tiny scratched, scarred door.

'Well done you!' Steve said in a low voice. 'Better make sure no one's watching . . .' He glanced quickly round, then reached down and pulled open the door. To Miranda's surprise it opened easily, without a squeak or a protesting creak, and though she turned towards Steve to remark on it, he pushed her through and shut the door behind the pair of them before turning to her and blowing out his cheeks in a parody of relief. 'Phew!' he said. 'Now I'll show you where I hide my gelt.' He turned towards the house, but Miranda put a detaining hand on his arm.

'Hold on a minute!' she whispered. 'This is a perishin' garden. Oh, I don't deny it's been let run wild, but it really is a garden, Steve. I didn't know there were gardens anywhere near Jamaica Close. Why, there's fully grown trees – flowers an' all. Someone could live here. I wonder who owns it? Oh, look, roses, really beautiful ones! Gosh, don't they smell sweet? And there's masses of black-berries, only they're still red berries now – and look at the rhubarb! The stems are as thick as my wrist; I bet they'd be really tough if you tried to put 'em in a pie.'

Steve followed her glance. 'Is that rhubarb?' he said, sounding surprised. 'I've never seen them big leaves on top of it when it's for sale in St John's market. But there's gooseberries, two or three different sorts, and I reckon there were strawberries once, only they've all gone tiny.

But the blackcurrant bushes, though the fruit is getting thinner, are still just about alive.'

Miranda drew in a deep ecstatic breath and expelled it in a low whistle. 'Oh, Steve, this place is just about perfect! We could come here every day and bring it back to what it was years ago. We could root out the weeds, harvest the fruit – I've already seen two apple trees, a Victoria plum and a greengage – and then we could sell the fruit and buy seed with the money. The first thing we ought to do is get rid of the weeds and dig over all the beds. I remember my mum saying you should always plant potatoes in ground that's new to cultivation, and before the crash came she was a farmer's daughter and knew what she was talking about. Oh, Steve, do let's.'

She looked at her pal and saw that he was laughing. 'Honest to God, Miranda, you're mad as meself,' he said approvingly. 'I had the same thought when I first found me way in, but it ain't possible, of course. Someone must own both the house and the garden, and I'll take a bet that if we started to interfere somebody would fetch the scuffers.' He pointed to the wall. 'See that loose brick? It's the one with the splash of white paint on it, which I put there so's to identify it. Pull it out.'

Miranda did as she was told and found that the brick had been hollowed out and contained an interesting number of coins and one beautiful, if dirty, ten shilling note. Hastily, she plunged a hand into her skirt pocket and produced almost a shilling in pennies and ha'pennies, which she slid into the hollow of the brick. She watched as Steve replaced it in the wall, then jerked her thumb towards it. 'Isn't it time we took a look at the house itself? You were kidding when you said someone would get the scuffers if we dug the beds over, weren't you?' she asked hopefully. 'No one's been here for years – ten, or twenty, or even more! The garden's a wonderful tangle, but we shan't be able to play in it until we've cut the weeds and brambles down. Goodness, Steve, there's a bed of nettles up agin that old door that's almost as tall as I am, and though the brambles are covered in berries, they're covered in prickles as well. We can't do much out here until we've armed ourselves with a scythe, a couple of spades and some garden shears. As it is, we'll have to be right careful, because the path's disappeared and if we aren't really clever we'll arrive at the house just about covered in stings and scratches. You'd better go first, because my legs are bare and you've got kecks. Look, that's where the path was once; it goes straight to the door, and . . .'

Steve gave a snort. 'If you think I'm goin' to walk, bold as brass, up to that door you're bleedin' well wrong,' he said roundly. 'I've not told you, because I didn't imagine you'd be daft enough to risk goin' into a tottering old house, but since you are I'll tell you why I won't go with you. It's haunted, that's why!'

Miranda stared at him, scarcely able to believe her ears. This was one of the rough Mickleborough boys, and everyone knew boys feared nothing, so why should he pretend that the house was haunted, unless he was simply saying it to frighten her? Well, he wouldn't succeed. She pulled a face at him, then tried to push him along the almost obliterated path. 'Don't be so stupid. If you'd said it might fall down and crush the pair of us to a jelly then I would have believed you, but haunted? Ha, ha, ha! You'll tell me next that it's the ghost of your great-uncle who lived in the house when he was a boy and got trapped in an old oak chest, like the woman in the story.'

She looked at Steve, waiting for him to begin to laugh, and to say that he was only kidding, but he did nothing of the sort. 'If you go in there, you go alone,' he said firmly. 'I've only ever been in once, and that was enough for me. Honest to God, Miranda, I never believed in ghosts until I discovered this place. I liked it so much that I fought my way through the nettles and brambles and went in through that door, the one you can see there. I crossed the kitchen – I think it was the kitchen – and went into the next room. It were pretty dark because the windows have been boarded up, though of course the wall goes all the way round the whole building so there ain't a lot of light anyhow. There's furniture in there; I reckon it were a dining room once, but no sooner had I took a look round than I heard someone singing. At first I thought it were coming from outside, but then I realised it were in the next room along. I'm tellin' you, Miranda, for two pins I would have cut and run . . .' he grinned unhappily, 'but I didn't have a pin on me, so I fumbled my way along a short corridor, which smelled horrible, until I found the doorknob of the next room, and . . . oh, Miranda, even remembering makes me go cold all over . . . and before I could turn the handle I felt it turn in my fingers. I swear to God I hadn't moved it, so I knew there was someone on the other side of the door. I can tell you I snatched my hand back as though the doorknob were red hot, but the door swung open and after a moment I peered inside. The singing had stopped, but I couldn't see no one; the room was empty and dark.

Then . . . someone started to laugh. It was a horrible laugh, the sort madmen give, you know? I took one last look round the room – it was empty all right – and then I ran like a rabbit and didn't stop until I had me hand on the outside door. Then I collapsed on to the grass and told myself that I'd imagined the whole thing. Only I'm not the imaginative kind.' He straightened his shoulders and grinned perkily at Miranda. 'So if you go into the house, you go alone,' he repeated firmly. 'And now let's have the bread and cheese me mam gave me. I wish I'd thought to bring a bottle of cold tea – even telling you about the ghost has dried me mouth.'

Miranda stared at him; he was the most down to earth person she could imagine, which meant that if he said he had heard mysterious laughter coming from an empty room then she simply had to believe him. He had said he thought the house was haunted, but Miranda thought this most unlikely. She knew sound travels in peculiar ways and decided it was quite possible that a tramp had moved into the old house, but did not want anyone to know the place was occupied. Being a child of the theatre she knew very well that it was possible for someone to 'throw their voice', so that the sound appeared to come from somewhere quite different. Therefore, she patted Steve's arm in a motherly fashion and sat him down beside her on a low wall. 'I know what I'm going to tell you sounds odd, but we have had variety acts in the theatre from time to time. All sorts of different ones – conjurers, tight rope walkers and mystery acts – and one of the latter is a chap called Cheeky Charlie, who can throw his voice. It's really odd; he can stand stage left, smiling at the audience, but his voice will come from stage right, and because he's also what they call a ventriloquist you won't see his lips move, not even a little bit.'

Steve snorted. 'Do you expect me to believe that a feller with a gift like that is wasting his time frightenin' kids so's they don't investigate a tumble-down old house?' he enquired, his voice vibrant with disbelief. 'Pull the other one, Miranda Lovage, it's got bells on! Tell you what, if you go in, and can find a logical reason for that awful laughter, then I'll give you a bag of Mrs Kettle's gobstoppers and not even ask for a suck.'

Miranda giggled. It was a good offer, and one she should have seized immediately, yet to her own surprise she did not do so. Instead, she got up and, skirting the worst of the nettles and brambles, made her way towards the house. Even as she did so, she found herself hoping that something would occur to save her from having to put her theory to the test. She looked back hopefully at Steve. 'If you come with me you'll be able to see that it's all moonshine and there's no ghoulies or ghosties or long-leggedy beasties waiting to jump out and shout boo,' she said. 'If you won't come in, how can I prove that I've even crossed the threshold?'

Steve chuckled. 'I'll see you go in, and I can guarantee that if you get into the room I told you about you'll come out of there like a rocket, and that'll be proof enough for me.'

That was scarcely reassuring, but Miranda took a deep breath, squared her shoulders and began to push her way through the waist-high leaves, having to stop every now and again to detach the clinging brambles as she approached the old house. As she got closer, two things occurred to her. One was that the door which she took to lead into the kitchen was sturdy and strong-looking; the other was that it looked quite modern, not at all in poor repair like the rest of the house. Insensibly, Miranda found this cheering. Indeed, she found herself hoping that the door would be firmly locked against her, which would be a cast iron excuse for going no further. When she reached it, however, her secret and unworthy hopes were proved false. The door swung open easily beneath her touch, with no eldritch shriek of old and unused hinges. Indeed it swung wide, letting in light which penetrated the room for several feet.

Behind her, Miranda heard a peculiarly nasty chuckle which made her blood run cold, until she realised that it was only Steve trying to frighten her. Then she walked steadily into the room, which was indeed the kitchen. It was, as Steve had said, very dark inside, because every window was covered by shutters, firmly closed.

She crossed the kitchen on silent feet, beginning to be aware of a rather unpleasant sensation. She felt that she was being watched, though there was no one in the room beside herself – she could tell that even in the semi-darkness – but she wasn't afraid, only annoyed with Steve, who had refused to back her up and search through the building with her. She glanced back at the open door and through it she saw Steve sitting on one of the low walls eating an apple, staring through the aperture at her. Miranda gave a little wave and was disproportionately glad when Steve waved back. She wished she had an apple, and for a moment contemplated returning to the garden and insisting that Steve share his ill-gotten gains, but then, with a resigned sigh, she decided to get her exploration over. She left the kitchen, mouse quiet, and entered the passageway of which her pal had spoken. Because there was no light at all, not even a crack from a badly shuttered window, the corridor was pitchy black, and though Miranda told herself over and over that she did not believe in ghosts, she still felt a frisson of something very close to fear when she stretched out her hand and laid it on the doorknob of the room which Steve had said was haunted. She moved her fingers very carefully, half believing that the door knob would be wrenched out of her hand by sepulchral fingers, but greatly to her relief it was only she who gently twisted the knob, opened the door silently and peered inside.

Blackness met her eyes, total blackness without one speck of daylight. Miranda took one faltering step into the room and even as she did so she thought she heard a low chuckle begin. It was, as Steve had said, an inhuman noise; it sounded as though it came from hell itself and all Miranda's courage and determination fled. She shot out of the door backwards, clouting her elbow so hard on the unseen door jamb that she emitted a startled shriek, and as she ran at top speed along the corridor, crossed the dimly lit kitchen at a gallop and burst into the warm and sunny garden she was only too willing to admit that there was something very odd indeed hidden away in the crumbling mansion.

Steve was laughing. 'Told you so,' he said mockingly. 'Did you hear that awful laugh? I've been sitting out here telling myself it was some sort of trick, like what you told me about the man who could throw his voice. Well, I dare say it is, but it's put me off and I bet it's put you off too.'

He had remained sitting on the low wall and Miranda

sat down beside him. She was still breathless, both from her fast run up the garden, heedless of nettles and brambles, and her fear over what had befallen her in the house, but she was beginning to calm down and to examine what had happened with a critical eye. 'What is really odd is that I still like the house, and the garden too. The garden's beautiful, somewhere I wouldn't mind spending a great deal of time. And I think, if we came back here with an electric torch each and threw open all the shutters in the house, and got to work cleaning it, then it would be a grand place to play. We could have it for our own, because no one else seems to want it. In fact we could kit it out – the kitchen at any rate – and stay here overnight, if we had a mind.'

Steve stared at her, and she read awe in his glance. 'You're a girl and a half, you are!' he exclaimed. 'Ain't you afraid of nothin', Miranda Lovage? I wouldn't stay in that bleedin' evil mansion, norrif they paid me a hundred quid a night. And as for likin' it – you must be mad! Don't tell me you wasn't scared, because I shan't believe you.'

Miranda snorted. 'I was frightened all right, when I heard that laugh,' she admitted. 'But I'll tell you something really weird, Steve. I know it sounds daft – quite mad, really – but when I was in the kitchen I kept having the oddest feeling that the house had something to do with my mother and her disappearance. The police stopped being interested ever so soon after she went, and though some of her friends, especially the Madison Players, tried their best to contact her, even their interest faded away after a few months. But I still believe somebody stole my mother away and if I hunt really hard I'll find her.' She looked hopefully at her companion. 'Will you help me, Steve? You've never met my mother, but she's ever so beautiful and the nicest person in the world. If we find her, she'll take me away from my aunt and reward you somehow, though I don't know how. What do you say to that, eh?'

Steve was sitting, elbows on knees, hands supporting his chin, but now he stood up, nodding slowly. 'I'd like to get you away from your perishin' aunt. That woman has some nerve, to knock you about when you aren't even her own child,' he said, and Miranda had to turn her head away to hide the smile. She thought it funny that Steve believed mums and dads had a perfect right to scalp you alive, but other relatives should keep their distance; still, no point in raising the matter now. Instead she got up and headed for the door in the garden wall.

'Let's be getting home so we can earn some money. Torches are expensive, but candles are pretty cheap. Suppose we come over here tomorrow with a few candle ends and explore the house that way? If we wait until we've saved enough for electric torches, we'll still be waiting come Christmas.'

'Shurrup,' Steve said briskly. 'I agree with you that the garden's prime, but I won't go into the house again, not if you were to pay me a hundred smackeroos. Not by torchlight, nor candlelight, not even by bleedin' search-light. Hear me?'

'Where have you been, Miranda Lovage?' Beth's voice was shrill with annoyance. 'You're supposed to be a friend of mine, as well as me cousin, but you bobby off without me whenever you've a mind, leavin' me to do

74

Mam's messages while you play with that nasty, dirty Mickleborough kid from Number Two.' She glared spitefully at the younger girl. 'Mam were goin' to take the pair of us to New Brighton tomorrow because she's got a load of starched tablecloths for one of the big hotels on the front, and she said if we'd carry half a dozen each then once they were delivered – and paid for, o'course – she'd let us play on the sand and paddle and have tea and doughnuts before we come home again. But when I tell her how you've been off wi' that scruffy Steve Mickleborough, that'll be you out.'

Once, Miranda would have jumped at the thought of such a delightful day out, but now she shook her head in pretended sorrow. 'Sorry Beth, I've got other plans,' she said briefly, and then, seeing the spiteful look deepen on her cousin's face, she broke into hurried speech. 'I'd come with you and give you a hand if I could, honest to God I would, but it just isn't on. I promised Mrs Mickleborough that I'd tidy round after they left, and then lock up. I told you, they're having a whole week at the seaside to make up for them all having the measles. They're renting two rooms down by the funfair; all she wants to do now is cook enough grub for the first three or four days of the holiday. I'm going to help her, I promised, and she's going to give me a sixpence if I agree to check the house every few days to make sure all's well.'

'You're a liar,' Beth said at once. 'Mrs Mickleborough's quite capable of doin' her own cookin'; she won't want you hangin' about. And if you told her you were needed to help with the tablecloths she'd probably say to leave the cleanin' till they're due back.' Her tone abruptly descended from demanding to coaxing. 'Aw, come on, Miranda, be a sport. You'll enjoy New Brighton, you know you will, and it'll be no fun for me if I have to go with Mam alone, 'cos she hates the seaside. If you've got any pennies we might have a go on the funfair – I'm rare fond of the swing boats – so why not be a pal and come with us?'

The two cousins were sitting on the steps outside Number Six, in Beth's case simply watching the other girls as they jumped in and out of the rope, chanting 'Salt, mustard, vinegar, pepper' as they played. Miranda, on the other hand, was waiting her turn to join in the skipping, so only had half her attention upon her cousin. She understood why Beth was so keen to have her company and was tempted to agree to go along, for though she and Steve had been saving up every penny they could they still had not got enough money to buy really strong torches. Miranda had finally persuaded Steve to relent, but though each had acquired a pocketful of candle ends and a box of Swan Vestas, they had only essayed one attempt to look round the house by candle-light and they both remembered, with a jolt of sickening horror, how the moment they had opened the door the invisible laugher had reached out an invisible hand and snuffed their candles, to the accompaniment of mad giggling.

Naturally enough, their retreat had been fast and terri-fied; Steve almost trampling Miranda underfoot as they had both fought to escape back into the garden, whilst the mad giggle behind them had gradually faded into silence. Later, without telling anyone why he was inter-ested, Steve had made some casual enquiries about the place and learned that a man who had made himself a huge fortune by dealing in slaves had lived here. That man had profited by the misery and degradation of the people whose lives he had ruined. And now, Miranda had thought dramatically when Steve told her the story, his restless soul was not allowed to enter heaven, but was tied for ever to the place where he had lived in uncaring luxury for so long.

'Miranda? What is it you and that feller get up to?' Beth whined. 'You never used to go off without me. Sometimes you used to hang around the Close, sometimes you went wanderin' off up towards the centre where the big shops are, sometimes I believe you even went home to the Avenue, though there's strangers livin' in your house now. Oh, and you went to the theatre of course, hoping they'd tell you somethin' about your mam, only they never did, 'cos they don't know nothin'. But after we'd all had the measles, you changed. You and that Steve went off just about every day, I dunno where. And now, when the Mickleboroughs are off to the seaside for a whole week, you might at least do things wi' me until they get back.'

Miranda sighed, and was about to agree to go to the seaside with Beth – it was better than hanging around the Close, after all – when something suddenly occurred to her. Steve was nice all right, probably the only real friend she had, but after that one ill-fated expedition he had refused point-blank to explore the slave trader's mansion again. Miranda herself had learned a good deal about the house lately. She had gone to what the school children called the museum of slavery and seen for herself the leg irons and manacles, the instruments of punishment, and talked to old folk who still remembered hearing how the slaves had been lined up in one of the city squares and auctioned to the highest bidder in those far off days. Miranda's soft heart had wept for the misery the slaves had suffered. Husbands, wives and children had been torn apart and Miranda, robbed of her own mother, thought she knew how they must have felt, the depths of their suffering.

One old man had told her many stories of how brutal and sadistic were the men who ran the sugar cane plantations on the island of Jamaica, where many of the slaves were destined to go. She had heard stories of dead or dying slaves being thrown overboard from the clipper ships, so many that sharks would follow in the ships' wake, eager for the 'food' thrown out by such uncaring hands.

Though the stories had horrified her, Miranda had been tempted to pass them on to Steve, but in the end had decided against it. She guessed he would show a ghoulish interest in them, but she also guessed that it would probably make him even less keen to enter the house. And now, with the summer holidays looming to a close and even the sheltered trees in the walled garden beginning to take on the tints of autumn, their free time would soon become severely restricted. Opportunities to visit their playground would be limited to weekends, and once the really bad weather set in she imagined that Steve's enthusiasm, always somewhat lukewarm even for the garden, would probably disappear altogether.

Before her conversation with old Mr Harvey, Miranda had told herself that since she most certainly did not believe in ghosts it was some trick of sound, perhaps from an underground stream, or even an echo, which had frightened her so. But now, with her new knowledge of the terrible past of the old house, she shared a good deal of Steve's apprehension, along with a growing feeling that, if there were a ghost, the ghost of some poor tormented slave who had suffered at the hands of the mansion's owner, it might recognise in her a kindred spirit.

For although it was perhaps unfair to compare living with her aunt to slavery, she was undoubtedly bullied and derided. Aunt Vi treated her like dirt, took pleasure in piling work on her weary shoulders, and the only emotion she showed her was dislike; never a hint of gratitude. Mr Harvey had called her 'Cinderella', though only in jest, but to Miranda the nickname was no joke; it was too close to the truth. Furthermore, she too had known the pain of loss when her dearly beloved mother had been torn from her arms. It occurred to her now that if she went into the house alone, and there really was a ghost living there, then she would be able to identify with the poor creature, which was more than Steve could do.

'Miranda!' Beth's whining voice jerked Miranda abruptly back into the present. In her mind's eye she had been seeing the tall white clipper ships and their miserable cargo as they sailed ever further from the country of their birth, and now here she was back in Jamaica Close with the girls playing jump the rope on the dirty paving stones and her cousin jerking at her arm. 'Miranda, *will* you answer me! If that horrible boy is off to the seaside then why can't you come to New Brighton with Mam and me?'

'I've *told* you . . . I promised to help . . .'

But Beth cut ruthlessly across her sentence. 'I don't care what you promised, and nor will me mam,' she said angrily. 'We can't manage all them bloody tablecloths without someone to give us a hand, so you can just make up your mind to it that you're coming to New Brighton with us; savvy?'

Miranda reflected with an inward smile that Beth was just like her mother. She never considered the feelings of others but simply went straight for whatever she wanted, either bullying or whining, depending which she thought would be more successful. Today, however, Miranda told herself, she was doomed to disappointment. She turned to her cousin, giving her a falsely sweet smile. 'Sorry, Beth, you and your mum are on a loser. Unless you intend to drag me to the ferry in chains, you're going to have to carry those tablecloths yourselves.' She got briskly to her feet, dusting down her skirt, but moving judiciously out of her cousin's reach before she did so. 'I can't even promise to help as far as the ferry because I shall be too busy. See you later, queen!'

'One, two, three spells out! You goin' to jump in, Miranda?'

Elsie Fletcher, one of the older girls, grinned encouragingly at Miranda and indicated that they would slow the rope if she wanted to jump in. Miranda ran forward and saw Elsie and the other girls grin as Beth began to sob. 'You're supposed to be me pal . . .' she was wailing, but when no one took the slightest notice she got heavily to her feet and went slowly through the front door of Number Six, still calling Miranda every bad name she could think of.

'That there cousin of yours is a right nasty piece of work,' Elsie said as the rope began to revolve smoothly once more. 'Dunno how you stand her meself.'

'She can be all right at times, and anyway she's not nearly as horrible as my aunt,' Miranda confessed ruefully. 'They want me to go with them to help carry a load of starched tablecloths back to one of the big hotels in New Brighton . . .' she grinned at Elsie, 'but I've other fish to fry, and won't my aunt be mad when Beth tells on me!'

Elsie returned her grin. 'I might have guessed she were a tale-clat as well,' she said. 'Still, a day in New Brighton ain't to be sneezed at. You might even get an ice cream cornet out of the old witch; mebbe even a dinner, or at least a paddle in the briny.'

Miranda snorted. 'If she bought me an ice cream she'd charge me for it, and the same goes for a dinner,' she said gloomily. 'Aunt Vi doesn't give anything away for nothing. But I've got business of my own to attend to, so I'll bypass New Brighton, just this once.'

Elsie nodded understandingly. 'Don't blame you; I only met your mam a couple of times, but Gawd above knows how she managed to have such a 'orrible sister as Vi,' she said. 'If I were you I'd sag off, find meself somewhere else to live . . . ever thought of it?'

'Heaps of times,' Miranda admitted. She and Elsie, being in different classes, had never had much to do with each other in the past but now Miranda realised she had an ally in the older girl. 'But I'm always hoping my mother will turn up again; she'd never leave me on purpose, honest to God she wouldn't.'

The other girl grinned. 'Course she wouldn't,' she said

firmly. 'Well, kid, if you ever need help in gettin' away from that aunt of yours, just let me know. I'd be tickled pink to put a spoke in her wheel, especially if it helped you. And one of these days your mam will return; I'm as sure of it as I am that you'll escape from the witch. Did you know we called her that – the witch, I mean?'

Miranda shook her head. Not only had she found a friend, but she was now aware of how much her aunt was disliked. She thought the nickname suited Vi admirably and could not wait to tell Steve. She must go round to Number Two straight away, and help her pal's mother – who so generously fed her on bread and cheese when Aunt Vi let her go hungry – to get ready for their longed-for holiday.

Chapter Four

Two mornings later, having made up her mind to take advantage of Steve's absence to visit the old house, Miranda slid out of bed as soon as the first grey light of dawn could be glimpsed between the thin bedroom curtains. She had had an uncomfortable night, with Aunt Vi taking up three quarters of the bed and Beth occupying the remaining quarter, so that Miranda was forced to cling on to the edge of the mattress and hope she would not be pushed out by either of the other two occupants. She had managed to sleep for the first few hours, too exhausted to remain awake, for her aunt, furious over her refusal to accompany them to New Brighton, had brought back a large quantity of dirty linen which, despite the heat of the day, she had taken straight to the wash house. After tea, she had refused to allow Miranda to leave the kitchen; had actually locked the door so that escape was impossible. Then she had built the fire up, stood a row of irons in the hearth and made her niece iron every single one of the huge white tablecloths. Miranda's arms, shoulders and back had ached agonisingly by the time she tackled the last one, and though she had done her best and worked as hard as she possibly could she had somehow managed to scorch the hem, causing Aunt Vi to slap her head resoundingly and say that, had it not been so late, she would have sent her niece back to the wash house to scrub away at the scorch mark and then made her iron the tablecloth again, wet though it would have been.

But the discomfort of her position had woken her long before the others were stirring, so she was able to slip out of bed without either of them appearing to notice that she had gone. She dressed quickly, not wanting to wash since the splashing might awaken one of them, and made her way down to the kitchen. There, the gingham curtains were still drawn across and the banked down fire showed red gleams where it was beginning to come to life. Miranda looked round the room; she could make herself some breakfast, but it would be best if she did not start to cook; just the smell of porridge might bring her relatives sleepily down the stairs. If so, they might start nagging again, or say she should stay at home to do the chores, or run messages; whichever it was, escape might become impossible, so Miranda cut a chunk off the loaf and spread it thinly with margarine, then generously with jam. She peeped into the pantry and saw a bottle of her cousin's favourite raspberry cordial standing on the slate slab beneath the window to keep cool. It was three quarters full. Miranda picked up an empty bottle, poured some cordial into it, went to the sink and added a judicious amount of water, capped the bottle and was about to investigate the contents of the large cake tin when she heard a slight noise from upstairs. It was probably only her cousin, or her aunt, turning over in their sleep, but Miranda was taking no chances. She glided across the kitchen and slipped out into the freshness of the morning. Closing the door behind her with infinite caution, she padded across the yard and let herself out into the jigger; then she headed for the old house.

It was the first time Miranda had ever been out alone this early; on the only other occasion when she had abandoned her bed at such an early hour she had been meeting Steve, but now she was on her own and able to appreciate the coolness and quietness of the streets. To be sure there were one or two people about, mostly making their way down to the docks, and she saw several cats, going about their mysterious business without so much as a glance in her direction. She saw a dog as well; a miserable skinny stray with sores on its back and a look in its eyes which caused Miranda to stop her onward rush. She knew that look too well, knew that her own eyes often reflected the desperation she could see in the mild gaze of the little brown and white cur. She held out a hand to it and it came slowly, clearly more used to kicks than caresses, but when she produced her jam sandwich and broke off a generous piece, hunger obviously overcame fear and it slunk closer, taking the food from her fingers with such careful gentleness that she could have wept. Instead, however, she squatted down on the pavement and fed the little creature a good half of the sandwich before tucking the food back into the pocket of her skirt. 'Tell you what, dog,' she said to it as she straightened up once more, 'if you're still around when I'm headin' for home later today – if the ghost hasn't killed me, that is – then I'll try to make do with a few apples, so you can have the rest of my bread and jam.'

It sounded like a generous offer but Miranda knew, guiltily, that she was unlikely to have to make it good.

Stray dogs don't hang around in one vicinity, they are for ever moving on, and she was sure this dog would be no exception. However, she was rather touched to realise, after half a mile, that the dog was still following her. She told herself firmly that it was not she the dog followed but the bread and jam, yet in her heart she did not believe it. The dog had recognised a fellow sufferer and wanted her company even more than he wanted food.

But he'll never stand the pace, Miranda told herself. I've simply got to hurry because I must be in the garden before the shift change, and I don't know when that is. Come to that I don't know if the factory works twenty-four hours because Steve and I only ever come here during the day, and then of course we avoid the times when we hear the hooter and know there will be folk about. I think Steve said he thought the chaps on the factory floor worked from 8 a.m. to 4 p.m., but for the office workers it's 9 to 6. Oh gosh, I wonder what the time is now? I really am an idiot; it's all very well coming early but I wouldn't want to be on the wrong side of the wall when there are crowds about. Someone would be bound to spot me and start asking questions, questions which I wouldn't want to answer, even if I could.

She told herself that there was no point in lingering, however, and she and the dog continued to twist and turn through the many little streets which separated them from the mansion. Presently her doubts were resolved when the breeze brought them the sound of a clock striking six times. Miranda smiled to herself, then glanced back at the little dog, trudging wearily along behind her, with what looked like a foot of pink tongue dangling from between its small jaws. Miranda slowed, then stopped, and addressed her companion. 'Am I going too fast for you, feller? Tell you what, when we reach the garden I'll get you a drink of water; I can see you could do with one.'

The dog glanced up at her, seeming to smile, definitely indicating that a drink of water would be extremely welcome, Miranda thought. And the dog wasn't the only one; as the heat of the day increased she grew thirstier herself and began to think longingly of the apples and greengages which still hung from the trees in the garden. She wondered if the dog's thirst could be slaked by fruit, but doubted it. Time, however, would tell, and if the little dog took to fruit then she would have no need to go into the kitchen in order to find him a drink.

Judging by the chimes of the clock she had heard, Miranda thought she must have left Jamaica Close well before six and it was still early – only around seven o'clock – when she and the dog slid quietly along the rosy brick wall and approached the garden door. No one was about, and Miranda paused to listen. She was relieved to realise that there was no sound at all coming from the big ugly factory next door, which during the daytime buzzed with every sort of noise: talk, laughter, the clattering and clash of machinery and many other sounds. It was pretty plain that whatever the factory made – Steve had told her he thought it was munitions, though why such things should be manufactured when the country was at peace she had no idea – they did not work twenty-four hours, which meant that if they were careful their presence need never be discovered. However, habit made Miranda open the garden door as softly as possible and take a quick look round the walled garden, which she thought should more accurately be called the wilderness, before closing the door behind her. When she glanced back she saw the little dog standing uneasily in the aperture, wearing the expression of one who has too often been rudely rejected to take acceptance for granted.

Miranda patted her knee. 'Come along in, little feller,' she said encouragingly. 'This here is our place – yours and mine, and Steve's too of course – so don't you hesitate, just come straight in.'

The dog did hesitate but then he trotted through the doorway and moved as close as he could to Miranda without actually touching. She could see he was shivering and put a protective hand on the top of his smooth brown and white speckled head. 'I told you it was all right for both of us to come in, and so it is,' she whispered. 'And now we're going to get you that drink of water. I wonder if there's a well anywhere in the garden which we've not noticed? If so, we could get the water from there.'

But even as she said the words she knew she was kidding herself, knew she was still none too keen on entering the house itself. That was why she had nagged Steve so relentlessly, begging him to accompany her. She, Miranda Lovage, was frightened of sounds which she did not understand. How ashamed her mother would be if she knew that her daughter was hesitating before giving a poor little dog a drink, just because of a noise which, after all, she had only heard once – she did not count the time she and Steve thought they had heard giggling in the kitchen because they had bolted out so quickly that it had probably been their imagination. She produced her bottle of raspberry cordial and took a quick swallow, and watched with guilty dismay as the little dog's eyes followed the movement of bottle to mouth with obvious wistfulness. Thinking back, Miranda realised that it had been at least a month and possibly more since it had rained. Puddles had dried up, gutters had run dry; a stray dog would have a long walk before finding even the tiniest puddle.

Miranda had come here determined to investigate the house. One pocket in her skirt contained half the jam sandwich and the raspberry cordial. The other was full of candle ends and a box of matches. Yet having arrived at her destination, she found she was still reluctant to actually walk into the house. If only it wasn't so dark! There were shutters at most of the windows, and the ones without shutters had been boarded up.

Miranda stood for a moment with her hand on the knob of the kitchen door. She wondered what Steve was doing, imagined him wading through the shallows with the hot sun on his back, then plunging into deeper water, whilst Kenny jumped up and down at the water's edge, shouting to his brother to give him a piggy back so that he too might get wet all over.

How Miranda envied them! How she wished that she too was on a beautiful sunny beach with the sea creaming against her bare feet and the whole happy day in front of her. But it was no use wishing; she had promised the dog a drink and a drink he would jolly well have even though it did mean entering the old house and fumbling her way across to the low stone sink. She had never been anywhere near it, had only glimpsed it as she had crossed the kitchen, heading for the corridor which led to the rest of the house, but now, she told herself firmly, she was going to stop acting like a superstitious idiot and get the dog some water. Resolutely she turned the knob and pushed the door open wide, letting in the dappled sunlight, making the place seem almost ordinary. Standing in the doorway, still hesitating before actually entering the room, she glanced cautiously around her. She saw the huge Welsh dresser which she had glimpsed on her first visit and a long trestle table; also the low stone sink with a pump handle over it. There was another door to her right which she imagined must once have opened on to the pantry, and a door to her left which she knew led to the passageway, and now that her eyes were growing a little more accustomed to the gloom she could make out piles of pans, dishes, and other such paraphernalia spread out upon the shelves which ran from one end of the room to the other. Good! She would fill a bowl or dish with water for the dog and then, if her courage held, use one of her candle ends to investigate the rest of the house.

She was halfway across to the sink, her hand extended to the pump handle, when once more she began to suspect that she was being watched. Uneasily, she glanced around her, then down at the dog, and she knew that had he shown any sign of wanting to bolt she would have been close behind him. But the little animal's attention was fixed on the pump and the enamelled bowl she held. Sighing, she seized the pump handle and began to ply it, and immediately two things happened: a trickle of water emerged from the big brass tap and something scurried across the sink, making for Miranda.

She gave a shriek so loud that she frightened herself.

The dog backed away, whining, and then ran forward, put his front paws on the side of the sink and began to lap at the narrow stream of water emerging from the tap, whilst Miranda, clutching the bodice of her dress against her thumping heart, backed away from the enormous spider which had been driven into activity by the action of the pump.

'Oh, oh, oh! You hateful horrible creepy-crawly!' she shrieked, unable to stop herself. 'Don't you come near me or I'll stamp on you and squash you flat.' She turned reproachfully to the little dog. 'Why don't you defend me?' She peered into the sink but could see no movement and, keeping well back, held the enamelled bowl beneath the trickle of water until it contained a reasonable amount. She looked all round her, but it was much too dark to see where the spider had disappeared, so she placed the dish on the floor with extreme caution, clutching her ragged skirts close to her knees as though she feared that the dreaded enemy would presently creep out of cover and climb up her bare legs. She stood very still, trying to convince herself that the spider was probably long gone, having spotted the open door and galloped into the sunlight. She wanted to pick up the bowl of water and carry it outside, but the little dog was still drinking and it seemed a mean thing to do, to interrupt him when he had had so many disappointments already in his short life. And anyway, Miranda was growing used to the kitchen. To be sure, she had felt she was being watched, but she now concluded that it must have been the spider and wondered why it had never occurred to her to open the shutters. There was light coming through the back door – sunlight, what was more

– but if anything it tended to make the rest of the room seem even darker in comparison, whereas if she were to open all the shutters . . .

She had actually stretched out a hand to the nearest pair when she realised that by opening up she might be letting in more than sunlight. Safely hidden away in the slats there might be whole colonies of spiders similar to the one which had apparently been living in the sink. Miranda decided that opening the shutters would have to wait until Steve returned from the seaside. Boys, she knew, were not afraid of creepy-crawlies. No, she would not touch the shutters, but as soon as the dog had finished drinking she would light one of her candle ends, protect it as far as she could with a hand around it, and investigate at least a part of the house. She had never seen the stairs, but today for the first time she'd noticed that the window of one of the attic rooms gaped black and open, neither shuttered nor boarded up. If she could find that room she might be able to see why it had not been blacked out like most of the other windows.

The dog finished lapping and glanced up at her, apparently to give her an encouraging grin; he actually wagged his disgraceful little tail, which had formerly been clipped so firmly between his back legs that Miranda had thought it had been docked, before giving one last sniff at the enamelled basin. Miranda took a deep breath and set off across the kitchen, and just as she entered the shaft of sunlight coming through the back door she discovered where the spider had gone. It was crouching in that very shaft of sunlight, its hateful legs forming a sort of cage around what looked like a sizeable moth. Poor Miranda gave an even louder shriek than the one which had heralded the spider's first appearance, and even as the echoes of her scream died away a soft voice spoke, seeming to do so almost in her ear. 'I no like spiders either,' the voice said sympathetically. 'I shriek like the factory hooter if I see one near my bed.'

Miranda nearly fainted and her heart, which had speeded up with the spider's reappearance, doubled its pace. She looked wildly round but could see no one, though she noticed that the door leading into the corridor, which had been firmly closed, now swung open.

There was no doubt that, had she been able to do so, Miranda would have cut and run, but fear nailed her to the spot. Once more her gaze raked the room, including the open doorway into the corridor, but she could see nothing, only darkness. 'Where are you?' she quavered. 'I – I hear your voice but I can't see you.'

The chuckle which greeted this remark no longer seemed threatening, but merely amused. 'I here, in the doorway,' the voice said. 'Can't you see me? Where your eyes gone?' The voice suddenly changed from mere curiosity to fear. 'I done nothin' wrong. Why you come here, take my water and eat my apples and plums?'

'I didn't know they were yours – the apples and plums, I mean – and if they are I'm very sorry,' Miranda said, trying hard to keep her voice steady.

There was a short silence, then the voice said: 'Why you come here secretly, instead of knocking on door like Christian?'

'Because we didn't know anybody lived here,' Miranda said, speaking each word separately and with great care. 'For that matter, why are you hiding? I can hear your voice plain as plain but I can see neither hide nor hair of you.' She hesitated, then decided to put the question uppermost in her mind. 'Are you a – a ghost?'

This time the pause was very much longer and the voice, when it spoke again, sounded extremely puzzled. 'Ghost? Why you think I ghost?'

Miranda shrugged helplessly. 'If you're invisible, and I think you are, then you must be a ghost.'

This time the pause was shorter. 'Can ghost own house? I told you this my house; you not believe me?' Miranda was growing accustomed to the voice now. Sometimes it sounded puzzled, sometimes unsure, but at other times impatience with her foolishness seemed uppermost. She shifted her position slightly, almost certain now that the speaker was standing in the corridor, but when she drew her candle out of her pocket and fumbled for the matches, the voice spoke sternly. 'This is old house and catch fire quick. Didn't your mammy tell you not to play wi' matches? Go away now and take candles with you; I'm best in dark. But come back another day and we talk more . . .'

Miranda thought she heard a soft sort of shuffling sound and then she became convinced that she was alone once more, save for the little dog. The ghost had gone without leaving any clue as to his or her identity. Indeed, did a ghost have an identity? Miranda was not sure; the only thing she was sure of was that the woman – thinking back she was positive that it had been a woman's voice – meant no one any harm. Perhaps she was a ghost, or perhaps she was just a very shy person who now owned the place. Miranda was about to return to the garden when her attention was drawn to the little dog. It was staring at the doorway which led to the rest of the house and wagging its poor little scrap of a tail, its shabby ears pricked and its tongue lolling out once more.

The Mickleborough family arrived home quite late on the Saturday, but as soon as day dawned on Sunday Steve was down in the kitchen helping his mother to prepare breakfast, since he was all on fire to get round to Number Six and see what Miranda had been doing in his absence. He had been surprised by how much he had missed her. She wasn't particularly pretty, or particularly clever, but she was grand company, and, despite her miserable home circumstances, game for anything.

Of course, he and his brothers had had a glorious time at the seaside. Little Kenny had watched with envy as the older boys splashed in and out of the sea and became totally at ease in the water. Then there were the wonderful fish and chip suppers, and perhaps best of all the new understanding between himself and his stepfather. Steve was not sure exactly why he and Albert Mickleborough had begun not merely to tolerate but to like one another. He thought it might be the fact that he had begun to call his stepfather 'Dad', whereas previously he had simply avoided calling him anything at all. And then he had greeted the news that his mother was expecting another baby with real enthusiasm; Steve liked small children and had no objection at all to looking after Kenny, whereas his other brothers, particularly Joe, had no interest in their mother's second family. When Albert expressed his hope that the baby would be a girl this time, Steve entered into the discussion with zest, suggesting names, and promising to take the new baby off his mother's hands whenever she and her husband fancied a night out.

All this had made the holiday one of the happiest Steve had ever known, and though normally he would have regretted it when they packed up and made for home, this time, though he knew he would miss the freedom the holiday had given him, his eagerness to tell Miranda all about it was a real compensation for the loss of the seaside he had so enjoyed.

'Wake up, Steve! Aren't you the one for dreaming. Got any plans for today? You've been such a good lad, lookin' after young Kenny so's your dad and I could have time to ourselves, that it's only fair to let you have time off to go around with your pals. If so, I'll pack you up a carry-out, enough for you and that poor little scrawny scrap of a girl what's livin' at Number Six.'

'Oh, Mam, that'd be grand,' her son said with real gratitude. 'But I'll help meself if it's all the same to you. Jam sandwiches, and your oatcakes and cheese, will be fine. I bet she's had a miserable time while we were away so I'll call for her and mebbe we can take a tram out into the country. Simonswood is her favourite place; we were dammin' a stream there to make ourselves a pool deep enough to swim in. She wants me to learn her how. I'd take her up to the Scaldy, but that's a place for fellers really, not girls.'

His mother smiled, and Steve reflected that she was still a pretty woman even though she was old; Steve considered anyone past forty to be over the hill. But now he returned her smile gratefully as he began to lay the table. 'I'll go and get Kenny up if you like, and give him his breakfast,' he volunteered, but Moira Mickleborough shook her head.

'It's all right, lad. You deserve some time to yourself.

And while I'm about it, I'd just like you to know that though I've said nothing, that don't mean I've not appreciated the way you've behaved towards my Albert. Life will be easier for all of us, particularly now that Joe's followed your lead and started calling him Dad too. I'm real grateful to you, 'cos sometimes I've felt like a bone between two dogs, and that ain't a comfortable way to feel.'

Steve chuckled. 'I know what you mean; I've felt the same meself now and then. I won't wait for breakfast. I'll cut myself a carry-out now, with enough spare for Miranda.'

Ten minutes later Steve left the house with the food in his old school satchel and a bottle of water sticking out of the top. He approached Number Six rather cautiously, and was glad he had done so when the front door shot open and fat Vi Smythe appeared on the top step, with Beth hovering close behind her. She was in the middle of shouting for Miranda to come in at once and give a hand with the chores when she spotted Steve, and immediately switched her attention to him. 'You're that blamed iggorant Mickleborough boy, what used to keep company with me niece,' she boomed. 'Aye, you're a nasty piece of work as I remember. So where's Miranda got herself to this time? Not that you'll know, 'cos we've scarce seen either of you for the past week. But now you're back from wherever your mam's fancy feller took you, you might as well be useful. Tell me niece she's to come back here immediate, no messin', else I'll see she gets the thumpin' she deserves.'

Steve did not even answer, though he smiled to himself. If Miranda had not been around Jamaica Close, then he could hazard a pretty good guess where she had been. Not that he intended to give her Aunt Vi any clue. He simply shrugged his shoulders and strolled past Number Six as though he had not even heard the fat woman's shout. However, he paused outside Number Eight when he heard his name hissed in a low voice. Turning his head he saw Jackie Jones gesturing to him. 'I dunno if it's any help, but I seen Miranda goin' off around six o'clock, or even earlier, most mornin's,' the boy said. 'I'm helpin' Evans the Milk to deliver – he pays me a bob an hour – and Miranda goes off real quiet, slippin' out of the front door and closin' it softly behind her. She gives me and Evans a wave, then puts her finger to her lips so we knows as she means we've not seen her, like. Any clues?'

Steve grinned. Jackie was only a kid, but like everyone else in the Close he hated Aunt Vi and pitied Miranda. 'Thanks, Jackie; I guess I know where she's gone,' he said, and set off towards the main road, reaching it just as a nearby clock struck eight. Steve sighed. It would have been more fun had he and Miranda met at six o'clock so that he could have told her all about his wonderful week at the seaside. He felt a trifle peeved, since he had impressed upon Miranda the fact that the family would be returning to Liverpool on Saturday, and had hoped she might have called for him if she wanted to go to the garden. Still, he supposed it was asking too much to expect her to linger anywhere near Number Six and risk being nabbed, either by her aunt or even by Beth, who was not only a year older than her cousin, but taller and a good deal stronger as well.

'Boo!'

Steve jumped quite six inches in the air and turned wrathfully to give whoever had scared him a thump, only to find Miranda, grinning from ear to ear and looking so happy that he nearly gave her a hug. However, he did not do so, merely punching her shoulder lightly and saying: 'Well, well, well! So you *did* wait for me. It was nice of you to hang about when you might have been grabbed by your 'orrible aunt; and there was me thinkin' you'd forgot all about me!'

Miranda's whole face was lit up by an enormous happy smile and Steve saw that she, too, had a shabby satchel on her shoulder, which he guessed must contain food. As he fell into step beside her, he pointed to it. 'Don't say you nicked some grub off of that fat old cow! But won't she take it out on you tonight, when you go home?'

Miranda giggled. 'Who says I do go home?' she asked mockingly. 'Well, sometimes I do, but I make sure it's so late that my aunt's abed, and I leave so early that her snores are still lifting the roof tiles. At first I was afraid she'd twig that food left the house at the same time as I did, but since I only ever take bread and jam and a tiddy bit of lemon water or raspberry cordial, I suppose she thinks it's cheaper than having to feed me a hot meal each evening. And of course there's fruit in the garden; the raspberry canes are awfully overgrown but I pick a good cupful each day, and aren't they the most delicious thing you ever tasted? And there's strawberries, too, and apples, and plums . . . oh, all sorts.'

'Yes,' Steve said, 'but bread and jam and raspberries won't keep you goin' for ever. You ought to have hot meals now and then, you know.'

'I do; once or twice I've stayed in and told my aunt

I'd do her messages, help with the chores and so on, but only in return for a good meal.' She chuckled suddenly. 'You should have seen her face! She was that furious I was quite frightened to go back into the house; but to be fair to Beth, she backed me up. Why, she even helped me with the cooking, though she mainly fetched and carried; didn't want to get flour and fat on her nice clean hands! I'm getting to know her better, and she's all right, underneath. In fact if she ignored her mum we might even be pals. Anyway, working around the house helped the week to pass quicker, which was a good thing, 'cos I don't mind telling you, Steve, that time didn't half drag while you were away.'

'That's nice,' Steve said absently. 'But I guessed you'd been goin' to the garden each day . . . well, you must have been, 'cos where else would you get raspberries?' He hesitated, then asked the question uppermost in his mind. 'Have you been in the house while I was away? Have you – have you seen the ghost?'

'No-oo, but I've heard it,' Miranda said cautiously. 'In fact I wonder if there are secret passages in the house because I don't believe it is a ghost; well, ghosts don't eat, do they? The day before yesterday I put a slice of bread and cheese on the draining board in the kitchen, and yesterday when I went back the bread and cheese was gone. There wasn't so much as a crumb left, so if the ghost didn't take it, who did?'

'Rats,' Steve said succinctly. 'Or mice, I suppose.' He glanced over his shoulder. 'I don't know if you've noticed, but there's a most peculiar-looking little dog following us.' He chuckled. 'Half dog, half rabbit, half rat, at a guess. Shall I shoo it away?'

Miranda stopped short, broke off a piece of whatever it was in her satchel and held it out. The extraordinary little dog came timidly forward, glancing cautiously at Steve as it did so, then reared up on its hind legs and took the proffered titbit so gently that Steve thought it must have been trained to do so. Miranda turned to her pal. 'This here little dog is mine; I call him Timmy. He's bright as a button and knowing as a human. I don't know where he goes at nights, he must have found himself a quiet spot somewhere, but the minute I reach the main road he comes trotting out and joins me. He stays with me all day, wherever I go, but when we get back to Jamaica Close he disappears.' She glared defiantly at Steve. 'I know he's an odd-looking dog but I'm rare fond of him and he's rare fond of me. And he's extraordinarily polite; he waited to be invited before he would come into the garden. Why, if he hadn't been with me I don't believe I'd ever have gone into the kitchen and got to know the Voice . . .'

'The Voice?' Steve interrupted. 'Do you mean the giggler?'

Miranda sighed. 'I'll begin at the beginning and go right up to this morning, when I popped out and said boo,' she told him. 'Timmy attached himself to me the day after you went away, pretty well as soon as I left Jamaica Close, but I'm afraid I walked rather fast and because he's a stray and had been living on any scraps he could pick up he got terribly tired and terribly hot. His tongue hung out a yard and when I had a swig from my bottle of raspberry cordial I could see how thirsty he was. As you know, there's no pond or water tap in the garden, but there's a pump over the sink in the kitchen . . .'

She told her story well, even imitating the strange accent in which she had been addressed, and telling Steve she was sure the voice was a woman's, which made it hard for Steve to believe that she had imagined the whole thing. His own Uncle George, who was in the merchant navy, had once visited Jamaica, and when he came home had often imitated the accent of the Jamaicans he had met on his trip. Hearing that same accent on his pal's lips added authenticity to her story, and when she finished Steve whistled softly beneath his breath. 'You aren't half brave,' he said admiringly. 'You wouldn't have seen me getting into conversation with a perishin' ghost. I say, Miranda, has it occurred to you that there must be some connection between the Voice and the house itself? Why else should a Jamaican be living in Jamaica House?'

Miranda stared at him, her eyes rounding. 'How do you know it's called Jamaica House?' she whispered. 'I suppose you aren't a ghost yourself, come back to haunt the old place and me?'

Steve laughed. 'I see'd a picture in an old book – that were the name carved over the main entrance door, before they built the wall which divides the house from Jamaica Close. I didn't take much notice at the time because I didn't know about the slaves then, but now it all fits, wouldn't you say?'

Miranda nodded slowly. 'Yes, I suppose you're right. Tell you what, we'll ask the Voice. Sometimes questions make her either angry or sad, and when that happens she just goes away and won't come back, no matter how often you say how sorry you are. But I don't see why she should mind talking about the name of the house.' By now they were approaching the little door in the wall and as they went through it, with Timmy close behind them, Miranda said enticingly: 'But now you're here, Steve, you can hear her for yourself. In fact we might be able to trick her into showing herself with two of us. If I engage her in conversation and you sort of go behind where you think she is . . .'

Steve gave a strong shudder. He would do a lot for Miranda, but he did not mean to become part of a ghost hunt. He told himself it was not cowardly to be afraid of ghosts. If she had been a flesh and blood woman, as Miranda had seemed to imply, then that was one thing, but a ghost was different. He knew from his reading of such authors as Edgar Allan Poe, Charles Dickens and even Oscar Wilde that ghosts could do unexpectedly horrible things. Walking through walls, clanking chains and whisking a human being through time and space were but three of their accomplishments, and Steve had no wish to find himself mixed up in such goings-on. But Miranda was looking at him hopefully, so he decided to disillusion her at once. 'I won't go ghost hunting with you, or anyone else for that matter,' he said doggedly. 'I said I'd never go into that perishin' house again, and I meant every word. I've brung a bottle of water to drink and if you and that horrible little dog wants anything out of the kitchen you can get it yourselves; so there!'

Miranda moaned. 'Oh, please, please, please, Steve, help me to find out whether the Voice is a real person or a ghost,' she said urgently. 'I'm not afraid of going into the house any more because Timmy always runs ahead of me now, with his tail wagging. I'm sure she's a real person, and I'm sure it's she who ate the bread and cheese. If only you'll give it a try . . .'

'Just you shut up and listen to me for a moment,' Steve said crossly. 'Suppose it was a real person who took the bread and cheese? If that's so, then how has she been living for the past goodness knows how many weeks on just one piece of bread and cheese? I don't believe she's ever picked any fruit in the garden since we've been coming here – or at least not enough to notice. So go on, tell me. How is she keeping alive?'

Miranda stared at him for a moment while a pink flush crept up her cheeks, then she stamped her foot, took the satchel off her shoulder and slung it down on the grass. Steve noticed that the garden looked a good deal tidier than it had done when he had first entered it, many weeks ago. He asked Miranda if it was her doing, which made her smile. 'Are you saying we're like Mary and Dickon in *The Secret Garden*? If so, you're wrong. Oh, I've done a bit of tidying, rooting out the weeds and clearing a path through the nettles so that I can reach the door without being stung to bits.' She looked around her thoughtfully. 'Do you know, I've not noticed, but you're absolutely right. Someone *has* been tidying up the garden. Well, I'm sure it's not someone from outside, so it must be the Voice. And if you've ever heard of a ghost who did gardening on the side, it's more than I have. Doesn't that convince you that the Voice is real?'

Steve shrugged, then grinned. 'You've got a point,' he admitted. 'And I'll come into the kitchen with you – maybe even further. But if someone starts giggling or walking through walls, or interfering with me in any way whatsoever, I'm off. Is that understood? Oh, and the dog has to go first, because dogs can sense things and if there was a ghost I reckon he'd bolt out of the kitchen howling like a banshee with his tail between his legs.'

Miranda beamed at him. 'And then, when we've both heard the Voice, we'll come out into the garden again and have our carry-out whilst you tell me all about your holiday,' she said. 'Oh, I meant to tell you. If you go into the big trees right up against the wall there's a swing. It's quite safe, I've tried it, and because it's beneath the shade of the trees you get a lovely cool breeze when you swing.'

Steve stared at her, then followed the direction of her pointing finger. It wasn't a proper swing, just a length of very thick rope with a couple of knots around a somewhat dilapidated piece of plank. But it was a swing all right, and Steve was pretty sure that it had not been there on his previous visits. He opened his mouth to say as much, then shut it again and caught hold of Miranda's hand. 'Come on then,' he said cheerfully, pulling her up the path towards the door. He would not have admitted it to Miranda for the world, but the sight of the swing, such a very mundane object, had reassured him as to the nature of the Voice. A ghost would not – could not – erect a swing, but a real person would only do so in order to encourage young people such as himself and Miranda to continue visiting the garden. What was more, Miranda had said it was not she who had attacked the weeds, and in his experience she was a truthful girl and unlikely to tell an unnecessary fib.

She was smiling at him, clearly delighted by his change of heart. 'I'm so glad you're going to come into the house with me; I'm sure you won't regret it,' she said eagerly. 'I've got a good feeling about today; today I think we shall find out why the Voice hides away in the old building and disappears whenever I ask a question which she doesn't want to answer.'

By this time they had reached the door and Miranda pushed it open, whereupon Timmy the dog trotted fearlessly into the darkened kitchen, then looked over his shoulder as if to ask why they were so slow. The three of them walked into the middle of the room and waited for a moment. It was pretty clear that Miranda, and Timmy the dog, expected something to happen, but nothing did, so Miranda crossed the floor and pulled open the door which led to the pitch black hallway, which was the only way to reach all the other rooms in the house. Despite himself, Steve felt a pang which, if not of fear, was definitely of discomfort. Miranda, however, seemed completely at ease. She put her head back and called softly. 'Coo-ee, where are you, Voice?' There was a soft chuckle and despite himself Steve felt the short hairs on the back of his neck bristle like a dog's hackles, but then, as his eyes began to get used to the dark, he thought he saw a slight movement.

'So you have come to visit the lady of the house; I real pleased to welcome you,' the Voice said, and Steve clung even tighter to Miranda's small delicate hand. 'But let us introduce us. I know dog is Timmy, and my friend is Miranda, but who you, boy?'

'I'm Steve Mickleborough,' Steve said awkwardly, and to his complete astonishment he suddenly saw hovering in front of him what looked like a half-moon of white in the darkness. It was so startling, so unexpected, that he gave a squawk of fright and jumped backwards, but Miranda, who had also gasped, suddenly broke into delighted laughter.

'You aren't a ghost, nor just a voice, you're a Cheshire Cat grin,' she said triumphantly. 'Open the shutters so we can see each other properly; you've had your fun, Voice, but it's time you came clean.'

The grin disappeared, if it was a grin, and for a moment Steve thought that the Voice had left the room, possibly annoyed by the fact that she was no longer a mystery to her two guests. But then one of the shutters creaked back a couple of inches and in the sunlight which poured through the gap Steve saw that the mystery woman was black as coal, and dressed entirely in black as well. Liverpool being a port, Steve was well used to the sight of black seamen roaming the streets. They were friendly and much addicted to the markets, where they spent lavishly on all sorts of strange objects. But by and large these visitors were men, whereas the person smiling uncertainly at them in the shaft of sunlight was most definitely a woman. She was tiny, even smaller than Miranda, and very skinny, which Steve thought not surprising considering that she must have been existing on any scraps she could find, plus a bit of fruit from the garden. Her face was wrinkled, her nose hooked, but her eyes twinkled at them and Steve was sure she was enjoying their surprise, and was even more sure of it when she grinned again. Her thin black hair was pulled into a tight little bun at the nape of her neck but Steve could not guess her age, though he thought she must be very old, fifty or sixty at least.

As soon as the light had entered the room, Miranda had bounded forward and seized the woman's hands in both of hers. 'So *that's* why we couldn't see you, and thought you were just a voice; we never thought you might be black,' she said. 'Do let's go into the garden to talk, though, because the house is awfully musty and I'm afraid if we start to open the shutters . . .'

'No,' the woman said quickly, shutting the one she had opened and plunging them into darkness once more. 'People come lookin'; mebbe he come again . . . at nighttimes I bolt doors and shutters. He not know I here, but if he did . . .'

She stopped speaking, looking anxiously from one face to the other, and Miranda spoke quickly, keen to calm any fears which the older woman might feel. 'It's all right, Voice, we won't touch the shutters. But who are you afraid of? No one comes here, do they? Well, not in daylight anyhow. So let's go outside, shall we? Oh, by the way, you know our names, but what's yours?'

As she spoke Miranda had been leading the way out of the dining room, through the kitchen and into the bright sunlight, to the place where she and Steve usually ate any food they had managed to bring with them. It was a long stone seat, set in a curved alcove in the great brick wall, and was a delightful spot. One could sit in the full sun on the right-hand side of the seat, or take advantage of the shade cast by an ancient cherry tree on the left-hand side. The three of them sat down and Miranda and Steve looked hopefully at their companion. 'Go on, what's your name?' Miranda repeated eagerly. 'It's not a secret, is it?'

The woman shook her head, flashing them a small, rather embarrassed smile. 'I Melissa. My family call me Missie, but men on ship call me Ebony.' She pulled a face. 'They meant to insult, but why should I care? In my own head I call them ruder names. Cap'n Hogg, I called Pig . . .' she chuckled, 'but you can call me Missie, as my children did.'

Miranda turned to Steve. 'Get out the grub and we'll divide it three ways; I'm sure there's plenty. And while we're eating, Missie can tell us her story.'

'And we'll tell her ours,' Steve said rather reproachfully. He was older than Miranda and had been the one to introduce her to Jamaica House, so he thought it should be he who took the lead, and decided to start with the question which fascinated him most of all. He produced the pile of jam sandwiches, oatcakes and cheese from his satchel and handed them round. Then he addressed Missie directly for the first time.

'If you don't mind me askin', what have you been livin' on all this while? You've been here ages to my knowledge, so what have you had to eat? Oh, I know there's fruit in the garden, but that hadn't even begun to ripen when I first found the place, and you were here then. I went into the kitchen and heard you giggling . . .'

Their new friend laughed. 'I saw you run like rabbit,' she said cheerfully. 'At first I scared you was Cap'n Pig, but when I saw you were stranger, I pleased and gave little laugh.' She repeated the giggle which had so frightened Steve the first time he had heard it. 'When you ran off, I thought I do it again if bad men come.'

Steve nodded wisely. 'Yes, I quite see that your giggle would put most people off exploring any further. But you still haven't said how you've been keeping body and soul together.' He saw her puzzled look, and rephrased the question. 'What've you been eatin'? Where did your food come from? You can't have existed on fresh air, nor on the odds and ends the factories chuck out.'

Missie glanced uneasily from one to the other, and Miranda gave Steve a scowl, before saying: 'You needn't tell us if you don't want to, Missie, only it seems so strange . . .'

'In summer, big factory leave window open just tiny bit. When it really dark and no one about, I get in to room where food is. I never take much, just a little.'

'What about winter? Or when someone notices and closes the window?' Steve asked. 'What do you do then?'

'I used to go down to docks and take from ships, or from boxes waiting collection,' their new friend said promptly. 'But better tell you my story from start.' She smiled at them both. 'I been here for many months, have seen seasons come and go, yet you first to come here in all that time.'

She looked enquiringly at them, but Steve shook his head. 'Go on,' he said firmly. 'Right from the very beginning, so that we truly understand.'

Melissa finished off the oatcake she had been eating, drew a deep breath and began. 'I come from small island in West Indies and for many years I work as nursemaid or nanny to children of man who own more than half of island. I happy then, I love job, but plantation owners send sons to England to get good education when they old enough. I lucky because Mr and Mrs Grimshaw, my employers, had large family and I look after them as they arrived, from birth until they went to school in England. When last child no longer need me, I was given cottage on shore and pension.' She sighed reminiscently, and Steve saw that her liquid eyes were dark with tears. 'But I miss my children, so I decide to help at village school. Each day I walk to work . . .'

Missie proceeded to tell them how she had been walking along the shore on her way to the village when she noticed a ship anchored out in the bay, and a small boat being rowed ashore. The men on it had hailed her, asking for directions to the island's only port. Suspecting nothing, she had waited until they came ashore before beginning to explain how they must proceed. She had scarcely begun her explanation, however, when she felt a stunning blow on the back of her head which plunged her into darkness. When she recovered consciousness, the ship was at sea once more, and one of the men, the crew called him Cripple Jack because he had a wooden leg, told her that their cook had been washed overboard in a tropical storm and Captain Hogg had kidnapped her to do the work the drowned man had performed.

Missie had tried to escape and had only desisted when the captain had threatened to put her in leg irons; had he done so she would not have dared to jump overboard, knowing that she would sink like a stone. So she had promised obedience if only he would take her back to her home island when he returned to the West Indies. He promised, of course, but she very soon realised that he was not a man of his word and would do no such thing. There were still places where human beings could be bought and sold, and she knew herself to be a very good cook, and an efficient maid of all work. There were people who would be happy to have her services without having to pay her a wage. She realised she must escape as soon as an opportunity offered itself.

When the *Pride of the Sea* berthed in Liverpool, every member of the crew wanted to go ashore, for Liverpool was famous amongst seamen for its many markets and consequently many bargains. It fell to Cripple Jack to be left on board to keep an eye on Missie, and make sure she did not escape. But by this time Missie was familiar with the whole ship, for she had cleaned and scrubbed every inch of it, so when the ship was deserted, save for Cripple Jack and herself, she went to the captain's cabin and unlocked the cupboard where he kept his supply of rum. She filled a large glass almost to the brim with the spirit and took it out on deck, telling Cripple Jack that the captain had left the bottle out on his table and this was her private treat to herself.

He had immediately taken the glass from her hand and put it to his lips. She pretended to try to get it back, which made him drink all the faster. The gangway had been drawn up, but this was no bar to Missie. She waited until Cripple Jack's snores were deafening, then climbed nimbly over the ship's rail and with the aid of a loose rope lowered herself on to the quay, and simply disappeared amongst the crowds of people thronging the dockside.

Drunk with the success of her scheme, for freedom is a giddying experience after weeks of torment and imprisonment aboard a not very large merchant ship, she had trotted along, heading away from the docks. She meant to hide up somewhere until the *Pride of the Sea* had left the port, then return to the docks and stow away on any ship which was heading for the Indies. She had no money on her, of course, not so much as a penny piece, so she could not buy a passage, which was a great nuisance, since stowing away depended on her ability to find some nook or cranny where she would not be discovered. But that was for later; at present all that mattered was that she not be taken back aboard the *Pride of the Sea*.

She was some way from the docks and was wishing she had had the forethought to provide herself with some food, apart from the handful of ship's biscuits she had put into the pocket of her shabby black dress earlier in the day, when she heard a shout from behind her and, glancing back, saw the first mate pushing his way through the crowds towards her.

With her heart beating overtime she still retained enough presence of mind to knock over a box of fish awaiting collection, and saw the mate slip, try to regain his balance and then go down with an almighty crash, uttering swear words at which even the most broad-minded of seamen would raise startled eyebrows. Terrified, she had set off at her fastest pace and very soon had left the docks – and the mate – far behind, though by now panic had her in its grip. She was running from she knew not what; she simply knew that she would keep on running until her breath gave out.

It was then that she had spotted an old house with an overgrown basement and dived into the tangle of weeds and rubbish. She heard the pursuit go past but stayed in her hiding place, watching, as darkness fell and the moon came up. She saw many things, including drunken members of the crew, some accompanied by women, heading back towards the docks. Captain Hogg and his first mate had come last, but by then all thought of leaving her hidden nook had been forgotten in her anxiety not to be recaptured. Even her thirst had not been sufficient to drive her out of cover.

When eventually morning came and the danger seemed less, Missie had come out of her nook and continued to head away from the docks. She had rounded a corner and found herself amongst factories instead of houses. Missie could see nowhere to hide, but she had been pretty sure there was no need; by now the men would all be back on ship, and the *Pride* would be heading for the open sea.

Indeed, she had been beginning to relax when she had heard someone shout behind her. Her heart had redoubled its frantic beating and she had hurled herself at a huge ivy-covered wall, finding the door quite by accident and shooting through it. Then she had collapsed upon the waist-high grass, wriggling deep into cover and staring at the door as though it might presently open to reveal the entire crew of the *Pride of the Sea*, come to drag her back into captivity. Nothing had happened, however, and she eventually realised that the shout she had heard had had nothing to do with her. As the days passed she had grown more confident, though she only left her sanctuary after dark, and never lingered outside the great wall for longer than necessity dictated.

The soft, sing-song voice ceased, and Miranda and Steve stared at the old woman with considerable admiration, which Steve was the first to admit. 'Gosh, that's the most exciting story I've ever heard and you're brave as a perishin' tiger,' he told her. 'But why do you go outside the garden, Missie? Especially if you still consider it dangerous to do so.'

Missie grinned, a flash of very white teeth in her dark face. 'I need food,' she said simply. 'I only go out in dark. First I make sure Cap'n Pig's ship not there, because he bear a grudge and I worth money as slave. I also look for ship to take me home.'

'And you've not found one?' Miranda asked incredulously. 'Not in all the time you've spent in England?'

Steve was watching Missie's face; it was difficult to read her expression but he thought a look which could almost be guilt crossed her face. 'I have no money for passage; if I stow away I at mercy of captain. I too afraid.' She smiled, first at Miranda and then at Steve. 'That why I so happy when you came, and came again. I begin to tidy garden . . . once, you gave me bread and cheese. I want help yet dare not ask until I sure you good people and my friends.'

Steve and Miranda exchanged a doubtful look. Neither had any idea of how much a passage from Liverpool to the West Indies would cost but both thought it would be a great deal. However, if they could find a ship bound for the West Indies and explain to her captain how Missie had been kidnapped, then surely a man of principle would take the old woman back home? Steve said as much and Missie nodded vigorously. 'Yes, yes, but I need someone to speak for me. The *Pride of the Sea* cannot be only bad ship. If I tell wrong person, they could offer me passage then sell me at another port. I dare not, oh, I dare not!'

Steve and Miranda both nodded; in Missie's position, having suffered once from such treatment, they too would have hesitated to take any sort of risk. But Missie was gazing at them, her eyes bright with hope as she continued her story. It seemed that despite her desire to leave England she no longer visited the docks, realising that she might easily end up worse off if she asked for help from a smiling scoundrel. She pointed out, however, that her new friends might, with safety, haunt the docks during daylight hours and ask openly which captain, on a ship heading for the West Indies, was to be trusted to honour any promise he might make.

When Miranda suggested that Missie might write to her former employers, asking for their help, she pulled a doubtful face, explaining that she had been absent for so long that everyone would assume she had been taken by a shark, and would suspect a letter from a woman they had mourned for dead was a forgery by a confidence trickster wanting money.

'I see. Then of course we'll help,' Miranda said warmly. 'Though if you have to buy a passage, I don't know how we are to find the money. You see, ever since my mother disappeared more than a year ago, I've had to live with my aunt, who's not only poor but mean as well, and Steve here has a great many brothers and his parents need every penny to feed and clothe their kids.'

Missie's face, which had been full of hope, fell, but Miranda leaned forward and squeezed her hand. 'It's all right. I've a friend who's a policeman; he might be able to tell us . . .'

Missie gave a small shriek and reminded Miranda that she was here illegally, with no papers, no passport, nothing to prove her story true.

'Yes, of course,' Miranda said slowly. 'Then you have no choice but to stow away. If we can find a crew member who's willing to help you . . .'

'Someone like that would need paying, though,' Steve put in firmly. 'But I think you're right, Miranda. Missie's best bet is to leave as quietly – and illegally – as she arrived.' He turned to the little old woman, whose face promptly lit up with hope once more. 'Don't you know anyone from your home island who might be willing to give a fellow countrywoman a helping hand? Someone visiting England? What about those kids, the ones you said were sent to school in England once they were old enough to leave their family; would they help if they knew you were in trouble?'

'But if they're only kids . . .' Miranda began, only to be immediately interrupted.

'If they are at a boarding school in England, they must be at least as old as us, probably even older,' Steve said. He turned to Miranda. 'Have you an address for them?'

Missie's face, which had lit up with hope once more, fell. 'No, no address,' she said sadly. 'Master Julian and Master Gerald stay with uncle during holidays.'

Steve frowned. 'The autumn term starts in a few days, probably a week or two later for boarding schools. But we can scarcely search the whole of England for two boys when we have no idea of their address.'

Miranda leaned forward and stared hard at Missie's tired, lined little face. 'Think hard, Missie,' she urged. 'Haven't they ever mentioned a town or a city, or a street even? The Grimshaws must have mentioned something about it.'

Missie shook her head slowly. 'No, only that it's the Browncoat School . . .' She looked startled as Miranda and Steve gave a yell of triumph, and Miranda jumped up and grabbed Missie by both hands, pulling her off the stone seat and whirling her round and round until they both collapsed back on to the bench once more.

'Missie, that's all we need to know,' Miranda said breathlessly. 'The Browncoat School is famous, and it's no more than ten miles from Liverpool, which is probably why the Grimshaws chose to send their sons to it. Gosh, it looks as though we're on the right track at last. But will Julian and Gerald have enough money to buy you a passage home? Do they have some way of contacting their parents?'

Missie's face was one enormous beam, and at Miranda's question she nodded vigorously. 'Yes, yes; they can send what they call a cable. I'm certain all would be well. They are very good boys and will believe my story.'

Steve stood up. 'Right, then I think we should have a plan of action,' he said briskly. The best thing is to wait until we're sure term has started at Browncoats. Then we can go up to Crosby, which is only a bus ride away. You'll have to come with us, Missie, because otherwise we won't be able to recognise Julian or Gerald, and might start telling your story to the wrong people, which would never do. I think we should go up to the school a week on Saturday.' He scowled at Missie, who was vigorously shaking her head once more. 'Now don't say you're afraid that the crew of the *Pride of the Sea* might be lurking around the Browncoat school, because that's downright silly. They can scarcely kidnap you when you're with us and miles from the docks!'

But at the mere suggestion of leaving Jamaica House during daylight, Missie, who had been so brave, broke into floods of tears and begged them not to try to take her away from the only place she knew. Miranda and Steve begged, pleaded and argued, to no avail. Finally, Steve said, bitterly, that if she was determined not to go with them then she had better give an exact description of both boys, and also write an explanatory note which they could show Julian and Gerald if their own word was doubted.

Missie looked from one face to the other, then spoke hesitantly. 'There is a way that is used on my island to show what cannot otherwise be seen,' she said slowly. 'It is frowned upon by the Grimshaws and many others, but . . . are you willing to try? It – it is a sort of magic . . .'

'I'll try; I believe in magic,' Miranda said eagerly. 'What do I have to do, Missie?'

Missie smiled at her, but shook her head, 'Eldest first, is rule,' she said. 'Close eyes, Steve, and think of nothing; make your mind blank or think of blue sky, and little white clouds . . . then I show you Master Julian.'

As she spoke she placed both hands on Steve's temples and began to mutter, and presently, to the boy's astonishment, he saw a face. It was less a boy's face than that of a young man, with thick, light brown hair bleached by the sun, a high-bridged nose and light blue eyes. Startled, Steve gave an involuntary jump. Missie's hands fell from his head and he opened his eyes to see her staring at him anxiously. 'What you see?' Missie asked.

'I saw someone who looked a lot older than me, with very thick light brown hair and a scar just above his left eyebrow; I'd recognise him again because I suppose you might say he was very handsome,' Steve said. He stared hard at the small woman, who was now smiling triumphantly. 'How the devil did you do that, Missie? Did I really see Julian, or was it just my imagination working overtime?'

'It was Julian; he wearing his light blue shirt,' Missie said. 'Did you see shirt?'

'The one I saw was white and open at the neck . . .' Steve began, and Missie gave a crow of triumph.

'That's right, that's right; just testing;' she said, grinning broadly. She looked consideringly at Miranda. 'You see Master Gerald? Perhaps it best.'

119

Miranda began to say that she was longing to try, but Steve shook his head warningly. 'It made me feel sort of fuzzy for a few minutes,' he warned. 'Still, as Missie says, we ought to be able to recognise both boys. Close your eyes then, goofy; I won't tell you to make your mind a blank, because it always is.'

Miranda, who had closed her eyes, shot them open indignantly, then closed them again and sank back on the seat. Missie's small fingers touched her lightly on each temple and Steve watched with some interest, and listened too as the old woman began to mutter and to move her fingers gently in a circular motion on both sides of his pal's head. He was startled when Miranda suddenly shot upright, gave a scream and grabbed Missie by both wrists. 'I saw – I saw – I saw . . .' She had gone very pale, and her eyes kept tilting up in her head, so that only the whites showed. Then she sank back on the bench and covered her face with her hands.

Steve rounded on Missie. 'What have you done to her?' he shouted. 'What did she see that frightened her so? What have you done, you old witch?'

'I done nothing, 'cept think of Master Gerald and pass picture I see to Miranda,' Missie said. She looked as frightened, Steve realised, as he felt himself. 'I didn't do voodoo, just made picture.'

But even as she spoke, Miranda had taken her hands away from her face and was sitting upright on the bench and giving them both a watery smile. 'What's the matter? Did I startle you when I shrieked?' she asked. 'I'm so sorry, but it was such a surprise! I saw a boy with dark eyes and curly hair. Was that Master Gerald? Only he wasn't really a boy, I should think he was fifteen or sixteen.'

Missie nodded slowly. 'What colour be his shirt?' she asked, and just for a moment she sounded quite different.

'It was blue and white check.' As she spoke she got to her feet, swayed a little and then smiled reassuringly at Missie. 'I'm all right, don't worry, but I'd love to know how you work that particular sort of magic. Come to think of it, you could use it to show us the captain and crew of the *Pride of the Sea* so we'd know them if we met.'

Missie looked horrified. 'No, no; it might give them power over you. It strong magic. I only know a little of what my grandmother teach me, because when my mother found out she made Grandma promise to tell no more. But you know boys now, and will recognise them again.'

After they had left Missie, having helped her with the composition of a short note explaining the situation to the Grimshaws, Steve looked curiously at his companion. 'You needn't think you fooled me into thinking that the only thing you saw was that Gerald chap,' he said. 'You saw something that scared the life out of you, just for a moment. Come on, you can tell me.'

'Well, you know I've said quite often that I'm finding it difficult to remember my mother's face, and have to keep looking at her wedding photograph?' Miranda said at last. 'First of all I saw Gerald, plain as plain. It was odd, wasn't it? It wasn't so much like looking at a picture as looking at a real person. Behind his shoulder I could see a hill, and the branches of the trees were moving . . . really odd; quite spooky in fact.'

'What's that got to do with your mother's

photograph?' Steve said crossly. 'I take it you saw her . . . only how is that possible? Missie's never seen her, has she?'

'No, that's what makes it so very odd,' Miranda confessed. 'One moment I was looking at Gerald and the next there was my mother with a black shawl thing covering her head, and her face was white and her eyes were closed. Then, just as I was going to scream, she opened her eyes and smiled and her lips moved, and though I couldn't hear what she said I'm sure it was my name. And then I woke up.'

'Gosh, no wonder you looked sick,' Steve said prosaically. 'But it must have been your imagination . . . or maybe your mother was what you really wanted to see and perhaps Missie knew it, and kind of helped the picture to come into your mind.'

'I expect you're right, but it was bloody terrifying and I don't want it to happen again,' Miranda said firmly. She glanced behind her, then tutted. 'Look at me, expecting to see Timmy, when I know very well he stayed with Missie. They really seemed to like each other, didn't they?'

'Well, once we're in school he'd be at a loose end, so it's best that he stays at Jamaica House,' Steve said. 'I say, I don't know why but I feel most awfully tired. Let's blow tuppence on a tram ride home. We deserve it after the day we've had.'

They were in luck; the very next tram which came along took them all the way to Jamaica Close, where they went their separate ways, having agreed to meet early next morning. Miranda entered Number Six expecting her usual reception, but found the house deserted, and the fire out. Sighing, she went to the pantry to get herself some bread and jam, and found a note propped against the meat safe. *Gone to Seaforth Sands to visit Great-aunt Nell. Bread in the pantry, water in the tap.*

Miranda pulled a face. Trust them to go off to visit her favourite great-aunt without a word to her. She guessed that Aunt Vi and Beth had planned to do this deliberately and decided that she wouldn't bother with the bread and jam, but would go straight to bed. She had told Missie and Steve that she believed in magic, but she had not really meant it, and the sight of her mother's face, so pale and strange, had upset her deeply. Now all she wanted was her bed, and she felt pretty sure that it was Missie's so-called magic which had worn her out.

Without even bothering to take a slice off the loaf she made her way upstairs. In the shared bedroom she glanced with distaste at the rumpled sheets, and at the clothing slung carelessly down on the dirty linoleum. She knew they would expect her to hang up clean clothes and carry dirty ones down to soak in the sink until she had time to wash them properly, but she did neither of these things. She made the bed as respectable as she could, undressed and put on her nightgown, then rolled into bed and was asleep within seconds.

Immediately, she dreamed.

She was on a beach of wonderful golden sand. Tiny blue waves, white-fringed, hissed softly at her feet, and when she glanced behind her there were great palm trees which she recognised from pictures she had seen in books. It was beautiful, but lonely. She walked into the sea until it covered her knees; it was warm as milk, and when she looked through the clear depths she could see beautiful shells and tiny fish. She would have liked to go deeper, for since this was a dream she should be able to swim, an activity which she had never tried in real life, but something stopped her. She was on this beach for a purpose, she felt suddenly sure, and that purpose did not include testing her ability to swim. Reluctantly, she returned to shore and saw two people strolling along the hard wet sand, heading in her direction. She glanced curiously at them, and when they were within a few yards was suddenly sure that the woman was her mother. Impulsively she began to run, shouting: 'Mum! Arabella! It's me, Miranda!'

As she got closer she realised she was being completely ignored, and when Arabella's eyes met hers their expression was that of a total stranger. Pain stabbed Miranda like a knife even as her mother became as insubstantial as mist and disappeared.

Miranda found herself sitting up in bed, her cheeks wet with tears, just as the bedroom door burst open, and Aunt Vi and Beth entered the room. They took no notice of Miranda, but began to undress, talking excitedly about the day they had enjoyed, the trip on the overhead railway, the dinner they had bought themselves at the café near the Sands and the wonderful tea provided by Great-aunt Nell.

At this point Vi seemed to notice her niece for the first time. 'The old gal axed after you, seemed downright upset when I told her you'd bobbied off with some young feller rather than visit her,' Aunt Vi boomed. 'Still 'n' all, you can take yourself off to the Sands whenever you've a mind, if you can find up the money for the train fare. Except, as I told her, you'd probably rather spend your time with a dirty thievin' young feller than with a borin' old lady.'

Miranda, still scarcely awake and still fighting tears, muttered something and hunched a shoulder. A couple of weeks previously Aunt Vi had decided that, because Beth was growing so rapidly, three in a bed was no longer possible. She had bought – second-hand of course – an ancient camp bed, provided it with sheets and blankets and told Beth that it was her new sleeping place. Beth, however, had objected vociferously, saying that her feet stuck out at the end, the covers were insufficient and she was darned if she was going to even try to sleep in such discomfort. Nothing loth, Miranda had willingly swapped with her and in fact much preferred the small creaky bed, with its inadequate bedding and rusty framework, to the big feather bed where Aunt Vi took up most of the room and Beth the rest.

So Miranda cuddled down once more and tried to wonder why, in the dream, her mother had not seemed to recognise her. When Arabella had first disappeared Miranda had dreamed of her practically every night and always in these dreams her mother's loving smile had warmed and comforted her. Sometimes they had hugged, sometimes exchanged stories of what had happened to them since they had last met, but always there had been warmth and affection flowing like a stream of happiness between the two of them. And the background to those dreams had been familiar, real; no golden sand or tropical skies. So why had this dream been so different? It was not only that her mother had looked straight through her, it was the unreality of the scene in which the dream had taken place. Looking back she realised that there had been something odd about both the shore and the sea itself. Screwing up her eyes she tried to recreate the scene.

At first it was difficult but then, all of a sudden, it came to her. The palm trees looked like cut-outs, the little waves like puffs of cotton wool, and the shells she had seen through the water were, she suddenly realised, the ones on her mother's theatrical make-up box. Despite herself, Miranda gave a relieved little smile. She did not understand why she should dream what amounted to a stage set, but it must mean that her mother, appearing not to recognise her, was as false as the setting.

Satisfied that the dream had come merely because Steve, Missie and herself had been discussing tropical islands, she turned her face into the pillow, and by the time her aunt and her cousin had stopped gloating over their day out she was fast asleep.

She did not dream.

Chapter Five

When term started, Steve and Miranda walked to and from school together, discussing many things, for, as Miranda told herself, she had no secrets from Steve. Naturally enough they talked a good deal about ways of contacting Julian and Gerald, and wondered how Missie was getting on. They guessed that she would have been out foraging each night, for now she had to feed not only herself but also Timmy, and though Miranda thought that this was rather hard on the old woman Steve disagreed. 'Having something to look after – or perhaps I should say somebody – is just about as good as being looked after yourself,' he told his friend. 'You mark my words, young Miranda, Missie will see that Timmy gets the best of everything, which means that she'll eat better herself as a result.'

'I don't see that,' Miranda objected. 'Dogs can eat raw fish, dirty old bones, scraps of food a person wouldn't look at twice.' She giggled. 'I can just picture Missie lying under the stone bench in the garden sharing a dirty great marrow bone with our little dog.'

Steve laughed too. 'Ah well, you may be right,' he conceded. 'By the way, I reckon the Browncoats have probably started classes again by now. The bus fare won't be more than a couple of bob and we've both got savings stashed away at Jamaica House, so I think we ought to go up to Crosby this coming Saturday. Have you any plans? If your aunt wants messages you'll have to slip out and let your cousin Beth do some work for once.' He raised his eyebrows. 'Where is she, incidentally? I've not seen her around since term started, come to think.'

Miranda grinned. 'Two reasons. One is that she's actually got herself a job! It's a big house on the outskirts of Speke and Beth has to be there quite early in the morning. She's a great one for her bed, which makes me wonder how long she'll stick it. She has to take a tray of early morning tea up to the old lady and help her to dress, and then she has to clean the house, cook some sort of meal at midday and take the old lady out in her wheel-chair anywhere she wants to go.'

Steve whistled under his breath. 'What's the money like?' he enquired with his usual practicality. 'And how the devil did she get such a job? I've heard my mam talking about girls going into service, but usually it's live-in.'

'Well, I'll tell you, though it's rather complicated,' Miranda said. 'Aunt Vi's pal, Flo, worked for old Mrs Seymour for years and she always did it as a day job because when she started the old lady's two sons still lived with her. Ned and Barry Seymour took it in turns to bring Flo to their mother's house, though she had to make her own way home. Then the boys married and moved out, and Flo discovered the sort of money that she could earn at one of the new factories making uniforms and that for the forces. She's a marvel with a sewing machine, is Flo. She knew her job at the big house was an easy one, knew that the moment she said she was quitting there'd be a queue of applicants a mile long, so the day she gave in her notice she took Beth with her and recommended her for the job, suggesting that Beth should work there on a month's trial. The old lady was only too pleased to take Beth on since Flo had given her a good character, so that's how it happened. The only difference is that she makes her own way to and from the village; when Flo started working there there were no early buses, but there are now. And guess what . . .' Miranda giggled. 'The other reason you haven't seen her is that she's got a boyfriend. Met him on the bus going to her new job, and discovered that he was employed a couple of days a week to help in the garden. It's huge, and very well kept, Beth says. And he asked her to go to the flicks with him one evening after work, and bob's your uncle.'

Steve stared, then pretended to faint. 'What sort of feller would go for a great lumpin' girl like Beth?' he demanded.

Miranda chuckled. 'Now she's got a boyfriend Beth washes her hair once a week, same as everyone else, and means to spend her wages on nice clothes and make-up.' She sighed. 'I wonder what it's like to have a boyfriend? I wouldn't go wasting the ready on make-up or frocks, though. I'd buy cakes and ice cream and pork pies and sausage rolls . . .'

By this time they were nearing their school and Steve gave her a friendly punch in the ribs. 'You have got a boyfriend. What d'you think I am?' he asked plaintively. 'Don't I walk you to school, take you to the Saturday rush at the Derby cinema, mug you to a sticky bun when I'm in the money . . .'

Miranda gave a scornful snort. 'Huh, you're my pal

– my bezzie if you like – but you ain't my boyfriend. And Beth's feller is Spotty Wade; you must know him. When we were in primary they called him Tadpole because he had such a big head for such a little body, but now he's just fat and spotty.'

'Well, you *are* my girlfriend . . .' Steve was beginning when the school bell sounded. 'Cripes. Let's gerra move on, chuck, 'cos it'll look bad on my report if I'm late,' he said, breaking into a run as he spoke. 'Is it agreed then? That we go up to Crosby this Saturday – day after tomorrer – and see whether we can still remember what them two boys look like?'

'Are you certain the Browncoats are back, though?' Miranda said a trifle breathlessly, running along in Steve's wake. 'We'll look awful fools if we get up there and find the school's still closed – or worse, that the boys are kept on the premises even at weekends.' By now they had reached the school gates and Steve paused in his onward rush to shake his head reprovingly at Miranda.

'What a one you are for raising objections and followin' the rules,' he said airily. 'I reckon the lad weren't born who couldn't escape from a school if he wanted to. And anyhow I've been to Crosby several weekends during term time and it always seems to me that the pavements are thronged with them boys. Still, I reckon we'd best gerroff early, so your aunt can't tie you to the kitchen sink, 'cos that would ruin our chances.'

Neither Aunt Vi nor Beth worked on a Saturday so the alarm was not set. However, Miranda was rudely awakened soon after seven o'clock by her cousin briskly pulling the covers off her sleeping form to the accompaniment of a shouted 'Gerrup, you lazy little slut!' which had Aunt Vi mumbling a protest.

Miranda was about to add her own objection to such treatment when she remembered that Beth was not the only one who wanted to be up betimes, so she rolled out of bed with no more than a mumbled protest, grabbed her clothes off the hook by the window and made for the kitchen. She then realised why Beth had woken her so crossly; whoever had been last to bed the previous night had failed to make up and damp down the fire in the range, with the result that it was almost out and one could not possibly boil a kettle, let alone make the porridge, until it was brought back to life once again.

From upstairs, Beth's voice reached her. 'Bring me hot water up as soon as you've got the fire going,' she shouted. Miranda heard their bedroom door crash open and saw Beth's round, pasty face appear at the top of the stairs. 'I'm meetin' Herbert early, so's we can have a day out.' She gave Miranda an ingratiating smile. 'Sorry I had to wake you kinda rough like, but I can't abide washin' in cold water and I want to look me best for Herbert. Yesterday I seen a dress in Paddy's Market what was only twelve 'n' six; it suited me a treat, so I bought it. Herbie's callin' at eight, so if you could just make me some sarnies I'll get meself washed and dressed while you're doin' it.'

'Okay, Beth. As it happens I'm goin' out myself so I'll put up a few sarnies for me as well,' Miranda said, pulling the kettle over the now briskly burning range.

Miranda enjoyed the bus ride out to Crosby, for though she knew the early part of the journey, the rest was strange to her. Steve chatted easily as they went, and told her that if they had time they might go down to Crosby beach and paddle in the long seawater pools which formed whenever the tide went out. He seemed confident that they would soon achieve their objective, which at this stage was just to identify the two Grimshaw boys. 'If we have a chance we'll suggest that they meet us another time to discuss Missie's plight,' he explained. 'But I don't think we should rush them, because they're bound to be suspicious of two total strangers trying to get them away from their schoolfellows.'

When the bus drew up in the middle of the small town, Steve and Miranda hopped off and turned towards the street where the school was situated, looking for brown blazers trimmed with gold braid with a very imposing crest upon the breast pocket. They saw boys large and small, boys fat and thin, boys who wore their caps tilted rakishly on the backs of their heads and boys who pulled them so far forward that they had to raise their chins to look before them. In fact after five minutes Miranda grabbed Steve's arm and pulled him into a convenient doorway. 'We're never going to find them, not if we search for a hundred years,' she hissed. 'There are hundreds of them and they all look exactly alike. Oh, if only Missie would come with us, finding them would be so simple. She could point them out and then go and hide herself somewhere . . .'

'Yes, but you know very well she won't come out in daylight, let alone travel on a bus which goes perilously close to the docks at times. And, you know, I don't altogether blame her. She had a real horrible experience with them men on the *Pride of the Sea*; it's only natural

132

that she don't want to walk into trouble again,' Steve said.

'If only there were some sign that we could look for,' Miranda moaned. 'If one of them had a wooden leg or an eye missing . . .'

Steve laughed and gave her a friendly shove. 'Don't give up so soon, Miranda,' he urged. 'What do you remember about the pictures of the lads which Missie put into our heads? I'm sure Julian's hair was light brown and I think he had a scar above one eyebrow, and didn't you say Gerald had curls?'

'I can't remember,' Miranda wailed. She had been thrown completely off balance by the fact that, in uniform, all the boys looked so similar. 'All I really remember is the colour of his shirt, and . . . oh!'

A small group of boys was approaching them, the tallest two in earnest conversation which stopped abruptly as Miranda grabbed one of the boys' arm. 'Are you Gerald Grimshaw?' she asked breathlessly. 'I've a message for you from an old friend.' The other boys were staring at her curiously – one or two sniggered – and she felt a hot blush burning up her face, but continued to cling doggedly to her target's arm. 'You are Gerald Grimshaw, aren't you? It's – it's a private sort of message . . .'

But the boy was shaking her off and frowning, his cheeks also beginning to burn. 'I don't think I know you, young woman,' he said coldly. 'Good day.'

Miranda, feeling the most almighty fool, fished the sheet of paper upon which Missie had written her message out of her pocket and tried to thrust it into the boy's hand, but he evaded her. She thought that he had cold eyes and a superior expression and wished very much that she had asked Steve to speak to him. Then she remembered that of course he had not seen the same image as she, and fixed the cold-eyed one with her most pleading expression. 'I'm sure you are Gerald Grimshaw, aren't you? This letter is most awfully important; I promised the – the writer that I would hand it to you personally. Oh, please, please read it!'

The boy, however, clapped his hand firmly over his breast pocket so that she could not insert the letter. 'I'm *not* Gerald whatsit,' he said, and then snatched the paper from her, screwed it into a little ball, and dropped it down the grating at his feet. 'We aren't allowed to talk to girls, especially ginger-headed gypsies,' he said nastily. 'Please go away; if I were seen talking to you I should be in real trouble.'

Miranda, her whole face burning by now, dropped to her knees and peered through the grating, but the note had disappeared. Scrambling to her feet, she fired one parting shot. 'You're a nasty stuck-up snob!' she said furiously. 'I was only asking you to read a letter from someone you're supposed to be fond of. When I tell Missie how horrible you've been she'll be disgusted.'

If she had expected the boy to show some sign of interest when she spoke the name she was disappointed. He simply continued to walk, speeding up slightly, and when he had got well ahead poor Miranda gave vent to her pent-up feelings in a burst of angry tears. She turned back to where she had left Steve, but could not see him anywhere and for a moment sheer terror gripped her. Steve had provided the money for the bus fares and had the two return tickets in his pocket. To be sure, she had a packet of jam sandwiches in her own pocket, but she could scarcely use them to bribe a bus conductor to take her home. And she had played her cards all wrong! She should never have tried to engage Gerald – if indeed the boy had been Gerald – in conversation whilst he was with a group of his schoolmates. Now she had spoiled the whole thing and they would have to return to Jamaica House this evening with only failure to report. Of course, it was Missie's own fault for refusing to accompany them, but Miranda understood how she felt, particularly now she had been so comprehensively snubbed. But perhaps if they told Missie what had happened she would pluck up her courage and accompany them to Crosby on their next visit.

But right now Miranda had a problem of her own, and she was about to start searching for Steve when she saw him strolling along the pavement towards her, a broad grin on his face. 'You got lucky, didn't you?' he asked as they met. 'I saw you talking to that boy – was it Gerald? Apparently they're on their way to the school playing fields, so they've got teachers with 'em, keepin' an eye; I guess you didn't have time to explain much. Shall we follow 'em up to the playin' fields and wait until Gerald's had time to read the letter? I thought I saw you put it in his pocket. Hey up, what's the matter? Don't start cryin', you idiot! What have I said? You done well. I didn't see anyone who looked like Julian.' He took her hand and gave it a squeeze. 'Look, there's a seat by that monument. If you don't want to follow them now, then we might as well have a sit down while you tell me what's upset you.'

Miranda gave an angry sniff and knuckled her eyes

to get rid of the tears which were forming. It wasn't fair! She had done her very best, had tried to explain . . . and the boy had called her nasty names and refused to listen. She had put on her only halfway decent dress and had braided her hair into two thick plaits besides having a jolly good wash, yet he had called her a ginger-headed gypsy; oh, how she hated him! But the thought of having to admit her total failure brought the tears rushing back into her eyes and she realised she was in no state to approach the Browncoat boys again, even had she wished to do so, so she followed Steve to the bench and sat down beside him. Without further preamble she told her story, including the fact that the letter over which she, Missie and Steve had taken such pains had been thrown down the grid before she had a chance to rescue it.

She half expected Steve to say she should not have offered the letter until she was certain that the boy she had accosted really was Gerald, but instead he fished out of his pocket an extremely dirty piece of rag, pressed it into her hand and told her to mop up her tears. 'It weren't your fault; we should have remembered that uniform kind of changes people,' he said comfortingly. 'Of course we'll have to rewrite the letter – or get Missie to do so, rather – but at least it will be a case of repeating what the first letter said which will be much easier than writing a new one. And next time it might be best to go straight up to the playing fields and ask someone, quietly, to point out the Grimshaws, then wait until they've been bowled out or wharrever and ask for a quiet word. So cheer up, kid; we're all but home an' dry.'

Miranda gave a watery sniff. 'So it probably wasn't even a Grimshaw who chucked our letter down the drain,' she said. 'I'm an idiot, I am! What's that thing about rushing in where angels fear to tread? That's me, that is. But I'll make up for it next week, I promise.'

Steve cleared his throat and Miranda saw that he looked distinctly uncomfortable. 'Look, queen, you've been great, much braver than what I was, but next week I think I'd do better by meself. The teachers have got it into their heads that the boys shouldn't talk to girls . . . well, you told me that the boy you spoke to said he'd be in trouble if someone saw him with a girl. So I honestly think I'd stand a better chance if I came alone.'

Miranda sighed. She had not enjoyed her encounter with the snooty Browncoat boy, who had not only insulted her – ginger-headed gypsy indeed – but made her feel small. Yet even so she did not want to be left out of the adventure, if adventure it could be called. But Steve was looking at her anxiously, probably guessing how she felt, and waiting for her reaction, so Miranda forced a smile. 'I know you're right, so next Saturday I'll spend the day with Missie,' she said with as much cheerfulness as she could muster. 'I do hope we can get her away before winter comes, though.'

Steve looked doubtful. 'It don't do to rush things,' he said, pulling her to her feet. 'You're a grand girl, you are, so let's go down to the beach and have a paddle before setting off for home.'

I never expected it to be easy, but I never thought it would be this perishin' difficult, Steve said to himself as he approached the playing fields a week later. Missie had been bitterly disappointed that they had not managed to contact one of the Grimshaw boys on their first attempt, but when Steve had explained his plan she had agreed that it was a good one. Even so, she had been reluctant to write out the letter again. She thought it would be very much easier for Steve to persuade Julian and Gerald to come to Jamaica House so that they could see for themselves that she really was in Liverpool. Steve and Miranda, however, had explained that the boys were strictly guarded and must be convinced that Missie really needed their help before they would even begin to consider venturing so far from school.

Now, Steve knew that he was unlikely to be mistaken for a Browncoat boy as they marched through the streets towards their destination, but he thought it would be easier to mingle once they were in their sports gear. He had persuaded his mother to give him a short haircut, borrowed – without his brother's knowledge – Joe's Sunday shirt, and was wearing his most respectable kecks.

Once they reached the playing fields, there was a good deal of milling around and shouting and at one point Steve rather feared he might be picked for one side or the other, but they managed to get two teams together, with half a dozen boys left disconsolately on the sidelines, and it was one of these whom Steve approached. He was a short, red-faced, cheery-looking boy, and responded at once to Steve's friendly overture. 'Gerald Grimshaw is second row forward . . .' He pointed. 'He's in the upper fifth. His brother's in the upper sixth.'

'Which one is he?' Steve said quickly. 'I'd like a word with both of 'em, but I dunno if that's possible.'

The cheery one grinned. 'I can see you don't know much about the Browncoats,' he observed. 'We have the playing fields by years; today is upper and lower fifth, next Saturday will be upper and lower fourth, and so on. The mighty men of the sixth play midweek; they get much more freedom than the rest of us, so you might find it easier to have a word with Julian than with Gerald.'

'But I don't know him from Adam. I shan't be able to recognise him even if I could get up here during the week, which is real difficult,' Steve said miserably. He suddenly thought of the letter, and fished the folded sheet out of his pocket. 'Look, if you could get this to Gerald, he could show it to Julian and they could decide what's best to do.'

The boy took the sheet of paper rather gingerly. 'I reckon I'll have to read it,' he said apologetically. 'For all I know you might be telling him to blow up the Houses of Parliament, or to aim a rocket straight through the windows of the headmaster's study.' He laughed but raised his brows. 'But you don't know me from Adam either – I'm Henry Prothero, Hal to my pals. So – shall I read it, or shall I give it back to you so you can give it to Gerald yourself?'

Steve did not even hesitate. 'Read it!' he commanded. 'And if you can see any reason for not handing it to Gerald, you tell me here and now. It's a rather complicated story, though, and if you agree to pass on the letter I'll explain anything you don't understand.' The two boys had been standing on the sidelines, watching the game in progress, but now Hal jerked his head towards a clump of trees and bushes at the perimeter of the field.

'Let's go over there where we're less likely to be spotted,' he said. 'After the first half, those who didn't play to begin with have to swap with someone who's had a game already. I hate rugger – I hate most sports, actually – and Mr Elliot, the games master, knows it, so I'll be first substitute if he catches my eye.'

Steve followed his new friend into cover and watched with some interest as Hal spread out the sheet and began to read. Watching his face, Steve saw perplexity but no trace of disapproval, and when Hal looked up and grinned at him he raised his brows. 'Well? Do you feel you can pass it on to Gerald? Is there anything in it which worries you?'

Hal shook his head, then began to read the letter aloud.

'Dear Julian and Gerald, I trust you have not forgotten your old friend Missie. I write because I am in Liverpool, having arrived here without money or papers and thus with no means of returning to the island we all love. I know your parents would help me if they knew of my plight, but they are far away and you are near.

I am writing this letter to ask for your help and have entrusted it to my friend Steve. He and his friend have helped me write this letter and supported me, but it is to you I turn for the means to buy a passage back to the West Indies. I am living quietly but long to see you both and explain how I came to be here.

You know I would not ask for your help except in great need and I pray to God you have not forgotten your old nurse.'

'Well, what more explanation do you need?' Steve said rather impatiently, as Hal came to the end. 'She's not a young woman – Missie, I mean – and she needs their help to get home.'

'Yes, but how did she end up in Liverpool? Did she come to England to look for work?'

Steve took a deep breath, trying to sort out how best to explain, then decided that it was unnecessary. Instead, he smiled and nodded. 'That's it. But her new employers were unscrupulous and mean. When she told them she wanted to leave they confiscated her papers and wouldn't pay her the money they owed her. So my friend and I helped. But we don't have the money to get her a return passage to the Indies . . .'

He stopped speaking as Hal nodded understandingly. 'Ah yes, I see. She'll want papers, a passport and so on, which you obviously cannot provide. But I expect the Grimshaws' uncle could help there. He's an old Browncoats boy and I know he's a lawyer.' As he spoke he was refolding the letter and pushing it into his trouser pocket. 'I say, that poor woman! I'm sure the Grims will be glad to help. Gerry's a wizard fellow and Julian's okay, though he's the quiet studious type, unlike his brother. But how to get you together I really don't know, because apart from coming to and from the playing fields we can't officially leave the school premises, except for some definite reason.'

'Like what?'

'Oh, a trip to the dentist, a Scout meeting, or sometimes a special exeat to see a relative of whom the school authorities approve. Tell you what, when Mr Elliot blows the whistle I'll go straight across to Gerry, pass the letter over and tell him you're in the bushes. Maybe you can arrange something then.'

Steve was so delighted that he could have hugged the other boy but contented himself with uttering profuse thanks. 'You're brilliant, you are; I never thought I'd meet someone so willing to help,' he said. 'When it's all over and Missie has been seen off safely back to her island, then I'll tell you the whole story. I wish I could do something to repay you in the meantime, though.'

'I wish I could help you more,' Hal said, his rosy face split by a wide grin. 'Wish I had a relative in Liverpool and could go a-visiting a couple of times a term. I s'pose you couldn't arrange that?'

Steve pulled a face. 'I wish I could,' he said sincerely, 'but though my mam's a grand woman, I doubt your teachers would think her respectable enough to entertain a Browncoats boy. Still, I'll see what I can do.'

Just as they emerged from the bushes the whistle blew and Mr Elliot began charging about and shouting. Hal made his way straight to Gerald Grimshaw and gripped his arm. Steve did not actually see the folded paper change hands, but guessed that it had done so when Gerald's eyes turned in his direction and he began to nod. He walked off the pitch, exchanging remarks with the other lads, and presently he joined Steve and shot out a hand. Steve shook it, taking a good look at his new companion. Gerald Grimshaw was a hefty young man who looked more than his fifteen years. He had short curly hair which stood up all over his head, broad cheekbones and twinkling brown eyes, a thick neck and broad shoulders. He grinned, then fished the letter out of his pocket. 'Are you certain sure that the woman you've been helping is really our Missie? Melissa Grundy? Only when we were at Uncle Vernon's for the Easter vac he told us that Missie had disappeared in a bad thunderstorm on her way to help at the village school. The locals said she must have gone into the sea for some reason and been taken by sharks – it does happen, especially during a storm when they have what we call a feeding frenzy – but she was certainly no longer on the island. Her house was given to someone else, and it did seem as though something like a shark attack must have been the reason for her disappearance, because nothing was missing, not so much as a pair of shoes or a teapot. And there was no – no body.'

Steve pulled a face. 'She was afraid people would think that,' he said ruefully. 'But you'd better read the letter first and then I'll fill you in on what we felt was too complicated to try to put into writing.'

'Right,' Gerald said unfolding the paper. 'How did you come to know Hal, by the way? He's a decent chap, one of the best, but he comes from somewhere north of the border and doesn't have any friends outside school so far as I know.'

'Luck,' Steve said. 'Read the perishin' letter, or your teacher will blow the whistle and our chance to arrange another meeting will be gone. And Missie is very much alive, as you'll see.'

Gerald scanned the page quickly, whilst a slow smile spread across his face. 'That's the best news I've ever had, and it'll be the same for Julian,' he said happily. 'But look here, lad, it's been a long while since Missie disappeared. How the devil did she get to Liverpool? She don't know a soul here apart from us. Can you explain a bit more?'

'Well, I could, but I think it might be better coming from Missie herself,' Steve said rather apologetically. 'But Hal mentioned that you had a relative in the legal profession. I wonder why Missie didn't think of him.'

143

'Oh, she wouldn't,' Gerald said at once. 'She never knew him. He's a great gun. If anyone can sort out papers, passports and so on it's our uncle, and I'm sure he'll do it as quick as a flash when we explain that it's for Missie. They never met, but he knows all about her, of course. And now you'd best explain to me what she's doing in Liverpool.'

Steve hesitated. The more he thought about Missie's capture and slavery aboard the *Pride of the Sea* the less likely it seemed. He was sure that if he told the tale he would not be believed, or at any rate a listener would take it with a grain of salt, as the saying went. They had all agreed on this, even Missie, and tempting though it was to tell all to this cheerful and friendly young man, Steve decided he had better stick to their original plan. 'Look, I promised Missie she should tell her own story,' he said firmly. 'I'm here to arrange a meeting, if that's possible. For reasons she'll explain when you see her, she will only leave her refuge after dark.'

Gerald grinned. 'Yes, Missie always was a snappy dresser. She loved brilliant colours and exotic materials,' he said reminiscently. 'I suppose she would stand out like a parrot amidst sparrows in Liverpool, where people tend to wear black or dark brown.'

Steve sighed. This was going to be even more difficult than he had supposed. 'No, it's not like that at all. Missie wears the only clothing available to her, which is black and pretty much in rags. She wouldn't stand out at all in the area near the docks, but . . . oh dear, when you meet her you'll see for yourself. And honestly, it should be as soon as possible. My pal and I worry all the time that someone will start to take an interest in Jamaica House and Missie will find herself . . .'

'Jamaica House? Our family used to run a business of some description, in Liverpool, and I think their head-quarters were called Jamaica House – in fact I'm sure of it. So that's where Missie is holed up, is it? I've never seen it myself, the family haven't been involved in that particular trade for generations, but from what I've heard the house is little better than a ruin. Look, I don't know the way there but I do agree with you that we must meet Missie, and the sooner the better. Julian is a prefect, so though he would do everything in his power to help he won't want to break any rules.'

'In that case it might be best if you came to Jamaica House on your own, preferably after it's begun to get dark,' Steve said. 'Fortunately your brown blazers and grey kecks can look pretty anonymous, so if you take your cap off and get hold of a dark-coloured muffler you're unlikely to be spotted as a Browncoat boy. I guess you think I ought to bring Missie to you, but it would be really difficult. I'll tell you what bus to catch and which stop to get off at, and I'll meet you there and take you straight to Jamaica House. But can you get away? Without being caught, I mean.'

Gerald thought the matter over. 'If Hal covers for me after the supper bell – we're in the same dorm – I can be with you by say half past eight in the evening. Then I can spend an hour or so with Missie and still get back to the dorm before anyone has checked that it's me curled up under the covers and not my pillow.'

'Well, if you're sure, I'll meet all the buses from Crosby between eight and nine o'clock. If you're not on any of them, we'll have to think again,' Steve said. 'Now, do you need to know anything else? Missie felt that the letter she wrote might not be enough to convince you that we weren't playing what you might call an under-game, though why she would want to entice a couple of bleedin' Browncoats into a ruined house is more than I can tell you.'

He expected his companion to laugh scoffingly, but Gerald did not do so. 'Extortion,' he said briefly, then grinned. 'But you don't look the type to drag me off, chuck me into a cellar and demand a ransom from parents a thousand miles away. So you can tell Missie that one of us, at least, will be with her . . . what day did we say?'

Steve laughed. So that was what 'extortion' meant! 'We didn't, but what about Monday? Or would tomorrow be better for you?'

They were still discussing the details of their plan when Mr Elliot's whistle shrilled and the boys, both players and spectators, began to amble back towards the wooden building. Gerald started to follow them, turning at the last minute to say: 'Monday evening, eight to nine. Cheerio for now.'

Steve did not hang about until the boys were back in uniform once more, but set off immediately towards the nearest bus stop. He was elated with the success of his plan, and looking forward to Monday evening. He and Miranda had grown fond of Missie, but Steve realised more than ever now that she was a real responsibility. He worried that someone would spot her when she went down to the docks to pick up any food she could find. He worried she would be seen leaving or entering the walled garden, or that one of the factory workers might follow her into her retreat, or perhaps inform the scuffers that a vagrant had taken up residence in the old house.

No, though he and Miranda would miss her, the happiest outcome of their strange friendship must be that Missie should return to the West Indies and the home she loved.

As he climbed aboard the bus which would take him into the city centre, Steve remembered Timmy. He could not go with Missie when she left, nor could he stay at Jamaica House by himself. He could imagine the screams of outrage from her aunt if Miranda tried to introduce a dog into Number Six, and whilst his own mother and father were both easy-going and generous, they would say that they needed every penny they earned to feed and clothe their own family, and could not afford the luxury of a dog. But now that he was regularly fed, groomed and exercised, Timmy was an attractive little chap. I dare say Mum and Dad would take to him if I promised to pay for all his food out of the money I earn doing odd jobs, Steve told himself, moving down towards the back of the vehicle as it slowed at his stop. He jumped down and was delighted as well as surprised to find Miranda, hands in pockets, strolling idly up and down the pavement, with Timmy close at her heels. She grinned at him as he joined her.

'Fancy meeting you!' she said gaily. 'I guess it were you who got lucky this time, judging by your grin.' She drew him out of the hurrying crowd. 'Here, Timmy! Don't you go wandering off; the butcher gave me a lovely marrowbone for you, so just you stick close to your pals, and you shall have it, as soon as we reach home.'

Back at the old house, Missie was waiting anxiously for them, knowing that Steve had believed he would meet the Grimshaws today. Despite the chill in the air she was sitting on the curved stone bench in the garden, and jumped to her feet eagerly, her big liquid eyes full of hope. 'Did you meet my young gentlemen?' she asked. 'Oh, but I can see you did. Tell me! I expect you told Miss Miranda already; it good news, it written on your face.'

By the time Steve had finished his story it was getting dark and Missie led the way down the garden and into the kitchen. This was now a much cosier and pleasanter room altogether, for a small paraffin stove stood in the hearth and the three of them had brought comfortable cane chairs through from the rest of the house. Missie and Miranda had ransacked drawers, chests and cupboards, and the result was cushions, rugs, and old-fashioned cloaks, which they had hung over the shutters at the windows. There was also food; Missie had told them she had found a bakery whose workers at the end of the day threw out cakes and loaves which they felt were no longer saleable, so now the three of them settled down to eat and chat and to discuss the future. Miranda enjoyed the cakes, despite a lurking fear that Missie had probably stolen them. Well, so what? Everyone has to live, and a baker wouldn't go hungry because of the loss of a few sticky buns, a small loaf and some cake, whereas Missie must eat to live.

'So, Gerald is coming here on Monday to meet you, just to make sure that the letter isn't a cunning forgery,' Steve said. 'Then nothing much will happen until next Saturday, when Gerald and Julian get this exeat thing and go off to their uncle's house to tell him the story.' He turned to Missie. 'Would you go with them? I really think you should. After all, you'll be heading away from the docks, not towards them, and the chances of anyone recognising you are pretty slight. I know the village where the Grimshaws' Uncle Vernon lives; it's very quiet and rural, not at all the sort of place wandering seamen want to visit.' Missie looked doubtful but Steve, catching Miranda's eye, gave an encouraging smile. 'I think we must somehow provide Missie with more suitable clothing than the things she's wearing at present before she meets Mr Grimshaw,' he said tactfully. 'I know dark clothing is fine for raiding the docks but it really won't do for visiting Holmwood.' He turned to Missie. 'I'm afraid you'd be far too conspicuous.'

Miranda had not thought of it before, but now she nodded vigorously. 'Steve's right, Missie. But even if we go to Paddy's Market, we don't have the sort of money to buy a decent dress. Oh, if only we'd thought of it earlier Steve could have arranged to borrow some cash from Gerald. I suppose we could ask your mam if she could borrow us a skirt and blouse, Steve, but . . .'

But Steve was grinning, flapping a hand at her. 'I've a better idea. I've heard two of the lads talking about the big rubbish skips at the back of Paddy's Market. It's a sort of yard at the corner of Maddox Street and Bevington Hill. The stallholders chuck anything they think they won't be able to sell into the bins on a Saturday night and on Monday morning the dustcarts collect them and carry them away. But the lads say some of the stuff is quite decent. They go there Sunday nights and either cram a sack with rags to sell to the rag and bone man – Packinham's or King's – or pick out the best stuff and sell it cheap to anyone willing to buy. If Miranda and meself nip down there tomorrow night with a couple of sacks, we can either help ourselves to anything we think will fit you, Missie, or we can fill the sacks and sell the stuff next day, like the fellers do, and by a dress wi' the gelt.'

'I'm surprised no one's twigged what's going on,' Miranda said, giggling. 'If old Kingy only knew, he'd cut out the middle man and go straight to the rubbish bins himself. He's far too mean to want to part with his money needlessly.'

Steve laughed too. 'You're right there. The fellers were sayin' someone were bound to find out soon, but I reckon if you and me go as soon as it gets dark tomorrow night, Miranda, we'll clean up.'

Missie beamed from face to face. 'Shall I come too?' she asked eagerly. 'I know where Paddy's Market is, on Scotland Road. I been there often.'

Both Miranda and Steve shook their heads firmly, however. 'No, Missie. You'll have to trust us to pick something respectable,' Steve said firmly. He gestured to Miranda. 'Time we were off. With a bit of luck your aunt and Beth will be in bed by the time you get home, and won't start asking questions.'

They said their farewells and made their way out to the main road to catch a tram back to Jamaica Close. As Miranda had expected, Number Six was in darkness, so she said goodbye to Steve and crept quietly to her bed.

Next day, in order to lull any suspicions that her aunt might be harbouring, she helped prepare and cook Sunday dinner and spent the rest of the day cleaning the house. Aunt Vi, coming in through the back door and narrowly avoiding the bucket of water with which Miranda was scrubbing the kitchen floor, swore loudly and would have given her a cuff, except that Miranda

150

ducked and raised her brush threateningly. Aunt Vi took evasive action, grumbling as she did so. 'What ails you, you miserable little bugger? If you want to clean the place up you should do it on a Saturday. I'm in me best coat and shoes; if they've got splashed I'll know who to blame.'

Miranda finished the floor with a final swirl of her cloth and stood up. 'I'm always busy on a Saturday, earning meself a few pence, so if you want floors scrubbed and cooking done it's got to be on Sunday,' she said firmly. She glanced at the clock above the mantel, which was showing five o' clock. 'I'm off now, Aunt Vi. I won't bother to stay for tea.'

Vi had been heading across the kitchen, clearly intending to go to her room and change out of her decent Sunday clothing, but at her niece's words she stopped in her tracks. 'You're going nowhere, not unless you tell me what you're up to . . .' she began, but Miranda was already out of the back door and hurrying across the yard. Heading for Steve's house, she felt quite excited. If they could acquire a decent skirt and some sort of blouse, Missie would be able to meet Mr Grimshaw, and then it was just a matter of time before her troubles would surely be over.

Chapter Six

Despite their hopes it was almost a month before the Grimshaws managed to arrange to take Missie to Holmwood, and Missie insisted that Miranda and Steve should accompany them. 'I shall want Mr Vernon to meet my friends,' she said firmly. 'We shall be respectable group, all in Sunday things, and Mr Vernon will arrange my passage home at once.'

Sitting on the bus which would take them to Holmwood, Miranda thought back over the past four weeks. The raid on the rubbish bins had started it, she thought, and that had not been all plain sailing by any means. For a start, it had begun to rain as they arrived at their destination, heavy rain which soon had both Steve and herself soaked to the skin, and had made the clothing they had crammed into their potato sacks extremely heavy. They had intended to select respectable garments both for Missie and for Miranda herself, but they soon abandoned that idea, simply filling their sacks with any clothing they could reach, for the bins were huge and deep. They had been heading back towards the big wooden double doors which led on to the road when these had creaked open and four boys, all a good deal larger than Steve, had shouldered their way in and stopped, staring with disbelief at Steve and Miranda.

Steve had tried to push past, but the biggest boy had

shoved him in the chest and kicked the door shut behind him. 'You ain't goin' nowhere, Steve Mickleborough,' he had said gruffly. 'You've been listenin' at doors you have, you sneaky little bastard. Me and the fellers ain't told no one about this here back yard so you'll hand over them sacks and clear orf before I clacks you so hard you'll be asleep for a week.'

'Aw, come on, Muffler, there's plenty for all of us,' Steve had wheedled. 'As for listenin'. . . well, I admit I did hear someone say as how the yard door wasn't locked, but you can't call that listenin', exactly . . .'

The large boy had given a scornful laugh. 'Oh no?' he had said jeeringly. 'I'll call it what I bleedin' well like, and I say you've been earwiggin'.'

But Miranda, seeing that the other three boys were already digging into the bins and shouting to their leader to get a move on so that they could get out of the perishin' rain, had sneaked round behind Muffler, pulled open the door, screamed to Steve to follow her and set off at a gallop. Her loot had been fearfully heavy and she might easily have been caught had not Steve swung his sack at Muffler's legs, causing him to crash to the ground. Horrified, for she guessed that Muffler would take it out on her pal next time they met, Miranda had hesitated, wondering whether she ought to help the big fellow to his feet and let him have her sack of clothing, but Steve had had no such qualms. 'Gerra move on, you idiot, and don't you *dare* leave that sack behind,' he had screamed, clearly guessing her intention. 'If we get a fair sum from old Kingy, I'll give Muffler a couple of bob to keep him sweet. Come *on*, Miranda Lovage!'

Soaked to the skin and fighting a wild desire to burst

into tears, for the rain had been so heavy that she could scarcely see more than a few feet ahead, Miranda had obeyed. She was panting and breathless, but when they reached Jamaica Close and lugged their sacks round the back jigger and into Steve's yard they had both been grinning. They knew they would have to dry the clothes out before they could present them to be weighed at the rag and bone man's yard, but that could be dealt with the following day. They had pushed their sacks into the shelter of the coal shed, exchanged promises to meet as usual the following morning, and made their weary way up to bed.

It had taken longer than they had anticipated to dry everything out because Monday and Tuesday had also been wet, but by Saturday it was dry at last and, as Miranda remarked, it was also very, very clean. They had sold most of it, save for a grey pleated skirt and a green jumper for Miranda, and then they had gone to a stallholder in Paddy's Market who was a friend of Steve's mother, who had agreed to lend them both clothing and shoes in different sizes, so that Missie might choose which she felt suited her best. Then Steve had returned to the market with the unwanted garments while Missie peacocked about Jamaica House, admiring her reflection in the long cheval glass in one of the bedrooms, and persuading Miranda to brush out her greying black hair and braid it into a coronet on top of her head.

'You look like a queen, dear Missie,' Miranda had said, astonished at what decent clothing and a new hairstyle could do for their little friend. Now, as Missie sat between Steve and Miranda on the bus, she presented quite a respectable appearance. Oddly enough, she seemed to have cast all her worries and doubts to one side, and had climbed aboard the bus quite merrily, chatting away to Miranda and Steve, though she did keep her voice very low, and appeared to be eager not to stare at her fellow passengers. The Grimshaw boys, who were already aboard, had grinned at them, but they had arranged not to join forces until they reached Holmwood, where Vernon Grimshaw and his family lived. No matter how respectable she, Steve and Missie might appear in their own eyes, she guessed that folk would stare to see two Browncoat boys in such odd company.

Soon the bus was drawing to a halt and Julian and Gerald were getting up from their seats, so the others followed suit. It was not raining, but the sky was overcast, and as Miranda alighted from the bus she looked around her with interest. They were in a village street with half-timbered thatched cottages on either side of the road, several of which were small shops. Miranda saw a blacksmith's, a bakery and what looked like a post office, but Steve was catching her hand, pulling her forward to where Missie and the boys stood. 'We'd better introduce ourselves,' he said briskly. 'Gerald we know, but . . .' he grinned at the older of the two boys, 'my vivid intelligence tells me that this tall feller must be Julian. Am I right?'

Everyone smiled; Julian nodded, but looked around him rather uneasily. 'We're a bit obvious standing about in the middle of the village street,' he observed. 'Let's wait until we reach Holmwood Lodge.' To Miranda's astonishment, he bent down and kissed Missie's cheek. 'It's grand to see you alive and well, dear Missie,' he said gently. 'But we're not out of the wood yet, so let's waste no more time. Uncle's house is about a quarter of a mile outside the village, so we'd best get going. Auntie is going to have tea and crumpets waiting . . .' he smacked his lips, 'and if I know my aunt there'll be a big fruit cake and scones with jam and cream as well.'

When the small group reached Holmwood Lodge, Miranda hung back. She had imagined a neat, detached house with a small front garden and a brightly painted front door; instead, Holmwood Lodge was set well back from the road, at the end of a long gravelled drive which was lined with tall trees. Steve too had not expected anything as imposing as the house they presently approached, but he grabbed Miranda's arm and gave it an admonitory shake. 'Don't look so scared, you silly twerp,' he hissed. 'It's not as though they ain't expectin' us. We're here by invitation and don't you forget it.'

'Oh, but it's huge,' Miranda said distractedly. 'I've never even imagined a garden could be so big, let alone a house.'

'Oh, don't be so daft,' Steve said crossly. 'You haven't come to buy the perishin' place, you've come to have tea, and talk about Missie. Or were you thinkin' about puttin' in an offer? I dare say they'd mebbe accept a couple of thousand quid, if you've got that much to spare.'

Miranda giggled. She did like Steve; he gave her courage, made her see her fears for what they were: groundless. So when they reached the front door – a solid slab of oak with a long bell pull and a knocker – she tugged on the bell pull so hard that even outside the house it sounded as though a fire engine was approaching. Gerald laughed. 'It is a big house, but I'm pretty sure the bell rings in the kitchen, and will be heard by the maids, so you've no need to tug the thing off the wall,' he said cheerfully. 'Of course in the old days a butler would have come to the door but now, because everyone says there's going to be a war quite soon, my uncle was telling me it's just about impossible to get domestic staff. But they've got a couple of girls who come up from the village each day, and a cook-housekeeper who makes wonderful fruit cake . . .'

'Shut up, blabbermouth,' Julian hissed. 'Someone's coming!'

Miranda listened, and heard footsteps approaching the front door. As it creaked open, she felt Missie's hand clutch hers, and realised that the older woman was even more nervous than she was herself. Missie was used to big houses all right, but only in what you might call a menial capacity. Now she was entering as a guest and felt just as awkward and embarrassed as Miranda did.

The Grimshaw boys must have realised how the old woman felt for they both turned to smile at her, and Gerald took the hand that was not gripping Miranda's even as the door swung wide and a fat, elderly woman with crimped grey hair, gold-rimmed spectacles and a broad smile appeared in the aperture, beckoning them inside. 'Come in, come in,' she said cheerfully. 'Mrs Grimshaw said to take you straight in to the drawing room, because it's a chilly day and you'll all be glad to get close to a good log fire. I've got the kettle on the stove and the crumpets will be cooked to a turn in another five minutes, so you won't have long to wait for your tea.' She ushered them into a large hallway, with a woodblock floor and elegant paintings on the panelled walls. Then she threw open the door, saying as she did so: 'Here's your guests, sir and madam. It's chilly outside, and no doubt they'll be glad of a warm whilst you talk.'

Steve and Miranda were at the back of the group, and found themselves entering a very large room indeed. Wide windows overlooked a glorious garden at the back of the house, but Miranda had no eyes for the view, the roaring log fire or the elegant furniture. She was staring very hard at Mr Vernon Grimshaw and his wife, both of whom came forward, smiling, clearly intent upon putting the visitors at their ease.

Julian performed the introductions, whilst Miranda could still only stare. The solicitor was a small thin man with a sharp intelligent face and a determined chin. Despite the fact that the boys had referred to him several times as elderly, he did not seem so to Miranda, for he had thick brown hair neatly trimmed, and a pair of very shrewd brown eyes which looked her over thoughtfully and were then lightened by a charming smile. 'It's very nice to meet you, Miss Lovage,' he said as they shook hands. 'Let me assure you that any friend of Missie's is a friend of ours. But you must let me introduce you to my wife. Mrs Grimshaw has never visited the West Indies, but she has heard me speak of Missie many times, and was as distressed as I was to learn that Missie had been only a few miles away and in great distress for all this time. Had we but known, she could have come to us straight away – heaven knows our home is big enough – and perhaps even remained here until we had managed to sort out her papers, and to get her a passage back home.' He turned to the lady at his side. 'Fiona, my dear, this is the little lady we've heard so much about: Miranda Lovage.'

Mrs Grimshaw looked taller than her husband, with a mass of beautiful dark red hair, which she wore in a French pleat. She had a heart-shaped face and very large red-brown eyes, the same colour as her hair, and when she smiled, revealing perfect white teeth, Miranda thought her truly beautiful. She was elegantly dressed in a coffee-coloured lace dress and shoes of exactly the same colour, with very high heels, which was probably why she seemed so much taller than her husband. She held out one hand to Miranda and one to Missie, and led them to a comfortable sofa.

'Sit down and make yourselves at home while I go and help Mrs Butterthwaite to bring through the tea,' she said. 'We sent the maids home, since we felt that the fewer people who knew about Missie's plight the better. Butterthwaite, of course, has been with the family for many years and is totally to be trusted.' She turned to the three boys, who were holding out icy hands towards the blazing logs. 'You must be Steve. Julian told me that you were the first to discover that someone was living in Jamaica House.' She gave a little purr of amusement. 'My husband tells me you thought Missie was a ghost, which makes it all the more impressive that you continued to visit the place, and of course eventually you met each other. When you're warm enough, come and sit down, because I think we won't discuss ways and means until we've all enjoyed Mrs Butterthwaite's cooking. Ah, I think I hear her approaching now. Open the door for her, Julian, and you can help hand plates and cups . . . dear me, Mrs Butterthwaite, I can see you've done us proud.'

Miranda looked at the heavily laden tea trolley, almost unable to believe the lavishness of it; there were cakes and scones, long plates filled with various sandwiches, and when Mrs Butterthwaite lifted the lid from a large silver salver piles of buttered crumpets, steaming gently, were revealed. 'Please help yourselves, only start off with the crumpets because they're hot,' their hostess commanded them. 'I very much hope that when Mrs Butterthwaite pushes the trolley back to the kitchen it will be a good deal lighter than it is now.'

Miranda doubted that this was likely, but when she saw the enthusiasm with which the boys and Missie attacked the food, she realised that she would only be conspicuous if she failed to take advantage of her hostess's kindness, and very soon – far sooner than she would have believed possible – Mrs Grimshaw's hopes were realised. Mrs Butterthwaite was rung for to wheel out the remnants of the feast, and Mr Grimshaw gestured them to take their places around a large and shiny table.

'And now to business,' he said. 'To start with, I want Missie's story from the very first moment she saw the *Pride of the Sea* putting out a boat to come ashore, right up to when you knocked on my front door.' He smiled round at them, a small, rather sharp-featured man who somehow inspired confidence.

Miranda had taken care to sit between Missie and Steve, though she had decided that she liked Gerald Grimshaw very much and did not feel at all awkward in his company. Julian on the other hand was still very much an unknown quantity. He had not addressed her once, and though his brother had said that he was shy, she felt that he thought himself superior to everyone in the room, save his uncle and aunt. But Missie was beginning to speak, and Miranda saw that Mrs Grimshaw, seated opposite her, appeared to be writing something in a large notebook. Mr Grimshaw must have noticed Miranda's stare for he raised a hand to stop Missie speaking whilst he explained. 'Many years ago, when I was a young solicitor just starting up in practice, I had a young secretary named Fiona Sayer. She was quite the prettiest and brightest girl I had ever met, and after a couple of years we decided that we were made for each other, and got married. Fiona's excellent shorthand has come in useful several times, so now, if you don't object, she's going to take down everything Missie tells us. Then she will go into my office, which is the room opposite this one, and transcribe it on to the typewriter. She will do the same when each of you tells your story, so then we shall have a complete record. I trust this is agreeable to everyone?'

Everyone nodded and Miranda, watching Mrs Grimshaw's pencil fly across the paper, thought that she would like to be a secretary one of these days, especially if it meant marrying one's boss and becoming mistress of a beautiful and elegant house.

Missie's recital was a long one, but it was amazing how the questions put to her by Mr Grimshaw clarified things. By the time everyone, even Miranda, had told their own story the sequence of events became clear; clearer than they had ever been before. Indeed, Miranda began to get quite excited, and decided she must ask for a transcript of Missie's story, so that she could be sure of certain facts. When Mrs Grimshaw returned with a sheaf of neatly typed pages, she was beginning to pluck up her courage to ask if she might have one when she realised there was no need to do so. Mr Grimshaw gave everyone a copy of the transcript, asking them to add or delete as necessary, for, as he said, reading it over one of them might well remember an important fact which someone else had missed. Then he told Missie that he had arranged for her to live in a property he had heard was coming vacant, until such time as she could be repatriated to the West Indies. 'You need a respectable address,' he told her. 'It's nothing very grand, my dear, just a couple of rooms above a bicycle shop on Russell Street, owned by a young man I used to employ. My wife would prefer that you remain with us – and so would I, of course – but I'm afraid that would not help your cause. We shall visit you frequently, and if you do exactly as I tell you we'll have you on a ship bound for the West Indies before you know it.'

Miranda thought that Missie would be delighted at not having to live at Jamaica House any more, but her friend looked terrified. 'I best where I know,' she said obstinately. 'Jamaica House not good address?'

Mr Grimshaw laughed. 'It's a very good address if you don't know Liverpool, but any Liverpudlians who know the house associate it with bygone days and assume it to be a total ruin. No, no, Missie my dear, you must be guided by me. I'm going to ask our young friends Miranda and Steve to keep you supplied with food and to take you around with them at weekends so that folks get used to seeing you. Don't worry, Russell Street is a good way from the docks so you won't be spotted by wandering sailors. I intend to make enquiries about the *Pride of the Sea*, but I should be very surprised indeed to find that they have ever returned to Liverpool.' He smiled at Missie. 'Why should they come back here? They will assume that you have reported their behaviour to the police and that they would be hauled before a judge and jury on a charge of kidnapping should they ever return. They might have abandoned Britain altogether and traded from the West Indies to North America, or Mexico; almost anywhere other than here. They might have changed the name of the ship. But whatever they have done, I'm certain you need no longer fear them.' He glanced at the ornate clock on the mantel. 'Time is getting on. Missie will remain here for a few nights since I can't take possession of the flat until Monday or Tuesday.' He turned to Miranda and Steve. 'I'm going to give Missie a sum of money which should last her until she leaves England, but I've written down the name, address and telephone number of my office so that if you need to contact me for any reason, such as Missie needing more money or some other worry, then you can do so.' He gave Steve a folded piece of paper as he spoke, then turned to his nephews. 'You're quite capable, I'm sure, of getting back to Crosby on public transport, but since I want to show Miranda and Steve where Missie will be living for the next few weeks, you might as well come with us in the car. Then I'll run you back to Crosby and make sure that the school understands that you will be visiting me on a regular basis.'

Missie cleared her throat. 'It very good of you, Mr Vernon, very kind,' she said timidly. 'But I rather live in Jamaica House until time to move into flat. I have little dog who waits for me. I shut him in dining room with bowl of water and biscuits, so I must return to Jamaica House. When I leave, Timmy come too.'

Mr Grimshaw's eyebrows shot up. 'A dog! Well, I shall do my best to find a good home for him, because if you were hoping to take him with you I think that is more than I can arrange,' he said. 'Very well, once I've shown you the flat in Russell Street, I'll drive you round to Jamaica House, and when I've made all the arrangements I'll return there to pick up you and your little companion.'

Julian cleared his throat. 'I've not liked to ask before, but did our family once own Jamaica House?' he asked. 'And if so did they benefit from the slave trade?'

There was an uncomfortable silence before Mr Grimshaw nodded reluctantly. 'Yes, Julian, I'm afraid you've guessed the truth. It's a period of our history of which our family are rightly ashamed, so it is never mentioned. But the family had ceased trading in slaves long before it became illegal to do so, I can promise you that.' He smiled across at Missie, who was staring at him, round-eyed. 'It was a filthy trade, dear Missie, which makes it even more important to see you a free woman, and back in your own place once more.'

Miranda, watching Julian closely, saw the worry fade from his face. 'Thank you for telling me, Uncle,' he said quietly. 'And now let us get on with the business in hand, which is making Missie comfortable and returning her to her island.'

Later that evening, as she made her way across to Number Six, Miranda reflected that everything had gone according to plan. Not knowing the area as well as Steve did, she had not realised that they would pass Russell Street every time they went to the city centre, though Steve had pointed this out to Missie. 'We'll be able to visit you on our way to and from Paddy's Market and that,' he had told her. 'And after what Mr Grimshaw said, you needn't fear meeting anyone from the *Pride of the Sea.*' He had shaken his head in self-reproach. 'Weren't we daft not to realise that the last place on earth Captain Hogg would want to visit would be Liverpool? It might be different if he had realised you'd be too afraid to go to the authorities, but I don't suppose that even crossed his mind. No, Mr Grimshaw was right. Probably this is the one place on earth that the *Pride of the Sea* dare not visit.'

Miranda approached Number Six with rather less than her usual caution, because her mind was full of the happenings of the afternoon and their plans for the future. At first her aunt had nagged her about her frequent absences, but when she realised that her niece was still doing her share of the housework, yet was seldom present at mealtimes, she had stopped expecting her to come straight home from school. The fact that Beth's boyfriend often accompanied her cousin home also made Miranda's life easier. In front of Herbert Wade, her aunt was on her best behaviour, treating Miranda, if not with affection, at least with civility, and anyway she was usually in bed by the time Miranda returned to the house.

This evening, however, when she went to open the back door, it was locked. Miranda stared. True, she was a good deal later than usual, but her aunt had never locked her out before. Naturally lazy and knowing that there was nothing worth stealing in Number Six, she never bothered to lock up. Miranda stepped back and looked up at the bedroom windows. No light showed, and she hesitated to knock. If she could have roused Beth without waking Aunt Vi, she would have done so, but there was little chance of that. Miranda heaved a sigh; one way and another she had managed to keep on the right side of her aunt recently, but she knew that if she woke her the least she could expect was a clack round the ear. She glanced towards the coal shed; she didn't much fancy trying to sleep in there, nor in the noisome little privy.

It was beginning to rain, and it was both cold and windy, which meant a night in the open was out of the question. The only alternative was to walk back to Jamaica House, wake Missie, wrap herself in one of the blankets and spend the night there. Miranda glanced hopefully at the downstairs windows, but they were all tightly shut. Oh well, it's a walk I've done often enough, and as I go I'll try to think of some solution to the problem of Timmy, she told herself. She wondered if the Grimshaws might take him in. They had a marvellous house but no pets, as far as she had been able to tell, and surely once they had seen Timmy they would be as eager to give him a home as she had been herself. She would still have loved to keep him, but knew that that would be impossible. Later, when I've got a proper job, I really will have a dog of my own, she mused as she walked, but until then I must just make sure that Timmy doesn't lose out.

By the time Miranda reached Jamaica House, the light rain had turned heavy and she was glad to open the door in the wall, cross the garden at a tired trot and approach the kitchen door. She knew Missie slept in a tiny box-like attic room on the top floor because she said she felt safer up there, and she knew that Timmy usually occupied the foot of Missie's bed. Normally he would rush downstairs, tail going nineteen to the dozen, eyes bright, ears flattened in welcome, but she had no idea how he would greet someone coming in the middle of the night. She hoped he wouldn't bark and scare Missie out of her wits, but perhaps it was not as late as she had imagined, for when she opened the kitchen door and slipped inside she saw that the room was lamp-lit, the fire glowed in the hearth and Missie was sitting at the big kitchen table eating some sort of stew from a large plate, whilst Timmy, at her feet, was destroying a large bone which Steve had wheedled from the butcher on Scotland Road.

Missie looked up and beamed when she saw who had entered, and Miranda, smiling back, thought how the visit to Holmwood Lodge had calmed all her friend's fears. Once, she would have shot out of her seat and disappeared into the rabbit warren of other rooms, but now she simply greeted Miranda as though night-time visits were commonplace.

'Have some stew, Miranda. Late for visiting,' she chuckled. She got up and fetched a second plate from the sideboard, then ladled stew into it and pushed it towards her unexpected guest. 'Go on, take bread,' she said. 'Timmy got bone; he ate his stew. Why you here?'

Miranda explained and Missie nodded wisely. 'I thought it something like that,' she said. 'Your aunt holy terror. When you finished, I get you blankets.' She beamed at Miranda; a small face shining with childlike happiness. 'It be nice and warm here; we damp down fire and both sleep on floor. Mr Vernon take me away soon.'

'I'll come with you and help you carry the blankets,'

Miranda said eagerly as she finished the stew on her plate. It was just a mixture of vegetables, but Missie had been living mostly on vegetables over the summer and knew how to make them tasty.

The two of them climbed the stairs by the light of the lantern Missie carried, and very soon the pair were back in the kitchen and making a bed on the floor, well supplied with blankets and cushions. Then they settled down, with Timmy curled up between them. Rather to her surprise, however, Miranda did not feel tired, but found herself wanting to talk over the events of the past couple of days. 'I wonder why you didn't sleep down here in the warm before, Missie?' she said, snuggling down. 'Were you too afraid of Captain Hogg and his merry men to sleep on the ground floor?'

Missie nodded. 'Yes. Mr Vernon, he no understand. Those men bad through and through; ship is evil. On very night I escape from ship, before I find Jamaica House, I make myself sort of nest in basement of other house, some way from docks. Moon was shining like daylight and I saw Captain Pig and first mate pulling woman along. She wore long white gown, hair loose. She not look bad woman, yet she with bad men . . .'

Miranda had only been half listening but on hearing those words she jerked upright and interrupted without ceremony. 'Missie, that poor woman might have been my mother! Can you recall what day it was? What street? Was the lady very beautiful? Oh, Missie, you know I live with my aunt? Well, I only moved in with her because my mother had disappeared – I don't think I told you because it upset me when people said she had gone away with a man. I knew that wasn't true. If she had wanted to go away with someone she would have taken her clothes, her books, all the things she loved, and me as well, of course, but she left in the middle of the night and I couldn't see anything missing from her wardrobe, so she might have been wearing just her nightdress. Oh, Missie, I'm sure you must have seen my mother being kidnapped by Captain Hogg! Was she bound or gagged? Were they carrying her? Please, Missie, tomorrow morning you must come to the police with me and tell them what you saw!'

Missie looked confused and worried. 'She not cry for help. Men have arms round her,' she said.

'Are you sure she was walking and not being carried?' Miranda said desperately. 'If only you will come to the police station I'm sure they will ask the Port Authority when the *Pride of the Sea* tied up at the quay, which would tell us for certain whether it was the day my mother disappeared. Oh, Missie, I beg of you to come to the police with me. Or if you won't do that, would you tell Mr Grimshaw what you saw?'

Miranda watched as the worry slowly cleared from her companion's face, to be replaced by a tentative smile. 'Yes, that good idea,' Missie said, clearly relieved. 'Mr Vernon would say I must not go to police.'

Miranda opened her mouth to argue, then shut it again. She suddenly realised that the first thing the law would ask would be for Missie's name and address. Also, it would be useless for her, Miranda, to tell the police what Missie had seen; that was not evidence, but hearsay. No, Missie was right. Mr Grimshaw would know what to do. Miranda settled back in her blankets. Missie had doused the lamp and the two had been talking in the fire's glow and now Missie turned to Miranda, her face alive with curiosity. 'It long time ago; have you been with your aunt long time?' she asked.

'Yes, I have; it seems like a lifetime,' Miranda said gloomily. 'Oh, my poor darling mother! What will they have done with her? Would they keep her on the ship as they kept you, to cook and clean for them?' She smothered a chuckle. 'If so I imagine they would very soon regret it. She isn't much of a cook and she hates housework.'

She glanced at Missie as she spoke and saw how Missie's eyes refused to meet her own. 'If was your mother, she mebbe escape, like me,' she said evasively.

'Yes, but if she did escape, why hasn't she come home?' Miranda said uneasily. 'I suppose it might take time to get people to help her if she's in a foreign country where they don't speak English, but as you say, a great deal of time has passed. Oh, Missie, I can't wait to tell Mr Grimshaw what you saw, and to get his opinion on what we should do next.'

Next day Miranda was so excited that she would have gone straight to Holmwood, but this Missie refused to do. 'You must go to your aunt's home and find out why she lock you out,' she said. 'There could be many reasons.'

The two of them were drinking tea and eating toast in the kitchen. Outside, the rain had really got into its stride and was pelting down and Miranda did not fancy the long walk back to Jamaica Close in such weather, but Missie produced the purse of money which Mr Grimshaw had given her and insisted that she should take the tram fare. 'And if your aunt ask where you spend night, tell her it with a school friend,' she instructed, and went on to explain that though she knew Miranda wouldn't give her away on purpose, she was so excited over the possibility that Missie had seen her mother that night that she might give something away. 'If you leave at once you be back here in time for us to catch two o'clock bus out to Holmwood. Perhaps rain will have stopped by then. Are you going to tell Steve what I saw?'

Miranda shook her head. 'I won't tell him today. As it is, we're going to have our work cut out to convince Mr Grimshaw.' She stood up, drained her teacup and headed for the back door. 'I'd best be making tracks.' Timmy shot across the room, his tail wagging so fast that it became a blur, for he did love a walk. However, Miranda had to disillusion him. 'Not today, old chap; you stay with Missie until I get back,' she said. She turned to the older woman. 'Do you think we could take him to Holmwood Lodge this afternoon? Only if they fell in love with him it would solve at least one of our problems.'

Missie laughed. 'You never know luck,' she said. 'See you later, Miranda.'

A couple of hours later Miranda, now clad in an old mackintosh with a scarf tied round her head, scarcely bothered to look round her before approaching the door in the ivy-covered wall. Quite apart from the fact that the rain was so heavy she could only see a couple of yards ahead, she knew that the factories did not work on Sundays, so did not fear being seen. The trees dripped and the flowers hung their heads so that the garden was no longer a paradise but looked neglected and rather sad. And neglected it soon would be, Miranda mused ruefully, for once Missie was gone she did not suppose that she and Steve would come here often. Steve would shortly be leaving school and getting a job, and she herself intended to follow his example as soon as she could. There were hostels for girls working in Liverpool, and once she found work she meant to leave the house in Jamaica Close, move into a hostel and start looking for Arabella in earnest.

As soon as she opened the back door Timmy rushed to meet her and Missie, peeling potatoes at the low stone sink, turned to give her a smile. 'Well?' she said eagerly. 'Why they lock you out?'

Miranda chuckled. 'As you know, we are Number Six. Further up the road at Number Ten there's a family with three sons, all working. It being Saturday they took themselves off for a river cruise and apparently had a grand day out, which included a great many bevvies – that means drinks – and a great deal of grub . . .'

'That mean food,' Missie said, giggling. 'So why your aunt locking door?'

Miranda laughed as well. 'Whilst they were out their house was done over – robbed – so they alerted the scuffers and one of the young constables came round to the Close. He visited every house, including Number Six of course, warned them all that the McDonalds had been robbed, and advised everyone to lock up with special care. Of course Aunt Vi swore they thought I'd come in earlier, which would have meant they were locking me in, not out. I won't say Aunt Vi apologised, because she didn't, but my cousin Beth said she were real sorry and why hadn't I chucked gravel at the bedroom window or battered on the kitchen door to be let in. She's not bad, Beth; I do believe if it wasn't for Aunt Vi she and I could have been friends. So you see it wasn't just spite, as I thought. In fact, if they hadn't locked me out you and I might never have spent the night talking, so I should be grateful to them.'

Missie nodded. 'Well, that one mystery solved,' she said cheerfully. 'We will have some of that vegetable stew for midday meal. Mrs Vernon will give us supper once we've told story to Mr Vernon.'

On their way to school next morning, Miranda regaled Steve with her doings. 'Mr Grimshaw didn't scoff once, but listened to every word Missie had to say,' she told him. 'And now that they've got the name of the ship, the police will go to the Port Authority and find out when the *Pride of the Sea* put in at Liverpool.'

Steve pulled a face. 'But it's so long ago, Miranda! I don't want to put you off or make you miserable, but if I were a detective in a book I'd say the trail had gone cold.'

Miranda scowled at him. They were both members of the nearest library and enjoyed detective stories but, as she pointed out, these were works of fiction, and what she and Steve were discussing was real life.

'Ye-es, but you can't deny that a year is a long time, and memories are short,' Steve argued. 'Still, if the ship has returned to the 'Pool, at least we'll know about it.'

'Yes. Mr Grimshaw's a man of his word, and the police will take him seriously, which is more than they would have done had you and I turned up on their doorstep,' Miranda agreed. 'And as for Missie telling her story herself . . .'

By now they were approaching their school gates and

Steve shouted to a group of boys ahead of them to wait for him. Then he turned to Miranda. 'Are we going to Jamaica House after school?' he asked. 'I know it's going to take Mr Grimshaw a day or two to fix up the flat in Russell Street – especially now you've given him another job of work, poor man – but there might be something we can do to help Missie get ready.'

In fact it was some time before Missie moved into her new abode. She was very nervous at first and begged Mr Grimshaw to allow her to share her grand new premises with Miranda and Timmy. 'Miranda very unhappy with aunt and Timmy unhappy without Miranda,' she said, and went on to explain that she still feared Captain Hogg would discover her whereabouts and burst in to carry her off.

Miranda had listened hopefully, for already she loved the neat little flat and would have been happy to live in it even for a few weeks, but Mr Grimshaw, though he understood their feelings, had shaken his head reluctantly. 'No, no, my dear Missie. Her aunt may not value Miranda as she should, but she would be as curious as anyone else if her niece suddenly found a flat share with an unknown West Indian woman! Now, it seems your Captain Hogg is suspected of a good many misdemeanours, though the Port Authority knew nothing about any kidnapping activities. Apparently, he only came into Liverpool for an engine part. That was his declared reason, anyway, and he left on the tide the day following his arrival, so very little interest was taken by the authorities on this occasion. But the date matches your mother's disappearance, Miranda, and once they started asking questions it soon became clear that the ship was notorious for slipping in and out of harbour without paying her dues, for loading shipments meant for other vessels, and similar offences.' He had smiled kindly at Miranda, and patted her on the shoulder. 'I think it's quite possible that your mother was seized by the captain, my child, but until we can trace the ship's movements we have no way of ascertaining her present whereabouts, if indeed it was Mrs Lovage Missie saw that night.'

Later, when Steve, Missie and Miranda were alone in the flat, with Timmy curled up on the hearthrug, they decided that discussing the matter was pointless. Instead, they would wait for solid news of the ship's first port of call, for Mr Grimshaw had promised that his investigations would start there. 'And as soon as we've seen you off on a ship bound for home, Missie, I shall leave school and get a job in one of the factories, and start saving up,' Miranda planned. 'I know there's been a depression – still is – but everyone seems convinced that there's a war coming and factories are being built to make uniforms and guns and wireless sets, that sort of thing. Beth is talking about leaving her job and going into either the services or a munitions factory, because they pay twice what she's getting from old Mrs Seymour, so I mean to do the same. If my mother is like you, Missie, desperate to get home but unable to raise the cash, then I shall jolly well get on a ship as soon as I've saved enough, and take her the money myself.'

'Three cheers for Miranda Lovage!' Steve said ironically. 'I never knew your mother, but that scuffer, the one who caught you sleepwalking, told me she was a real beauty with primrose-coloured hair, clear blue eyes and a very curvy figure. If you ask me she could get a job even if she'd landed on the moon!'

Miranda noticed Missie giving Steve a warning look, and for the first time it occurred to her that her mother's beauty might not be the asset she had imagined. She gave Steve a penetrating stare but he met her eyes frankly, his own faintly puzzled, and she realised that he had not understood Missie's glare either.

'What's up?' he asked, and then, as neither of his companions answered, he shrugged. 'Have your secrets then,' he said huffily. 'And it's time we were heading home, Miranda.'

As Mr Grimshaw had warned them, arranging for Missie to travel legally from England to her home took time. She had been presumed dead and had to prove that she was not an impostor, though this seemed daft to Miranda; what was the advantage in perpetrating such a fraud? Autumn was well advanced when at last Missie's passage was arranged, and when Mr Grimshaw disclosed that his brother had been overjoyed to hear that Missie was still alive, and had immediately offered to take her back into his employment when she returned, Miranda knew that her visits to the little flat above the bicycle shop would soon be a thing of the past. Regretfully, she guessed that this would also mean she could scarcely keep popping over to Holmwood Lodge; she did this a lot, particularly at weekends when the boys were visiting, and she had grown friendly with them both. Julian and Gerald seemed to enjoy Steve and Miranda's company, despite their different stations in life. For one thing, Steve had got a job upon leaving school, at one of the big factories making parts for aero engines, and talked of joining the Royal Air Force as soon as he was eighteen, whereas Julian and Gerald knew nothing of the world of work, though they had both joined the junior division of the OTC.

Steve had always been generous, and now that he was earning he bought little presents for Miranda and took her on theatre and cinema trips, for meals in cafés and similar treats. Miranda felt guilty for accepting his hospitality so often and confided in Mrs Grimshaw her plan to leave school and apply for a factory job as soon as Missie had gone home. 'At first I thought of getting a room in a hostel, but there are lots of girls in the city looking for a flat share,' she told the older woman. 'Perhaps two or three of us could club together and take on Missie's place. I wonder if my cousin Beth might want to join us. Of course living at home is much cheaper because she doesn't have to pay her mum rent, and not a great deal for her keep either, but there was a big row the other day over Beth's telling whoppers. She told Aunt Vi she'd been to a dance at the Grafton with Spotty Wade, and then Aunt Vi discovered that Herbert had been working that night so Beth had gone by herself and picked up some foreign sailor whose ship was in port. Aunt Vi wouldn't have known anything about it only Curly Danvers, who lives further up the Close, met her in the fish shop and commented that Beth seemed to have got herself an officer, and a good-looking one at that.' Miranda hesitated; there was something she longed to ask but she was not sure whether it would be polite to do so. However, she and Mrs Grimshaw were companionably washing up the tea things whilst the boys played snooker in the games room, and she decided to take a chance. She and her hostess had grown easy with one another during the past weeks, so now Miranda braced herself and voiced the question. 'Mrs Grimshaw, would you mind telling me what sort of rent the owner would ask for the flat?'

'My dear child, I've no idea what the rent of the flat would be, but I'm sure my husband could tell you,' Mrs Grimshaw said. 'But, you know, Mr Grimshaw and I have talked about your future many times, and we think it would be a great waste for you to abandon your education without even attempting to get your School Certificate. I can understand your wanting to earn money of your own . . .'

Miranda interrupted her. 'I wouldn't be abandoning my education, honest to God I wouldn't,' she said eagerly. 'My mother was always on about the importance of what she called "that little bit of paper", so I thought I'd enrol at the technical college for evening classes. You can get all sorts of qualifications from there whilst earning at the same time.'

Mrs Grimshaw nodded. 'Yes, I know.' She emptied the water in her bowl down the sink, dried her hands on a tea towel and patted Miranda's cheek. 'My dear, Mr Grimshaw and I are willing to help you establish yourself with a career and a place of your own; so we would arrange for Mr Huxtable – he's the young man who owns the bicycle shop – to let you take on the flat at a reasonable rent. Mr Grimshaw needs an office girl, and though the salary is small the hours are nine till five, much more suitable than a factory for a girl studying for her certificate.'

Miranda stared at Mrs Grimshaw open-mouthed, and when she spoke her voice was husky. 'You've been so good to me already that I feel quite guilty,' she said. 'But I can't accept a cheap rent at your expense, it really wouldn't be fair. And I know all about key money! If you can tell me how much we should be expected to pay, I'm sure I can get two or three girls interested in flat sharing; then we could pay the rent between us. And I'd work very hard at my evening classes, honest to God I would.'

Mrs Grimshaw began to collect the clean cutlery and crockery and replace it on the shelves. She said, without looking round: 'Suppose we were to call the key money a loan? Would you feel more comfortable with that? I think a flat share is a grand idea, but not with three or four of you sharing the place. You and one other could be comfortable, couldn't you?'

'Oh *yes*,' Miranda said eagerly. 'And we'd pay you back just as soon as we could.'

Miranda awoke. She twitched back the bedroom curtains to let in the early sunshine, then wondered for a moment why she had not immediately rolled out of bed, for usually she liked to be downstairs and making some sort of breakfast for herself before Beth and her aunt woke up. Then she remembered. Today was leaving day; Missie's passage was booked, her packing done, and the little flat cleaned to within an inch of its life, for Missie was determined that the Grimshaws should not find one speck of dust in her dear little flat. They had all arranged to be down at the docks when Missie left, although it meant that the boys would have to sag off school. However, Steve had arranged to get a day off from his factory and Miranda herself was what you might call 'in between', since she had left school at the end of the previous week and would not start her job in Mr Grimshaw's office until the following Monday.

Since the Grimshaws had been determined to do everything properly, Mr Grimshaw had visited Aunt Vi to explain that he and his wife intended to help Miranda as she began to gain her independence. He had somehow made it appear that he had known Miranda's mother and was doing it for Arabella's sake; at any rate, that was the explanation which Aunt Vi gave to everyone, adding that the kid had certainly fallen on her feet, since the Grimshaws were also giving her a job and had offered to pay for her to attend evening classes.

So now Miranda lay on her back contemplating the pale sunshine and the blue of the sky which she could see through the crack in the curtains, and thinking that Missie would at least start her voyage in cold but pleasant weather conditions. But presently, despite telling herself that she deserved a lie-in, for the ship did not depart until noon, she rolled out of bed, padded to the wash-stand and began vigorously washing. She had ironed her best cotton frock the night before and thought that she would wear the little red jacket which Steve had bought her from Paddy's Market with his very first wages. She had noticed how his face lit up whenever she wore it, and she reflected that meeting Steve and becoming his friend was the best day's work she had ever done. He had never let her down, and continued to accompany her to the Port Authority when she went each week in the hope that the *Pride of the Sea* might have berthed somewhere along the British coast. Others had given up, but Miranda knew that Mr Grimshaw had not, and was beginning to believe that Captain Hogg must have changed the name of the ship. 'I've written fifty or sixty letters and contacted just about everyone who might be able to give me some information,' he had told Miranda. 'But ships need papers, just as people do, and sooner or later, whatever they call her, we'll root her out and bring Hogg to account. No doubt he'll claim ignorance, but with a crew such as his there's bound to be one of them who can be bought. Yes, once we've run the ship to earth, I'm very hopeful we shall find out what happened to your mother.'

But that day had not yet arrived, although Miranda still could not help connecting Missie's plight with Arabella's. Missie had remained hidden for a very long time, so why should not Arabella also be tucked away somewhere out of sight? Accordingly, Miranda had got one of the actresses who had worked with her mother to sketch Arabella's likeness and had pressed the picture into Missie's hand. 'If you see anyone, anyone at all, who looks like this, will you ask her if she's Arabella Lovage?' she said urgently. 'Steve said the captain and his mate might have given her some sort of drug, and she might have lost her memory. If you do see her, Missie, and tell her about me, surely that would be enough to make her remember?'

Now, having washed and dressed as quietly as possible so as not to wake Beth and Aunt Vi, she tiptoed down the stairs and into the kitchen. It was the work of a moment to put the kettle on the range and cut herself a thick wedge of bread which she spread with the jam Missie had made from the fruit in the garden of Jamaica House. Having breakfasted, Miranda made a pot of tea and carried it upstairs. Beth had just woken and greeted the tea with enthusiasm, but Aunt Vi just grunted and rolled over. 'I aren't gerrin' up yet,' she mumbled. 'Bring me some hot water up, and mebbe I'll have a wash.'

Miranda bit back the words 'That'll be a first' and went quietly out of the room. She did not wish to get on the wrong side of Aunt Vi, for in a couple of days she would be taking over the flat, and once that happened she doubted she would return to Jamaica Close, except to visit Steve.

She let herself out of the kitchen, closed the door gently behind her and headed across the back yard, then along the jigger and out into Jamaica Close. It was early but men and women were already walking briskly towards the main road, where they would catch the trams or buses which would take them to work.

Steve answered her knock, one cheek bulging, and pulled her into his mother's kitchen. 'Here, have some brekker,' he said thickly. 'It's a bacon sarnie; that'll line your belly until dinner.'

His mother, frying bacon, smiled a greeting. 'Mornin', queen,' she said cheerfully. 'Today's the great day, I gather. Done your packin' yet?'

Miranda giggled. 'Missie leaves today, but I shan't move into the flat until the weekend,' she explained. 'As for packing, I've got my old school skirt and jersey, my winter coat and the dress I've got on, and some underwear, so I don't think I'll need a suitcase to carry my belongings from Jamaica Close to Russell Street.' She smiled at Mrs Mickleborough. 'As soon as I'm settled I hope you'll come a-visitin', you and Mr Mickleborough. I'll get a big pot of tea ready, 'cos I know what big tea drinkers you two are, and a couple of dozen penny buns, the sort with pink icing on the top, and we'll have us a little party.'

'And you'll see Timmy, Mam,' Steve said, his tone reproachful. He had begged his mother to take the little dog in, but, whilst she was still considering, Mr Huxtable had asked Miranda if he might become Timmy's new owner.

'He's a grand little chap,' he had said appreciatively. 'I've always wanted a dog, and livin' above the shop you'll be able to visit him reg'lar like.'

Both Steve and Miranda were very grateful to the dark-haired young man, but Steve put into words what they were both thinking. 'That's real kind of you, Pete, but what will happen if you're conscripted into one of the forces?' he asked. 'Or have you already volunteered?'

Pete grinned. 'I volunteered right at the start, but they turned me down 'cos I'd broken my ankle and were still in plaster when I went for the medical. They said when the hospital released me as fit they'd be in touch again, and I dare say they will, but in the meantime I'm sellin' cycles and doin' repairs, and if I do go into the services I've a cousin who'll take over here. He's gorra dog of his own and will look after Timmy here like a mother, don't you fret.'

So very soon now they would all be settled: Missie on the ship which would take her home, Miranda in her brand new flat, and Timmy in the bicycle shop, and though Steve had said he would leave home if his mam wouldn't take Timmy in, everyone knew it was an idle threat. No family was happier than the Mickleboroughs. Not even my mother and me, Miranda thought to herself, and was surprised and even slightly shocked when the thought entered her head. Naturally she remembered Arabella through rose-coloured spectacles, but she was a practical girl and knew there had been times when her mother had voiced the wish that she did not have to work every hour God sent in order to keep her daughter and herself. Then there had been all the usual arguments as Miranda grew up, which came, she supposed, from two females sharing a house. Arabella had grumbled over the state of her daughter's bedroom, saying that at her age Miranda should not simply sling dirty clothing down on the floor, but should take it downstairs, possibly even wash it. Miranda realised, guiltily, that she had not been a very good daughter; in fact she had been both selfish and lazy. Now that she had begun to think back, she thought of all the things she might have done to make her mother's life easier, some of the things her aunt had taken for granted she would do as a sort of return for living in her house. Only Aunt Vi had carried it to extremes; Miranda had been expected to do not only her own washing, but that of Beth and her aunt as well. Aunt Vi had expected her to make the bed and to do all the housework, yet even then it had not occurred to Miranda that she had treated her mother as unfairly as Aunt Vi treated her. Oh, when Arabella comes back I'll wait on her hand and foot, Miranda dreamed. I'll cook beautiful meals, keep the house clean as a new pin and buy her little presents from my salary at the end of each month. When she comes home . . .

'What are you thinkin' about, dreamy? You've gorra real soppy look on your face.' Steve's voice cut across her musing. 'What'll we do till it's time to fetch Missie?

We could go to Jamaica House and collect any windfalls so's my mam can bottle them, or make jam. Unless you want to spend the time with Missie, that is.'

Miranda jumped, then turned to smile at him. 'Sorry, Steve. I was thinking how much you help your mum, and realising how little I helped mine. You're a lad, and a lot of lads do next to nothing in the house, not even the messages. But you do all sorts without even having to be asked. It makes me ashamed that I wasn't a better daughter when I had the chance.'

Steve looked gratified. 'There you are, Mam, a recommendation,' he said, laughing. 'Ain't you glad you've got me?'

He puffed out his chest as he spoke and smirked, but Mrs Mickleborough gave him a shove. 'You ain't a bad lad, but if I'd had the good sense to give birth to a girl first I reckon you'd be like all the other young fellers round here, and wouldn't raise a finger whilst your sister was there to run messages, clean the house and do a bit of cooking on the side, so you can take that silly grin off your face and fetch my marketing bag down off its hook. I don't want a deal of stuff, just a big bag of spuds, a cabbage and Mrs Evans's laundry delivered, so mind you don't go buyin' the spuds first an' lettin' the laundry get dirty.'

Steve groaned. 'Oh, Mam, can't I do the messages later?' he asked hopefully. 'We meant to go straight round to Russell Street to see whether Missie needed any help in gettin' her stuff down to the quayside.'

Mrs Mickleborough laughed, but shook a reproving finger. 'And this is the feller who asked his pal what she wanted to do until it was time to take Missie aboard her ship,' she said. 'Oh, go on with you! Take the laundry round for me, there's a good lad, and I'll fetch the veggies myself. It'll do me good to get a breath of fresh air on such a lovely day.'

'Well, if you really wouldn't mind . . .' Steve was beginning, but Miranda cut him short.

'We'll take the laundry on our way to Russell Street and fetch your messages on the way back,' she said, smiling at Mrs Mickleborough.

Miranda, who had never been aboard a ship, was assured by Steve that they would have a good chance to look round the vessel whilst all the passengers boarded, and she was glad she'd put on her best dress and her most respectable pair of sandals. When they got to the flat, having dropped the laundry off at Mrs Evans's small tea room, she saw that Missie, too, was clad in her best. When they had first known the little woman, she had been dressed in black clothing which was little better than rags, but the Grimshaws had seen to it that she had decent garments for her stay in Liverpool, and a case of lighter clothing for the voyage and her return to the island. When Steve and Miranda ran up the metal staircase which led directly to the flat they were greeted by Missie, incredibly smart in a navy coat and skirt and a crisp white blouse. She had said she would be happy with clothing from Paddy's Market which she could wash, iron and darn where necessary, but the Grimshaws had taken her to T J Hughes and kitted her out with the very best. Miranda congratulated her on her appearance and Steve agreed that she was as smart as any lady of his acquaintance.

Missie beamed. 'I knew you would come, best of my

friends,' she said gratefully. 'Mr Vernon said he would call, but I say no need; my friends will come. But first we will have cup of tea and bun and I show you special cake, Miranda, so when I am gone you must come back here and have tea and cake.'

Missie bustled about, pouring boiling water from the kettle on the Primus into the teapot and producing some buns, which she said proudly she had made herself. Once the buns were eaten and the tea drunk, Missie fetched her hat and coat and Steve leaned towards Miranda, his brows rising. 'There's no oven in the flat,' he whispered. 'She couldn't possibly have made those buns, could she?'

Miranda giggled. 'It just shows how little you know,' she said derisively. 'Folk without ovens take their cake or bun mix, in its tin, round to Sample's, the bakery, and pay a small sum to have it cooked for them. Aunt Vi did that once in a while, when she was too lazy to light the oven.'

Steve leaned back, satisfied, then got to his feet and went over to the sink. 'I'll just wash up these few things . . .' he was beginning, when Missie came back into the room. Her hat was perched on her head and she was pulling on her gloves.

'All set; let's go!' she said briskly, then glanced around the kitchen. 'I happy here,' she said musingly as they headed for the stairs, 'yet I glad to leave. Mr Vernon take me to Jamaica House yesterday evening and I said my goodbyes. Now I must forget past and think of future.'

The three of them clattered down the stairs, Steve swinging the suitcase, and Missie with her handbag clutched beneath one arm. It was a leather one, shiny and new, a last present from Mrs Grimshaw, and Miranda knew that her little friend valued it highly. Accordingly she warned her not to wave it around when they neared the docks, and suggested that Missie should walk between herself and Steve. 'It's better to be safe than sorry,' she said sagely. 'Goodness, how the morning has flown! If we don't hurry, we'll be the last people to board the ship and I shan't have a chance to look round before they're pulling up the anchor and saying that all visitors must leave.'

When they reached the quayside, however, the Grimshaws were waiting and they all boarded the ship together. She was called the *Island Princess*, and though she was not a large craft Mr Grimshaw had been assured that her crew were experienced, her captain friendly and the passengers' quarters both comfortable and commodious. Unlike Miranda, Steve did know ships, since one of his brothers was in the Royal Navy, aboard a sloop, and Steve had visited several times when it had been in port, but he was very impressed by the *Island Princess* and told Missie that she was a lucky dog to have quarters so luxurious. 'My brother slings his hammock along with a dozen or so others, with almost no room for his own stuff,' he assured them. 'Missie's cabin could hold half a dozen, I'm sure; and she'll eat her dinner at a proper table with a white cloth and silver knives and forks. Oh aye, this is the way to travel!'

Miranda, thinking of her mother, asked Missie whether this ship was very different from the *Pride of the Sea*, but Missie shook her head. 'I dunno; it a long time ago and I a slave aboard her,' she muttered, and when a member of the crew shouted through a megaphone that they would soon be casting off and advised visitors to leave the ship, Miranda was aware that Missie was relieved.

Reaching the quayside once more, Julian and Gerald said they would stay to wave Missie off, but Mr Grimshaw wanted to get back to his office and said that if the boys could leave at once he would run them back to Crosby in his car. Julian looked thankful and Miranda guessed that his strong sense of propriety had made him reluctant to sag off school, but Gerald shook his head.

'I'm going back to Russell Street with Miranda and Steve,' he said firmly. 'Missie told me she'd left one of her magnificent fruit cakes and I just fancy a slice of it.'

'You're a greedy pig; that cake was left for me, not you,' Miranda said, but she spoke without much conviction, and even as she did so the senior Grimshaws said their goodbyes and moved away to where the car was parked.

Miranda gave them one last wave and turned back to the quayside. 'Oh, look, the ship's beginning to swing away from the quay; your parents and Julian might just as well have stayed!' she said. 'Missie is on the deck; can you see her waving? Oh, I forgot to remind her to show everyone the sketch of my mother Betty Prince made! But I'm sure she'll remember; she's not the sort to forget her friends.' She turned to Steve. 'She's promised to write, and will post a letter as soon as she can. Oh, isn't it sad saying goodbye to a friend you'll probably never see again? Oh, dear, and I was so determined not to cry . . . '

Gerald flung an arm round her shoulders and gave her a squeeze. 'Everyone cries when they're waving a friend off, even if they're going to meet again in a few months,' he said reassuringly. Seeing the look on Steve's face without fully understanding it, Miranda wriggled out of Gerald's embrace and smiled at Steve, though her eyes were still brimming with tears.

'It's all right, I'm okay now,' she said huskily. 'Let's get back to that cake; crying always makes me hungry!'

Chapter Seven

By the time Christmas was over, Miranda had received several letters from Missie, only one of which had come whilst she was still aboard the ship. On an international level, the war which had been spoken of vaguely when Miranda had first joined Grimshaw, Scott and Carruthers, Solicitors and Commissioners for Oaths, was now thought by most people to be inevitable, despite Mr Chamberlain's 'piece of paper' announcing peace for our time. And Miranda had not wasted her time at work. With a good deal of help from Mrs Grimshaw at weekends, she had learned to type and to take down simple letters in shorthand and Mr Grimshaw had increased her salary accordingly. 'Not that you're liable to be with us for long, because I dare say the government will want young women to do war work as well as young men,' he told her. 'But for the time being at least, the firm will take advantage of your many abilities.'

Miranda had beamed, delighted with the praise which she honestly felt she had earned, for despite attending evening classes in both typing and shorthand she had continued to study for her school certificate, and was always working at her desk or doing some other necessary job well before nine o'clock in the morning.

Since moving into the flat and on Mrs Grimshaw's advice, she had spent a good deal of her salary on the sort of clothes she could not have dreamed of buying before – not dance dresses, though she intended to purchase one as soon as she felt she could afford it – but what she thought of as sensible office clothing: a green pleated skirt, a crisp white blouse and a dark green cardigan. Steve, still working in his factory, also spent some of his wages on what he thought of as 'suitable clothing' for taking a young lady – Miranda – out to the cinema or the theatre, or for similar treats.

And Steve was not the only young man who took her about. Gerald Grimshaw, though still at school, managed to see her at least once a week and made it plain that he enjoyed her company. Miranda thought Steve did not altogether approve of this friendship, though he never said so, and Miranda did her best not to favour one above the other, though, as she told him, Steve would always be her bezzie.

Right now, however, the two were in the tiny kitchenette of the flat in Russell Street engaged in the tear-jerking task of pickling onions. Miranda had procured a promise from a stallholder in the Great Homer Street market to sell, on Miranda's behalf, as many jars of pickled onions as she could provide, and naturally she would make a small profit herself on every jar. When she had told Steve that this was going to be her way of paying for various little extras, like a dance frock, he had agreed at once to come round on weekends and evenings and give her a hand. So now the two sat on opposite sides of the kitchen table, packing the peeled onions into jars, adding vinegar, and sealing and labelling the jars ready to be ferried to the market on the stallholder's handcart.

Steve topped the jar he was filling with vinegar, closed

the lid and got up. 'I'll put the kettle on; I reckon we deserve a cup of tea after so much hard work,' he said. 'And just you remember, queen, who it is what's ruinin' his eyesight so's you can buy a dance dress; it's Steven Mickleborough, not Gerald Grimshaw.'

'Well, I enjoy going around with Gerald because we talk about lots of things I'd never have heard of if he hadn't told me,' Miranda explained. 'You're much more practical, Steve.' She chuckled. 'You took me horse racing, and to the football matches, so now I'm an Everton supporter and I know a bit about racing as well. But Gerald's helped me to understand why we're liable to go to war quite soon, for instance.' She grinned at her old friend. 'So you see, I value you both very highly, but in different ways. And Gerald will be off to university in a couple of years, so no doubt he'll lose interest in a little shorthand-typist and take up with an undergraduette, if that's what they call them.'

Steve sniffed. 'Well, so long as you don't let him take you dancing, I suppose I can't grumble.'

'Why don't you take me dancing yourself?' Miranda asked, knowing the answer full well. 'I know I don't have a decent dress yet, but I'm sure I don't mind going to the Grafton or the Daulby Hall in my office skirt and jumper.'

Steve grinned but shook his head. 'What, make a fool of myself in front of half Liverpool?' he said derisively. 'I can't dance; me brother Ted, the one what's in the Navy, says he'll learn me next time he's ashore for more than a few days . . .'

'*Teach* me, not learn me,' Miranda said instructively. 'If I've told you once, I've told you a hundred times.'

'What does it matter? You nag on when I asks you to borrow me half a dollar, but you know full well what I mean,' Steve said crossly. 'Stop tryin' to educate me, woman, or I'll forget meself and give you a clack round the ear. Oh, that reminds me, your horrible Aunt Vi stopped me as I was coming home from work yesterday and axed me why you'd not been to see them, nor you hadn't give them your new address. I lied in me teeth and told her I didn't know and she give me a right glare, and nodded so hard that her chins wobbled. Then she said it weren't right, that woman keepin' you away from her kith and kin. She meant Mrs Grimshaw, of course. Then she said Beth wanted to know, because you cousins had always been fond of one another.' He pulled a face at Miranda. 'How I kept meself from laughin' out loud I'll never know, but I just managed it. Anyhow, she puffed off, mutterin', but I thought I'd better warn you.'

'Thanks, Steve, you're a real pal,' Miranda said gratefully. 'But in a way Aunt Vi's right; she really ought to have my address, and I wouldn't mind Beth seeing my new place, especially since I've got a flat share, which means Beth can't expect to be taken in.'

Miranda had met Avril Donovan at her shorthand and typing classes. Avril was a very large girl indeed, both tall and broad, with flaxen hair cut in a shining bob and merry blue eyes. She had been brought up in children's homes since her parents had been killed in a road accident when she was thirteen, and she was living in a hostel, but as soon as Miranda mentioned that she was looking for a flat share Avril had begged to be allowed to see the flat and, if Miranda was agreeable, to share it on a month's trial. Very soon the two girls realised that they were getting along famously, for Avril was an easy-going, hard-working girl, always willing to do more than her fair share of the work, since she was so grateful to Miranda for letting her live in the flat. To add to her other accomplishments, Avril was a good cook, having worked in a big bakery, so they took it in turns to prepare meals, and once they had had a small party, the guests being Steve, Julian and Gerald and, to make numbers even, one of the girls who worked with Avril at her clothing factory.

Very much to Miranda's surprise, Julian had liked Avril, and Miranda, who had secretly thought of him as rather a snob, had to change her mind. Avril was sweet, but she talked with a broad Liverpool accent and knew nothing of books, seeming almost proud of the fact that reading was a chore she had never really cared for, whereas Julian, who was working hard for his exams and hoping to go to university in the autumn, talked of things that had even Gerald mystified.

The party had been a great success but it had also cost a bit more than the girls expected. Since both of them were saving up, though for different reasons, they decided that parties would have to be rare events.

Very early in their relationship – in fact when Avril, sprawling across the kitchen table, had been writing a letter to one of her pals – Miranda had told her new friend all about her mother's mysterious disappearance. 'So whilst I'm saving up for a dance dress, it'll come from Paddy's Market, the same as all my clothes have,' she had admitted. 'Because what I'm really saving up for is my mother's return. I know she's not disappeared for ever, but I do think she may be in a similar condition to that of the friend who lived in this flat before I took over. Missie was kidnapped . . .'

When the story was finished, Avril had nodded understandingly. 'Of course, if your mother was kidnapped, like your pal Missie, and is now in a foreign country, she might well find it real hard to make folk believe her story, and lend her money to buy a passage home,' she had agreed. 'But if you find out where she is and go over there with all your cash, you'll be able to rescue her. That's what you're hopin', ain't it?'

'That's right,' Miranda had said after an appreciable pause. 'The thing is, when she first disappeared I was frantically worried and cross, so that when people thought she'd just gone off with a man of her own free will I stopped thinking logically. You see, I – I wasn't a very good daughter to her, only I didn't realise it until quite recently. My friend Steve – you've met him – does all sorts for his mother, and never a word of complaint. I took it for granted that Arabella would do all the housework, even iron my clothes, and give me pocket money for doing nothing but grumble when things didn't go my way. She liked me to call her Arabella, by the way, instead of Mum.'

Avril, laughing, had said she understood. 'I were real difficult at that age; I can't think how me mam stood me,' she had assured Miranda. 'If she said black, I'd say white; if she said go, I'd say stay; and if she asked me to do something – shoppin' or givin' a hand wi' the cleanin' – I'd do me best to wriggle out of it somehow. But I'm sure your mam wouldn't have run off to escape from you, kiddo. So if that's what's botherin' you . . .'

'Oh, it's not,' Miranda had said at once. 'As I told you,

I'm ninety-nine per cent sure she was kidnapped. No, I'm a hundred per cent certain that it was Arabella Missie saw being dragged down to the docks. But whatever happened, I'm sure she's alive and well, though naturally I can't explain why she doesn't seem to have made any effort to come home . . . or perhaps I should say that her efforts haven't been successful.'

'You mentioned memory loss, and the fact that she was probably sleepwalkin' at the time of her disappearance,' Avril had said thoughtfully. 'Oh, I'm sure you're right and she'll turn up again sometime . . .' she had grinned at her friend, 'and then I'll lose me lovely flat share and be cast out on the world. Or perhaps you'll let me have a shakedown in the livin' room until your mam sets you up like a queen in a proper house like the one you lived in before she disappeared.'

Now, however, Steve was handing her a steaming mug of tea and suggesting that they might take the jars of pickles along to the Great Homer Street market whilst there was still some daylight left. Miranda agreed that this was a good idea. 'Avril's gone to have tea with a friend, so we've got the flat to ourselves until nine or ten this evening,' she said. 'So when we've dumped the pickles, what do you say to fish and chips for supper?'

Steve agreed that this sounded good and the two set off, carrying the many jars of pickled onions down the stairs and stacking them on the borrowed handcart.

'Good thing you've got a pal with plenty of muscles around,' Steve said, tapping his chest with a forefinger. 'You'd of been hard put to it to get this thing over cobbles without cracking any of the jars, if I hadn't been with you.'

Miranda, heaving manfully at one of the handles, reminded him that Avril was pretty strong and that, at a pinch, she might have persuaded Gerald to give a hand, but as they reached the market and puffed to a halt beside Mrs Inchcombe's stall Steve made a derisive noise. 'Oh, ha, ha, that's a likely one!' he said. 'As you said yourself, earlier, Gerald is a good one to talk, but it's me that's good at doing.'

A lively argument might have developed, but at that moment the stallholder came out to greet them, and began to unload the handcart on to her stall. She was an enormously fat woman clad in a voluminous striped overall, with a thick scarf tied cornerwise over her hair, a muffler round her neck and large boots on her feet. She made admiring remarks about the onions, said they would all be sold within a week and waved them off with promises to take any more that they might produce, as soon as the ones that they had delivered were sold.

They were turning away from the stall, well satisfied, when Mrs Inchcombe called them back. 'You'll want some cash to buy more onions and vinegar,' she said breathlessly. 'Here's ten bob.' She chuckled richly. 'Shows I trust you, so don't you go lerrin' me down, queen.'

Miranda pocketed the money gratefully and tucked her hand into Steve's arm. 'When we get the money for the first lot of onions I'll share it with you,' she said. 'And you're right, of course; Gerald's a good pal in many ways but I can't see him pickling onions whilst tears plop on to his hands.' She pointed to the brightly lit window of a baker and confectioner's shop. 'Seeing as how I've got some money and it's a bit early for fish and chips,

I'll pop into Scott's and buy half a dozen sticky buns. We can have them as pudding after the fish and chips.'

Emerging from the shop, Miranda was unprepared when Steve suddenly shouted: 'Race you to the next lamppost!'

'Anyone would take us for a couple of kids,' she panted as they hurtled along the crowded pavement, causing a good few outraged shouts as they dodged folk hurrying along. They galloped into Russell Street, Miranda remarking that the run would have done them good after being shut up in the flat for most of the day, and saw a slim figure standing at the foot of the staircase which led to the flat. For one unbelieving moment Miranda thought it was Arabella, but the woman turned her head to smile, and even in the faint glow from the streetlamp she recognised Mrs Grimshaw. They stopped at the foot of the stairs and Miranda addressed her friend.

'What's up, Mrs Grimshaw? I wasn't supposed to be coming out to Holmwood today, was I? I'm pretty sure I told you that Steve and I were going to pickle onions . . . but how rude I am! Do come up to the flat, and we can boil the kettle and have a couple of the buns I've just bought. How nice it is to have a visitor! But I'm afraid the whole place probably reeks of onions, though it won't be quite so bad in the sitting room as in the kitchen.'

Smiling, Mrs Grimshaw followed them up the flight and into the small flat. After the fresh air the kitchen did indeed smell strongly of onions and Steve flung all the windows wide, though they only remained so for a few moments since the cold was crippling. Then he carried the tea tray through into the living room, whilst Miranda lit the lamp and Mrs Grimshaw arranged the buns on a pretty plate. She said nothing about her reason for calling on Miranda until the tea was poured and the buns handed round, but when she spoke her face was serious. 'Miranda, my dear, have you ever heard of a typhoon?'

The secret hope that Mrs Grimshaw had cheerful tidings to impart began to fade. 'Yes,' Miranda said, her voice no more than a whisper. 'Go on.'

The story did not take long in the telling. Apparently Missie had had cause to go with her employer to a neighbouring island, on plantation business. Once there, she bought some of the shellfish for sale in the market whilst Julian and Gerald's father went off with his manager, leaving Missie to wander around the harbour. True to her promise, she began to ask natives of the island whether they knew anything of the *Pride of the Sea*. Several of them did; indeed they seemed surprised that Missie had not heard. 'She foundered in a typhoon, two days out from her last port of call,' the harbour master had told her. 'Lost with all hands. There was one survivor, but he was just being given a lift from one island to another, so was not a member of the crew. But it's all history; it happened ages ago, and memories are short. No one was truly sorry that the *Pride* had gone, and the survivor, Ned Truin, said that for the short time he was on board most of the crew were drunk. They'd taken on a consignment of rum and someone had broached a bottle or a barrel, I don't know which. If you want more details, Ned Truin's working aboard a fishing boat which will be in harbour before dark. These old seamen never go far from the sea, but when he comes ashore I'll point him out and he'll tell you the story as he experienced it.'

Missie had sought out Mr Grimshaw and explained that she owed it to her English friends to get the full story, and Mr Grimshaw had agreed to delay their departure from the island until she had had a chance to do so.

The full story, as heard from Ned Truin, was a mixture of foolishness, downright wickedness and bad weather, for though Ned admitted that most of the crew were drunk and incapable, he thought there was little they could have done to save the ship once the typhoon had hit them. Within moments the sea, which had been blue and relatively calm, had become a raging inferno of ten-foot white-capped waves, which smashed down on the *Pride* until she was little better than matchwood. When the ship went down – largely in pieces – he himself had managed to cling on to a spar. He had had a terrible and frightening time over a period of two days and nights, for sharks were busy in the vicinity and he thought he had only been saved from being torn apart by managing to scramble into the ship's dinghy, whence he was rescued at last by a passing fishing boat.

Naturally, Missie's first hope had been that Arabella might already have left the ship, but when she asked Ned Truin if he knew of anyone's doing so he could only shrug. Mr Grimshaw had explained that they were searching for a woman who they believed had been kidnapped by the captain and his mate, but again Ned Truin could not say for certain what had happened on board the ill-omened ship before the typhoon blew up. 'I had only been aboard two days when the storm came,' he had told Missie. 'I realised the crew were a bad lot, but that was all.'

Mrs Grimshaw rose from her chair as her sad story

ended and went to sit beside Miranda on the couch, putting a comforting arm around her shoulders. 'My poor child, I've dreaded giving you this appalling news ever since Missie's letter and the report from the harbour master arrived in the mail this morning. At first Mr Grimshaw wanted to keep it from you, wanted to let you to continue to hope, but in his heart I'm sure he knew that to say nothing would have been cruel in the long run.'

Miranda did not speak, but the slow tears formed and fell, formed and fell. She knew Mrs Grimshaw's arm was round her shoulders, but she could not feel it. Arabella could not have drowned! She would not believe it, no matter how convincing the story. But Steve was speaking – she must listen. 'But suppose, like Missie, Miranda's mum escaped and hid herself away whilst the men were loading or unloading somewhere, and then could not be found?' Steve said at last, and even in her deep distress Miranda could hear the quiver in his voice. 'That's possible, isn't it?'

Mrs Grimshaw heaved a deep sigh. 'You must understand, my dears, that the islands which the *Pride* visited are all small, with few inhabitants. It seems to both my husband and myself highly unlikely that she could have got ashore unseen by anyone and stayed hidden for even the smallest amount of time. If such a thing had happened someone must have helped her, and why should such a person not admit to their good deed? Saving anyone from the sea and from men such as Captain Hogg is surely something to boast about, not to keep quiet? I'm afraid, my dear, that such hopes have no basis in reality. According to Missie's letter, my brother-in-law carried out a rigorous search on all the islands within reach of the one to which Ned Truin was taken, and found no indication that any stranger had landed on any of them.'

There was a silence. Miranda sat on the couch as if turned to stone, her wide eyes fixed unseeingly on Mrs Grimshaw's face as though it were a picture on the cinema screen; as though if she stared hard enough she would see her beautiful golden-haired mother being pulled ashore and rescued.

Steve, having given the matter some thought, went over to Miranda and knelt beside her, taking her cold hands and squeezing them comfortingly. 'No one can be certain that your mam was still aboard,' he said bracingly. 'And no woman's body was cast ashore. Isn't that proof of a sort that she wasn't aboard when the *Pride* went down?'

'No; Missie said there were – were sharks,' Miranda mumbled. She gave a convulsive shudder, then straightened and glared defiantly from Steve's anxious face to Mrs Grimshaw's. 'I can't – and won't – believe Arabella is dead,' she said loudly. 'If she is, I'm sure I would know in my heart, because Arabella and I were close, even though we had our bad moments when we shouted at one another and – and said things we didn't mean.'

'Of course you did; mothers and daughters are always falling out and then falling in again,' Mrs Grimshaw said comfortingly. 'And I'm sure you're right; but at least we now know that it is useless to try to find the *Pride of the Sea* or any member of her crew. However, there are a great many islands in the Caribbean. Your mother might have swum from the wreckage to any one of those islands, so we still have a great deal of ground to cover before we need give up.'

Miranda gave the older woman a watery smile. 'My mother can't swim, any more than I can,' she said sadly. 'She wasn't a very practical woman, not in that way. But you're right; I shall never give up hope of finding her alive.'

After Mrs Grimshaw had left them Steve looked at his friend's woebegone face, and decided that she must not be allowed to mope. After all, her mother had disappeared a long while ago, and though his pal claimed to think of Arabella every day Steve knew that this was probably her conscience talking. She had entered the world of work, was meeting new people and changing from an awkward child to a striking young woman. Her carroty curls had darkened to a shade between chestnut and auburn, the dusting of golden freckles across her nose gave warmth to her complexion, and she was developing a proper figure. Like it or not, he was sure her obsession with her mother's disappearance had begun to fade, though now of course the discovery that the *Pride of the Sea* had been lost with all hands had brought Arabella to the forefront of her daughter's mind once more. Probably she'll never quite lose the hope that her mother will miraculously turn up again and claim her, Steve told himself. But the Grimshaws are good people; they'll see that she lives her own life, and stops living in a fool's paradise.

Steve took his coat from its peg, slipped it on and helped Miranda into hers. 'You were goin' to buy us fish 'n' chips, Miss Moneybags,' he reminded her. 'Oh, but we've ate the buns what were intended for our pudding, so shall us pop along to the market and buy a couple of them big oranges you're so fond of?'

Miranda shrugged. 'I don't care,' she said listlessly as they left the flat and clattered down the iron stairs.

Steve blew out a steaming breath into the icy air, then glanced up at the lowering grey sky above. 'Reckon we'll have snow before morning,' he remarked. 'If there's a decent fall, shall us take my old sledge up to Simonswood and see how far we can travel on it?'

'Whatever you like,' Miranda said shortly, and Steve couldn't help giving an inward grin. She was clutching her unhappiness to her bosom, trying to make him see that the news Mrs Grimshaw had given them had affected her deeply. Well, he knew it had, of course, but he also knew that she was in the same position after Mrs Grimshaw's news as she had been before it. True, she now knew that the *Pride of the Sea* had foundered, and that there was a possibility that her mother had drowned with the rest. But if you were honest she was really no worse off than she had been before Mrs Grimshaw's revelations.

Steve sighed. 'Miranda? If it snows all night . . .'

He was interrupted. 'Snow? What does it matter? I don't care if it snows ink,' Miranda said dully. 'I keep thinking of my poor Arabella, struggling in an icy sea, perhaps even seeing approaching sharks . . .'

Her voice ended on a pathetic hiccup, but this was too much for the practical Steve. 'Oh, for God's sake, be your age and use your brain,' he said crossly. He took hold of her hand, tucking it into his elbow. 'However your mam died – if she *did* die – it wasn't in icy water. Okay, this typhoon thing blew up, but the water would be warm, probably quite pleasant . . .'

Miranda tore her hand away from his and turned on

him, eyes flashing. 'How dare you speak to me like that when I'm in such distress! I hate you, Steve Mickleborough, you're cruel and wicked and unfeeling! If it was your mother eaten by sharks you wouldn't be so offhand about it.'

Steve gave a smothered giggle; he couldn't help it. Just the thought of his cosy, smiling mother struggling in a Mersey full of enormous sharks was so absurd that he could only laugh. 'I can just see me mam punching a shark right on its hooter,' he said, trying to choke back the laughter and failing dismally. 'Anyway, you don't know that your mam was eaten by sharks. I thought you believed she was still alive and kicking somewhere. You said . . .'

Miranda rounded on him, her cheeks flushed with anger and her tear-filled eyes bright with rage. 'I *do* think she's alive, I do, I do,' she said vehemently. 'And you're cruel and hateful to scoff.'

Once again, laughter bubbled up in Steve's throat. 'If we're going to talk about scoff, let's buy them fish 'n' chips, take 'em back to the flat and scoff them, instead of scoffing at each other,' he said. 'Don't be an idiot, Miranda. You can't have it both ways: either you're going to mourn your mother as dead, which is understandable, or you're going to insist she's alive and safe on some island or other, but simply hasn't managed to get in touch. Now tell me, which is it to be?'

Miranda tightened her lips and said nothing. She speeded up, and when the fish and chip shop was reached she joined the queue, fishing out the money the stall-holder had given her. Steve chatted amiably as they inched up towards the counter, saying that he would buy a bottle of Corona to go with their meal, and asking Miranda whether she would like him to buy a slab of cake to take the place of the buns they had eaten earlier.

Miranda, however, still clearly in the grip of annoyance, tightened her lips once more and said nothing, and Steve fell silent as well. In fact they bought the chips, a bottle of cherryade and a slab of plain cake and carried everything back to the flat without exchanging another word. When they got there Miranda unlocked the door, ushered Steve inside, and divided the fish and chips between two china plates. Then she went into the small pantry – it was more like a cupboard – and produced salt and vinegar and a couple of glasses for the cherryade, all of this in complete silence. Steve, beginning to be really annoyed with his old friend, decided to follow her example and did not say anything either whilst they polished off the food and drink in record time, for it had been a long day and they were both extremely hungry.

When all the food was gone and the kettle hopping on the hob, Steve used half the water to wash up their plates and cutlery. Then he turned to Miranda. 'I can see you're still in a nasty mood, but I was brought up to be polite even when others were rude,' he said calmly. 'Good night, Miranda, and thank you for my share of the fish and chips. I'm sorry if I upset you by saying the wrong thing, but I truly meant it for the best. You're me bezzie, so that means I ought to be able to speak me mind and trust you not to take it wrong. Will you forgive me?' He had already put on his coat and hat and had his hand on the doorknob waiting for – indeed expecting – Miranda to speak, but she said nothing. Steve sighed. He supposed she had a reason for behaving so badly but none of it was his fault, so why was she taking her ill humour out on him? It was scarcely because of him that the *Pride of the Sea* had foundered. All he had really done was try to make her see that she was behaving illogically and making her situation worse. He turned to open the door and glanced back over his shoulder, but Miranda was now at the sink collecting the plates and mugs to replace them on the dresser, and took no notice of him even when snowflakes blew in through the doorway. She just stood with her back to him, stacking the plates, and he felt maliciously pleased when the cold wind roared into the room and attacked Miranda's pinafore-clad form. He saw her give a little shiver, and for a moment was tempted to go back and give her a hug. Perhaps he had been wrong to try to make her choose between accepting that her mother was dead and believing that she was still alive, but even as he hesitated, wanting to turn back, his pride rose up and refused to let him eat any more humble pie than he had already digested. He went out on to the top of the steps, closing the door softly and gently behind him. She'll have come to her senses by tomorrow, he told himself. Poor old girl. Although we've all been half expecting such news, it's obviously hit her hard. But she's sensible, is Miranda; I bet by tomorrow she'll be full of plans. She'll talk about setting off for the West Indies as soon as summer comes, and why not? If she doesn't go soon the war they're all talking about will start and she won't be able to go anywhere.

Sighing to himself, Steve clattered down the flight and into the snowstorm. Tomorrow's Sunday, so if the snow builds up real good then I reckon it'd be worth a gang of us making our way out to Simonswood and taking my sledge and any sturdy trays we can lay hands on, he told himself. Miranda will have got over her sulks by then; she loves sledging. We went last year and she loved every minute. If I get up early enough I'll get Mam to pack up a carry-out. She's bound to have bread and jam and that, and I can buy another slab of cake and another bottle of Corona. Oh aye, if the snow continues, Miranda won't go on bearing a grudge. He grinned to himself. She'd better say she's sorry, 'cos I've done it once and now it's her turn.

Making his way along the snowy and deserted streets, he decided that he would tell his mother what had transpired as soon as he reached home. She was a grand woman, his mam, and always knew what was the right thing to do. She'd feel rare sorry for Miranda, of course, but that wouldn't stop her seeing his point of view. Thinking back, he was glad he had apologised and tried to make things right, because he knew his mother would tell him to do just that. He guessed that she would also tell him off for pointing out that Miranda had got the temperature of the sea all wrong. He really shouldn't have said that; he was lucky she had not battered him across the ear, even though it was true.

Steve turned the corner and the full force of the storm hit him, hurling snowflakes into his face with stinging force. He turned up his collar and pulled his cap lower over his brow. Not much further, he told himself. Soon be out of this horrible weather and in Mam's kitchen. Wonder what she's got for supper? Hope it's scouse. He plodded on, all memory of the fish supper he had recently eaten disappearing under the onslaught of the storm. Scouse would be nice, but what he most wanted at the moment was a big mug of hot tea with two sugars and possibly one of Mam's shortbread fingers. He turned into the jigger and actually had difficulty in recognising his own back yard through the whirling flakes, but he made it at last and burst into the kitchen looking, no doubt, just like a snowman for his mother, seated comfortably by the fire in her old wicker rocking chair, gave a squawk of protest, and his stepfather, seated in the chair opposite and working away at his weekend task of mending the family's shoes, begged him tersely to 'Gerrinto the yard, lad, and brush off that perishin' snow; us don't want the kitchen like a pond when it melts.'

Steve obeyed. Then he came back into the kitchen, hung his outer clothing on a peg by the door and turned to his mother. 'Have you had supper yet, Mam?' he asked hopefully. 'I'm that hungry me belly thinks me throat's been cut. But if you've et . . .'

'I saved you a dish of scouse and two big boiled potatoes,' Mrs Mickleborough said at once. 'It's on the back of the stove keeping warm. I guessed you'd be glad of a bite after fighting your way from your young lady's place to Jamaica Close.'

'Thanks, Mam, but she ain't my young lady, nor likely to be,' Steve said gloomily, emptying the contents of the saucepan on to a tin plate. 'There's been news of that ship – the *Pride of the Sea* – what Miranda thinks her mother may have been aboard . . .'

When the story was finished – and the scouse also – Steve looked hopefully at his mother. 'I reckon you'll say I did wrong to try to make her see she weren't no worse off than before,' he said apologetically. 'Lookin' back, I can't think what come over me. I said I was sorry of course, but she never said a word, not even when I thanked her for the fish 'n' chips . . .'

His stepfather, who had not appeared to be listening with undue attention to the story, looked up, brows rising. 'Fish 'n' chips?' he said indignantly. 'And then you come here and guzzle a big plate of scouse and spuds! You've got hollow legs, young man.'

Steve laughed, but his attention was fixed on his mother. 'I'll go round tomorrer and tell her I'm sorry and mebbe we'll sit down and write a lot of letters for Missie or the Grimshaws to hand out to any islanders they think might know something,' he said. 'Poor old Miranda; she feels guilty, you know, because she wasn't nicer to her mam when she had the chance.'

Mrs Mickleborough sniffed, but Mr Mickleborough nodded slowly. 'That's what you call *what might have been*,' he said. 'It's allus the same when someone goes out of reach; those that are left wish they'd been kinder. Ah well, no doubt your little pal will come to terms with what's happened. And now, my lad, you'd best wash up that plate and mug and gerrup to bed, 'cos I know you. Tomorrer bein' Sunday, a whole gang of you will go off to Simonswood, snowballin', mekkin slides and sledgin', so you'd best get a good night's sleep.'

'Okay, Dad,' Steve said, but his eyes were still fixed on his mother's face. 'I thought I'd ask Miranda to come sledging with me; we could have a whole day away if you'd make up a carry-out for us. I don't mind takin' Kenny if you think I ought.'

He was relieved, however, when his mother shook her head. 'You'll have your work cut out to get back on the right side of young Miranda,' she said sagely. 'And now

211

gerroff to bed, young man; I'll let you have a bit of a lie-in, but if the snow's still thick I'll wake you around nine o'clock. And once you're in bed you can work out how best to make up with your pal.'

After Steve had left, Miranda simply sat in the kitchen fighting the despair which threatened to overcome her. She acknowledged that she had probably overreacted to Mrs Grimshaw's news, and she knew in her heart that it had been no reason to turn on Steve the way she had. He was her bezzie, had never faltered in his championship of her, had listened patiently whilst she went over and over the last day that she and her mother had spent together. He had never criticised her for her behaviour, and even after Mrs Grimshaw's dreadful news he had been supportive. In fact the only thing she could blame him for was his callousness regarding the water in which her mother had drowned – *if* there had been a woman aboard, and if that woman had been her mother, of course. Going out for the fish and chips and feeling the cold wind trying to tear the hair from her head, it was natural that she had thought of her mother struggling in an ice-cold sea, but it was also foolish. She and Steve both knew from talking to Missie and the Grimshaw boys that the weather in the West Indies was tropical, that the sea was blue and warm as milk, and that in any case sharks would not venture into the icy waters that surrounded the British Isles.

Yet still she could not help feeling furious with Steve. He simply did not realise that her mind was still in shock from the story she had been told. He had been right when he had pointed out that she could either mourn her mother as dead or believe that she was still alive somewhere, but he should have understood that she couldn't think logically at the moment.

When Avril returned from her evening out, she was so full of chat that Miranda did not have to open her mouth, and presently Avril made both of them a cup of cocoa, and then went to bed. If she was surprised at Miranda's short answers to her questions she gave no sign of it and presently, sitting on the hard chair in the kitchen, her mind aching with worry and confusion, Miranda looked up at the clock and saw that it read midnight. Sighing, she damped down the fire and went through to bed, suddenly realising that she was totally exhausted, too tired even to prepare herself properly for bed. She slid between the sheets in her underwear and was asleep almost as soon as her head touched the pillow.

First there was a sensation of falling which seemed to go on for a long time, and then she was in the water. Waves as high, it seemed, as a house picked her up and threw her from one to another as though she were the ball in some wild, cruel game. She started to cry out and was gagged by the water pouring into her open mouth. Something hit her a numbing blow and she grabbed for it just as another wave, bigger than the rest, smashed down on her, but she hung on, thinking how often she had heard of a drowning man clutching at a straw, wondering whether that was what she was doing, but continuing to cling nevertheless. When the next wave crashed over her she realised she was holding on to a plank of wood; wood floats and will stay on the surface, she told herself, even in the worst and most violent sea.

Then for an instant she felt her foot touch something; was it land? But just as she was beginning to hope, a huge wave snatched her up and once more there was only darkness and water, though she was aware that there was flotsam all around her; the remains of the ship on which she had been travelling when the storm hit.

But she had no time for conjecture; the only thing that mattered was clinging to the spar of wood and praying that someone would find her before her strength gave out, before her numb fingers were torn from the spar by the strength of the attacking waves, and she was dragged into the depths.

Mostly she had scarcely bothered to look around her in the pitch dark, but presently she thought she saw a lightening of the sky overhead, and it seemed to her that the sea grew calmer as dawn, cool and grey, lit the sky. She was beginning to hope, to think that she might drag herself ashore if she were lucky enough to be carried on her friendly plank to terra firma, when she felt something nudge her dangling legs. For a moment she remembered stories of friendly dolphins helping shipwrecked mariners to gain the nearest land, but then another image arose, and she kicked out convulsively, terror in every movement. Sharks!

Desperately, she tried to haul herself aboard the plank and almost succeeded, but then her weight tipped the plank right over. For a moment she clutched it, but then the water entered her gaping mouth and she spiralled down into darkness.

Miranda awoke. She had a vague feeling that she had been dreaming and suspected that it had not been a particularly pleasant dream; why should it be pleasant, after all? Mrs Grimshaw and Steve had tried to make light of the fact that the *Pride of the Sea* had foundered in a storm somewhere in the Caribbean and that her mother might possibly have been aboard. There had been one survivor, the man who had paid to be taken aboard as supercargo in order to reach the next island at which the *Pride of the Sea* would drop anchor. Miranda sighed and sat up, glancing towards the window. For a moment she was honestly surprised to see, through a crack in the curtains, snowflakes whirling past; odd! For some reason she had expected to see bright sunlight and blue skies, and as she jumped out of bed to feel warm linoleum beneath her feet. Instead the whole room was freezing cold, and when she went over to the washstand ice had formed on the jug.

Miranda frowned. The events of the previous evening were somewhat vague, but she did remember that she had been very angry with Steve because he had not seemed to sympathise with her conviction that her mother was still alive. However, she also remembered – or thought she did – that he had promised her some sort of treat; whatever had it been? Judging by the weather she could see through the window it must have been some sort of indoor activity, and since today was Sunday she supposed that the most she could expect would be an invitation to share the Mickleboroughs' Sunday dinner, which was nice but not her idea of a special occasion.

Having ascertained that she would have to go and boil some water in order to get a wash, Miranda donned dressing gown and slippers and went through to the kitchen. She had not wound the alarm clock the previous night and had no idea of the time, but as she entered the kitchen she saw that it was nine o'clock, and when she tapped the kettle it was warm, so she guessed that Avril had been up at the usual time, breakfasted and gone off to church, no doubt guessing that her friend had been late to bed.

Miranda carried the hot water to her room, washed and dressed and returned to the kitchen. She made herself a mug of tea and several slices of toast, still aware that she was confused as to just what had been arranged the previous evening. In fact she was on her last piece of toast when she heard feet clattering up the outside stair and she got up and opened the door, imagining that it would be Steve.

But she was wrong; it was Gerald, pink-cheeked and breathing hard. He grinned at her, then knocked the snow off his cap and brushed it from his shoulders before entering the kitchen. 'Morning, Miranda. You all right?' he said, and Miranda heard the anxiety behind his cheerful words, and was grateful. He had obviously been told by his aunt or uncle about the *Pride of the Sea* and had guessed she would need cheering up. However, she did not intend to let Gerald know how desperately unhappy she had been, so she smiled and went over to the teapot.

'Want a cuppa?' she asked brightly. 'You can have toast an' all – I've cut plenty of bread – but you'll have to make it yourself. Why have you come round so early?'

'I wouldn't mind some toast,' Gerald said, rubbing his hands together. 'It's most dreadfully cold out there, what we call brass monkey weather at Browncoats. And I'm

216

early because I thought you might like to go sledging; the buses are still running, so the roads can't be too bad. We could get out to Simonswood and I thought it might take your mind off – off your troubles. Julian and I are spending the weekend at Holmwood Lodge which is how I came to hear about the *Pride of the Sea*.' He patted her arm. 'Poor old Miranda. What a frightening story. But Auntie told me you believe your mother is still alive, and I'm sure you're right. It may take time, but us Grimshaws know all sorts of people in the West Indies, and I'm sure if your mother is on one of the islands we'll hear about it in due course. So you're to stop worrying and start getting on with your life.'

'Oh, Gerald, you are kind, and sensible as well,' Miranda said gratefully, but the mention of Simonswood had brought Steve's suggestion rushing back. He had wanted her to go to Simonswood with him so that they could sledge. Well, she hadn't said she would, though she hadn't said she wouldn't either. She decided it was time that Steve was taken down a peg or two; taught that he was not the only person on whom she relied. Accordingly, she gave Gerald a big smile. 'That would be lovely. Where's your sledge? And shall I make a carry-out? I've got a flask which I can fill with tea so we can have a hot drink . . .'

'You'll come? Oh, that's wizard,' Gerald said. 'As for my . . . er, my sledge, it's in the boot of Uncle's car. He's letting Julian drive it now he's passed his test. Don't bother with a carry-out – Uncle telephoned one of his tenants to see if she was still doing farmhouse teas and light lunches, and she is. So he booked a meal for four people and we'll eat at her place.'

'Four?' Miranda squeaked. 'Who's the fourth? You aren't going to suggest taking Steve, are you?'

Gerald looked surprised. 'Why not? But actually we thought Avril might enjoy a day out; if she's got no other plans, that is.'

'She's gone to early service so she should be home in about ten minutes, but I'm sure she'll come with us,' Miranda said. She knew she was being mean by excluding Steve, but whenever she thought of his behaviour the previous evening she felt sore and upset. And she was sure he had not dreamed of inviting Julian or Gerald on his sledging trip, so it was fair enough that they should plan a trip and not invite him. But Gerald was talking, and Miranda dragged her mind back to the present.

'. . . and you'll need warm clothes, your wellington boots and a good solid tray. That tin one advertising Guinness would be fine,' Gerald was saying. He read her startled look and grinned apologetically. 'We do have a sledge, a great big old-fashioned thing, but it won't fit into the boot of the Rover, so Auntie is letting us use a couple of her trays. We thought it would be more fun if we could have races, which means we'll need a tray each. I told Julian to give me ten or fifteen minutes to persuade you and then to come round here to pick us up, so maybe this is him arriving,' he added, as they both heard the clang of someone beginning to climb the stairs.

Miranda shot open the back door, suddenly wondering what on earth she would say if it was Steve, but it was not. Avril cast off her snowy coat and headscarf, then went across to the fire. 'Brrrr, it's perishin' icy out there,' she said breezily. She turned to Gerald. 'You're early, ain't you? And your brother's sitting in a car a couple of doors down, readin' a book. What's up?'

'Oh, Avril, they've come to ask us if we'd like to go sledging and have our dinners at one of those farmhouses who do food,' Miranda said happily. At the thought of the treat in store, all the misery she had felt the previous evening had disappeared. She still felt very cross with Steve, though, and thought it would serve him right when he discovered she had gone sledging with somebody else. 'Are you on?' Avril was thrilled, and in an incredibly short space of time the four of them – and their trays – were packed into the Rover and Julian was driving with great care along the snowy streets towards their destination.

Despite his mother's promise to wake him if it continued to snow, it was quite ten o'clock before Steve, wrapped up to the eyebrows, ascended the metal stairs and rapped on Miranda's door. Then as he always did he tried to fling it open, only to meet resistance. Steve grinned to himself; she was probably still in bed, lazy little monkey. Well, he would keep knocking until she answered, because he was sure by now she would have got over her temper and be as eager for the treat as he was himself. Five minutes later, with a worried frown, he was descending the stairs again, his feet touching the pavement just as Pete Huxtable, with Timmy at heel, came out of the shop and turned to lock the door behind him. Turning back, he spotted Steve and broke into speech. 'Mornin', Steve! As you can see I'm takin' his lordship for his mornin' constitutional. I let him out earlier – bein' Sunday there were no one much about – and he played in the snow as though he'd never seen such a thing before; well, I bet he hasn't, at that. He were tryin' to eat it and when Miranda chucked a snowball at him he thought it were a real ball and kept tryin' to pick it up. We all had a rare laugh, I can tell you.'

'Mornin', Pete; hello, Timmy,' Steve said. 'I've been up to the flat, but though I knocked real loud no one came. Are the girls out, then?'

'Oh aye; they're all out all right. When I sez all, that includes them two chaps from the Browncoat school,' Pete informed him, looking wistful. 'I don't know what Avril sees in the la-di-da one, but there's no accountin' for tastes.'

As he spoke he pinched the bridge of his nose with thumb and forefinger, a gesture which Steve had seen him use before when troubled. Steve smiled to himself: he had suspected before that Pete had fallen for Miranda's flatmate; now he was sure of it.

'I axed 'em where they were off to,' Pete went on. 'The la-di-da one was drivin' a car and Miranda said they was goin' to Simonswood to go a-sledgin' an' have their dinners at a farmhouse.' He pulled a rueful face. 'No wonder the gals was all pink and excited. All I can offer is a ride on the carrier of me racin' bike, which don't compare with a Rover.'

For a moment Steve was literally bereft of speech, and stared at the other man, his jaw dropping. Then he pulled himself together. 'Ah well, if she's gone off with the Grimshaws there's no point in my hangin' around,' he said. 'And you say they're havin' dinner somewhere and will be out for the whole day? Then I'd best look up one of me other pals.' He gestured towards his sledge. 'As you can see, I'm off to find a good slope meself.'

Pete had been looking rather anxious, but now he smiled. 'That's right, Steve, why not gerron a bus an' join 'em?' he enquired jovially. 'But I mustn't forget me duty to his lordship here.' He jerked a thumb at Timmy, who was now straining at the leash and whining. 'He's a right knowing one, is Timmy. I gives him a good walk every day afore I opens up the shop, but Sundays is special. We go all the way to Toxteth Park and I lets him off the lead and throws the ball until he's tired of retrievin' it. Then we goes to my Aunt Eva's and she makes us a Sunday dinner fit for a king. She's rare fond of Timmy so he always has his share, roast spuds, veggies an' all. She even gives him a bit of apple pie and custard for his afters, and he gobbles it up like winkin'.'

He paused, evidently expecting a reply, and Steve dragged his mind back from what he'd like to do to Miranda for her treachery to the present. 'Lucky old Timmy,' he said hollowly. 'Well, as Miranda's not about I'll be on my way. Enjoy your dinner, Pete.'

Heading for Jamaica Close once more, Steve grew angrier and angrier. It was true that the Grimshaws had arrived earlier at the flat than he, but he knew jolly well that his invitation had been extended first. True, Miranda had not accepted it, but neither had she refused it. In fact she had been in such a nasty mood that she had not even acknowledged the suggestion. For a moment Steve wondered if she had simply gone with the Grimshaws because they had a car and could take her out in style. But by this time he knew the boys well enough to guess that they would willingly have included him in their day out had Miranda explained the situation. That she had not seen fit to do so was evident, so although he felt no animosity towards Julian or Gerald he felt a good deal towards Miranda. Girls, he thought with disgust. You couldn't trust them, not where their emotions were concerned. A lad would never behave so shabbily, but that was women for you. They could take offence over the most trivial thing – he seemed to remember it was a disagreement over the temperature of the water in the Caribbean which had made Miranda screaming mad – and how they could bear a grudge! He could remember various occasions when Miranda had been so pigheaded that he had wanted to shake her, only good manners did not allow a feller to shake a girl, unless they were related, of course.

Striding out along the pavement, which was still covered by a good six inches of snow, he all but walked into someone striding in the opposite direction, and would have passed by without a word, save that the other pushed back the hood of his duffel coat and grabbed Steve's arm, saying as he did so: 'Hello–ello–ello, where's you off to in such a rush that you don't reckernise your ol' pal?'

Steve stared; then a slow grin spread over his face. 'Cyril Rogers, by all that's wonderful! Where the devil have you sprung from? I've not seen you since school. You joined one of the services, didn't you? I keep sayin' I'm goin' to do just that, though I've not got round to it yet. But we can't stand here talkin' whilst we freeze to the spot; come back to Jamaica Close and we can have a good old jangle in the warm.'

'Grand idea,' Cyril said, falling into step with Steve. 'I'm on leave, as I reckon you've guessed, but today me family have gone off to visit me gran what lives over the water in Birkenhead. She's a right miserable old codger, so I thought I'd call round and visit young Emily Sutcliffe, the gairl what I used to take dancin' when I lived at home. I thought mebbe I'd tek her sledgin' in Prince's Park, but she had other plans, it seems.' He pulled a face. 'I can't blame her I suppose, but she's found herself another feller, one who lives a good deal closer than two hundred odd miles, so I'm at a loose end. Wharrabout you, Steve? Gorrany plans of your own?' His eyes fell on the sledge which Steve was still dragging behind him. 'Oh, I see you have.'

'Well, I were goin' to go sledgin' if I could find someone to come with me,' Steve admitted. 'Tell you what, I know a couple of girls, good sports, what'd come sledgin' like a shot if you and me was to ask 'em. Remember Pearl and Ruby? Them sisters what live near the school? If we paid their bus fares and bought 'em a meal, they'd come along, no question. What d'you say we give it a go?'

Miranda kept telling herself that she was having the time of her life. She and Avril had each brought along a tin tray, but when they reached the slope which they'd judged best for sledging down, they found several people were before them and somehow this made the expedition even more fun. They organised some races, descending both singly and in pairs, but if the truth were told Miranda was missing Steve and was miserably conscious that she had behaved badly. However, she would not let her companions down by showing that she was not perfectly happy. She felt quite envious of Avril who clearly was having the time of her life, teasing the rather staid Julian until he was in fits of laughter and behaving,

Miranda thought, just like any other young fellow out with his girl. So when she happened to glance to where a new party were clambering on to their trays, she was momentarily thrilled to recognise Steve. In fact she was walking towards him, a broad smile on her face, eager to apologise for having come on ahead of him, when he flung his arms around a girl she remembered from school, gave her a kiss on the cheek and a smack on the bottom, and then jumped on the back of her tray so that the two of them disappeared down the hillside in a flurry of snow and shrieks.

Miranda turned away, misery speedily swamped by fury. How dared Steve kiss another girl when he was supposed to be her bezzie? In all the time they had known one another Steve had never kissed her, nor had she expected him to do so. Friends, she reminded herself, did not do anything as soppy as kissing.

'What's up, Miranda?' Gerald's voice cut across her thoughts. 'I see Steve's arrived. Are you going to suggest that he come to lunch with us? I'm sure there'll be plenty of food for one or two extra. By the look of it, that girl in the blue knitted cap is with him, so he'd probably want to bring her along.'

Miranda gritted her teeth but managed to reply airily, 'You mean Pearl? Yes, I think he's with her. She and Ruby – they're sisters – were in my class at school. But no, I wouldn't dream of suggesting that Steve come along. In fact it's the last thing I'd do.'

Gerald looked mildly surprised. 'Really? Well, you're probably right. Now, are you going to share my tray for one last swoop before we go to the farm for something to eat?'

Despite the best of intentions, Miranda could not help watching Steve, an older feller she also remembered from school, and the two girls, whenever she thought herself unobserved. And the more she watched, the crosser she grew. In fact she gave an inward sigh of relief when Julian and Gerald insisted that she and Avril leave the slope so that they might drive to the farmhouse. 'Mrs Higginbottom will be expecting us,' Julian reminded them. 'If I know her she'll make us a hot meal, for though she only provides salads in the summertime she'll guess we need something to keep the cold out and will cater accordingly. Gosh, if this lot knew that a hot meal was being prepared only a quarter of a mile or so away they'd probably insist upon coming along as well.'

As they climbed into the car, red-cheeked and bright-eyed, Miranda cast a glance around her and spotted Steve in earnest conversation with the feller whose name she could not remember, but then they were all in the Rover and Julian was driving carefully along the snow-covered road, and very soon they were in the Higginbottom farmhouse enjoying the magnificent meal which their hostess had prepared.

Chapter Eight

For the rest of the day Miranda brooded, trying to decide how she should treat her pal when they next met, for he had never before shown any interest in Pearl or Ruby; in fact he had never shown an interest in any girls. True, he was certainly interested in Miranda, but she now realised that this was not the same thing at all as the interest he had been showing in Pearl. Both sisters had the reputation of being what they called 'good time girls', and if anything Steve had rather despised them, yet here he was taking them sledging and ignoring Miranda completely. The thought that Miranda was also ignoring him occurred, only to be dismissed. She had walked towards him, smiling in the friendliest fashion, had she not? She told herself, untruthfully, that she had intended to ask him to accompany them to Mrs Higginbottom's, had only not done so when she saw him kissing Pearl. Well, she hoped that by now he was regretting his behaviour and would apologise to her the next time they met. The trouble with this pious hope was twofold, however. First, she knew very well that she could not possibly have extended an invitation to Steve without first discussing it with Julian and Gerald, and second that she had been at fault from the moment she had accepted their invitation, knowing full well that Steve had asked her first.

Despite the excellence of the meal Mrs Higginbottom put in front of them, Miranda found that her usual hearty appetite had fled, and she had to force herself to eat. They did not leave the farmhouse until darkness had fallen and Julian crept along, headlights blazing, clearly worried that the car might skid and deposit them all in the ditch. However, this worry proved groundless, and soon enough Miranda and Avril were thanking the brothers sincerely for a wonderful day and promising to entertain them, in their turn, to what Avril described as a 'splendiferous high tea' in the flat the following weekend.

'And with a bit of luck you'll of got out of your bad mood by then and be pals wi' Steve again,' she said airily, filling the kettle at the sink. 'I dunno what were the matter wi' you and Steve, but I could see you'd both got a cob on when not a word was exchanged, and I wasn't the only one to notice; Julian asked me what was up.'

Miranda felt her cheeks grow hot. 'I don't know what you mean,' she said feebly. 'What makes you think I was annoyed with him? He's my best pal . . .'

Avril gave a disbelieving laugh. 'No one treats their best pal the way you treated poor Steve,' she said roundly. 'And no matter how hard you tried not to show it, any fool could see you were in a bate. For a start, whenever you thought no one was looking you had a face like a smacked bum, and so did Steve.'

Miranda began to mutter that Avril had misread the situation but, having started, Avril did not intend to let the matter lie. 'Don't try to pull the wool over my eyes, 'cos it won't work,' she said firmly. 'I don't know what's been goin' on betwixt the pair of you but it's pretty obvious you've had an almighty great quarrel, probably your first from what I know of you, and I guess seeing poor old Steve give that girl a peck on the cheek just about put the lid on it.' She grinned widely, then stretched across the table and tapped Miranda's hot cheek. 'No use getting in a rage with me, 'cos I've read the situation like a perishin' book,' she said breezily. 'I don't know who was in the wrong to start with, but you couldn't get a sweeter-tempered feller than that Steve, so if I were you I'd go round to his house early tomorrer mornin', before he sets off for work, and admit you were in the wrong and apologise.'

Miranda was about to say that she knew Avril was right and would do as she suggested when, all unbidden, a picture rose up before her inner eye. It was a picture of Steve – *her* Steve – kissing Pearl's infuriatingly pink cheek and then slapping her resoundingly on her neat little bottom. 'Shan't!' she almost shouted. 'It's up to him to say he's sorry for kissing that little tart. Why, everyone knows she'll do anything for a bag of crisps and a bottle of fizzy lemonade, and if that's the sort of girl he wants . . .'

Avril was beginning to reply when the kettle reached the boil, and she took it off the Primus and began to pour the contents into Miranda's hot water bottle. She pressed the bag until all the air was out, then screwed the top on tightly and handed it to her still simmering flatmate, before beginning to fill her own bottle. 'Don't go losing your temper wi' me, luv, or you'll end up wi'out a friend in the world,' she advised kindly. 'It started last night, didn't it? The row, I mean? I knew you were upset about summat; was it the letter you and the Grimshaw boys were talking about at teatime? If so, I'm awful sorry, but it won't do you no good to turn on your pals, you know.' She squeezed the air out of the second hot water bottle, made to head for the bedroom and then turned and gave Miranda an impulsive hug. 'Oh, Miranda, I'm sure your mam's alive and kickin' somewhere,' she said gently. 'But when you're in trouble that's the time to value your friends, not drive them away from you. Just you take my advice – remember, I'm older than you, with a great deal more experience of life – and make it up wi' Steve first thing tomorrer. Unkind words fester and produce more unkind words; you can do wi'out that. Will you promise me you'll go round to Steve's place as soon as possible?'

At Avril's kind and understanding words, the ice seemed to melt around Miranda's heart and with a choking sob she ran round the table and cast herself into her friend's welcoming arms. She wept convulsively for several moments, then stood back and gave a watery smile. 'I'm really sorry I was horrid to Steve and you're quite right, I should tell him so,' she admitted. 'We had a stupid quarrel over something so trivial that I'm ashamed to mention it, but I'll go round as soon as I'm up and dressed and tell him he was right and I was wrong. Will that do, do you think?'

Avril thought that it would do very well, but unfortunately the best laid plans usually go awry. First Miranda overslept on Monday morning, and though she hurled her clothes on, snatched a slice of bread and butter to cram into her coat pocket and ran all the way to Jamaica Close, Steve had already left when she arrived. Considerably flustered, and fearing that Steve had probably told his mother how badly she, Miranda, had behaved, she left no message, merely saying that she would meet him at the factory after work. That afternoon she hung around Steve's workplace and was both cold and cross by the time one of his workmates stopped by her, eyebrows rising. 'Hello, queen. Who's you waitin' for?' the young man asked curiously. 'You're young Mickleborough's pal, ain't you? He come in late this mornin' an' went straight in to see the boss and got give a day off. Gone to London, I gather. I dare say he'll be here tomorrer, but there's no point in you waitin' now.'

Miranda mumbled her thanks and left, wondering why Steve should have gone to London now, particularly since he worked shifts and she knew that he would not be at the factory towards the end of the week. However, there was nothing she could do about it, so she returned to Russell Street and when Avril came in she had prepared vegetables to go with the two mutton chops she had bought for their tea. Avril bounced into the kitchen, slung her thick coat on the hook by the door and sniffed at the delicious smell of cooking. 'You've got the tea on early; does that mean Steve's comin' round later to take you to the flicks?' she asked, peeping into the oven of the Baby Belling Mr Grimshaw had given Miranda as a house-warming present. 'Hey, mutton chops! Is there any of that dried mint what the old lady on the Great Homer Street market give us a couple of days ago?'

It was tempting to pretend that she had made her peace with Steve, but Avril was far too canny to be taken in. As the other girl straightened up, Miranda nodded. 'Aye, there's some mint, and I didn't catch Steve, though it wasn't for lack of trying,' she assured the other girl. 'I went round to his place first thing this morning but he'd already left, so I went to the factory as soon as I'd finished work and one of his mates told me that he'd gone to London and wouldn't be in till tomorrow.'

Avril's brow puckered. 'Very odd,' she said slowly. 'I wonder why he's gone? Not with either of them girls he were with yesterday, I'd put money on it. Oh well, tomorrow he'll be full of whatever scheme he's hatched, and eager to bend your ear with his doings. But if I were you I'd set the alarm for six, lay out your clothes all ready and be on his doorstep by the time he wakes up. He's a good bloke is Steve; you don't want to lose him to young Pearl.'

Miranda sighed, but she nodded too. 'I reckon you're right, and I'll do as you say. I just wish I knew what it was all about, though. Me and Steve have never had secrets from one another, and I can tell you I don't like it.'

But though she took Avril's advice and hung around Jamaica Close until well after Steve's normal leaving time he did not appear, and though she contemplated going to the house and asking Mrs Mickleborough when he would be back her pride would not allow her to admit that she was no longer in his confidence. Instead she returned to the flat and did a few small tasks before setting off for the office, wishing the quarrel had never happened. With no other course of action open to her, she simply settled down to her work, and waited.

Steve had felt just as furious with Miranda as she had with him; probably more so. He had spotted her on the sledging slope before she had seen him and had deliberately plonked a kiss upon Pearl's hot cheek, knowing how it would infuriate his old bezzie. He had been truly hurt by the fact that she had spurned his invitation, but accepted a later one from Julian and Gerald. It was a dirty trick to bring them to the same spot where he had intended to take her, and from what he had seen of her a good deal of her animation had been put on to upset him. He and Cyril had talked for a long time when they got back to Jamaica Close after seeing the girls home and Cyril had laughed when Steve had told him how he longed to join the air force, as Cyril himself had done. 'Then why not do it?' his old friend had said. 'I took me uncle's advice – he were in the Royal Flying Corps during the last lot – and he said the sensible thing were to get in early because once war was declared there'd be a rush and them as was already in would get the plum jobs.'

Steve had nodded wisely, agreeing that he had heard other fellers say the same thing, but had Miranda come a little earlier to Number Two on Monday it is doubtful whether Steve would have gone off early to call for Cyril, who had offered to go along to the recruiting office with him. There he had filled in many forms and answered many questions, and the feeling of resentment and pain which had haunted him over Miranda's defection began to lessen. He was doing what he should have done all along, refusing to let her affect his life. He was a man, wasn't he? Well, he looked old enough to join the Royal Air Force, at any rate.

The helpful sergeant behind the desk had advised him to take his completed papers along to somewhere called Adastral House, in London, not very far from Euston

Station. Handing in his papers personally might speed things up a bit, the sergeant thought.

Feeling that his future was mapped out for him, he hurried to work to see his boss. Mr Richmond was not best pleased, but agreed that it was every fit young man's duty, in time of war, to do his best for his country. Steve was rather startled to hear his boss talking as though war were already a fact, but when he saw the hum and bustle at Adastral House he knew that he was doing the right thing. Cyril, who had accompanied him to London and was looking forward to a night on the town with his old pal, reminded him of the old saying 'One volunteer is worth ten pressed men', and he thought that this was probably true. He was given papers to take to a medical centre the next day so that his health could be checked. If all was well he might find himself in uniform within the month.

When he got home on Wednesday morning, full of excitement, Mrs Mickleborough cried, Mr Mickleborough clapped him on the shoulder and wished him success in this adventure, and his brothers stared round-eyed, though Reg and Joe reminded the family that they both intended to follow Ted into the Navy, and Kenny wept bitterly at the thought of being the only boy living at Number Two.

Steve laughed, and Kenny's tears disappeared as if by magic when his brother reminded him that he would soon have a new baby to play with, and promised that on his next trip to London he would bring back a model Spitfire for his little brother; a toy which Kenny had longed for.

'And now all I've got to do is tell Miranda. Has she

been round asking for me?' Steve said with pretended indifference.

Mrs Mickleborough wrinkled her brow. 'She came round Monday morning, after you'd left for Cyril's,' she said rather doubtfully. 'She said she would meet you at the factory after work. Didn't you tell her what you were going to do?'

'No,' Steve said airily. 'Didn't want her hangin' round me neck in floods of tears and beggin' me not to leave her.' He grinned at his mother. 'Some perishin' chance o' that! The mood she was in she'd probably have said good riddance to bad rubbish!'

Mrs Mickleborough tutted. 'What a horrible thing to say! She's a grand girl your Miranda, and when she does hear I dare say she'll be upset. She'll miss you something awful – so will us, won't us, Dad? But there, Steve luv, I'm sure you've done the right thing. You'll find your carry-out by the back door, so off you go and don't be late this evenin' 'cos it's Lancashire hotpot, and I know you love that.'

Having learned that Steve had gone to London, apparently for some reason which he had not seen fit to confide either to his pals at work or to herself, Miranda fully expected him to come thundering up the stairs which led to the flat on Tuesday evening. But this did not happen. In fact Miranda lost patience and decided to go round to Jamaica Close the next day, ostensibly to visit Aunt Vi and Beth, but really so that she might meet Steve by accident on purpose, so to speak. But on Wednesday morning Gerald telephoned her at work, suggesting that they might go to the cinema together that night. It was a film she very much wanted to see, and she was tempted to leave visiting Jamaica Close till the following day. She wondered how Gerald had got permission to leave school and come into the city, but he explained that his teachers thought he was going with his classmates to see another film, one which was part of their School Certificate curriculum and so would be helpful to them. 'But surely the other boys will report that you left them?' Miranda objected.

Gerald laughed. 'It's clear you know nothing about fellers at public school,' he said reprovingly. 'We drew lots; one of the fellers will actually go to the other film and take notes. Then, on the bus going back to Crosby, he'll fill the rest of us in. Everyone else wants to see *A Day at the Races*, but luckily the chap who drew the short straw is a swot, so he's quite happy to miss the Marx brothers and watch boring old Shakespeare instead.' His tone changed from explanatory to wheedling. 'Do say you'll come, pretty Miranda! I've already told the fellers that my girl will be one of the party. I'll look the most almighty fool if you turn me down.'

Miranda sighed. She would have loved to see the film, especially in Gerald's company, but she was forced to shake her head. 'Thank you very much, Gerry, but it's out of the question, unfortunately. I've not seen Steve since he got back from London and I must do so this evening.'

Gerald's voice sharpened with interest. 'He went up to London? Did he go with Julian? My big brother means to go to Sandhurst for officer training, and had an interview last week. Don't say your Steve was doing the same?'

'He's *not* my Steve,' Miranda said crossly. 'You say I don't know nothin' about public schools; well you don't know nothin' about Liverpool, if you think that havin' a bezzie is the same as having a boyfriend, 'cos it bleedin' well isn't. In fact I'm not even sure that Steve's my bezzie any more. If he was he wouldn't have gone off to London without a word to me.'

'Aha, I thought there was a rift in the lute when we went sledging. The pair of you were glaring at each other like a couple of angry cats quarrelling over a mouse,' Gerald said. He spoke rather unwisely, as it happened, since Miranda shouted into the receiver that he shouldn't leap to conclusions and now she certainly would not accompany him to any cinema, no matter how badly she wanted to see the film. Gerald began to apologise, but at that moment a member of staff entered the hallway where the telephone hung on the wall and Miranda slammed the receiver guiltily back on its rest and turned to face Mr Hardy, who was coming towards her, eyebrows raised.

'I trust you were not taking a personal call, Miss Lovage,' he said reprovingly. 'You know we frown on personal telephone calls. Whilst you are on the line our clients might be clamouring to get through.'

'No, it was a business call for Mr Lawrence, only he's not come in yet,' Miranda said, crossing her fingers behind her back. 'I gave the caller Mr Lawrence's extension number and told him to try it in about half an hour.'

Mr Hardy grunted, then handed Miranda a sheaf of papers. 'I'll take your word for it,' he said grumpily. 'And now have these typed up for me, please. If you're too busy to do it yourself give them to Miss Okeham; she's always very accurate and quick.'

236

'Certainly, sir,' Miranda said through gritted teeth. It was just her luck that Mr Hardy had been the one to catch her using the telephone for a personal call. She knew he disliked her, and thought she had got the job of office junior not through excellence but because she was some connection of Mr Grimshaw's. Unfortunately there was enough truth in this assumption to make it impossible for Miranda to deny it, so now she took the papers from Mr Hardy's hot little paw and hurried back to the typing pool, where she had a desk at the extreme end of the long room.

All that day she worked hard and tried to forget that Gerald must be wondering why she had put the phone down on him, but it was the sort of day when things keep going wrong. As office junior, she pushed a trolley round from department to department at eleven in the morning, offering cups of tea or coffee to the assembled staff, and because she was in a hurry to get back to her desk – Miss Okeham was too busy to take on Mr Hardy's work – she forgot to avoid the loose board at the entrance to the typing pool. She grabbed the tea urn just in time to stop a real calamity but, alas, not quickly enough to prevent tea from puddling all over the trolley. She had only just finished mopping up the mess when several of the men sent her out for sandwiches. She was supposed to buy two ham and pickle, one egg and cress and four beef with mustard, and she would have done so had the baker and confectioner not sold out of beef. He assured her that her customers would like pork just as well, so she followed his advice and bought pork and mustard, only to discover on her return to the office that Mr Rosenbaum, because of his religion, was not allowed to devour any part of the pig.

Miranda sighed, and her friend Lucy, who sat at the next desk, came and took some of the letters which Miranda should have been typing, and gave her friend a sympathetic grin. 'Haven't you ever noticed old Rosie wears a little cap thing in his hair?' she asked. 'He explained to me once – he's ever so nice is Mr Rosenbaum – that Jewish men call that cap thing a yarmulke and they're supposed to wear it all the time; well, not when they're in bed I s'pose, but whenever they're up and doing. Anyway, Jewish people aren't allowed to eat pork, so do you want me to type up some of your letters while you go and buy him something else?'

Miranda thanked her sincerely and scurried off to the bakery to buy another sandwich; at Mr Rosenbaum's suggestion, another egg and cress.

Naturally enough this made her late and being late made her cross, and being cross led to mistakes in her typing, which normally never happened, so by the time she was about to start her last task – collecting and stamping all the letters that had been typed that day – she was simmering with annoyance, very unfairly directed at Steve because he had not told her, his best friend, either that he was going to London, or the reason for his trip.

She was somewhat mollified on finding, when she eventually left the building, that Steve was waiting for her on the pavement. She was carrying an enormous sack of stamped mail to be posted in the nearest pillar box, and managed to give Steve a small smile and a mutter of thanks as he began helping her to push the letters through the flap. But even this friendly act could not remove her sense of ill usage nor make her forget what a horrid day she had had. During the course of it she had actually wondered if Mr Hardy might demand her dismissal, for she knew very well that Mr Hardy had hoped one of his nieces would get her job. However, until today he had really had nothing to complain about so far as her work went, so she tried to dismiss such thoughts from her mind and turned expectantly to Steve. 'Well? Where have you been?' And then, before Steve could open his mouth, she added: 'Not that I need to ask; you've been to perishin' London for some reason, so are you going to tell me, or would you rather tell that horrible Pearl?'

Steve's eyes opened wide with astonishment. 'Now what makes you say that?' he asked in a wondering tone. 'I've not seen the girl since Sunday.'

'Nor you've not seen me,' Miranda interrupted ungrammatically. 'You've made a right fool of me, Steve Mickleborough. I thought we was bezzies, but . . .'

'So we were,' Steve said. 'I asked you to come sledgin' but you chose to go with Gerald instead. Of course he's gorra car and I've only got buses and trams, but I asked you first, you can't deny it.'

'I never said I'd go, though,' Miranda said huffily. 'You'd been horrible to me, so why should I go sledging with you?'

The two had been standing on the pavement by the letter box, but now Steve took her arm and turned her towards the busy main road. 'I can see you're still in a bad mood, so if we're going to quarrel we might as well do so over a cup of tea and a bun,' he said resignedly. 'Oh, Miranda, do come down off your high horse and admit it was a rotten thing to do, to go sledgin' with the

239

Grimshaw boys in the very same place that you knew I wanted to take you.'

Miranda tried to snatch her arm away, but Steve hung on. 'No, you aren't goin' to walk away from me until we've had our talk, so make up your mind to it,' he said grimly. 'You must have guessed that Cyril and meself only invited Pearl and Ruby to come along because we thought you'd give me the go-by; well you had, hadn't you? You thought you were punishin' me for darin' to argue with you; well, I suppose I thought I was punishin' you by taking the girls sledgin'.'

Miranda stopped short and drew herself up to her full height. 'You know very well that Gerald and Julian are just friends, but from what I've heard Pearl and Ruby are a different matter altogether. Why, if anyone wanted to punish anyone else it was you, kissing that horrible Pearl. Not that I care,' she added quickly. 'You can kiss anyone you bloody well please, so long as it isn't me.'

Steve shook her. 'I'd as soon try to kiss a spitting wild cat, which is what you are,' he said grimly. 'Here's the tea room; furious though I am with you I'm prepared to mug you to tea and a bun whilst we sort things out. Oh, Miranda, don't be a fool. Don't just chuck away months and months of good friendship just because of one little falling out.'

Miranda began to protest but Steve ignored her. He pulled her into the small tea room and made her sit at a quiet table in the furthest corner. Then he ordered tea and cakes and the two sat in brooding silence until their order was delivered, when Miranda almost forgot her grievance at the sight of the cream cakes temptingly displayed on a three-tier stand. Her hand hovered between an éclair positively bulging with cream and a meringue, but when Steve advised her to take the éclair first and to have the meringue next she returned her hand to her lap and glared at him. 'Perhaps you're confusing me with that little tart you took sledging,' she said frostily. 'I've heard it said that she'll do anything for a packet of crisps and a fizzy drink; well I'm not like that so just in case you get the wrong impression I'll take the custard tart.'

If Steve had merely passed her the custard tart all might still have been well, but instead he gave a loud guffaw, snatched the éclair and plonked it on her plate. 'Don't be so daft, Miranda Lovage, and don't be so unfair to Ruby and Pearl. I don't know what folks say about them but to my way of thinkin' they're just a couple of girls full of energy and fun, without an ounce of vice. And since you'd been invited to come sledging and didn't even have the good manners to say yes or no, why shouldn't I ask a couple of girls I've known most of me life? Now, for God's sake eat it, and drink your tea; here's hoping it'll sweeten your temper. And then you can tell me what's wrong.'

Miranda ignored the tempting éclair. 'All right, I was wrong to fall out with you and not agree to go sledging,' she muttered. 'But next day I went round to your house to say I was sorry only you'd already gone to work. I did try to catch you there but I had no luck. So go on, I know you were in London but you've been away for three days and I don't know why you had to go there at all.' Despite her intention to treat his trip with indifference she could feel her brows beginning to draw together. 'Well? Are you going to tell me or aren't you?'

241

Steve took one of the cakes and bit into it. He chewed and swallowed infuriatingly slowly, before picking up his cup of tea and taking a long swig. When he spoke it was slowly and distinctly, as though to a small child. Miranda gritted her teeth and took a bite out of the chocolate éclair, not deigning to say a word, but waiting for Steve to speak first.

'Well, after I'd called for you on Sunday and you weren't there, I were walking along the Scottie headin' for Jamaica Close when someone shouted me. It were Cyril Rogers; do you remember him? Tall feller, wi' a big conk and what you used to call a puddin' basin haircut.'

Miranda giggled. 'He's changed a lot,' she observed. 'I saw him on your sledge. He's got himself a proper haircut for a start and he was wearing pretty nice clothes considering he was sledging with you and those two – young ladies.'

'Yes, well, he's joined the air force,' Steve explained. 'We talked about it all the afternoon – when we weren't actually on the sledge, I mean – and then he came home to Jamaica Close and Mam gave us both pie and chips and we went on talking. He's rare keen on the service, and it made me think I could do worse than join up as well. You see, everyone knows there's a war comin' despite what Mr Chamberlain said, and Cyril told me what I've heard others say – that them as volunteers before war is declared get the best choice of jobs – so I went to the recruiting office and filled in about a hundred forms . . .'

Miranda gasped. She suddenly realised that if she had missed Steve so badly when he was only away for three days, she would miss him a whole lot worse if he joined the forces and left Liverpool, if not for good, then for a very long time. 'Steve Mickleborough, if you've joined the Royal Air Force then it's the most unfair thing I ever heard,' she interrupted, her voice rising. 'It's not fair! I can't do the same because I'm too young. Oh, do say you're just kidding. Do say you've not committed yourself!'

Steve grinned. 'Well if I said it, it'd be a lie,' he announced cheerfully. 'I took the recruiting sergeant's advice and went up to London with Cyril. We booked ourselves into a YMCA hostel – it was quite cheap – and I went to a place called Adastral House where I filled in even more forms, and had an interview, and then they sent me to somewhere in the suburbs where I had a medical. I passed A1 – well I would, wouldn't I? – and I'll get a letter telling me where to report for training in a few weeks.'

Miranda's mouth dropped open. 'Without telling me?' she said. 'Without a word to your bezzie, just because we'd had a teeny little falling out? Steve, how *could* you? Oh, if only I were a couple of years older . . .'

Steve began to say that he had only forestalled the authorities by a few months because he was sure they would start recruiting his age group very soon, but Miranda was not listening. She pushed her teacup and the plate with its half-eaten éclair away from her, put her head down on her arms and began to weep in earnest. Steve, clearly alarmed, for everyone in the tea room was staring at them, reached across the table and tried to brush the hot tears from Miranda's reddened cheeks. 'Stop makin' an exhibition of yourself, and me too,' he hissed. 'Everyone will be thinkin' I've done or said somethin' bad to make you carry on so. What's so wrong with me joinin' the air force anyway? I don't want to go into the Navy, 'cos I'm always seasick, and I don't fancy the army either. But I'm interested in aero engines, because that's what we make at the factory. Oh, Miranda, do stop!'

Miranda sat up; she was red-eyed and the tears still brimmed over, but she muttered something inaudible and reached for her cup.

'What did you say?' Steve asked, rather apprehensively. 'Look, Miranda, it's no use blamin' me because what's done can't be undone . . . oh, dear, don't start again! Here, take this.' He offered her a moderately clean handkerchief, with which Miranda began mopping-up operations, whilst continuing to mutter.

'It's always the same,' she said in a small, hoarse voice. 'Nobody really likes me, not enough to stay with me, at any rate. First it was my mum; she pushed me away by making me call her Arabella, and left. Then it was Missie, who went off to her island, then Pete Huxtable took Timmy, and now it's you!'

'And next it will be you,' Steve pointed out. 'You've said yourself that as soon as you're old enough you're going to join one of the forces. So all you've got to do is wait a while, and you'll be off yourself. And remember, I'm joining the air force. From what I've heard the chaps in the air force don't necessarily go abroad. I might be posted to somewhere within a few miles of Liverpool; think of that!'

Miranda gave her eyes one last rub then handed the now sodden handkerchief back to Steve. Then she picked up the remainder of the éclair and began to eat it. 'You're right, of course,' she said as she finished the last delectable mouthful. 'I was being silly. The truth is, knowing that you had kept something a secret from me made me feel left out, rejected if you like. Why *didn't* you tell me, Steve? You could have come round to Russell Street before you left, or you could have come to the office.'

'Oh yeah? And have you either bury your fangs in my throat or burst into floods of tears and try to stop me going?' Steve said, grinning. He leaned across the table and rumpled Miranda's already rather untidy hair. 'Besides, I wasn't sure whether I'd be accepted or not.' He eyed the remaining cakes on the stand. 'Want another one?'

Miranda shook her head. 'No thanks; now that I've pulled myself together I really should be getting back to the flat, since it's my turn to do the spuds and get some sort of a meal together. Want to come to tea with Avril and me? If so I dare say we could run to fish and chips.'

Steve paid the bill, agreeing to forgo his mam's Lancashire hotpot and have supper in Russell Street, and they left the tea room. Outside on the pavement Steve gave Miranda's hand a squeeze. 'Are we pals again? Bezzies? Or are you still cross?'

Miranda gave a watery giggle and shook her head. 'No, I'm not cross; I was a fool to be annoyed. Of course you should join up, and I'll do the same when I'm old enough. Can you come straight round to the flat now, or do you want to go home first?'

Steve considered. 'I'd best nip back to Jamaica Close and tell Mam I shan't be in for tea,' he said. 'Come back with me, why don't you? Mam's always glad to see you and you can have a good old moan about me leavin' home, 'cos Mam was just as upset as you were when I told her I'd joined the RAF.'

Miranda suspected that he was crossing his fingers behind his back, for she thought Mrs Mickleborough far too sensible to object to her son's joining up; his elder brother was in the Royal Navy, after all. But as he had said, she did like Steve's mum, so the two of them set out together for Jamaica Close, the best of friends once more, their differences forgotten.

Chapter Nine

Miranda got into bed on the night of 3 September, aware with an uneasy chill that what everyone had talked and conjectured about was now a fact: they were at war with Germany. According to the popular press Hitler would start by overrunning France and the Low Countries, and would, within a matter of weeks, have an invasion force ready to cross the Channel and occupy Great Britain, whilst the skies above would be full of paratroopers disguised as nuns, carrying the war into even the remotest parts of the country.

Cuddling down, she allowed herself a little smile at the thought of a burly paratrooper landing on one of the Liver Birds, or having to disentangle his skirts from the tower of St Nicholas's Church, for she found it impossible to believe that even Hitler, clearly a madman, would be fool enough to send a force of men disguised as women across the Channel.

Soon her mind drifted to other things; to Steve, who was being trained as a mechanic, and to the fact that she meant to go and meet him at the village nearest his airfield as soon as it could be arranged. He was in Norfolk, rapturous about some sort of lake or river called the Broads, insisting that she should come over when he could get a forty-eight. Together, they could explore the countryside, prowl round the old city of Norwich, reputed to have a pub for every day of the year, and spend time on the beach, for though the government intended to sow all the shores with landmines they had not yet done so.

Dreamily her thoughts moved on; to the moment when she would be old enough to join the WAAF and meet Steve on his own ground, so to speak. She imagined herself in the blue cap, tunic and skirt, her legs in grey stockings, her feet in neat black lace-ups. How amazed Steve would be the first time he saw her in uniform! But of course if Hitler really did send paratroopers and an invasion fleet the war might be over before she was old enough to join up. She had heard a stallholder on the Great Homer Street market saying that he remembered how folk had thought the Great War would be over by Christmas. 'And now I hear fools sayin' the same about this little lot,' he had said bitterly. 'But that war, the last 'un, went on for four perishin' years and I reckon Hitler and his Panzers and his Lootwharrever – his air force, I mean – are a deal tougher than the Huns, so I reckon we're in for a hard slog before we've kicked 'em back over the Channel where they belongs.'

Miranda burrowed her head into her pillow. So mebbe I'll get a chance to show myself off in uniform to Steve and his pals before we've kicked 'em back over the Channel, she told herself now. I don't want a war, I'm sure nobody does, but we've got no choice; war has arrived and we've all got to do our bit towards winning it, because judging from the newsreels living under the Nazi jackboot would be a terrible thing; we'd be better off dead.

But by now excitement and tiredness had caught up

with Miranda and she sank into slumber with the words *better off dead, dead, dead* ringing in her ears.

Miranda was preparing a meal in the flat's small kitchen when she heard someone running up the metal stairs and grinned to herself. She guessed that it would be Avril, whose shift had ended half an hour ago, eager to gobble her supper so that the two of them could go Christmas shopping at Paddy's Market, for the holiday was rapidly approaching and they had not yet managed to get all their presents bought.

Despite the dire warnings in the press and on the wireless, nothing much had happened since the start of the war three months earlier. No paratroopers had descended from the sky, no invasion fleet had begun to cross the Channel, and no bombs had rained down on them from the Luftwaffe. Steve, now a fully trained mechanic on Wellingtons, would be coming home for a forty-eight over Christmas, and she and Avril were looking forward to hearing what he thought was about to happen. Folk were already referring to the first three months of the so-called 'conflict' as the phoney war, but Steve had warned Miranda in his letters that this was unlikely to last. Hitler and his generals must have some reason for delaying their onslaught upon Great Britain and the Commonwealth and Steve, who was in daily contact with the men who flew the big bombers over France, the Low Countries and Germany, had heard them say that the delay was due, not to a lack of preparation, but to Hitler's declared wish to join forces with the British against the rest of the world. Whilst he still hoped, Steve had written, whether Hitler knew it or not he was giving

Britain time to arm, train and begin to work on their defences, which at the moment were almost non-existent.

Trust us to do nothing to build up our own war machine despite knowing that Hitler's forces were already infinitely superior, both in strength and experience, to our own, he had written. *But it's always the way, so the chaps tell me. The British Bulldog lies quiet and watches until it's ready to pounce.*

Miranda had thought this downright comical since Mr Jones up the road owned a bulldog, a lazy animal, bow-legged and obese, who waddled slowly up and down the road at its master's heels, its stertorous breathing audible half a mile away. The thought of its pouncing on anyone or anything was so ludicrous that Miranda had to smile, but just at that moment the stair-climber rattled the door, then opened it, and Avril entered the kitchen, laden with paper carriers. She grinned widely at her friend, dumped her carriers on the kitchen table and sniffed the air. 'I smell Lancashire hotpot with a load of spuds and the rest of that jar of pickled cabbage,' she said dreamily. 'You're home early. I came up Great Homer and since I didn't think you'd be back yet I bought a couple of them pasties for us teas. Still, we can take one each to work tomorrow, save us makin' sarnies. Any word from Steve? Wish I had a boyfriend in the air force what could give us news of what's goin' on.'

Miranda, who had been laying the table, stared at her friend, wide-eyed. 'Avril Donovan, you've got half the crew of that corvette – the *Speedwell* – writing to you; what more could you want? And yes, I had a letter from Steve this morning. He has to be careful not to give any classified information, of course, but he did say that it's mostly leaflets which get dropped at present and not bombs.' She peered inquisitively at the nearest paper carrier. 'Looks like you've been buying up everything you could lay hands on. Heard any rumours? All I know is rationing will start in earnest once Christmas is over. And even before that no one's allowed to buy icing sugar. Fortunately, however, we had a bag left over from your birthday cake last summer so if we just ice the top and not the sides of the cake I made last week, it'll do very well for Christmas.'

'Clever old you; and I got some made up marzipan from my pal what works in Sample's,' Avril said happily. 'And being as it's only a couple of days till Christmas the boss paid us all a bit of a bonus so I spent it on goodies from Great Homer . . . look!'

As she spoke Avril had seized the largest of the paper carriers and tipped its contents on to the table, making Miranda give a protesting yelp as various items rolled and bounced across the cutlery and crockery already set out. But then she gave a squeak of excitement, for Avril had bought a packet of balloons, another of tinsel and some candy walking sticks to decorate the tiny tree which stood in their living room. 'Oh, Avril, you are clever! I particularly wanted it to be really Christmassy because Steve seems certain that the phoney war will soon become a real one, and future Christmases will be pretty thin on treats,' she said as her friend drew from another carrier a bottle of some sort of spirit, three large oranges and a bunch of bananas. When Miranda put out a hand to the next bag, however, Avril pushed her away, shaking her head.

'No, no, you mustn't look in that one, it's me Christmas presents,' she said proudly. 'I couldn't get anything much, but I don't mind tellin' you Steve's gettin' ten Woodbines, only you ain't to tell him, understand?'

'As if I would,' Miranda said indignantly. She peeped into the remaining paper carrier. 'Oh, you bad girl. The government have told us not to hoard goods against rationing starting and I spy sugar and butter – oh, and that looks like quite a lot of bacon – gosh, Steve will think he's died and gone to heaven because meals in the cookhouse are pretty basic, he says. They get dried egg but not the sort of eggs you can fry – I think they call them shell eggs – and great chunks of fried bread to make up a decent plateful. Oh, and I didn't tell you, did I? He'll be home late on Christmas Eve and has to leave again by lunchtime on Boxing Day. It's not long, but apparently they're giving the chaps with wives and young families longer.' She turned to her companion, knowing she was grinning like a Cheshire cat. 'Oh, Avril, telephone calls are all very well – and letters, of course – but it'll be grand to see Steve face to face again. He tells me he's talked to one or two Waafs and they say that provided you aren't already doing war work a girl can sign on before she's even seventeen. It's not as if girls will be actually engaged in conflict, though if you ask me the jobs they do will take them into just as much danger as the men. Now, let's get on with this meal because Steve will be back in two days' time and I want to have everything ready for him.'

Avril began to shovel her purchases back into their paper carriers and looked across at her companion, her expression a touch guilty. 'I've a confession to make, chuck. The young feller what works as a supervisor at my factory, the one who was in that dreadful accident where he lost his leg and the use of one eye, won't be goin' home for Christmas. Well, as you know, he's not got a home to go to no more. So I – I axed him back to our place, knowin' you wouldn't mind. He's okay is Gary; you'll like him. He says he'll bring some of the holly he cut for the girls in the factory, and a piece of ham which he meant to have for his own Christmas dinner. Since he'll be sharin' our chicken now, he says we can have the ham for Boxing Day with a tin of peas and a baked potato.' She gazed anxiously at Miranda. 'You don't mind, do you, chuck? It 'ud be downright mean to condemn him to a lonely Christmas after all he's gone through.'

'Of course I don't mind,' Miranda said at once. She knew Gary's story, knew that he had been working in a timber yard when something had gone wrong with the mechanism of the machine he was using and he had been dragged into the works. He had been in hospital for months, and had been fitted with a wooden leg, but according to Avril never referred to it and was always cheerful and optimistic. He had tried to join the Services – all of them – but had been turned down, so had gone to Avril's factory and started work on the bench, speedily rising to his present position as supervisor. So now she grinned encouragingly at her friend. 'Tell him he's as welcome as the flowers in May, and you can tell him as well that he won't be playin' gooseberry 'cos Steve and I are just bezzies, so there!'

Steve telephoned Miranda by dialling the number of the box on the corner at the agreed hour, for though the Mess was on the telephone the flat was not. Sometimes he was unlucky and someone at Miranda's end who was already waiting for a call snatched the receiver off its hook, breathing some other caller's name. This called for diplomacy to make sure that at the sound of an unfamiliar voice the girl, or feller, did not crossly slam the receiver down, thus cutting the connection before Miranda was able to intervene. Tonight, however, it was Miranda's own small voice which came to him as soon as the operator said 'You're through' and left them to get on with their conversation, having first reminded them sternly that it was wartime and many other people were waiting for a chance to use the instrument.

'Steve? Oh, it *is* you! I've got so much to tell you, but since we'll be together in a couple of days I won't waste telephone time. Avril's asked her supervisor to join us on Christmas Day itself, and since he's providing the food for Boxing Day I suppose he'll have to come along then too. I've never met him myself but Avril says we'll get along, and I'm sure she's right. Have they told you what time your train gets into Lime Street? And how's your mam and the little 'uns?'

Mrs Mickleborough, Kenny and the baby had been evacuated way back in September when the war had started and were now comfortably ensconced in a farmhouse somewhere in Wales, which was why Steve would be having his whole forty-eight with Miranda. Naturally, Steve would have liked to see his mam, Kenny and the baby – his stepdad had joined the Navy – but he quite agreed with the government feeling that Liverpool, once the war really got going, would be a major target, and anyone living there ran a far greater risk than if they allowed themselves to be sent to the relative safety of the countryside.

Steve cleared his throat. 'Mam's doin' fine, Kenny loves the local school and Flora has settled down well,' he said. 'I can't say much about Dad, or the others – classified information, I guess – but I'll spill the beans when we meet. As for train times, cross-country journeys are hell; I could have up to five changes, but I reckon I should be home before midnight.'

'Oh dear, and you'll have to leave on Boxing Day . . .' Miranda was beginning when the operator's voice cut in.

'You've had your three minutes, caller. Others are waiting for the line. Please replace your receiver.'

Miranda and Steve began simultaneously to say their farewells, while the operator, infuriatingly, tried to shut them up. In fact she did so just as Steve bawled 'Love you Miranda' into his receiver, and he crashed it back on its rest before Miranda could remind him that they were supposed to be just good friends.

Miranda and Avril's preparations for Christmas proceeded smoothly. Miranda was one of the few people still left in the typing pool at Mr Grimshaw's office. There was an elderly lady, a Miss Burton, and another known as Miss Phyllis, who had been called out of retirement as the other typists either joined the forces or went to work in the factories which paid very much better than even the most generous of office jobs. Miranda had missed her friends at first but soon realised that Miss Burton and Miss Phyllis were well up to the work, and proved both faster and more efficient than the staff they had replaced. Miranda might have been lured by the high wages one could earn in, for instance, a munitions factory, save that she had it on good authority that applying to join one of the forces whilst employed in such a post might well be doomed to failure. As it was, she and her two elderly companions managed to share out the work to everyone's satisfaction. They even bought each other tiny presents – Miranda gave each of her colleagues a very small bar of scented soap and they clubbed together to buy her rose geranium talcum, whilst Mr Grimshaw presented each woman with a ten shilling note.

'It may not be much of a bonus, but it's all the firm can afford at the moment,' Mr Grimshaw had said as he handed over the money. 'And we're giving you a whole week's holiday with pay, so I trust you don't feel too hard done by.'

Delighted with even a small amount of extra money, Miranda scoured the shops for Steve's favourite, choco-late ginger, and bought him the biggest box she could find. The rest of the money was spent on extras and a length of green ribbon with which she tied her hair back into a ponytail, getting Avril to knot the ribbon into a huge bow on the nape of her neck. 'Making sure he'll reckernise you?' Avril asked derisively. 'Better ring him up and tell him you're the lass with the green ribbon in her hair, just in case he's forgot your freckly old face.' It was Christmas Eve and they were in the kitchen at the flat, Avril cutting sandwiches so that they would have something to give Steve if he was starving after his long and complicated journey, whilst Miranda donned her thick navy blue overcoat and crammed a large floppy beret on her head, for at ten o'clock it was already very cold, with frost or snow threatening.

Avril looked up from her work. 'You off already?' she enquired. 'You're daft you are; the train's bound to be late, and you'll be waiting in the cold for ages.'

Miranda pulled a rueful face. 'I don't mind waiting – better that than miss him. And once I'm on the platform there's all sorts I can do – I could even go into the refreshment room and buy a cup of coffee.'

'Oh, you!' Avril said affectionately. 'Why can't you admit you're mad about the bloke? Why d'you have to keep pretendin' that you're just good friends? He's a nice feller is Steve; you want to grab hold of him while you can.'

Miranda opened the door, letting in a blast of cold air. 'Think what you like,' she said grandly, 'but I repeat: Steve and I are just bezzies!' And with that she stepped on to the top stair and slammed the door behind her before clattering down the flight and beginning to walk with care along the frosted pavement. Everyone was always complaining that trains were late, and Steve had told her that cross-country journeys in particular were fraught with difficulties and delays, so she should arrive at the station first.

She reached the main road and turned towards the city centre. Because of the blackout, crossing side roads was a dodgy business, but she had a little torch in her pocket and flashed it discreetly each time she came to a kerb, and presently arrived at the station. The concourse was crowded despite the lateness of the hour, and though she glanced wistfully towards the refreshment room the queue at the counter was a long one. Perhaps she might go in later and buy herself a coffee, but for now she would simply stroll around and wait.

Despite Steve's hopes it was after midnight before his train drew in to Liverpool Lime Street, and though the platform was by no means deserted it was not crowded either. Hefting his kitbag from the string rack, he jumped down, then turned to help an elderly lady to alight. She had told him as the train chugged slowly towards Liverpool that she was going to spend Christmas with her daughter and three grandchildren, and was hoping to persuade them to return with her when she left at the end of the holiday. 'My grandchildren were evacuated back in September – their mum works in munitions so she couldn't get away – but since there's been no bombings, nor no landings from over the Continong, she sent for them to come home,' she had explained, as the two of them sat side by side in the crowded compartment. 'I dunno if she were right, but the kids weren't happy where they was billeted. Said the woman didn't want 'em, made no secret of the fact. The eldest, Bessie, what's nine, wrote to her mam and said they weren't gettin' enough food for a sparra. She said the 'vacuation lady didn't like boys and picked on Herbie – he's five – no matter who were really at fault. So Maud, that's me daughter, decided to bring 'em home.' She looked hopefully at Steve. 'If the bombs start, like what some folk say they will, then they can come to me. I'd treat 'em right . . . only my cottage is right up agin an airfield.'

Steve had given all the right answers to reassure her and had confided that his mother, his little brother, and Flora, his baby sister who was four months old and a great favourite, had also been evacuated. 'They'd have liked to come home for Christmas once they knew I'd got leave – me brothers and me dad are in the Navy so no tellin' when they'll be in port again – but our dad got real angry when she wrote suggestin' it. So Mam give up the idea and I'm the only one of us Mickleboroughs who'll be in dear old Liverpool for Christmas.' He had grinned sheepishly at his companion. 'I'm goin' to stay with me girl,' he said proudly. 'She's only young but she's gorran important job as secretary to a firm of solicitors. Mind you, she's goin' to join the WAAF as soon as she's old enough; wants to be in the same bunch as me, of course.'

The old lady had murmured that everyone must do their best because old 'uns like herself could still remember the horrors of the Great War. 'I dunno how it come about that we ever let Germany get strong enough to take on the world again,' she had said sadly. 'Don't us British never learn nothin'? It's plain as the nose on your face that the Huns has been armin' and gettin' ready ever since the Spanish Civil War; why, I remember . . .'

The carriage had contained not only themselves but five soldiers, all of whom appeared to be asleep, and a woman whose nurse's uniform could just be glimpsed beneath her heavy overcoat. As the old woman said the words Spanish Civil War, one of the soldiers, older than the rest, opened a lazy eye. 'Careless talk costs lives,' he said reprovingly. He opened his other eye and fixed Steve with an admonitory glare. 'You should know better, young feller. Why, you all but give away where your mam and the kids have gone, and you mentioned where you'll be spendin' Christmas. Accordin' to what I've heard, perishin' Hitler's got his spies everywhere, so don't you forget it.'

The fat little woman who had been chattering so freely to Steve swelled with indignation and Steve could scarcely hide his amusement, for she reminded him of one of his mother's plump little broody hens when disturbed on the nest. Even so, though, he knew that the soldier was in the right even if his elderly companion was scarcely spy material. So he addressed the soldier in his most apologetic tone. 'Sorry, mate, you're absolutely right,' he said humbly. 'But I didn't lerron where me mam's stayin', nor what ship . . .'

'Leave it,' the soldier said easily, but there was a warning glint in his eye. He sat up straighter and pulled a pack of cards from the pocket in his battledress. 'How about a game of brag?' He lifted the blind a little to peer out into the pitch dark. 'There's no tellin' when we'll arrive at Lime Street, but I guess a game of cards will help the time to go faster.'

The little old lady gave the soldier the sort of glare he had given Steve, then settled back in her seat and folded her plump little hands over her shabby handbag. 'You can count me out, young feller. I's goin' to have a nap,' she said firmly, and spoke not another word until the train drew into the station. Then she had let everyone else get off the train before creaking to her feet and accepting Steve's offered hand. Having descended to the platform she looked all around her, then lowered her voice. 'Walls have ears, so they say,' she muttered. 'That perishin' soldier! Does I look like a spy, young feller? If he hadn't been so big I'd ha' been tempted to clack him across the lug. But thanks for your company and I wishes you a very merry Christmas.'

Steve, who had put his kitbag down on the platform whilst he helped his fellow passenger to descend, wished her the same. 'And I don't think that brown job meant he suspected *you* of spying,' he said, trying to conquer a quivering lip. 'There were others in the carriage, you know, all listening. I think he meant one of them.'

The old woman sniffed. 'Oh aye, I s'pose he were lookin' at that nurse, thinkin' she might be one of them paratroopers what they warned us about when the war first started,' she said. 'And her pretty as a picture! But there you are, I suppose; anything's possible in wartime.'

Agreeing, Steve hefted his kitbag up on one shoulder and, suiting his pace to her leisurely one, with her small suitcase in his free hand, made his way towards the concourse. Glancing up at the clock when he drew level with it he saw that it was a quarter past midnight, and the faint hope that he might be met disappeared. He knew Miranda would have been working all day – no one got Christmas Eve off – and having seen his companion trot towards the taxi rank he was about to start walking towards Russell Street when he heard his name called and, turning in the direction of the voice, was just in time to slip his kitbag from his shoulder and hold out his arms so that Miranda might fly into them. Hugging her tightly he began to kiss her upturned face, but instead of returning his kisses she gave a breathless giggle, put a hand across his mouth and told him not to be so soppy. 'I've been waiting since ten o'clock, you horrid person, so if you want cocoa and a bun before bed, we'd better get on the end of the taxi queue,' she said. 'Hey, Steve, there's someone waving at you.' She giggled again. 'So you've got yourself a girlfriend already? That's a nice state of affairs, I don't think!'

Steve grinned and raised a hand in response to the frantic beckonings from his erstwhile travelling companion. 'That old lady and meself were in the same compartment on the train,' he explained. He stretched and yawned. 'Lord, I'm that tired, and stiff as a board into the bargain. Shall we walk to Russell Street? It's not far and that queue's awful long, and I don't feel like standing around getting colder and colder. If we walk, it'll keep our circulation going, 'cos this is what we in the RAF call brass monkey weather.'

Miranda, clutching his arm, informed him crisply that it was not only the RAF who described the weather thus. Then she agreed that walking was by far the better option and the pair set off.

Steve slung an arm round her waist, pulling her close. 'If we keep in step we'll go faster, like in a three-legged race,' he informed her. He slid his hand a little lower and patted her bottom. 'My oh my, I do believe you've put on a bit of weight. About time if you ask me.'

He half expected Miranda to take offence, for she had always tried to keep him at arm's length, but either because she was so pleased to see him, or because she was too tired to quibble, she just chuckled sleepily and snuggled against him. 'Oh, you!' she said drowsily. 'Did I tell you you'd be sleeping on our sofa? I suppose if I were a real lady I'd offer you my bed, but since I'm nothing of the kind you're condemned to the sofa, my boy. Oh, Steve, it's so good to see you again and have a bit of a laugh together. You may only be my best friend, but I'm really fond of you, honest to God I am.'

Steve heaved a deep sigh and gave Miranda's waist a squeeze. 'Oh well, I guess it's better than nothing,' he said resignedly. 'And now tell me all your news. Have you been back to Jamaica House at all? I remember someone saying that since Mr Grimshaw had the deeds somewhere in his office he would be entitled to claim it, though he wasn't particularly interested in doing so, as I recall.'

'I've been far too busy to traipse all the way round there,' Miranda said rather indignantly. 'I told you I was a fire watcher – not that there have been any fires to watch yet – and I've joined the WVS; I do all sorts, never have a moment to myself, and Avril's the same. If you were home for longer we might go round and just check up that no one's found the door in the wall. When you think about it, a spy could set up a whole wireless network inside the old house and no one the wiser. I say, Steve, I never thought of that! Do you think we ought to nip round in the morning and check up?'

Steve laughed, but shook his head. 'No I do not! To tell you the truth, Mr Grimshaw said something of the sort when I got my posting and went round to Holmwood Lodge to say cheerio. He told me then that he would arrange for someone to keep an eye on the old place and would tell the authorities to check on it every so often once the boys left the area.' He peered at the pale shape of Miranda's face, turned enquiringly up to his. 'Are the Grimshaw boys still around?'

'Well, Gerald's still at school, of course, and Julian changed his mind about going to Sandhurst. He went to Africa instead, where he's flying Stringbags and happy as a sand boy. Before he went to Rhodesia he came over to see us, to say cheerio I s'pose, and I was working late and didn't see him, but he took Avril to the flicks and then out for a meal. Nice of him, wasn't it?'

'Very,' Steve said off-handedly. He squeezed her waist again. 'Glad it wasn't you. I've enough trouble keepin' tabs on Gerald without havin' to widen my scope to include Julian as well.'

Miranda pinched his hand. 'Rubbish; you're all my friends, all equal,' she said grandly, and ignored Steve's groan.

By the time Steve snuggled down on the sofa, he felt his cup of happiness was full. They had had a marvellous Christmas Day, starting with what he called a pre-war breakfast of eggs, bacon, sausage and fried bread, to say nothing of toast and marmalade and large mugs of tea. They had opened their presents earlier and Steve had been the recipient of ten Woodbines from Avril, and an air force blue muffler and matching gloves from Miranda. He had bought both girls attractive headscarves which were much appreciated, though Miranda told him that, should she wear hers at night, the oranges and lemons emblazoned upon a navy blue background would be noticeable enough to draw enemy fire.

Soon after breakfast Gary Hamilton had arrived. Avril had forbidden him to buy presents since, as she told him with all her usual honesty, she and Miranda had been far too busy to search for something for him, not knowing his tastes. However, he had brought a large cauliflower which one of the stallholders on the Great Homer Street market had sold him cheap the previous day, and offered it to Avril, blushing to the roots of his hair. 'You said no presents, but I thought you might make use of this,' he said, thrusting it into her hands. 'It's not what you might call a present . . .'

Helping him out of his coat and scarf and sitting him down before the fire, for it was bitterly cold outside, Avril assured him that the cauliflower was much appreciated and would be served next day, and then introduced him to Steve. 'He's only here until lunchtime tomorrow,' she explained, 'so we've got to make the most of today.'

And make the most of it they did, Steve recalled happily. They spent the morning preparing the chicken dinner they were going to enjoy, and as they peeled vegetables, made gravy and boiled the pudding, they talked and laughed, getting to know one another. After dinner they listened to the King's Christmas message and then played games before setting off, well wrapped, to make room for the tea which the girls had prepared in advance.

'Let's see if we can walk all the way to Prince's Park, and see if the lake is iced over. It's a pity it's not snowing because we could have a grand snowball battle between the four of us.' Miranda had sighed reminiscently. 'When I was at the Rankin Academy I had a friend called Louise, and she had two brothers, twins they were. The four of us used to have no end of fun when it was snowy. We'd make snowmen, and then a sort of snow castle, which two of us would defend and two would attack. Usually I got the smaller of the twins, Trevor, and Louise had Philip. Then whichever couple won would have to treat the other pair to tea and scones at the little café down by the orangery.' She sighed happily. 'I suppose we're too old now for snow battles, but I wouldn't mind a slide on the lake, if the ice is bearing.'

When they set out on the long walk, well muffled up, they had flinched against the icy wind, but by the time they reached the park they were glowing with health and warmth. Despite Miranda's hopes the lake was not completely iced over, and her fear that the café would be closed proved to be justified, but even so they thoroughly enjoyed the exercise. They did not indulge in races, because it would not have been fair on Gary, but they played guessing games, Chinese whispers and the like, and despite the enormous chicken dinner they had eaten were ravenous once more when they arrived back at the flat in time for tea. When the meal was over they played more games amidst great hilarity until Avril, saying she would accompany Gary part of the way back to his hostel, put on her outer clothing and wagged a finger at Miranda. 'Don't you take advantage of our being away to get up to any naughty tricks,' she said teasingly. 'I can see young Steve there is longing for a cuddling session.' She struck her head with the back of her hand. 'There, we never played postman's knock; that's a good game for a Christmas party.'

'We don't need games; we can have a cuddle for old times' sake, can't we, Miranda?' Steve said as the door closed behind Avril and Gary. He sat down in one of the creaking wicker armchairs and pulled Miranda on to his lap. 'Oh, you're lovely and warm and cuddly,' he said, pressing his cheek against hers. 'Tell you what, if we get up early you and me can go round to Jamaica House and make sure all's well there. I'd like to see the old place again; if it hadn't been for Jamaica House you and I might never have got together.'

'We've not got together now, not in the way you mean,' Miranda objected. 'I do like that Gary, don't you? Avril pretends there's nothing in it, but if you ask me, they'll be a couple by the time the winter's over. I'd better put

266

the kettle on, because when Avril gets back the first thing she'll want will be a nice hot cup of tea.'

'The first thing I'll want is more cuddling and perhaps a bit of kissing as well,' Steve said plaintively. 'I agree with you, though, that Gary and Avril look like becoming a couple.' He pulled a funny face, cocking one eyebrow and speaking in a transatlantic accent. 'How's about youse an' me follerin' suit, Miss Gorgeous?' he said hopefully. 'I *need* a girlfriend to keep up my reputation as a great lover. Come on, Miranda, say you'll be my girl.'

Miranda, pouring boiling water into the teapot, put the kettle back on the stove and gave Steve an indulgent smile. 'Give you an inch and you'll take a mile,' she said, and then, when Steve pulled a disappointed face, she chuckled, crossed the room, pulled him to his feet and kissed the side of his mouth. Steve moved his head quickly and was fielding another kiss when, at this inauspicious moment, the door opened and Avril and a blast of cold wind entered the kitchen. He and Miranda sprang apart as though they had been doing something far more interesting than just kissing, but Avril was oblivious. She rushed over to the fire and stood as close to it as she could, teeth chattering.

'I'm perishin' perished,' she announced, beginning to unbutton her coat, remove her headscarf and endeavour to fluff up her flattened hair. 'Does that teapot still hold enough for one?'

'It holds enough for three,' Miranda said, getting three mugs down from the Welsh dresser. 'Steve and I were just saying what a grand feller Gary is. You really like him, don't you Avril?'

Steve turned his head so that he could look at the older

girl, and saw her eyes begin to sparkle, and the pink in her cheeks to deepen. 'Yes, he's a grand chap,' she said. 'If you knew what he had to put up with when he was first in hospital . . . but no point in talking about that. He's the bravest bloke I've ever met, I admire him tremendously and – and he's invited me to go to the theatre with him when the pantomime starts in January. He says he doesn't care if he's the only feller in the audience over ten years old, and he says we'll have fish and chips afterwards. Oh, Miranda, I do like him so much!'

So now Steve, clutching his pillow and wishing it was Miranda, thought that the four of them had had a perfect day. There had not been a single disagreement and everyone, he knew, had thoroughly enjoyed themselves. Next day he would have to leave the flat no later than noon, but the girls had decided to combine breakfast and lunch, and have a meal at around eleven o' clock. Then they would all go to the station together and he would set out on the long cold journey back to his Norfolk airfield. As he contemplated the following day he found himself hoping that Avril and Gary would have enough tact to realise that he and Miranda would want to be alone – or as alone as anyone could be on a crowded railway platform – to say their goodbyes, which might have to last them for many months, since rumour had it that postings would be handed out as soon as everyone had returned from their Christmas holidays.

In fact, however, when they reached Lime Street the following day the train he meant to catch was drawing into the platform, and he almost hurled himself aboard, then let down the window and leaned out to grab as much of Miranda as he could hold. 'Write to me every week – every day – and I'll write back whenever I've gorra moment,' he gabbled. He tried to give her a really ardent kiss but even as he pursed his lips for action the train began to move, porters began to shout and Miranda was quite literally torn from his arms. Steve leaned even further out of the carriage. 'I love you, Miranda Lovage,' he bawled, not caring who was listening or what they might think. 'Take care of yourself until I come home to take care of you myself.'

He could see Miranda's lips moving but could not hear what she was saying, and decided to assume it was words of love. Why should it not be, after all? He knew she was fond of Gerald but sincerely hoped that her feelings for the other boy stopped at liking. And in the meantime, whilst he remained in Norfolk a telephone call a couple of times a month and as many letters as she could pen would have to do.

Steve withdrew from the window as the train began to pick up speed. It was a corridor train, and he had slung his kitbag on to a corner seat to save himself a place, for the train was crowded. He straightened his fore and aft, checked in the window glass that his uniform was all correct and went back to his seat, reaching up to put his kitbag on the overhead rack, and then settling into his place with a contented sigh. It had been a fantastic Christmas, the best he could remember since he was a small boy, and it occurred to him now that it was the first time Miranda had not gone on and on about Arabella; this, he thought, was a good sign. When he had first joined the air force, her weekly letters had been full of her inability to believe that her mother was dead. She had wanted constant reassurance and he had done his best to give it, because Mr Grimshaw had said that she would begin to accept her loss as time went by. Now, it seemed that Mr Grimshaw was right, for Miranda had not once mentioned Arabella from the moment she had met him off the train to the moment when he had embarked on his return journey.

Steve looked around the compartment; two sailors, four airmen, including himself, and two brown jobs, one a sergeant, all settling themselves for sleep. Steve chuckled inwardly; one thing the forces did teach you was to snatch a nap whenever you got the chance, so you would be fresh and rested for whatever trials were to come. Steve closed his eyes and began to relive his lovely Christmas. Soon, he slept.

'It's a jolly good thing we had such a wizard Christmas, because this perishin' weather looks like lasting for ever,' Miranda said discontentedly. She and Avril had quite by chance boarded the same tram, and were now hanging on to a shared strap as the vehicle began to lurch along the main road. 'Have you ever seen such conditions? Steve's last letter was full of it, but in a way he thinks it's a good thing. Norfolk is even worse than us, with the blizzards blowing the snow into huge mountains, blocking roads and breaking the branches off trees. I should think even the kids must be fed up with snowballs and snowmen when they're accompanied by freezing feet and icicles forming on your nose whenever you forget to wipe it.'

'True,' Avril agreed. 'But kids don't seem to feel the cold. I remember being indifferent to it when it meant playing in the snow.'

Miranda chuckled. 'I know what you mean. And Steve says we should be grateful, because apparently the weather's just the same on the Continent and that means no planes can take off, not ours nor the Luftwaffe. They're still calling this the phoney war, but if you ask me it's a blessing from heaven for us. It's giving us time to arm ourselves for what is to come. If the weather eases in February, which is only a few days off, then I bet there'll be floods and all sorts. Still, Steve says the weather has given us a breathing space and I reckon he's right.'

Both girls began to move towards the rear of the vehicle as the ting of the bell proclaimed their stop was approaching, and as they stepped from the comparative shelter into the teeth of the storm Miranda grabbed her friend's arm and spoke directly into her ear. 'You're out at the same time as me for once – because of the weather, I imagine – so why don't we do a flick? We might as well make the most of the opportunity because once it begins to warm up your shifts will return to normal. What do you say?'

'Good idea,' Avril said. 'Gary's taking me to the cinema at the weekend but he won't want to see a romance. He's more for action films – Errol Flynn, Douglas Fairbanks, that sort of thing.'

As she spoke they had turned into Russell Street and now they did their best to hurry along the frosted pavements, clattering up the metal stair at speed since they made a point of spreading salt on each step before they left for work in the morning.

Once in the kitchen Miranda unfolded the newspaper she had bought earlier, spread it out on the table and decided that they would enjoy seeing John Barrymore and Mary Astor in *Midnight*, because, as Avril remarked, it was bound to be a romance and she felt that they could both go for something really lovey-dovey. Avril had begun to take her coat off, then hesitated. 'It's not far to the cinema where *Midnight* is showing; we can walk there easily, so let's go out straight away. We can buy ourselves some sweets to suck during the performance, and if we hurry we won't miss more than a few minutes of the main feature.'

Miranda looked rather wistfully round the kitchen but agreed with her friend that the sooner they left the sooner they would be in the warmth of the cinema. Accordingly they clattered down the stairs once more and were shortly handing over their money and being shown to their seats by an elderly usherette. She was a friendly and garrulous woman and told them that they were bound to enjoy the film. She herself would be watching it tonight for about the tenth time, since it was the end of the week and tomorrow a new film would be showing. 'It's grand seeing all the stars for free,' she confided, flashing her torch along the almost empty rows of seats. 'Sit where you like, gairls, there ain't no one goin' to check tickets on such a night. Come far, have you?'

'Not far,' Miranda replied. She took off her damp coat and spread it out on the seat next to the one she had chosen. 'Aha, it's the newsreel, I see; we're earlier than we thought.'

'Thank goodness,' Avril muttered as the usherette moved away. 'I know Scousers are friendly but I were afraid she were goin' to plonk down in the seat next to mine, and talk all the way through the newsreel.'

Miranda chuckled, wriggling back into her seat and suddenly conscious of how tired she was. On the screen, pictures came and went. Men making battleships in a large factory up in Scotland somewhere, a warehouse blaze in the London suburbs caused by a carelessly dropped match, a number of Boy Scouts on their bicycles riding through the city streets as the new age messengers who would take the place of the members of the forces who had previously done such work.

Miranda could feel her eyelids beginning to droop as the commentator talked on. 'America may not have entered the war yet, but her citizens are working hard to show they are on our side; these women are making up food parcels for our troops . . .' The picture on the screen showed women in turbans and overalls at long benches, packing biscuits, chocolate and other foodstuffs into small brown boxes. Others were in factories, making aeroplane parts, whilst their sisters joined concert parties to raise money for their cousins across the sea.

Miranda tried to fight the desire to fall asleep and was jerked suddenly awake by Avril's voice. 'Gee whizz, ain't she just the prettiest thing you've ever seen?' Avril said. 'All that fantastic hair . . .' Miranda's eyes shot open. The screen was flickering, about to change, but she still managed to glimpse the woman to whom her friend had referred. Miranda rose in her seat like a rocket when you light the blue touch paper. She clutched Avril's arm so hard that her friend gave a protesting squeak. 'What's up, chuck?' she said.

But Miranda cut across her. 'It's my mother!' she shouted. 'Oh, won't somebody stop the film, wind it back? I was almost asleep, I just caught the merest glimpse . . . oh, Avril, did it give names, addresses, anything like that?'

But the newsreel had come to an end, the curtains swished across and their erstwhile friend came waddling slowly down the stairs at the back of the circle with a tray of sweets and ice creams round her neck. A few customers left their seats and, producing their money, went across to the usherette.

Avril, meanwhile, positively gawped at her friend. 'Wharron earth's got into you, Miranda?' she said plaintively. 'What do you mean, it's your mother? I thought you said she were dead . . . and anyway it couldn't possibly be your mam, because the feller talkin' was in America – well, I think he was – so what makes you think . . .'

Miranda gave a moan. 'Oh, Avril, don't you ever *listen*?' she demanded. 'Other people said my mother must be dead after it was discovered that the ship she had sailed on had been lost in a storm. But I never believed it, never, never, never! We were close, Arabella and I, so I was always sure that had she been drowned I would have known it in my bones and given up all hope. But I never did – give up hope, I mean – and now I'm certain sure that she's alive. Oh, how can I bear to sit through the main feature and the B film before I can see the newsreel again?' She had stood up when the newsreel was coming to a close but now she sat down with a thump and turned appealingly to Avril. 'Will you come with me to the manager's office to ask him to rerun the newsreel straight away? It's most awfully important that I have proof of Arabella's being alive, and of where she is at the moment. You say the women in the newsreel were Americans.

Well, the authorities would have to let me go to America if I explained. America's a neutral country, isn't it? Oh, surely they'll let me go on one of those ships that Steve told me about? They're taking airmen who want to become pilots over to the States so that they can be trained in a no war zone. If I swore I'd work my passage in some way . . .'

Avril cut across what she clearly regarded as her friend's ramblings. 'For God's sake, chuck, don't talk such rubbish!' she urged. 'Even if it was your mother you saw on the newsreel – and I don't think it was because I'd looked at you seconds earlier and you had your perishin' eyes shut – the authorities ain't likely to ship you halfway across the world on what would probably turn out to be a wild goose chase. And why do you want to go to her, anyway? If you're right and the woman on the screen really is your mam, then why hasn't she come home, or at least tried to get in touch? Look at you, straining at the leash to get to her, so why couldn't she have done the same? Dropped you a line, or even bought a passage and come back to Liverpool before the war started? What I mean is, I can't imagine any reason for her not contacting you and getting things straightened out. Can you?'

Miranda had tried not to think about the quarrel between herself and her mother for many months, but now it came into her mind as clearly as though it had happened yesterday. She felt her cheeks grow warm and tears rose to her eyes. 'Well, we did have an awful row the evening before she disappeared,' she admitted, and realised, with some surprise, that apart from Steve she had never mentioned the row to anyone. She had been too ashamed, because in her secret soul she had believed the quarrel might have been the cause of Arabella's disappearance. In fact her rage and blame-laying on that last evening might have been the straw which had broken the camel's back.

But Avril was shaking her head. 'No, no; it would have taken more than that to send her flying off to America,' she said. 'All mothers and daughters have barneys from time to time, but they don't go off without a word and never contact each other again. As for asking the manager to rewind the film, I wouldn't try it if I were you 'cos you'd be settin' yourself up for a dusty answer. I reckon if we just stay in our seats – hey up, the curtains are drawing back and the fire screen's rolled up – then you can see the newsreel through again. But if you really didn't see the bit about the American women giving concert parties to raise money for the war effort, then what makes you think one of them girls was your mam?'

Miranda hesitated. It sounded so daft to say that her mother's wonderful mass of curling primrose-coloured hair had been unmistakable, but now that Avril mentioned it she realised she had scarcely had time to focus on the woman's face before the picture was replaced with another. She knew that it would not do to admit this to her friend, however, and said briefly that she had recognised Arabella's glorious hair.

But now the usherette had reached the end of their row and was eyeing them curiously. Plainly she had seen Miranda leaping to her feet, probably heard the shouts as well. Miranda, blushing, opened her little purse and produced some coins. 'Two wafers, please,' she said humbly, 'and a packet of peanuts.'

It was snowing steadily by the time they left the cinema and both girls pulled their mufflers up over their mouths and linked arms as they hurried along the snow-covered pavements. It was impossible to exchange conversation under such conditions, but as soon as they were back in the flat with the kettle on the primus stove, Avril turned to her friend. 'Well? Are you satisfied now? I suppose you're still sure it was your mother and not just an extremely pretty blonde? Only if I'm honest, Miranda, that woman only looked about twenty, or thirty at the most.' She giggled. 'Unless gettin' away from you took twenty years off her age!'

Miranda sniffed. 'I shall ignore that remark,' she said loftily. 'My mother married at sixteen and had me at seventeen, or so she always claimed. But remember, the commentator said she was with a concert party, so she would have been wearing stage make-up. It can take years off you, can that.'

Avril shrugged. 'Have it your way, queen. Your mam is alive and well and living in America and I'm tellin' you straight that there's no way you're going to get there until the war's over. Even if America do decide to join in the war they won't let young women go to and fro across the Atlantic like they did in peacetime. Why don't you write? Only I'm not sure to whom.'

'That's why I want to go over myself,' Miranda said impatiently. 'As for why my mother hasn't written to me, I have a theory . . .'

Avril sighed. 'You can tell me all about it whilst I make the tea and cut some bread and butter. And you can get out them jam tarts I made yesterday. It was just our luck that they'd closed the café because of there bein' almost no customers, but we'll make the best of what we've got. Go on then, what's your theory?'

Miranda wondered how best to explain to Avril the sequence of events which had led her to believe that her mother must have lost her memory. Now that she came to think about it she realised that she had never told it from beginning to end, as though it was just a story. She knew she must have let fall bits and pieces to her flatmate, but had never told her the events in sequence. Now she really must do so if she was to gain Avril's belief. 'Well, I told you that she'd disappeared during the night,' she began. 'Next day everyone was very concerned – the scuffers as well – and at first they tried to find Arabella, tried very hard. There were advertisements in the press and notices down by the docks asking if anyone had seen her. But we got absolutely nowhere, and of course I couldn't stay in our beautiful house in Sycamore Avenue – I had no money for the rent for a start – so I was forced to move in with Aunt Vi and my cousin Beth. As the weeks passed I suppose folk forgot; then one night I was woken by somebody shaking my shoulder . . .'

Miranda told the whole story of her sleepwalking, and presently she finished off with Missie's revelation that she had seen a woman in a long white gown being dragged down towards the docks by two members of the crew of the ship which was later wrecked with the loss of all hands. When she finished she looked enquiringly at Avril, who whistled softly beneath her breath. 'Cor, that's a story and a half,' her friend said appreciatively. 'And do you mean that sleepwalkin' can be inherited, like blue eyes or freckles?' She gave a snort of

278

amusement. 'Pity you inherited sleepwalking and not long golden curls!'

'Shut up, you horrible girl,' Miranda said, unable to prevent herself from smiling. 'So you see, if I'm right and Arabella really was sleepwalking and was kidnapped by Captain Hogg and his merry men, then I should think it's quite possible that she has lost her memory. If she knew who she was, she'd know about me, and I'm sure she'd be desperate to get in touch. As you said, mothers and daughters may fight and disagree, but underneath there's a huge well of love. So I'm sure if Arabella could have written or even telephoned she would have done so. But if she's forgotten everything since the ship went down . . .'

'How dreadful it must have been, having to swim to the nearest land when she must have known there are sharks in tropical waters,' Avril said with feeling. 'She's a real heroine; no wonder you want to find her and claim her as your mother. But I'm tellin' you, queen, you won't do it until the war's over. Oh, you can write, probably put advertisements in American papers asking Arabella Lovage to get in touch, but if she's lost her memory . . .'

'If she's lost her memory the name Arabella Lovage will mean nothing to her, and I should add that she can't swim,' Miranda said gloomily. 'But I've got to try; what else can I do?'

'Tell me, queen, why did your mother insist on you calling her Arabella?' Avril asked.

'I don't know what that's got to do with it . . .' Miranda began, and then, meeting Avril's eyes, she capitulated. 'She didn't want people to know she had a daughter in her teens because when she auditioned for a part she would always tell them she was in her mid-twenties.' She saw the beginnings of a smirk on her friend's face and hastened to disabuse her. 'All right, all right, but as you've already said she doesn't look her age, and when you're auditioning for a part it's your looks they go on rather than the number of your years. Oh, Avril, I've tried and tried to put my mother's plight out of my mind, not to keep harping on about it, but I believe I'm getting somewhere at last!'

Avril agreed that knowing that Arabella was alive and living in America was a tremendous step forward. 'But you've been patient for so long that by now being patient must be second nature to you, so don't try to rush things, but let life take its course,' she added. 'Have you finished your bread and butter? If so, we'll start on the jam tarts.'

Miranda took a tart, but did not bite into it. Suddenly she knew that she wanted desperately to speak to Steve, to tell him all about the newsreel and how she was certain, now, that her mother was still alive. She glanced at the clock on the mantelpiece, which read ten o'clock; would Steve be in bed? Would there be anybody still awake to answer the telephone in the Mess? She was telling herself that she would simply have to wait until the following day to call Steve when her hand, seemingly of its own accord, replaced the jam tart on her plate even as she got to her feet. She went across the kitchen, took her thick coat, headscarf and muffler down from their hook and began to put them on. From behind her she heard Avril's chair squeak as her friend pushed it back, but she did not even look round.

Avril's voice sounded almost frightened when she

spoke. 'Miranda? Wharron earth are you doin'? Don't you go out like your mam did and get kidnapped by a beastly Nazi. It's bedtime – oh, damn it, if you must walk I suppose I'll have to go with you.'

Miranda, already at the door, turned and smiled at her friend. 'Don't be so daft. I'm just goin' down to the box on the corner to give Steve a ring, tell him about the newsreel. Once I've told him I'll come straight back, so I shan't be more than ten or fifteen minutes at the most. And you aren't to even think about coming with me, Avril, because I'm not a child and I'm not sleepwalking either. Just stay there and watch the clock.' As she spoke she was opening the kitchen door, then glanced over her shoulder at the other girl. 'It's all right, the snow's stopped. I've got my torch, though I shan't need it. See you later.' With that she closed the door upon Avril's half-hearted objections, clattered down the stair and ran all the way to the telephone box. Putting her money into the slot when the operator demanded it, she thought ruefully that she was being daft. Steve would have been in bed ages ago and she could not possibly ask for him to be told of her call because that would mean disturbing everyone else in his hut. Yet she had a strong feeling – you could call it a conviction almost – that he had not yet gone to bed, that in some mysterious way they were on the same wavelength, despite the distance which separated them, and when it was he who picked up the receiver she was not even surprised, particularly when she did not even have to give her name, because Steve said at once: 'Miranda? What's happened? I knew it must be you, ringin' at this ungodly hour, so what's new?'

'Oh, Steve, you are wonderful, and I'm sorry to ring

so late,' Miranda gabbled. 'Only I had to tell you, because I knew you'd understand. Avril and I went to the cinema this evening . . .'

At the end of the recital there was the shortest of pauses and then Steve's voice, warm and reassuring, came over the wire. 'Don't worry about disturbing me; the chaps and I have been talking and we are all still up. It's fantastic news that Arabella is still alive, and I'm sure you'll manage to get in touch with her somehow. And you can stop feeling guilty, queen, now that you know she's all right.'

Miranda hissed in a breath; how had he known that it had been guilt over their quarrel which had made her so desperately eager to prove that Arabella was still alive? She had never admitted to a soul that the quarrel, even if it had only driven her mother to take that solitary walk, might have been Arabella's downfall. And now, having told Steve and received his understanding, she was aware that she felt as if a great weight had been lifted from her shoulders. Avril had doubted her, but Steve had accepted every word of her story. Blissfully, Miranda realised that though she still meant to try to contact her mother it was no longer as essential to her happiness as it had once been. In the very nature of things she and Arabella would, by now, have begun to take their separate paths. Of course she meant to do everything she could to trace Arabella, but even if she failed she would know at least that Arabella lived, and, what's more, lived happily. But now Steve's voice spoke urgently in her ear. 'Miranda? I was going to send you a telegram asking you to ring me, but I might have known you'd sense my urge to talk and ring me anyway. I've got some news of my own which, as it happens, will affect you. In a week's time I'm being shipped along with a great many other fellers to America, where I'll be trained as aircrew; if I'm good enough, as a fighter pilot.'

For a moment, Miranda could not even speak. She felt as if all the air had been drained out of the telephone booth, leaving her gasping like a landed fish. But Steve's voice in her ear, sharp with anxiety, brought her back to life. 'Miranda, where have you gone? Have you cut the connection? I was just telling you . . .'

Miranda and the operator spoke almost simultaneously. 'Caller, your time is up.'

And Miranda's voice, small with shock and dismay: 'Oh, but Steve, you can't go. I can't lose everyone I care about . . .'

Steve's voice echoed in her ear, sounding strangely unlike himself. 'Can't change what's already happened . . .' he was beginning when there was a decisive click and the operator said crisply: 'Replace your receiver please, caller. Others are waiting for this line.'

Very, very slowly, Miranda put her receiver back on its rest, automatically pressed button B although she knew she had used all the money the operator had required, then stumbled out of the box, apologising to the young man in naval uniform who had obviously been waiting for her to finish her call. He moved to pass her, then must have noticed her pallor because he caught her arm. 'You awright, miss?' he asked. 'Not bad news, I hope. You've gone that white . . .'

Miranda conjured up what she guessed must be a rather wan smile. 'No, not bad news. But my boyfriend is being sent to America,' she said, and was about to add

283

the information that he was going to learn how to fly when she remembered the government posters and gave the young naval officer a watery smile. 'I'm fine, honest to God I am. It was just the shock. But thanks for your concern.'

''Sawright, gairl,' the young man said easily. 'Mind how you go.'

Miranda heard the door of the box click and stood for a moment, replacing her muffler, pulling on her gloves and doing up the top button of her coat, whilst the young man consulted a small notebook, spoke into the receiver and began to put pennies in the slot with a great clatter. Then she moved away when she saw his mouth move and knew he was in contact with the operator. No use hanging about whilst he got his call. Steve would probably be on his way to bed by now, and if the operator recognised her voice she might well refuse to put another call through; some operators were like that, thought themselves in charge of the whole telephone system.

Miranda was at the foot of the metal stair when the door above opened and Avril looked anxiously out, though the anxiety disappeared as Miranda began to climb. 'Did you get through, queen?' she asked. 'Poor old Steve, was he tucked up in his nice little bunk? I bet he cursed you, especially if whoever answered the phone had to wake the whole hut.'

Miranda trudged up the remainder of the stairs and was glad to enter the warmth of the kitchen and shut the door behind her. 'He wasn't even in bed, but he had some news of his own,' she said wearily. She took off her outdoor clothing and turned to Avril, trying to manufacture a cheerful smile and knowing that she failed. 'In fact, he was going to send me a telegram because next week he's being sent to America with a batch of other men, who'll all learn to fly fighter planes.' She turned to Avril and felt the first tears rise in her eyes to the accompaniment of a violent sob. 'Oh, Avril, it's true what I said when he first joined the air force; sooner or later, everyone leaves me. And now Steve's going so far away that there won't even be telephone calls, and letters which get sent from abroad are chopped to bits by the censor, if they arrive at all, which a lot of them don't. Oh, and convoys get attacked all the time; he could be drowned, or bombed . . . I can't bear it!'

Avril tutted. 'These things happen in wartime, to everyone, not just you, so stop feelin' so perishin' sorry for yourself,' she said crossly. 'When Steve was at your beck and call you kept denying that he was your boyfriend, but now he's going away you talk as if he were your only love. Be consistent, for Gawd's sake, you silly little Lovage. Pull yourself together!'

Miranda fished a handkerchief out from her sleeve, blew her nose resoundingly and then wiped her eyes with the backs of her hands. She gave another enormous sniff and a watery giggle, then turned a calm face towards her friend. 'First I find my mother isn't dead and am over the moon, then I find my best friend – and he's still my best friend and nothing more – is being sent half a world away. Next thing I know you'll be snatched up and sent off on a mysterious mission to Antarctica or somewhere and I'll lose you as well.'

Avril sniffed. 'And of course they'll choose me since I

speak Antarctic like a native,' she said sarcastically. She handed Miranda her filled hot water bottle, which her friend immediately cuddled gratefully. 'And now shall we go to bed before I drop in my tracks? If I'm tired – and I am – you must be absolutely jiggered.'

'True,' Miranda admitted. 'But I wonder why Steve isn't getting embarkation leave, like Julian? I remember that Julian came round and took you out for a meal before he took ship for Rhodesia. So why not Steve?'

'Can't you guess? Whilst the awful weather continues all flights are grounded, and even the ships are mainly in port, here *and* on the other side of the Channel. That means your precious Steve should have a safer crossing than if he waited for a few weeks. Be grateful, girl.'

'I *am*,' Miranda said. 'Grateful, I mean. And you're a real pal, Avril, to take the worry off my mind.'

Later, snuggling down in bed, with her hot water bottle strategically positioned to de-ice her freezing toes, she began to think about her day and realised that, though she knew she would miss Steve horribly, the warm glow which she had felt ever since seeing her mother on the silver screen had not dissipated. In fact with every moment that passed it felt stronger, and she realised that her chief feeling was a very odd one indeed. Because her mother was alive she, Miranda, would be able one day to apologise to her for all the horrid things she'd said during the course of that long ago quarrel. And of course the fact that Steve might be quite near Arabella merely made the feeling even better. If I have to wait until the war is over I shan't mind so much now, she told herself, pulling the blankets up until only her eyes were clear of them. I'll be able to give Steve money from my savings to pay for advertising in American newspapers – and he saw Betty Prince's picture, which was quite a good likeness. Yes, I'm sure Steve will run her to earth if anyone can.

Chapter Ten

1940

Miranda and Avril joined the queue for the tram, shivering and stamping their feet, for it was a freezing cold December day. Miranda, however, had more important things than the weather on her mind: namely, getting to Lime Street Station in time to meet Steve's train, for he was coming home at last, after almost a year away.

'Excited, queen?' Avril's voice was indulgent. 'I know you won't let me call Steve your feller, but you've been . . . oh, I don't know, sort of lit up . . . ever since he arrived in England.'

That had been a week earlier, a week in which he had been too busy to telephone, for on arriving from the States he had been immediately posted to somewhere called Church Stretton, where they were taking pilots who had flown bombers – Wellingtons mostly – to retrain on to Lancasters, and had not been allowed off the airfield until he had been thoroughly debriefed, whatever that might mean.

'Brrr,' Miranda said. 'It's perishing brass monkey weather again. Thank you for saying you'd come to the station with me – it'll be much nicer than waiting on my own, though I'm sure that if any of the Mickleboroughs are at home they'll be on the platform as well!'

Avril laughed. 'Well, you said his mam, Kenny and

the baby were coming home for Christmas, so if they're back by now I'm sure they'll be there. And his gran is still living in Jamaica Close, isn't she? So I take it she'll be feeding Steve whether or not his mam is here.'

Miranda shrugged. 'Who can tell? What with no trains ever arriving on time and being so crowded with members of the forces that civilians scarcely ever get a seat, you can't say for certain where anyone will be at any given time. Tell you what, if Steve's mam isn't on the platform then we might as well buy fish and chips when he arrives and take him back to the flat. He can go on to his mother's place later.'

The tram drew up beside them and the two girls got in. The long narrow bench seats were already full but the girls were used to strap hanging and continued their conversation as the tram rattled on. 'I believe the weather in Texas is really warm,' Miranda said with a shiver. 'Poor Steve, having to get used to our dear old English climate all over again! Of course I told him how lovely the weather was in the summer but there was so much I couldn't mention that I think my letters became rather stilted. And his letters were rather stilted too, because he had to admit he'd had no luck at all in finding my mother.'

'Well, you know he tried; he sent you copies of the advertisements he'd put in the papers,' Avril reminded her friend. 'And if you're talking about things like the fall of France and the evac—'

'Shurrup, you moron; loose lips sink ships,' Miranda reminded her. 'But yes, the American papers will have had all the major war news in every detail. No, what I meant was the things that had happened here – the raids last month, for instance. Liverpool will seem like a foreign city compared to the one Steve knew.'

The tram skidded to a stop on the icy rails and Avril gave a squawk as the man next to her stumbled, his elbows swinging round to catch her on her upper arm. 'Sorry, chuck,' he said, not sounding sorry at all. 'But it weren't my fault, the bleedin' tram driver needs a lesson in brakin', if you ask me. You gettin' off here? It's the station.'

'Oh, crumbs, so it is,' Avril gasped. 'You can't see a thing in the perishin' blackout, and it don't do to miss your stop with the pavements so slippery an' all.' She jerked on Miranda's arm. 'Come on, queen, gerra move on. Chances are you'll still be waitin' in an hour or two, but on the other hand the train really might be on time for once.'

The girls descended from the tram, crossed the pavement and dived into the concourse. As usual it was crowded, but Avril collared a passing porter and was told that the cross-country train for which they waited was a mere forty minutes late. 'Have yourself a cup of tea and a wad, and by the time you've queued for it and ate it, your feller will have arrived,' he said jovially.

Avril sniffed. 'I hope my feller is safely tucked up in his factory startin' the night shift,' she said, to the porter's retreating back. 'Why does everyone assume that if you're meetin' a train it must have some man on it what you're busy pursuin'?' She turned to Miranda. 'Look, love, if it's forty minutes behind time now, the chances are it'll be an hour and forty minutes by the time it gets here. There's no point in me hangin' around waitin' that long for a feller what's your concern and not mine. I'll go back to the flat, light the fire and get the place warmed through, and see if I can make some sort of meal for Steve, just in case his train don't get in till after the chippies close. Shall I make up the bed in the living room in case he wants to stay over? It'd be no trouble.'

Miranda pondered for a moment, then shook her head. 'No, don't bother. As you say, it only takes a couple of minutes. What have we got in the pantry if the fish and chips shops are all closed?'

The girls took it in turns to cook their main meal of the day, which was generally eaten at around seven o'clock in the evening, and since it was Avril's week she had done the marketing, though rationing made shopping a chore. Standing on the concourse with people all around them Avril ticked the contents of the pantry off on her fingers. 'Some sausage meat, a big onion, a few carrots and enough flour and marge to make a pastry case,' she announced. 'Will that do, chuck?' When Miranda nodded, she said, 'Righty ho; see you later.'

Glumly, Miranda headed for the refreshment room. As she went she glanced around her; how good it would be to see some member of the Mickleborough family or a friend from school, but all the faces seemed strange. Sighing, she joined the queue. At least if you bought a cup of tea you might be able to sit down whilst you drank it!

By the time Steve erupted from an overcrowded carriage it was well past ten o'clock. Miranda did not recognise him at first, seeing merely the only tanned face under an RAF cap, a tan which made his teeth look astonishingly white. He must have seen her at once, though, because she was still looking wildly around her when she felt herself seized and hugged. 'Oh, you good girl; how I love you!' Steve's voice said in her ear. 'My poor darling, you must have been here for hours, because in my telegram I said my train would be arriving at seven o'clock, not twenty past ten. Now why don't you put your arms round my neck so that you can give me a welcome home kiss? And don't start talkin' nonsense about bezzies because I'm as good as a Yank, I am, and we expect kisses and hugs from every girl we see.'

Miranda obediently put her arms round his neck, but dropped her face to snuggle against his tunic. 'I feel stupid,' she mumbled. 'You've changed. Goodness me, Steve, you've grown! You're actually taller than when you went away.'

'And broader, though it's mainly across the shoulders,' Steve said complacently. 'Oh, it's so grand to see you, Miranda. I've missed you something awful.' He caught hold of her hand as she released his neck, swung it up to his face and kissed the palm, and this made her give a little gurgle of shocked astonishment, which made Steve laugh. 'You daft kid,' he said affectionately. 'And my mam's comin' home for Christmas despite my tellin' her I'd rather she didn't. The Luftwaffe are bound to get Liverpool's measure sooner or later, and when they do, believe me, honey, they'll smash the place to smithereens. Oh, I know Churchill says we won the Battle of Britain, that two German planes were downed to every one the Royal Air Force lost, but the truth of the matter is we're still building up our defences and retraining the BEF, so I'd rather my mother and the kids were tucked away safely in Wales.'

He bent and picked up his kitbag, which he had tossed aside in order to have both arms free for Miranda, and began to lead her out of the station. 'Where am I spendin' the night?' he asked. 'I'm quite happy to share your bed, pretty lady, if that's the only accommodation available. As you know, my gran stayed in Jamaica Close when Mam and the kids were evacuated, and she's there still, but she's awful old and gets confused. A neighbour does her marketing, lights her fire and cooks her food, though Gran bustles about and helps a lot, or so she claims. But even if she was told that today was red letter day, she'll probably have forgotten by now and won't have so much as a sardine in the pantry to keep my strength up. So how about if I come back to Russell Street? Any chance of a bite? And I don't necessarily mean food either.'

'You've got awfully cheeky, Steve, since you've been away,' Miranda said reprovingly. 'Of course you're very welcome to come round to Russell Street for a meal, but no biting, if you please. I had meant to buy fish and chips but I reckon all the chippies will be closed by now. However, I think Avril means to make a sausage turnover and cook some carrots and that to go with it. Then there's the remains of a junket Avril and I had for tea, standing on the slate shelf in the pantry. What do you say to finishing that? I suppose you'll have to spend the night, because the trams will have stopped running by the time we've heard each other's news.'

Steve agreed eagerly that this was a great idea, and when they reached the flat and found Avril fast asleep in bed, but the sausage turnover still warm from the oven, he took off his greatcoat, cap and scarf and settled down eagerly to attack the plate of food Miranda placed in front of him. Whilst he ate she read him Missie's latest letter, which was almost equally divided between pleasure at being in her own home again and apprehension for her friends across the seas. After that, she asked about America, and tried not to feel jealous when Steve described the parties, dances, barbecues and picnics which had been arranged by local girls for the entertainment of their British guests. She told herself firmly that to feel jealous was absurd because Steve was not her boyfriend, but presently, when he had eaten and drunk everything Avril had provided, they settled on the couch for a nice cosy cuddling session whilst they talked into the night, and told each other of the more exciting events which they had not been able to share in letters.

Miranda was in the middle of a description of a dog fight she had watched between a Messerschmitt and a Spitfire when something in her companion's breathing made her stop speaking and stare into the deeply tanned face so near to her own. And not only deeply tanned, but deeply asleep. Miranda smiled and thought about what he'd said that night. He'd told her he loved her and she felt confused. Did she really think of him as a brother? Oh, she was too tired to think about it now. She closed her own eyes and wondered how much wearier poor Steve must be! He had come all the way from Texas in a troop-carrying plane, not renowned for its comfort. Then he had had a hectic debriefing session and an introduction to the Lancaster aeroplane. After that he was given a seven day pass and had undergone the hell of a cross-country journey in wartime. Meeting her must have been quite as much of a trial for him as it was for her, because he must have been as conscious as she of the changes that had taken place during their year apart. And now, well fed and warm, it had been the most natural thing in the world for him to fall asleep. But of course it would never do. They had not made up the sofa into a bed so the bedcovers were still rolled up beneath it, and soon enough the fire would go out, leaving the room as cold as the icy courtyard below. Clearly, it behoved her to wake him up and either set him on his way to Jamaica Close or get him to give her a hand to make up a bed on the sofa. Thinking of this, she realised that she was already feeling somewhat chilly and, with infinite care, reached under the sofa and dragged out a couple of blankets. She threw them over Steve, causing him to give a sleepy mutter, and then pulled them over herself. The sofa cushions would make a lovely pillow, but of course she could not actually lie on the sofa the way Steve would, once it was converted into a bed. Miranda wriggled into a more comfortable position and found rather to her surprise that her head fitted most comfortably into the hollow of Steve's shoulder. Anyone would think we'd been married for years, she told herself sleepily. For years and years and years and years . . . and Miranda was asleep.

Steve awoke. For a moment he lay perfectly still, thoroughly puzzled. Over the past ten days or so he had woken up in so many different places that he could scarcely count them, but this waking was different from all the rest. He shifted a fraction, forced himself to open his heavy lids and looked around him. It was still dark though he could see light coming through a gap of some sort; not very much light, and not the golden sunshine to which he had become accustomed in Texas. This was a faint bluish light, as though the moon was shining directly on the outside of what he now realised must be a blackout blind. He frowned; if he was in his hut at Church Stretton then the window had got up and moved during the night, which seemed unlikely. So if he was not in his hut, where the devil was he? He remembered the long cold journey in the train and the ecstatic moment when he had descended on to the platform at Lime Street Station, and had opened his arms to Miranda . . .

Miranda! At the mere recollection of her name, memory came flooding back. They had been too late to buy fish and chips but had returned to the flat in Russell Street and found a delicious supper which Avril had cooked for him. Avril had already been in bed and asleep, so he and Miranda had moved into the living room, intending to have a goodnight cuddle . . .

Cuddle! With the word, his arms tightened around Miranda's warm body, curled up against his chest. Guiltily he realised that the two of them must have been so tired that they had fallen asleep, and here it was, early morning, and they were still cuddled up on the sofa. Steve could not help grinning to himself. In future he would be able to claim that he and his girl had slept together, and at the very thought he felt pleasure and guilt in equal quantities assail him. She would be furious, of course, if he teased her by telling Avril that they had spent the night together, even though he would explain that it had been an accident, that sheer weariness had caused them to fall asleep. At the thought he dropped a light kiss on the side of Miranda's face, thinking he would tell her that, as in all the best fairy stories, his kiss had wakened her, but in fact he was unable to do so since Miranda slumbered on.

Steve had half risen on his elbow but now with infinite care he lay down against the sofa cushions and let his mind go back to the very first time he had seen Miranda. She had been standing in Jamaica Close staring up at the great twenty-foot wall whilst her lips moved soundlessly. He had thought she looked as though she was reciting some magical rhyme which would cause a door to open in the wall, so that she might go through. Steve remembered with shame that he had jeered at the scrawny kid with her topping of carrot-coloured hair, had teased her by pretending she was just a dog, but a dog who had managed to slip its leash. Then they had talked about their parents and he had seen the wistful resignation in her large hazel eyes and had offered her friendship, an offer she had grabbed with real enthusiasm. There were no boys in Jamaica Close around his age so palling up with the new kid was sensible, and he very soon realised that she had spunk, plenty of it. Despite the fact that she was younger than he they got on very well, and it was not long before he was proud to consider her his bezzie. In fact, he thought now, with the soft sweet-smelling length of her in his arms, he had fallen in love with her long ago without actually realising that his emotions had changed and deepened.

Her introduction to Jamaica House had been intended as a test but all it had really proved was that she was a lot braver than he, and from the moment that the two of them had begun to help Missie he had known that being bezzies would never be enough. She might not have known it then – might not know it now – but she was his girl and always would be.

The only trouble was that she did not seem to realise that he had got past mere friendship and was floundering in a sea of love which she refused to let him show. He had envied the Grimshaws – Julian must have looked so suave and handsome in the uniform of a flying officer – but Julian was in Africa, training other men to fly fighter aircraft, whilst he, at long last, was on the spot. And he intended to make the most of it. Only the elderly partners and the two old biddies Miranda had told him about were left in Mr Grimshaw's office, which meant that at least there was little fear of her becoming emotionally involved with a fellow worker. But he knew she occasionally saw Gerald, and the previous evening he had been dismayed when he saw pink colour flood her cheeks at the mention of his name, and her eyes, which had been staring straight into his, suddenly veil themselves in their long pale lashes. He had given a sheepish grin. 'I think Gerald might have his eye on you,' he said frankly. 'If only you'd let me buy you an engagement ring – just a tiny one – then I'd know he wasn't a threat.'

'Oh, Steve, what a fool you are! I like both of you, but in different ways. You've been like a brother to me.'

Infuriated, Steve had got to his feet, crossed the room in a couple of strides and plucked Miranda out of her chair as though she weighed no more than a kitten. 'I am *not* your brother, for which I thank God devoutly,' he had said crossly. 'I fell in love with you when you were a scrawny little stick of a kid climbing the trees in the Jamaica House garden and throwing the fruit down to me, and I'm in love with you still, so put that in your pipe and smoke it.'

He had waited for an indignant reply, and had been pleasantly surprised when Miranda had flung an arm round his neck, pulled his face down to her level and kissed first his cheek and then the side of his mouth, though she had moved back before he could take full advantage of her softened mood. 'Look, Steve, I'm not very old and neither are you. And Gerald is a lot of fun to be with . . .'

Steve had sighed. He had been standing with her in his arms, but then he sat her down again and took his own place at the table once more. 'All right, all right, I'm jumping the gun, but I just want you to know that you can't go off and get yourself tied up to any Tom, Dick or Harry because you're mine; get it?'

Miranda had pulled a face. 'I don't belong to anyone but myself,' she said firmly. 'And don't worry, no Tom, Dick or Harry – or Gerald or Julian for that matter – is going to want to sweep me off my feet. And now let's eat up so that we can both get to bed. I see the kettle's boiling so I'll make us both a hot water bottle as soon as I've finished my supper.'

'If you go pouring boiling water into a rubber bag you're liable to get an unpleasant shock in the middle of the night,' Steve had warned her. 'You'll wake up, thinking you've peed the bed, not realising . . .'

'Don't be so rude. I've been making hot water bottles for years and always pour cold in first,' Miranda had said reprovingly. 'And now you can stop going on about poor Gerald and tell me more about Texas.'

Now, Steve stroked Miranda's cheek, looking forward to the moment when she awoke and found herself in his arms, but though she murmured she still did not wake and Steve's thoughts returned to the past. *Why* did he love Miranda so desperately? He had to admit, though no longer quite so scrawny and with her carroty hair darkened to auburn, she was still no beauty. She had a pointy chin, a straight little nose and a generous mouth, whilst her big greenish-hazel eyes seemed almost too large for her small heart-shaped face. Steve could think of a dozen girls, many of whom he had taken around whilst in Texas, who were twice as pretty and half a dozen times as willing as Miranda Lovage. But she had, for him, an attraction which could not be put into words, and he supposed that Gerald and perhaps many other men were also aware of her charms. The thought made him jerk back on to his elbow. He was home in England now and could arrange for her to visit his airfield once he got a definite posting; then he would persuade her to start thinking seriously about marriage.

As though she had read his thoughts, Miranda gave a soft moan and sat up. She stared around her, eyes dilating. 'Where the devil am I?' she said in a bewildered voice. 'Oh my goodness, what's the time? Avril, have I missed the alarm? Oh my goodness!'

As she spoke she heaved herself clear of the blankets and wrenched herself out of Steve's embrace with such force that they both descended to the floor with a crash, Steve giggling helplessly and Miranda scolding. 'Oh, Steve, I must have fallen asleep . . . I was so tired, you wouldn't believe . . . oh, goodness, it's morning and it was my turn to make the breakfast.' She turned on him where he lay on the floor, still laughing, and punched him in the stomach. 'You beast, Steve Mickleborough, how dare you let me fall asleep! Oh, and we were both wearing all our clothes . . .'

'Not all of them; I took my tunic off so I was in shirt-sleeves, but I'm afraid you're right and my kecks are pretty crumpled,' Steve said ruefully. 'But I was about to wake you 'cos I hear sounds of movement coming from your kitchen. You'll want to wash and dress and so on in your own bedroom, whilst I'll have to make do with the kitchen sink.' He grinned at her. 'Do you realise what this means? We've spent the night together and folk will think that I must do the decent thing and marry you! What do you say?'

Miranda, trying to comb her hair with her fingers for it had got considerably tangled in the night, was beginning to tell Steve that if he breathed a word regarding where he had spent the night she would excommunicate him, when the door to the living room burst open. Avril stood there, round-eyed. 'Wharron earth . . .' she was beginning when Miranda, choking back a laugh, interrupted.

'Oh, Avril, can't you guess? We came through here to make up the couch as a bed for Steve. Only we both went and fell asleep and we've only just woken up.' She stood up, stretched and yawned. 'Thank the Lord Mr Grimshaw gave me the day off because Steve was coming home! But now we'd better get a move on because Steve will want to go back to Jamaica Close to see whether his mam really means to come for Christmas, and I intend to go with him.' As she spoke she had been tidying away the blankets, and Steve, scrambling to his feet, went to the window, pulled back the curtains and wound up the blackout blind, then turned to Avril.

'Much though I hate to admit it, nothing of an interesting nature occurred all night because we were so perishin' exhausted,' he said, grinning. 'But if I may have a borrow of your sofa again tonight I can promise you I'll stay awake if I have to prop up my eyelids wi' matchsticks.'

He was relieved when Avril laughed, came over and gave him a shove. 'Men!' she said scornfully. 'You're all talk and trousers, you. I know me pal better'n you ever did and she ain't the sort to give a feller what he wants just because she's knowed him years.' She looked at Miranda. 'It's perishin' cold still but I've put the kettle on for tea and poured hot water into the big enamel jug. So if you take that to your room you can have a wash and change. You can't wear that skirt and blouse; they look as though you've slept in 'em.' She turned her attention back to Steve. 'As for you, I'll go back to my room while you make yourself respectable. We've an electric iron and an ironing board what we got off Paddy's Market, so if you want to give your kecks a quick press you can do it whilst Miranda and meself check that our glad rags are in good repair.' She gave him a wicked grin. 'I take it you're going to invite us both out for some grub, lunchtime.' She pulled a pious face, though her eyes were still twinkling. 'You could call it buyin' me silence, or a spot of blackmail, whichever you prefer. If you treat me right I'll keep me gob shut.'

Steve sighed theatrically, but said he was very willing to mug them a meal at noon and arranged to meet outside Lewis's, though he told Avril he meant to go to Jamaica Close as soon as he'd had some breakfast. 'I think Mam's due to come back tomorrow, but I know Dad's written to her absolutely forbidding her to bring Kenny and the little 'un into danger, even for the sake of having a family

Christmas,' he explained. 'It ain't as though you can rely on the Luftwaffe to just drop the odd bomb whilst they're concentrating on wiping poor old London off the map. Any day now they could turn their attention to the next largest port in the country and begin to hand out the sort of punishment the Londoners have been facing. But you know women; once they get an idea into their heads it's powerful difficult to get it out again, and . . .'

'Shut up!' both girls screamed in unison, Miranda adding: 'Your mam's really sensible and wouldn't bring the little 'uns into danger. So shut up and give yourself a good wash whilst I do the same, then we can have some porridge and toast and start our day on a full stomach.'

Although she would never have admitted it Miranda had found waking up in Steve's arms strangely exciting, and she had been aware of a slight sense of disappointment when he had not tried to take advantage of the situation. In fact she felt quite peeved. He said he loved her, which presumably meant he wanted her, yet there she had been, in his arms and at his mercy so to speak, and he had not tried to cajole her in any way, save to suggest teasingly that, having spent the night with him, she might want to marry him, thus regularising the situation. However, she supposed that it was really a sign of Steve's respect and decided she should be grateful. She had heard various stories from girls in the factory about what happened when you 'gave your all', and it sounded rude, embarrassing, and even rather painful. Definitely not the sort of thing which one did casually, especially when one knew that the door to the room in which one lay might suddenly burst open to reveal the shocked face of one's best friend.

Having convinced herself that all was well Miranda got on with the task in hand. Only the previous week she had treated herself to a thick and far from new seaman's jersey in navy blue wool, for it was already obvious that they were going to be in for another very cold winter. The jersey had been shrunken, with both elbows out and holes in various strategic spots, but Avril had been taught the art of darning and sewing whilst at the children's home and had offered to put it right. Not one hole remained, and Miranda had embellished the garment by embroidering lazy daisies round the crew neck. She put it on now with a thick woollen skirt, also in navy, and went through to the kitchen where Avril was already dishing up the porridge, and Steve, fully dressed, was turning away from the sink. He grinned at her. 'Hello again, queen. It's perishin' cold out,' he greeted her. 'I went down to the privy for the usual purpose and there's a big puddle frozen solid right at the bottom of the stair, so if you need to go you want to watch out.'

'I'm all right, thanks,' Miranda said, having shot down to the privy before going to her bedroom to change her rumpled clothing. 'Gosh, the porridge smells good; oh, and toast as well.' She grinned at Avril. 'Good job bread isn't rationed.'

The three sat down to their meal and presently, the girls clad in their thick coats and hats, they left the flat, descended the stairs and decided to go their separate ways, since Avril, who was not on shift till the following evening, still had a couple of presents to buy and Miranda wanted to go back to Jamaica Close with Steve. Her main reason for this was to learn whether Mrs Mickleborough had decided against returning to the city for Christmas. If she had, Miranda intended to ask Steve and his gran back to the flat for the day itself, but of course she would not do so should Mrs Mickleborough and the little ones be coming home. There simply would not be sufficient room in the flat for five extra people, and though Miranda had not seen Kenny since the previous September she remembered him as being lively and demanding, to say the least, whilst Flora was surely toddling about under her own steam by now.

So when they reached the main road Avril went off towards the city centre, whilst Steve and Miranda caught a tram and were presently knocking on the door of Number Two Jamaica Close. They heard Gran's slippered feet shuffling along the front hall, and presently the old lady was exclaiming with delight and ushering them into the kitchen, where a bright fire burned in the range and the kettle was hopping on the hob. 'Eh, it's grand to see thee, lad, real grand,' Granny Granger said. She beamed at Miranda. 'And you've brought your young lady along! Eh, I'm honoured! Now sit down the pair of you and you shall have tea and a bit of me seed cake, 'cos it's mortal cold out there.' She chuckled richly. 'When I visited the privy earlier me bum near on froze to the seat; imagine that!' Her visitors laughed, but as soon as they were settled with tea and cake the question which Miranda guessed was uppermost in Steve's mind was voiced. Gran, however, shook her head. 'I dunno whether they'll take the chance, but if her good man's letter reaches her in time I reckon she'll give up the idea. If you ask me she'd be downright foolish to take the risk. It ain't as if she were unhappy in that little Welsh village, 'cos she ain't. Her letters is full of country talk, and she says after the war's over she means to try for a country cottage. I dunno as she'll ever get one, 'cos her hubby has to be near his work, but it's good that she's goin' to try. More toast? Another cup?'

Steve accepted, but Miranda, shaking her head, got to her feet. 'Thanks, Mrs Granger, but I believe I ought to visit my aunt and my cousin Beth. I've not been round since war broke out – I've been too busy – but now I'm actually in the neighbourhood I really should say hello. And I've got a little present for Beth, and one for my aunt, so if you don't mind I'll just nip up the road.'

Granny Granger nodded her understanding. Steve reminded Miranda to give a knock on the door when she was ready to leave, and then he and the old lady settled down to talk of aunts and cousins he had not seen for many months, whilst Miranda walked along to her aunt's house and knocked on the door, aware of a tiny shudder of distaste at the memory of her time spent living here under her aunt's despotic rule.

When the door was answered, however, her aunt's grim mouth softened a little, though she said accusingly: 'Slummin', ain't you?'

'Don't be nasty or you shan't have your Christmas present,' Miranda said promptly. 'I haven't come all this way to be insulted, you know.'

Her aunt sniffed. 'You haven't come all this way very often,' she said, but in a milder tone. 'If you remember, young lady, you left without givin' us your new address, so you're lucky to get any sort of present off of Beth and meself. However, bein' the souls of generosity, we've bought you a little somethin' in the hope that you might deign to come round, bein' as it's the season of goodwill and all that.'

'I'm sorry, Aunt Vi, but we're so short-staffed at the office now that it's all I can do to get my messages and have a sleep,' Miranda explained. 'Well, I reckon you must understand, because a few weeks ago I met Beth in St John's fish market, and she told me she was working in a factory making parachutes, so I guess her time off is pretty limited too. And I did tell her I lived in a flat over a bicycle shop on Russell Street; didn't she pass the news on to you?'

Her aunt sniffed again but stood aside, beckoning her niece to enter. 'I dunno as she might have done,' she admitted grudgingly. 'Fact is, Miranda, that she ain't here all that often; she kips down with a pal when she's on a late shift so she's only under my roof, oh, one week in four, I suppose.' She pulled her mouth down at the corners. 'Truth to tell, I gets lonely, so if you're ever lookin' for a place to lie your head there's a spare bed here you'd be welcome to use.'

Miranda had to bite her lip or she might have reminded her aunt of the way she had been treated when she had lived in Jamaica Close, might also have added that if the factory making parachutes was too far from Jamaica Close, her own place of work was even farther. Instead she said: 'Thanks, Aunt, I'll remember your – your kind offer.' Then she rooted around in her pocket and produced the presents, both well wrapped. 'Not to be opened until Christmas Day; yours is the one in red paper and Beth's is in the green,' she said, with a gaiety she was far from feeling. One glance round the dirty neglected kitchen and one sniff of the smell of stale food and rotting vegetables was enough to convince her that her aunt had not changed. She was still lazy, greedy and a bad housewife, and she, Miranda, would have to be desperate indeed before she crossed this threshold again.

Outside once more, she took a deep breath of the icy air and was approaching the Mickleborough house when Steve emerged from it, giving her his broadest grin. 'Didn't think you'd hang around there for long,' he greeted her. 'I bet the old biddy hasn't changed at all. Did she ask you to come over and cook her Christmas dinner? I bet that was her first thought!'

'You're not far out; apparently even Beth doesn't spend much time at home now. Did I tell you she was making parachutes at a big factory on the outskirts of the city? No, probably I didn't, because of the censor. Well she is, and Aunt Vi says she kips down with a pal when she's on late shifts. She said she and Beth had a present for me, but whatever it was she didn't hand it over. Now, what else did Granny Granger say about your mam and the kids coming home for Christmas?'

'Norra lot,' Steve said cheerfully as they swung into the main road and headed for the tram stop, 'just that Mam didn't mean to come until the day before Christmas Eve, so she's still got time to make up her mind. But I think she'll be sensible; my mam is sensible, wouldn't you say?'

'She's very sensible,' Miranda agreed. 'What'll we do today? If you're not too tired I've got some last minute shopping to do, and this evening I really would love to go dancing. It's difficult for Avril and me, because of

Gary. Those two really are in love and want to marry as soon as they've saved up enough money to rent a couple of rooms somewhere. Avril used to love dancing but of course Gary can't do even the simplest steps, though he tells Avril that he wouldn't mind if she wanted to dance with other blokes, but she won't do it. You can understand why, can't you, Steve?'

'Course I can,' Steve said at once. 'She's a grand girl, your Avril. But I take it she won't mind if you and I go dancing? I'm no great shakes, but there was a girl in Texas who took me in hand and now I can waltz and quickstep with the best of 'em, though the foxtrot and the tango are still beyond me. Do you think Avril will want to come with us? Even if she won't dance for fear of hurting Gary's feelings, I suppose she could watch.'

'And play gooseberry?' Miranda said scornfully. 'Of course she won't, you idiot. Besides, she's very pretty, you know, even if she is a tiny bit overweight. She'd be besieged by offers and turning a chap down can be really uncomfortable. No, if we go dancing it will just be you and me.'

They caught a tram into the city centre, Steve admitting that he had heard so much about the shortages in England that he had scoured Texas for any foodstuffs or luxuries he could afford, to give to all his loved ones as Christmas presents. 'So we've no need to go shopping on my account,' he assured Miranda. 'Where do you want to go for yours?' He glanced at the heavy watch on his wrist. It had several different dials, which had intrigued Miranda until he had explained its various uses. 'Ah, but it's twenty to twelve; we'd best make tracks for Lewis's and a really good, pre-war lunch!'

Avril and Miranda were in Miranda's room, Avril sitting on the bed and watching as her friend tried on a dance dress she had borrowed from a pal whose own boyfriend was on one of the ships in the transatlantic convoy and would not be back home in Liverpool for another two weeks at least. And anyway, the dress would never have fitted her, Miranda thought to herself, remembering how her plump little pal had sighed as she handed the dress over in a stout paper carrier, explaining that her mother, a first rate needlewoman, had made it herself several years before the war started, and had only worn it twice. Miranda, pulling the soft chiffon out of its bag, had gasped with pleasure. It was a smoky blue-grey shade with a low-cut bodice and floating sleeves, and with it her friend's mother had worn delicate blue silk sandals. These were too small for Miranda, but her own white sandals looked almost as good, and when she turned to Avril her friend's widening eyes was all the confirmation she needed that the dress both fitted and suited her. Carefully she picked up the gossamer stole with its embroidery of silver stars and turned once more to Avril. 'Isn't it the most beautiful thing you've ever seen?' she enquired breathlessly, 'I shan't dare to have a drink even if I die of thirst, because suppose I dropped a spot on it? I could never replace it, not if I had all the money in the world. Oh, Avril, do you think I should just let Steve see me in it when he arrives and then change into my old green dress? After all, Steve hasn't seen the green one either.'

But Avril, though she laughed, shook her head. 'No way! Your pal meant you to enjoy it, and anyway the only drink they serve at the Grafton is weak orange squash. You could probably pour a gallon of that stuff down your front and it would come out the minute you put the dress in water. So stop worrying and enjoy yourself.'

Presently a knock on the door heralded Steve's arrival and his expression, when Miranda floated into the kitchen in the borrowed dress, was almost unbelieving. 'Oh, queen, you look like the Queen,' he gabbled. 'No, you look like a film star! God, I know they say love's blind, but I'm tellin' you, you're bleedin' well beautiful and I never knew it before.'

Not surprisingly, Miranda bridled. 'They say clothes make the man, and I suppose you're telling me they make the woman, too,' she said frostily. 'It's not me or my carroty hair that's beautiful, but my pal's dress.' She regarded her swirling skirts proudly. 'It is fantastic, isn't it? Her mother made it for a Masonic function before the war, and only ever wore it twice. My pal is quite a lot heavier than either her mum or me, so I doubt she'll ever get to wear it, but I'm going to treat it like gold dust, see if I don't.' She grinned at Steve. 'So you'll have to learn to dance without actually laying your greasy hands anywhere on this wonderful creation.'

Laughing, Steve promised to scrub his hands within an inch of their lives as soon as they reached the ballroom. Then he and Miranda told Avril to be good and to have the kettle on the boil by eleven o'clock, and clattered down the steep iron stairway. At the foot of it they met Gary, carrying a parcel which he explained was a bag of sprouts. 'I've a pal with an allotment out at Seaforth, and he told me that the sprouts are ready to eat after the first frost. It's a cold old job cutting them, though, so he said if I'd give him a hand I could have a bag of them for our Christmas dinner.' He stared at them inquisitively. 'You off somewhere?'

'Oh no, I always wear my best shoes to queue for fish and chips,' Miranda said sarcastically. 'I know my dress is covered by my old winter coat but surely you can see my elegant footwear!'

Gary grinned. 'So you're off for a dancing session, are you? Great news, because that'll give me a whole evening to keep Avril company,' he said at once. 'I was supposed to be on shift this evening but because of cutting the sprouts I did a swap with Billy.'

'Nice for you and even nicer for Avril, because she thinks she's going to spend the evening alone,' Miranda said. She slipped her hand into the crook of Steve's arm and they set off across the courtyard. 'Cheerio, Gary. See you later I expect.'

The pair of them hurried, carefully, along the icy pavement. Above them the dark arc of the sky blazed with stars, reminding Miranda of the stole around her shoulders. They reached the dance hall and joined the line of people waiting for admittance. Steve greeted a couple of old friends from school further up the queue whilst Miranda rubbed her cold hands together, stamped her chilled feet and wished she had done as other girls did and worn her boots, bringing her dancing sandals in a paper carrier to change into inside. But already the queue was beginning to move and very soon she and Steve were rushing to claim a couple of the little gilt chairs set out around the gleaming dance floor. As soon as the orchestra struck up they tipped their chairs forward to indicate that they were taken, as was the small round table, and set off. It was the first time they had ever danced together and Miranda found it a very pleasant experience, but unfortunately, without thinking, she said something which spoiled the moment for them both. 'The last time I was here with Gerald . . .' she began, her cheek resting comfortably against Steve's tunic, and was astonished when she found herself suddenly pushed away from him and held at a distance.

'Did you have to say that?' Steve growled, giving her an admonitory shake. 'When did you go dancing with Gerald? Why didn't you mention it in any of your letters?'

Miranda, jerked out of her pleasant daydream, scowled at her companion. 'Don't be so silly, Steve. I've danced with all sorts of people these past months . . .'

She stopped speaking as Steve put a hand across her mouth. 'What was that noise?' he asked curiously. 'A sort of wailing noise. And why is everyone streaming off the floor?'

Miranda gasped and grabbed his hand. 'That was Moaning Minnie,' she said. 'In other words, the air raid warning. Sometimes the men on watch don't see the planes till they're almost overhead, though, so we must get a move on or we shan't get into the shelter. If we were in the flat we could go down to the basement under the cycle shop, but it's too far to go from here.'

They joined the pushing, jostling crowd and once on the pavement Miranda pointed at the moon, brilliant in the blackness of the night sky. 'See that? I expect you know it's called a bomber's moon. Well, with luck they'll be heading for some other destination, but you can't take chances. Here comes the first wave. Quick, give me your hand and run like hell.'

313

Steve complied, saying as he did so: 'I've often heard the expression bomber's moon, and now I understand what it means. It's as light as day, I bet those buggers up there can see us clear as clear, like ants scurrying out of an anthill when a foot comes too near the nest . . .'

He stopped speaking and Miranda, gazing up, saw that the first planes were indeed overhead. The ack-ack guns were blazing away; she saw one of the enemy aircraft stagger, then seem to recover, saw something descending to earth, and dragged Steve hastily into the shelter of a shop doorway. 'Incendiaries,' she told him, as the dreaded firebombs began to rain down. 'Oh, come *on*, Steve, run before the next lot come over. Look, there's a warden. He'll tell us which shelter to make for.'

The warden, uniformed and helmeted, came towards them, and had to raise his voice to a shout above the whistle of descending bombs. Just as he reached them there was an almighty explosion somewhere in the vicinity of the Adelphi Hotel, an explosion violent enough, Miranda knew, to have caused enormous damage. The warden reached them and grabbed Miranda's arm, then peered into her face and grinned. 'Oh, it's you. Not fire watchin' tonight, then? There's a shelter not twenty yards ahead; you'll be all right there. Gerra move on, though. This is no night to be out on the streets.'

'Thanks, Jim,' Miranda said, and would have set off at once, but Steve held her back.

'Is there anything I can do to help, mate?' he asked as the warden turned away. 'I'm on leave, but . . .'

The warden laughed. 'Get into the bloody shelter and stay there until you hear the all clear,' he commanded. 'Once the raid's over . . .'

Another enormous explosion rocked the three of them, and caused Miranda to give a yelp of impatience. 'Do as the man says and get a move on,' she commanded. 'This war doesn't need dead heroes. Ah, I can see the shelter and the feller in charge is beckoning us . . . come *on*, Steve!' To their right a large building was already in flames, the firelight competing with that of the moon, but neither Miranda nor Steve so much as glanced towards the conflagration. They pushed aside the smelly sacking curtain at the bottom of the shelter steps and entered into the usual scene of confusion: children howling, mothers trying to quiet them, and old people, eyes dark with fright, trying to pretend that this was all part of a day's work. Miranda glanced sideways at Steve, remembering that this was his first experience of a severe air raid – and she knew from the number of dark shapes overflying the city that this was a severe raid indeed. Steve caught her glance and grinned sheepishly, taking his place on one of the long wooden benches which lined the shelter. Miranda sat down beside him and took his hand.

'Awful, isn't it?' she said softly. 'Poor Steve, you really have been chucked in at the deep end, haven't you? For the rest of us it's come gradually, with each raid worse than the last. Yet somehow one never gets used to it. The kids are petrified simply by the noise, and when one of the parachute mines lands too close you get the most horrible sensation, as if your brain is being pulled out through your ears. I'm told that's the result of blast, and apparently if you're near enough blast can kill you just as effectively as a direct hit. If it weren't for the fact that while we're in the shelter we're not makin' work for the wardens I'd far rather be out in the open, and I expect you feel the same.'

Steve put his arm round her and gave her a gentle squeeze, then kissed the side of her face. 'You're right, Miranda; that's exactly how I feel,' he said quietly. 'It's an odd thing, because when I'm flying I don't feel confined in any way, but now I feel boxed in and helpless.'

Miranda chuckled. 'Everyone does, I'm sure,' she said. 'But don't worry – tomorrow, when the fire service are trying to douse the flames and the wardens and anyone else who offers are digging out survivors and roping off dangerous buildings, your help will be very much appreciated. I've never managed to sleep in a shelter, though lots of people do, so I usually go back to the flat after the all clear has sounded, get a couple of hours' kip and then go and offer my services at the nearest ARP post.' She grinned at him. 'Care to follow my example? You can have the sofa again, or you can go home to Jamaica Close and get yourself a proper eight hours.'

Steve returned her grin, then winced and ducked as a whistling roar announced the arrival of yet another high explosive bomb. 'I'll stick with you, babe,' he said in a mock American accent. 'I just hope to God my mam is still safe in Wales.'

'You said she wasn't setting out until the day before Christmas Eve, so the news that the city has been targeted will reach her in time for her to make the right decision,' Miranda pointed out. 'Oh, Steve, I'm so sorry that your first trip home looks like being spoiled. So long as the skies stay clear – and there's a building standing in Liverpool – they'll keep up the attack, because everyone says after they've flattened London it'll be the turn of the busiest port in the country, and that's us. Ought you to cut your leave short? I know you're not due to go back to your airfield until Boxing Day, but you could go tomorrow. I expect you'd be more use attacking the Luftwaffe.'

But Steve was shaking his head, his expression grim. 'I'm going to stay here and do my damnedest to help,' he said. He glanced towards the end of the shelter where the warden in charge was trying to start a communal sing-song, though at present the noise from outside made such a thing impossible, and suggested that he might just slip through the curtain, steal up the smelly dank steps and take a look around, but Miranda assured him that this would not be allowed.

'Once the warden lets one person go out there would be a concerted rush. And even if you don't realise it, Steve, it's tremendously dangerous out there. People run back into their houses to fetch a wedding photograph or a terrified cat, and never run out again. The building may collapse on them, or escaping gas from a fractured pipe catch them unawares, and there's one more death to add to the Luftwaffe's haul. So just behave like the good citizen I know you are and wait for the all clear.'

Steve sighed, but after another hour, during which Miranda leaned her head against his shoulder and actually managed to snooze, he gave her a shake.

'Miranda, I've got to go outside for a moment. I – I *need* to go outside.'

Miranda stifled a giggle. 'You want to spend a penny, don't you?' she asked. 'Haven't you noticed people getting up and going behind the curtain? There's a heavy leather one behind it, which the warden draws across as soon as the shelter's full. He keeps a couple of fire buckets in the space between them which can be used in an emergency.' She saw Steve hesitating and gave him a friendly shove. 'Oh, come on, don't be shy! When we were kids you told me you used to swim in the Scaldy in the altogether, yet now you feel embarrassed having a pee in a bucket. It's much easier for you men than us girls; at least you don't have to squat on the edge of the thing whilst the warden pretends he's got business at the other end of the shelter. Besides, why suffer? We're all in the same boat and it may be another hour or more before they sound the all clear.'

Steve sighed but got stiffly to his feet. 'If you're planning to make me look a fool . . .' he began, but before Miranda could assure him that she was telling the simple truth an elderly man in a patched army greatcoat and a much darned balaclava got to his feet and shuffled towards the warden. He was ushered through the curtain, which was swished shut behind him, and when he emerged again Steve was quick to jump to his feet and follow his example. Miranda was amused to see the obvious relief on his face as he returned to her side, but was too tactful to say so. Instead she hauled a small child, a girl of four or five, on to her lap and announced that it was story time, and that she would tell them all the tale of Timmy Tiddler, a very small fish who lived in a pond in the heart of a magic wood . . .

Soon Miranda was surrounded by tiny listeners, and though the noise from outside did not stop, it began to lessen as the roar of the aircraft overhead became fainter, though it was three in the morning before the longed for notes of the all clear reverberated through the shelter. People began to rub their eyes, for many had slept once the worst of the raid was over. Belongings were collected, children claimed by parents, and the evacuation of the shelter began.

Out on the pavement, Miranda and Steve looked around them at a scene of devastation. Fires raged, and buildings which had toppled still gave off clouds of dust. Miranda sighed and tucked her hand into the crook of Steve's elbow. 'It's worse than I thought. Those dreadful incendiaries cause fires which light up the city so that the bombers have something to aim at,' she said. 'Steve, would you be happier if we went straight to Jamaica Close and checked that your grandmother – and my Aunt Vi, I suppose – are okay? I wouldn't mind a bit of a walk in the open air, having been penned up in the shelter for hours.'

Steve began to brush at the shoulders of his greatcoat, then gave it up, because the very air was dust-laden. 'There won't be much open air as you call it, more like open brick dust,' he observed, 'but I do believe you're right. We'd better check on Gran and your horrible old aunt, and once we know they're all right we can go back to your flat, get ourselves some breakfast and snatch a couple of hours' sleep. Then I mean to offer my services at the nearest ARP post.'

'All right: Jamaica Close first, and then breakfast. Best foot forward! I wonder how Avril and Gary got on.' She chuckled. 'Poor Gary, he was so looking forward to having Avril and the flat to himself for a change; maybe the whole building if Pete Huxtable decided to trek when he realised that the skies were clear and the moon would be full. Have you heard about trekking? Londoners began it, I believe. You take some grub and a couple of blankets and as soon as your work finishes for the day you lock up your house and go as far into the country as you can get and stay with anyone who'll let you sleep on their floor until morning. The raid is always over before the sky gets truly light again, and if you're lucky you can catch a bus back into the city, though otherwise you have to walk. But at least you'll have had a proper night's sleep and be fit for work next day.'

'Yes, I've heard of it, and having suffered a night in the shelter I think trekkers are doing the right thing,' Steve said. 'I can't imagine why the government tries to discourage them . . . well, they wouldn't if they had to put up with the sort of night we've just lived through. If you ask me only a lunatic would choose to stay in a city under attack if they could possibly get away from it. But I'm just a simple sergeant-pilot.' He looked at her seriously. 'Couldn't you trek, queen? I'd feel a deal happier if I knew you were safe out of it before the bombs begin to fall.'

They were heading along Great Homer Street, already finding it difficult to breathe the dust-laden air, and Miranda coughed before she replied. 'Oh, I couldn't possibly. I'm a fire watcher. They position us on top of high buildings and give us either a messenger boy or what they call a field telephone so that we can report any fires in our vicinity as soon as they start. Besides, I don't have any friends or relatives living in the country, so for me – and many like me – trekking is out of the question.'

Steve nodded reluctantly. 'I see,' he said. 'The trouble

320

is, queen, what I've seen tonight has made me realise that we really are all in it together. I thought being on my station was the most dangerous job of all, but at least we don't simply sit there waiting to be shot at. We have the satisfaction of knowing we're both protecting our civilians and attacking the enemy, which is a good deal preferable to being sitting ducks.'

As they neared the turning which would lead them to Jamaica Close, there were fewer and fewer people on the pavement. Out here those who had been in communal shelters had returned to their homes and others, Miranda assumed, had come up from their cellars to snatch a few hours in bed before day dawned. They turned into the Close and went straight to the front door of Number Two, where they hesitated. Steve stared at the front door, hauled the key on its string up through the letter box and looked enquiringly at Miranda. 'Do you think it's too bad of me to wake her? Gran, I mean?'

'There's no need to wake her,' Miranda whispered, gently taking the key from his hand and inserting it in the lock. 'You can just check that she's safely asleep in her bed, and then write a little note telling her that you're fine, and will come back later. Agreed?'

Steve was happy with the idea, but as it happened their creeping about was not necessary. As soon as they entered the hallway Granny Granger appeared, coming towards them from the kitchen with a big smile. 'There's tea in the pot,' she said cheerfully. 'There's nothin' like a hot cup of tea to set me up for wharrever the new day may hold, but you're early callers, ain't you?' She had ushered them into the kitchen and now jerked a thumb at the clock on the mantel, whose hands pointed at ten past four. 'Take off your coats, else you won't feel the benefit,' she instructed. And as Miranda obeyed she looked down at herself and gasped with horror.

The beautiful borrowed dress was torn and filthy, the stole with its twinkling stars ruined. Miranda groaned. 'Oh, Steve, and I promised I'd take such care of my borrowed finery,' she said. 'Whatever shall I do?'

'You can't do anything, of course, but a dress is just a dress. Life and limb are much more important,' Steve said comfortably. 'Your pal will forgive you; she'll know there was nothing you could have done to keep the dress immaculate.'

Granny Granger bustled out of the pantry, carrying a tin with a picture of the Tower of London on the lid. 'There's still some cake left and I brewed the tea not ten minutes ago,' she said. 'Now set yourselves down and tell me if there's anything left of dear old Liverpool. Were it as bad a raid as it sounded?'

Reflecting on the resilience of the old, Miranda sank gratefully into a chair and accepted a cup of tea with eagerness, even agreeing to nibble a slice of seed cake, though it was by no means a favourite with her. 'Yes, it was dreadful. There are fires and firemen everywhere. I guess when they post the casualty lists later in the day, we'll know just how bad it was in terms of people getting killed. As for damage to property, well, the mind boggles, but it's difficult to judge in the dark.'

Granny Granger nodded. 'And you'll be glad to hear, young Steve, that I had a telegram from your mam yesterday evening saying she wouldn't be coming after all. It seems she'd had the letter from your pa, and had seen the foolishness of leaving Wales. So If you want to see her, Kenny and baby Flora, you'd best gerron a bus or train and visit them, instead of the other way round.'

They chatted with the old lady for a bit, agreed to do some shopping for off-ration food, if they could find any, and accepted her invitation to have tea with her. Then Miranda ran down to Number Six and would have tapped on the door, except that as she raised her hand to knock, Mrs Brown from Number Eight appeared on her front doorstep.

'Mornin', Miranda. You're up and about early,' she remarked. 'But if you've a mind to wake your aunt, I'd suggest you think again. She spent the best part of the night searchin' for Beth's cat what has been stayin' at Number Six whenever Beth's on shift. She found it in the end because once the raid was over it come home, the way such critters do, so she shut it in the kitchen and went off to catch up on her night's sleep.' She chuckled. 'And I pity anyone what disturbs her,' she finished.

Relieved to have got out of an encounter which she knew was unlikely to bring her anything but grief, Miranda asked Mrs Brown to tell Aunt Vi that she had been asking for her. Then she and Steve trudged wearily back to the main road, and caught the first bus heading towards the city centre, though it was crowded with folk going to work so they had to stand. As always, Miranda was impressed by their cheerful acceptance of the terrible night they had endured, and saw that Steve, too, admired their fortitude. When they reached the first of the big factories the bus almost emptied and Miranda and Steve slid on to a seat and held hands as the vehicle clattered onwards. 'I hope we don't wake Avril and Gary,' Miranda said absently, as she tried to stifle an enormous yawn.

'They won't have stayed in the flat – that would be madness – they'll have been in the basement under the cycle shop. Pete has told us to make free of it. He gave us the key when the war started, and we've used it several times.' She smiled reminiscently. 'When it starts to get noisy it seems to go to poor Timmy's bladder and he whines at the door to be let out. We always joke that the all clear should be called the free to wee, because Timmy charges up the steps and barely reaches the courtyard before his leg is lifting.'

Steve smiled and said that he would like to see the little dog again, not having done so since before the war. 'You ought to buy him wax earplugs or woolly earmuffs,' he teased. 'If he couldn't hear the bangs he'd probably go off to sleep quite happily.'

They were still laughing over the idea of Timmy in fluffy earmuffs when the bus deposited them at their stop, and they hurried along towards Russell Street, planning the breakfast which they hoped to enjoy presently. It was too early for any of the shops in the street to be open, but that was not the only reason for the unfamiliar quiet. The air was thick with dust, and despite the householders' precautions there were several glassless windows, and shop doors swinging wide. Miranda began to hurry. 'I hope to God they're all right,' she said breathlessly as she ran. 'Oh, I do hope they're all right!'

Chapter Eleven

Avril and Gary had barely settled down to their fish and chip supper when Moaning Minnie set up her wail. Timmy, under the table awaiting any scraps which might come his way, moaned softly as well, but Gary and Avril fell into their usual routine without a moment's hesitation. The fish and chips were rewrapped in their paper and shoved into Avril's air raid basket along with some rather dry cake and sandwiches from the previous day and two bottles of cold tea. Then she and Gary raided her bedroom for two blankets and a pillow each, donned their winter coats, hats and scarves and set forth.

The basement was reached from the back of the bicycle shop, through a heavy oak door at the foot of a dozen steps. This would be the first time that Gary had seen it, for usually when the warning sounded he had to hurry off either to act as a shelter warden or to take messages from one post to another on his trusty old bike, for despite the fact that one of his legs was made of wood he could ride a bicycle as well as any able-bodied man, thanks to a special pedal into which his false foot fitted.

He looked appreciatively around the underground room, which was empty as they had known it would be. Pete had warned them that he meant to go out to his uncle's farm on the Wirral and get at least one decent night's sleep, for the moment he looked up at the clear sky and the great disc of a moon he knew it was on the cards that the raiders would soon be overhead. Avril and Gary had said they would look after Timmy, since the little dog was terrified by the sound of falling bombs and would hear very little if he was in the cycle shop basement, which was deep and well protected. Avril put the basket on the small table Pete had provided and closed the door. Gary stood the little dog down on the uneven floor and began to spread his blanket out on the wooden bench which ran along the wall.

Avril smiled as she took in Pete's latest attempt to make the basement homelike: an ancient alarm clock had appeared on one of the shelves he had built some time before. There was also a Primus stove, a kerosene lamp, a couple of ancient but comfortable chairs, and wooden benches on the two longest walls, so that, when just two of you were sharing the basement, you could stretch out on a bench each, wrapped in your blanket with your head on your pillow, and make believe you were in bed. 'What do you think?' she asked. 'All the houses and shops on this side of the street have basements, but I bet no one has gone to greater lengths to make theirs comfortable than Pete has. I can never sleep in the public shelters – too much noise and too many people – but I've slept down here a couple of times. That door is solid oak; you can't hear much through it, unless a bomb drops awfully near. The only thing that really worries Pete is fire, so every now and then he just has a quick look out, but so far we've been lucky. Go on, what do you think?'

'It's grand,' Gary said appreciatively. 'Shall I light the Primus? I think the fish and chips will still be warm, but I don't fancy cold tea if we can have it hot.'

'Well, all right,' Avril said rather uncertainly. 'I don't believe anyone's ever lit it before, though. Pete always says that, what with the floor being so uneven and the stove pretty old and wonky, he's afraid it might tip over and set fire to the basement. It's really for emergencies only, so if you don't mind, Gary, I think we'll stick to cold tea.'

'Of course I don't mind,' Gary said immediately, and presently they were seated on opposite sides of the small table eating fish and chips with their fingers whilst Timmy, fears apparently forgotten, laid his head in Avril's lap and accepted chips, small pieces of fish and larger pieces of crisp golden batter. They finished their meal in record time and went to their respective beds, though Gary, looking uneasy as the noise from outside grew in intensity, did not immediately wrap himself in his blanket. 'I feel I ought to be out there, because it sounds like a bad one to me,' he said. 'I know I'm off duty tonight, but if the noise is anything to go by the fellows might be glad of an extra pair of hands.'

Avril sighed. 'You know what they say: folk wanderin' about durin' a raid, even if they're tryin' to help, simply cause the wardens more work. So just settle down and try to get some sleep. Morning comes a lot quicker if you've managed to nod off for a while at least. We'll leave the lamp on, but I'll turn the wick right down.'

For twenty minutes or so both Gary and Avril lay quiet, but Avril soon realised that sleep would not come. The noise was dreadful. The bombs seemed to be bursting all around them; several times the basement rocked, and what Pete had feared came to pass: the Primus stove fell over and rolled tinnily back and forth, whilst Timmy, who had been lying on the foot of Avril's bed, suddenly elevated his nose to heaven and howled.

Avril sighed and sat up. 'It's no use; no one could possibly sleep through this,' she announced. 'I'm going to turn up the lamp, find my book and have a read. What about you? There's yesterday's *Echo* in my basket as well as a couple of children's books – *The Secret Garden* and *Humpty Dumpty and the Princess*. When there's a bad raid I find it easier to read a children's book which I know well so I don't have to think.'

'I'll have whichever one you don't want,' Gary was saying, when someone knocked on the heavy oak door and then pushed it open. Two frightened little faces peered into the warm and well lit basement.

'Can we . . .' the older child, a boy of perhaps ten, began, but before he could say any more Avril pulled him and the little girl who clung to his hand into the basement and slammed the heavy door shut. 'Where have you come from, and what are you doing in the street when there's a really terrible raid going on?' she demanded. 'It's lucky you saw our door; lucky we were here. Where are your parents? I don't want to frighten you, but . . .' A tremendous explosion cut the sentence off short and both children jumped and winced before the boy answered, his voice coming out in a squeak.

'We was goin' home. We've been evacuated, me and Maisie, only the lady hated us and didn't feed us proper. We stuck it as long as we could, only at teatime yesterday she wouldn't give us no bread, said it were on ration now and we'd ate our share at breakfast. Maisie was so hungry she were cryin' so I told her we'd go home – we live in Bootle – only we didn't have no money so we had to walk. We axed the way and got lifts a couple of times. We told folk we'd missed our train . . .'

'Well, never mind that,' Avril said. 'You'll be safe enough here until the raid's over and then me and my friend will take you home to your parents. I'm sure you know your address and which tram to catch.'

The boy nodded eagerly. 'Thanks, missus,' he said. The little girl suddenly clutched him and pulled his head down to her level.

'Ask the lady if there's food,' she pleaded, and there was a wealth of longing in her voice. 'Any food 'ud do, Dickie. I's so hungry . . . and thirsty . . .'

Gary leaned forward, took the sandwiches out of Avril's basket and wordlessly handed them over, watching as the children devoured Spam, jam, and paste sandwiches indiscriminately and with every sign of enjoyment. 'You can give the crusts to Timmy,' he said, then laughed as he saw that the two little visitors were eating the sandwiches in great starved bites, indifferent to crusts.

'Fanks, mister,' the boy said, and took the offered cup of cold tea, holding it for his sister and not drinking himself until her thirst was satisfied. Then he looked up at Gary. 'Who's Timmy?' he asked curiously. 'Is that you, mister?'

'No, I'm Gary, this is Avril and the little dog is Timmy . . .' Gary began at the same moment as Avril gave a cry of dismay.

'Timmy's gone!' she said, her voice rising. 'He must have slipped out when the door opened, and we didn't notice. Oh, Gary, he'll be killed for sure! Even if the bombs don't get him he'll die of fright.' She rushed across to the door and began to tug it open, hoping that the little dog would have got no further than the foot of the stairs, but there was no sign of him. Avril climbed halfway up the flight and got the impression, in the only glance she was allowed, that the whole city was in flames and that the bombers were still attacking, black against the stars. Then she was peremptorily snatched back by Gary, who caught her round the waist and pulled her back to the relative safety of the basement.

'I'll go and call Timmy. If he's out there and I can see him I'll fetch him back,' he shouted above the whistle of descending bombs and the terrible crashes as they came to earth. 'It's all right, silly, I won't take any risks, but I know you won't be happy until you know Timmy's safe.' He was climbing the stairs as he spoke and Avril called to him not to be a fool.

'You know what they say – if you go back into a bombed house for a cat or a dog, they'll have found a safe spot but you'll wake up dead,' she cried distractedly. 'I know we all love Timmy, but he'll be hiding away somewhere . . . please, please, Gary don't go out there!'

Gary glanced back at her and grinned. 'Can you hear me, Mother?' he said in a passable imitation of Sandy Powell whose catchphrase it was. 'Get back into the cellar and look after those two kids; I shan't be a tick.'

Avril was tempted to ignore him, but when she turned and saw Dickie and Maisie she changed her mind. She closed the door on the horror outside and produced slices of cake and a bag of boiled sweets from her emergency supply. The two little faces turned so trustingly towards her were white with exhaustion and streaked with tears and dust. Of course she loved Timmy, often lured him up to the flat with scraps so that she could have a cuddle, but these two children had had an even worse time than the little dog. According to Dickie – and she had no reason to doubt his word – both he and his sister had been half starved by their so-called foster parent and had taken desperate measures. Fate had flung them in her way and now it was her duty – hers and Gary's – to see that they got safe home to Bootle, where their real parents would make sure they were fed and loved as befitted children so young.

She stared hopefully at the heavy oak door, but realised that it might take Gary five or ten minutes to search the places to which Timmy might have fled. She turned back to the children, about to suggest that she read them a story, then changed her mind. 'Take your coats and hats off and I'll wrap you up in a blanket and you can have a bit of a snooze,' she said tactfully. When the two children continued to stare blankly at her, she sat down, took Maisie on her knee and undressed the little girl down to her liberty bodice and patched knickers.

But when she put out a hand to help Dickie, masculine pride made him say, gruffly, 'I can manage, fanks, missus,' as he shed coat, balaclava and much darned jumper. Then he climbed up on to the bench where his sister was already wrapped in blankets, thumb in mouth and eyes tightly closed, and cuddled down beside her. Avril opened her mouth to bid them goodnight and closed it again. Her unexpected visitors were already fast asleep.

For the next half hour Avril read her book, but after every two or three chapters she found herself glancing towards the door. She realised she was in a difficult position. She longed to go in search of Gary and Timmy, but knew that if she did so she would be acting against her own advice, and in a thoroughly foolish manner. Besides, she could not possibly leave the two children. Gary was so sensible; she imagined he had gone further than he intended and had either found Timmy or given up the search, for the time being at any rate. Then he must have realised how far he had wandered and would either have been ordered down a shelter by a passing warden or have gone down himself, knowing that without his tin hat or his bicycle he would be of very little use to the emergency services until the raid was over and the clearing up operation was beginning.

Wondering what time it was, Avril picked up the alarm clock and examined it closely, sure that it must have stopped. But its tick was steady and when she tried the winder mechanism she realised that Pete must have set it going just before he left, which meant that the time really was around two o'clock in the morning. She knew she should get some sleep, but had to fight an almost irresistible urge to slip through the doorway and climb the stairs so that she could get some idea at least of what was going on. Surely the Luftwaffe must have dropped all their bombs and incendiaries by now? But going to investigate meant leaving the safety of the cellar, and suppose one of the children woke and followed her, or slipped out as Timmy had done? No, the sensible thing to do, and well she knew it, was to stay where she was until the all clear sounded. Then and only then could she and the two children emerge to make their way across the city to Bootle.

Avril gave a deep sigh, picked up her book and began to read, but after several more chapters she glanced at the lamp. Damnation! The wretched flame was beginning to waver, which had her chewing her fingernails. If she turned it down to save what oil there was in the hope of retaining some sort of light in the cellar, then it might go out altogether and prove difficult to relight. If she left it turned up full, however, it might still go out, and possibly at an even worse moment. She had just decided that she would turn the lamp as low as it could go without actually going out when two things happened. She remembered she always kept a small torch in her handbag, which nestled in the bottom of her emergency basket, and just as she got to her feet to fetch the torch there was an even bigger explosion than the ones she had been hearing all night, and the lamp was blown out.

Avril stood very still for a moment, her heart thundering. That had sounded far too close for comfort. She fumbled in her basket, found the torch and switched it on. Instead of being brilliant white, the torchlight was pale and yellowish, a sure sign that the battery was on its way out, but the ceiling above them, though it was raining dust, was not actually coming down. Not a direct hit, then, but something pretty near. With trembling fingers she found the matches Pete always kept within easy reach. After four or five attempts she shook the lamp and realised that it was almost out of oil. She knew Pete kept a small supply somewhere in the cellar, but could not remember exactly where, and she did not want to use the torch more than she must. She decided she would just nip over to the door, climb perhaps halfway up the stairs and see what was happening at ground level. Cautiously, she swung the beam of her torch across the children. They were both sound asleep and she guessed that if they could remain slumbering through the sort of raid the city had just suffered the chances were they would sleep the clock round; at any rate she need not worry about them for the time being.

Cautiously, she went across to the heavy oak door, put her hand on the handle and gave an experimental shove. It did not move. She stopped, puzzled. Had she locked it after the children's arrival? For that matter, had she locked it after Gary had gone in search of Timmy? But she knew very well, really, that the last thing she would have done was lock this door. How else could Gary possibly come back triumphant, with Timmy in his arms? And what if some other unfortunate soul should be looking for a place of refuge? No, she knew very well that neither she nor Miranda, nor Pete, would ever lock the door whilst they were inside, or if a raid was in progress. She gave the door another push; it was like pushing at Snowdon. Before she could stop herself, Avril hurled herself at the door, beating uselessly at the stout panels, and even as she did so she heard a crashing rumble and part of the ceiling – thank God it was the far end – came down. Bricks, rubble, a wooden beam and, oddly, a bicycle came crashing into the cellar. Avril glanced involuntarily at the two children, but though Dickie stirred and muttered neither child woke.

Relieved of one worry, for she had no wish to have two terrified children on her hands, Avril made herself sit down once more, and began to think logically. Gary knew she was here. Miranda, Steve and probably Pete Huxtable would guess. As soon as the raid was over and there was daylight the rescue services would begin their unenviable task. Damaged buildings would be cordoned off for fear somebody would try to enter and be trapped beneath falling masonry. The army would be brought in from Seaforth Barracks to sift through the rubble in search of survivors. From the glimpse she had already seen, Avril guessed that the fire service would be fully occupied and would probably be requesting aid from as far away as Manchester and Blackpool. And there must have been mayhem amongst the shipping, which meant mayhem also in the docks and the warehouses which clustered close to the water. Sooner or later Pete would come back from his uncle's place on the Wirral to find, judging from the great pile of rubble at one end of the cellar, that his beautiful shop and the flat above it were no more. And he would immediately remember the basement. It might take a fair while to move the rubble which was so effectively blocking the door, but it would be done at last.

Avril's wavering torch beam was getting fainter, so she switched it off, hoping that as soon as it was daylight – and daylight could not be long in coming now – a beam of it would somehow enter the cellar. Gingerly she crossed to the pile of rubble and stared upwards with watering eyes, for the dust here was dreadful, catching at your throat, making you long for fresh air as one usually longs for a cool drink. But to her disappointment no light came from above. Sighing, she returned to her chair but did not attempt to light the lamp or switch on the torch. Time might drag its feet, but even as she had gone over and tried the door she was pretty sure she'd heard the all clear, and she thanked God that her ordeal would soon be over. Volunteers would dig her out quickly, especially when Gary told them that there were two small children buried with her in the cellar beneath the cycle shop. Yes, release would come quite soon now.

And since she was terribly tired she leaned back into her chair and let sleep overcome her.

A soft whimpering awoke her. For a moment she thought that it was Timmy, but then the whimpering became a small voice. 'Where is we, Dickie? Oh, Dickie, I's frightened.'

Immediately the events of the night sprang fully fledged into Avril's mind. The two children seeking refuge, Timmy bolting out of the basement and Gary going in search of him. And now that she was properly awake she could see a beam of light, dust-laden to be sure, but light nevertheless. It was coming from the hole in the ceiling above the pile of rubble at the far end of the basement, and far off and faint she thought she could hear voices. Hastily she fumbled in her pocket and produced the torch, clicking it on to reveal the two children, both now wide awake and sitting up, Dickie with his arms protectively around Maisie's small shoulders. 'S'all right, nipper, the lady'll see us home now it's daytime,' he said reassuringly. He glanced curiously around the cellar in the faint torchlight. 'You said you'd take us home, didn't you, missus? Can we go now? Our mam will be worried if Mrs Grimble has writ to say we've run off.'

Avril got rather stiffly out of the chair in which she had been sleeping, and took the last slice of cake out of the basket. She broke it in two, gave the children a piece each and then spoke reassuringly. 'We can't go out just yet, because there's something against the door. I tried to open it earlier but it wouldn't budge, and I don't believe we should try to get out from where the daylight

336

is getting in because it wouldn't be safe. But Gary – the friend who was with me when you arrived – will tell the rescue people we're here, and they'll get us out in a trice, just you see.'

Dickie swallowed a mouthful of cake, then addressed his sister. 'Do the warning, Maisie,' he commanded, and before Avril could ask him what he meant both children threw back their heads whilst from their mouths, shrill and demanding, came the sound, first, of the air raid warning and then of the all clear. It was so piercing that Avril, laughing, clapped her hands to her ears, whilst Dickie patted his little sister on the back and told her to take a deep breath and 'give 'em one more go of the warning, just in case they've not noticed the first 'un.'

Avril laughed again, ferreted in the basket and produced the remaining boiled sweets. 'You're a couple of little marvels,' she said admiringly, handing each child a Fox's glacier mint. 'Yes, I hear voices; thanks to you, we'll be out of here in no time.'

Dickie chuckled, but Maisie turned wide eyes upon Avril. 'I'd rather be out in five minutes than in no time,' she said. 'I don't like it here. There's a funny sort of smell and my hair's all dusty.' The two children had been sitting up on the bunk bed but now Maisie cast aside the blankets, slid on to the floor and went towards the door. She gave it a kick with one small, wellington booted foot, and even as she did so the door began to tremble, and a man's cheerful voice hailed them.

'You okay down there? We'll have you out just as soon as we can. Your feller didn't mention you'd got the red alert and the all clear down there as well.'

Avril was laughing and beginning to explain when the

door gave a protesting creak and opened six or seven inches. Maisie could have squeezed through, but the man's voice warned them to keep clear. 'You aren't out of the wood yet,' he told Avril. 'Let us clear the stairway. As soon as it's safe we'll tell you.'

Avril stepped back from the door. Dickie was dressing himself, Maisie was trying to struggle into the garments she had worn earlier and they were both clear of the door and able to see quite well now that daylight was pouring in through the increasing gap the rescuers were making. The work ceased for a moment while a flask of hot tea and some jam sandwiches were passed through and the three captives sat down on a bench and had what Avril called their breakfast, though the alarm clock had disappeared when the end of the cellar had collapsed so she had no idea of the time.

It seemed ages before the man who had been chatting reassuringly to them as he worked announced that they might come up now, and Avril and the children crawled up the steep stairs, getting filthier with every step, but not caring. What did a bit of dirt matter? What mattered was escaping back to normality. They were helped up the last few steps and stood in what Avril imagined had once been the courtyard, though it did not resemble its old self in any way. She cleared her throat and touched their rescuer's arm. 'Where's my pal, the man who told you we were in the basement?' she asked. 'Is he – is he hurt? Is that why he didn't dig us out himself?'

'That's right, queen, but he ain't too bad. Stood too close to a collapsing building. A brick got him on the noggin' – head wounds bleed like fury – and they reckon he's bust his arm, but he still wanted to dig you out himself; they had to all but carry him to the ambulance, protestin' all the way . . . ah, here he comes! Is that your feller, the one with the bandage round his head and his arm in a sling?'

Avril ran towards the approaching figure. 'Did you find Timmy?' she asked anxiously. 'Oh, Gary . . .' Her voice faded into silence as Pete Huxtable pushed impatiently at the bandage which hid his dark hair and obscured the sight in one of his eyes. Then he put his free arm round Avril, and gave her hand a squeeze.

'Thank God you're all right. I were that worried I tried to stop them takin' me up to Casualty, only one of the wardens said they'd heard voices . . .' He shuddered. 'And now you'd best come wi' me, queen.'

He led her back into what had once been the courtyard and over to a silent figure lying with several others on the cobbles.

Avril gasped. 'Is he much hurt?' she asked anxiously, seeming not to realise the significance of the sheet which Pete was gently folding back to reveal Gary's dirt-smudged face and, as the sheet was pulled lower, the little dog curled up in the crook of his arm.

'I'm sorry, queen,' Pete said quietly. 'I know he were your feller and a better man never lived, but there's nowt we can do about it. I reckon he went out after Timmy, ain't that so? God, I'm goin' to miss Timmy.'

Avril gulped. Tears, she knew, stood in her eyes, but she could not let them fall in front of the two children who had followed her into the courtyard and were now pressing close to her. She turned away blindly whilst beside her Maisie's voice, sounding slightly puzzled, came to her ears. 'Is they sleepin'? The feller and the little dog? They ain't hurt, are they?'

It was too much. Avril gulped back the tears, but could not answer the child's innocent question. Instead, she said huskily: 'Time to get going, little 'uns. If there's a tea room still standing I'll buy us some breakfast – oh no I won't, I haven't got any money, but I dare say someone will lend me a couple of bob – and then we'll have to make our way to Bootle.'

As she left the courtyard – what had once been the courtyard – she tripped and would have fallen but for Pete Huxtable, who grabbed her arm and pulled her to a halt. 'There's a WVS van at the end of the road what'll feed and water you for free,' he said. He lowered his voice. 'And if it's any comfort, love, they would neither of 'em know a thing. Blast's like that; it kills without leaving so much as an eyelash out of place. Who are your little friends, anyway?'

He was interrupted. 'Oh, thank God! When I saw the flat and the shop so badly damaged, with the roof gone and the windows all out, I thought . . . but of course I should have realised you'd have all gone to the basement as soon as the raid started. Steve and I spent the night in the big shelter near the Grafton Ballroom on West Derby Road. Where's Gary? That guy's incredible. I bet he went straight out and started helping the rescue teams . . .'

'Steady, Miranda; Gary's bought it,' Pete said with a brusqueness Avril had never heard in his voice before. 'And I'm afraid Timmy . . .'

Miranda put both arms round Avril and hugged her tightly. Tears ran down her face and mingled with the dirt. 'Oh, my love, I'm so sorry,' she whispered. 'I won't ask you what happened, because I can guess. Let's find a tea room where we can take stock.' She suddenly seemed to notice the children for the first time, both now clinging to Avril's skirt, and raised her brows. 'Who the devil are they?'

'They were in the basement with me when – when the place collapsed,' Avril said wearily. 'We're takin' them – I mean I'm takin' them – back to Bootle, to find their parents. Where's Steve, by the way?'

'Fighting fires down by the docks; there are several warehouses ablaze, and someone's reported an unexploded bomb. And you can forget the *I'm* takin' the children, because that *should* be we, since I don't intend to let you go off by yourself. And then I suppose we shall have to think about finding a place in a hostel. Incidentally, your beloved workplace has been badly damaged and may not be fit for work again for many weeks, if it ever is again . . .'

Avril cut across her friend's sentence. 'I'm not stayin' in the city. I couldn't bear it. I've already applied to join the WAAF; I shall pretend I got a letter of acceptance but it went up in smoke at the same time as the flat in Russell Street. You'll have to do whatever you think best, but I just want to get away from here.'

Beside them, Pete nodded his bandaged head in agreement. 'That's right, chuck, get right away from here, put it all behind you and start a new life in the air force. I'm goin' to do the same, though I guess they won't take me until my arm's out of plaster and the stitches are out of my head. But keep in touch, won't you?' His glance encompassed both girls but Miranda knew he was thinking of Avril. 'We'll all have to report to an ARP post, see if they can find accommodation for us for a few

341

nights. I don't mean to trek tonight; I reckon I'll be needed here.' Very much to Avril's surprise he gave each girl a kiss on the cheek before turning away and disappearing in the direction of the nearest ARP post.

'Pete's real fond of you, Avril,' Miranda said gently. 'But I guess you know that.'

'As you are so fond of saying, he's just a pal,' Avril said wearily, pushing a wing of blonde hair off her forehead.

They joined the queue of dazed and dirty people at the WVS van and after some thought Miranda said that she would join the WAAF as well. 'I'm sure Mr Grimshaw will understand. And he'll still have Miss Burton and Miss Phyllis.' She gave a rather wan chuckle. 'It will solve the dilemma of what to wear now that we haven't even got a pair of knickers or a hair ribbon left. The WAAF will kit us out, feed us, find us beds and train us for whatever work needs our skills . . .' She reached the head of the queue in mid-sentence. 'Oh, can we have four mugs of tea and four sandwiches or buns or whatever, please?'

Presently the four of them, still chewing, jumped on a bus. The children were understandably excited as the vehicle upon which they were travelling reached familiar territory. Maisie, with her nose pressed to the window, was the first to shout 'Our stop's comin' up!' and but for Avril's staying hand would have bailed out before the vehicle had actually come to a halt. Dickie told his sister sternly to behave herself, but Avril saw how his eyes sparkled and guessed he was quite as excited as Maisie, just, being older, more capable of restraint.

Once on the pavement she took Maisie's hand and

Miranda took Dickie's and they followed the children's instructions through a maze of small side streets until they reached Quarry Lane where they were towed impatiently up to the front door of Number Six. Avril looked for a bell, but seeing none would have used her knuckles on the wooden panel, only Dickie bade her follow him, and went down the side of the small house. Before he could knock on the back door it shot open and a weary-looking woman with tear stains on her cheeks stumbled across the tiny cobbled yard and grabbed both children in a comprehensive embrace before turning to the two older girls.

'Oh, thank you, ladies,' she gasped. 'I had a visit from the scuffers this mornin', said the kids had run off yesterday, though their foster mother swore she'd been kindness itself, and said they was ungrateful and wicked, which, as I told the scuffers, weren't anywhere near the truth.' She lifted Maisie up and lodged her on one hip, then held out a hand to Dickie. 'Come along, big feller; I'll make a brew of tea and your new pals can tell me what's been happenin'. The scuffers was worried in case you'd reached Liverpool 'cos of the big raid last night, but I thought you'd likely found yourselves an air raid shelter or a garden shed and kipped down in it long before the Jerries had even begun to come over.'

The two girls followed her and the children into the house, but Avril, taking the lead for once, said that though they would be glad of a cup of tea they knew very little more than she about the children's reason for running away. 'They told me that their foster mother didn't feed them properly, and I gather she was pretty quick-tempered; not the type of person to look after children at all. But I expect you'll get more out of them than we had a chance to do. Only they were in Liverpool at the height of the raid and knocked on our door . . .'

She told the whole story clearly and precisely, as far as she knew it, but glossed over what had happened to Gary and the dog. Remembering her own childhood, she knew how easily Dickie might talk himself into believing that it was his fault, because had he not knocked on the basement door both Gary and Timmy might be alive today. If the dog had not scooted past them up the stairs Avril knew, ruefully, that Gary would never have left the security of the basement.

But it did not do to think like that; what's done is done, she told herself, and nothing in this world was certain, except that death comes to us all in the end. In such dangerous times she and Miranda would not be any safer than the citizens of Liverpool wherever the air force might choose to send them. Folk who stayed behind in the city, or trekked into the country when the moon rode high in the clear sky, were all at risk. And war, she told herself, was the biggest uncertainty of all.

Mrs O'Halloran proved to be a delightful person. Barely five foot in height she was correspondingly skinny, with greying hair pulled back from a tiny, bright-eyed face, and an endless fund of stories about her children. She insisted that her guests should take a freshly baked scone with the cup of tea she had already set before them, exclaimed with horror when Avril told her that their flat had had its roof blown off, and actually offered her sofa, if the girls were desperate, though the little house only had two small bedrooms, one for herself and Mr O'Halloran, and the other, little more than a box room, for Dickie and Maisie.

'And what I'll do when they's older, and it wouldn't be right for 'em to share, is more than I can say,' she admitted. 'We stays here because the rent's cheap and it's near my husband's work, but one of these days I'd like to move into the country. The only good thing about that Mrs Grimble was the village she lived in: plenty of space for kids, a nice little school with only thirty or forty pupils, and even a stream at the end of her garden where the kids could paddle or try to catch tiddlers . . .'

Avril and Miranda exchanged glances; outside it was still freezing cold, not at all paddling weather, but of course the children might have been there for some time, though they doubted it, and Dickie confirmed their doubts. 'At first we was at a lovely place, real nice, with a fat jolly farmer's wife, and a granfer what smoked a pipe and told us wizard stories about that other war, what he called the Great War. Only Auntie Ethel – that's what we called the farmer's wife – got appendic . . . appendiss . . . two months ago and couldn't keep us no longer.' He sighed heavily. 'We wanted to go and live wi' the baker's wife – she offered to have us – but Mam said . . .'

Mrs O'Halloran cut across the sentence. 'They was in Devon, what's a devil of a way off. I only visited 'em once and it took a whole day to get there and a whole day to get back, besides costing a small fortune,' she explained. 'Oh, dear, it's all my fault. I said I wanted 'em closer, so's I could visit mebbe once a month, and the authorities found Mrs Grimble what had no evacuees and sent 'em there. Oh, if only I hadn't interfered, they'd be in that little village in Devonshire, happy as Larry, and writin' regular, which they never did from Mrs

Grimble's, which should've made me wonder . . . oh, what a fool you are, Suzie O'Halloran.'

Both girls assured her that she could not have known how unsuitable Mrs Grimble was, and then, catching each other's eye once more, they rose to their feet, thanked their hostess for her hospitality, kissed the children and made them promise to become evacuees once more, for though this second experience had been horrid their mother would make sure that they went somewhere pleasant as soon as she could get them away from the city. 'If you need to escape from somewhere again, just run as far as the nearest scuffer, and tell him you're being badly treated,' Miranda instructed. 'Be good, and write to Mum every week. And don't forget us!'

Back in the city once more, the girls got beds in a hostel and went to the nearest recruiting office where they told their story and gave the sergeant in charge the address of the hostel. They were assured that because of their situation they would receive their postings within a week to ten days. Then they went down to the docks, where they found Steve working to help fight the many fires which still blazed. Before he could put his foot in it and ask about Gary, Miranda took him to one side and explained. 'It's still too raw and painful for Avril to want to talk about it, so the less said the better,' she explained. 'Later, when she's begun to accept that Gary's gone, she'll want to talk about him, but not yet.'

When she told him that they were joining the WAAF she wondered if he would think that they were running away in a cowardly fashion, but he gave his approval at once.

'Without bed or board or so much as a stitch of your own clothing, you'd be nothing but another mouth to feed if you stayed here,' he told them. 'As soon as they can spare me I shall go back to my airfield and start teaching the Jerries that they can't attack Liverpool with impunity.' He smiled at Miranda. 'And the moment you get an address you must drop me a line with the telephone number of the Mess. You'll go to a training camp for starters and be there for about six weeks while they kit you out, train you to march with a heavy pack on your back and decide what you're best suited for . . .' he grinned, 'and then they'll post you to somewhere entirely different.'

Miranda heaved a sigh. 'I can see we shall be writing a great many letters to all the people who've been kind or helpful, or both,' she said ruefully. She looked up at the sky, which was clear and filled with wintry sunshine, and turned to Avril. 'It wouldn't surprise me if there was another raid tonight, so let's get back to the hostel and have a zizz while we've got the chance.'

Chapter Twelve

1944

Miranda and her fellow Waafs were in their hut, preparing for a kit inspection. Knowing how fussy their officer was they always tried to arrive at least ten minutes before the inspection was due to take place, and today was no exception. The rest of the air force might be whispering excitedly about the invasion which was such a big secret, but which everyone knew would be taking place very soon, but the Waafs had their minds fixed on the forthcoming inspection and nothing else.

'Hey, has anyone seen my respirator? Oh, it's okay, it's under my bed.' That was Doris, whose bed was on the right-hand side of Miranda's. Doris was always in a flap about something. On Miranda's other side, Tiddles Tidsworth was trying to arrange her grey stockings so that the huge hole in one heel was out of sight. Miranda checked that her own kit was as it should be, then sat cautiously down on the end of her bed and addressed her neighbour.

'Oh, Doris, this time tomorrow Sarah will be off to the north of England and my friend Avril will be settling in here. She'll find it strange after her beloved balloon site, but oh, it will be wonderful to have her around again.'

Tiddles gave a snort. 'Isn't that just typical of the air force?' she demanded. 'First they put girls on balloons, one of the hardest jobs there is, and let them slog away at it for two or three years without apparently even noticing the casualty rates. Then, when it suits them, they decide to close just about all the balloon sites, and the ones that remain go back to the fellers.' She stood back and regarded her kit with approval. 'Still, they have played fair in one respect; they let the redundant balloon ops retrain for the trade of their choice, though why your pal should chose MT is more than I can fathom.'

Miranda puffed out her chest and seized the lapels of her tunic. 'I told her what a great thing it was to be an MT driver,' she said, grinning. 'So naturally she went off to Wheaton for training same as I did. It was just sheer luck that she got posted here, though. It's months and months since we last met. I reckon she's as excited as I am.'

'And I expect you'll want me to move my bed so that your pal and you can be next door to one another,' Doris said somewhat sulkily. She had already moved several times to accommodate friends who wanted to be together and was always threatening not to do so, but on this occasion at least the move, Miranda thought, would surely be to her advantage. Doris was a parachute packer and so was Sarah's neighbour, so Doris ought to welcome the change.

To the dismay of them both, Miranda and Avril had been separated after their initial training down in Gloucestershire, where they were kitted out with uniform and accessories such as knives, forks and spoons – usually known as 'irons' – gas masks and button sticks and taught to march, to wear the correct uniform for every occasion, and to keep everything immaculate. At Wheaton Miranda was taught to drive, to maintain engines and to become, in short, a mechanical transport driver. She and her fellow MT drivers might drive trucks, salvage wagons, ambulances, tractors or mortuary vans as well as staff cars, and very soon Miranda found herself on an airfield in Norfolk, learning the practicalities of her trade. Sitting on the end of her bed, now, and thinking about the past three years, she remembered ruefully that, upon passing out as a fully trained MT driver, she had thought it would be a cushy job. That had soon proved to be an illusion, for at times drivers had to find their way in almost pitch darkness across countryside from which all signposts and other means of identification had been removed. Furthermore, they had to find their destination with virtually no headlights, since these were masked, with only a little slit of light to make them visible to others allowed.

She soon discovered that East Anglia was covered in airfields and as a driver she had to visit all of them, sometimes carrying messages, sometimes officers and sometimes aircrew. She drove the liberty truck into the nearest big town, loaded with off-duty airmen, and on more than one occasion she drove their group captain up to London for an important meeting. On her first long drive it was winter, the snow thick on the ground, and though she managed to find her way to her destination she got hopelessly lost trying to get out of London, and was almost ready to burst into tears when, having stopped to try to find some indication of their position, she was hailed by a passing lorry driver, who had slowed and leaned out of his cab to see if she needed help. 'Are you lost, lass?' he asked in a strong Scottish accent. 'Where are you bound?'

Miranda hesitated; should she say, or would she get into trouble if she did? But a voice from the back seat reassured her. 'Tell him,' the voice said impatiently. 'He's not likely to be a spy in the middle of London with snow on the ground.'

'Righty ho, sir,' Miranda had said thankfully. She put her head out of the window and gave the required information.

The lorry driver chuckled. 'Got you,' he said cheerfully. 'Just follow me, only not too close, and I'll take you through the suburbs and out on the right road. When I pip my horn and veer off to the right you go straight on.' Miranda thanked him from the bottom of her heart, but expected a rocket from the officer when at last they drew to a halt outside his headquarters. Sometimes the men she drove scarcely bothered to acknowledge her presence at all, but this one, it seemed, was different.

'You've done very well, aircraftwoman. Despite the conditions you drove so smoothly that I was able to snatch quite an hour of sleep.'

'Thank you, sir,' Miranda said, gratified. 'But I'm sorry I got lost.'

The man chuckled. 'You weren't the only one,' he admitted ruefully. 'I'm a Londoner, but with the snow down and no lights showing you could've driven me into Buckingham Palace and I still wouldn't have known where we were. What's your name? I shall ask for you next time I'm needed for a meeting.'

Doris's voice brought Miranda back to the present with a jolt. 'Do you want me to move my bed or don't you?' she demanded. 'Honest to God, Miranda, you're such a dreamer.'

Miranda apologised hastily and admitted that it would be grand to have Avril beside her. 'Otherwise we'll keep trotting up and down the hut exchanging bits of gossip and news and disturbing everybody . . .' she was beginning when the hut door was abruptly opened by their flight sergeant and the officer was ushered into the room. Miranda jumped hastily to her feet and went and stood at the head of her bed, saluting stiffly until they were told to stand at ease, and the kit inspection began.

When it was over and no one had been called to account for missing equipment or clothing, she walked across to the cookhouse with the others, glancing at the large watch on her wrist. It was essential for drivers to know the time since their work was planned by the clock, and now she saw that she would have to get a move on or she would be late for her next job.

The girls straggled into the cookhouse, taking a plate each from the big pile at the end of the counter nearest the door. Miranda held hers out to the fat little cook who plopped a generous helping of mashed potato on to it, whilst another girl slapped on a ladle of the much despised corned beef stew. There was tea in a bucket and Miranda dipped out a mugful, then went and sat down at a table where girls she knew were already tucking into their food. 'Room for a little one, Hazel?' she asked politely, not waiting for a reply before she took her place at the table and began to eat. All around her there was clatter and chatter, and when Hazel suddenly addressed her Miranda, whose thoughts had been far away, jumped. Hazel laughed. 'I was just asking you about this pal of yours who's coming up to use her training as a driver after two years on barrage balloons,' she said. 'All the girls are leaving the balloon sites, aren't they?' She snorted. 'Now that the air force have maimed the flower of British womanhood with the beastly things, they simply change their minds and make the girls re-muster. It's too bad, so it is.'

Miranda laughed, but shook her head. 'No, you've got it wrong. Apparently, if your job simply disappears, you can choose which branch of the WAAF you transfer into. Avril – that's my pal – trained as a C and B, but went over to balloons after her first year because they were recruiting strong girls and she hated working in the cook-house. They gave them men's rations, because they were doing men's work, and men's clothing too: trousers, special gloves, balaclavas – all sorts, in fact.' She laughed. 'The fellers will like Avril; she's one of those Nordic types; blonde hair, blue eyes . . .'

'. . . and white eyelashes,' Hazel said, giggling. 'What time's she arriving? Will she come by rail?'

'I dunno,' Miranda said, shrugging, 'but I shall be hanging round the airfield until she arrives. I'm driving the liberty truck into Norwich this evening, so I just hope she gets here before then.'

Avril sat in the train, peering out through the dirt-smeared window and reflecting that although re-mustering was probably always a bit of a strain, re-mustering from balloons was weird. Balloon opera-tives were the only people who were allowed two kit bags because of the great mass of equipment they had to carry around with them, so travelling without the extra weight made her feel strange, almost naked. She knew that the air force was constantly posting Waafs from one station to another, seeming indifferent to the fact that this was the part of service life which the Waafs found hardest to take. To be removed from friends and from the familiarity of work and workplace seemed to them totally unnecessary; certainly the powers that be would not dream of splitting up the crew of a bomber, though she supposed the fighter pilots might find themselves flying from a variety of different airfields in the course of their work.

'Hey, Avril! Want a sandwich? I'd do a swap, because mine are all dry and curling up at the edges. I couldn't believe it when Cookie told me that all we got for the whole journey – apart from the rail pass – were two lousy Spam sandwiches, a bottle of cold tea and a bit of cake so stale you could resole your shoes with it. It's not as if we could hop off the train and buy something from the refreshment room because if we miss our connection they'll probably court martial us.'

Avril gave a snort of laughter, but turned away from the window to answer. She and the other aircraftwoman had met whilst waiting for the connection and Avril had speedily discovered that they were both heading for Norfolk airfields. Now she shook her head at the suggestion of a court martial, though it was perfectly true that arriving after your leave had expired was a punishable offence. It had to be, otherwise members of the forces would use the unreliability of the trains and the various vicissitudes which beset all travellers in war time as an excuse for prolonging their leave by a day or two.

'You're daft, you are!' she said. 'Next time the train stops we'll look out and see if there's a grub trolley on the platform. I can manage without food but I'm desperate for a drink, and if I have a drink I shall have to visit the bog, unless you think I ought to use my tin hat?'

The other girl laughed. 'Tell you what, when the train stops next we'll both hop out, I'll hold the door open – the engine can't move until every door is closed – and you can nip along to the bog, and if you see someone selling drinks . . .'

'Right you are,' Avril said. 'God, this train is barely moving at walking pace. At this rate it'll be midnight before we get in. Good thing the weather's lovely, because I've not got enough money for a taxi . . . but surely they'll send a vehicle of some sort to meet us? I saw other Waafs and aircraftmen on the train when we got on, so I'm hoping there'll be a gharry or even a bus waiting for us. I know the days are long at this time of year, but they'll want to see us into our huts and get bedding and so on sorted out whilst it's still light, don't you think?'

It was her companion's turn to shrug. 'Dunno. This is my first posting, apart from when I first joined of course, and that took place with twenty or thirty of us all heading in the same direction.' She looked curiously at her companion. 'You said you were on balloons. Did you like it? I reckon I'm too short – maybe even too fat – but I wouldn't mind having a go. They say you get special rations and have a much freer life on a balloon site, with only the odd officer prowling round a couple of times a month, than you do when you're on a real RAF station. So why did you decide to re-muster?'

'I didn't,' Avril said patiently. She felt she had already explained at least fifty times why she was heading for pastures new. 'The air force looked into the number of balloon ops who were in hospital with hernias or broken wrists or . . . oh, all sorts, and when they realised how many of us got injured one way or another they closed down most of the balloon sites, conscripted men to run the ones which were left and advised us to re-muster. I don't deny that it was hard and dangerous work – it truly was – but I think we all loved it. It wasn't too good on the city sites because it was the devil of a job to get the blimp up when it was surrounded by tall buildings, flats, churches and the like. Getting it down was even worse; that's when most people got injured. I copped a broken wrist and two smashed toes on my right foot, but apparently I'm a quick healer and was only off duty for six or eight weeks. But I loved it – as I said, I think most of us did. I'd never have re-mustered of my own accord, but of course we had no choice.' She smiled at the incredulity on the other girl's face. 'It would be hard for other people to understand, but the comradeship, the closeness, the feeling that we were all in it together, and the sheer beauty of the countryside surrounding some of the sites . . . it made up for the hard work and the danger.'

'But all the airfields are surrounded by countryside,' her companion pointed out. 'And though they're pretty dangerous places there are plenty of dugouts and shelters and such, whereas on the balloon sites you had to be outside working with the balloon all through the raid until well after the all clear had sounded. I don't fancy that, I'm telling you.'

Avril sighed, knowing that it was impossible to explain how she felt. She remembered a wild night when the cable which tethered the balloon to the ground had snapped and she, the sergeant in charge of the winch, and the entire crew of Site 36 had chased across the London suburbs in the windy darkness, finding the balloon eventually and staring helplessly up to where it roosted, like an enormous broody hen, over the roof of a fire station. Poor Belinda Boop – the girls always named the balloons – had been rescued eventually but the damage was too extensive for mending and she had been taken away on a tender. The new balloon arrived the very next day and the girls, worn out from their exertions in pursuit of the errant Belinda, had to begin the task of readying the new balloon in case a raid occurred the following night.

Avril told the story of the escaping balloon amusingly and well, and pushed to the back of her mind the sad memories which she could not bear to recall. There was Erica, who had tripped over a guy rope and failed to see the concrete block which secured it. She had bashed her head open, and because the night was wild and the concrete block in shadow had not been discovered until she had bled to death. The girls had been shocked and horrified and had not appreciated the dressing down they had received for not noticing Erica earlier. Later, their sergeant had told them that their fellow operative could never have recovered, was probably dead within seconds of her head's meeting the block, but Avril knew for a fact that two of the girls – the ones who had first found Erica – had asked for transfers to other, less hazardous work as a result.

But the train was slowing and the ghastly image conjured up by memory faded as their carriage drew to a juddering halt. Avril stood up and let the window down, then turned to her companion. 'Are you sure you'll be all right, Daisy? I'm sure if you explain to the porter that this isn't a corridor train he'll let us nip out to the bog. If we take it in turns then whoever remains here can buy a cuppa or whatever. How much money have you got? I've got two half crowns, which won't buy much, but . . .'

'I've got the same,' Daisy said, ferreting around in her gas mask case and producing a small red leather purse. She jumped down on to the platform and gave Avril, who was already down, a shove. 'Go *on*,' she urged. 'There's folk getting off but no one in uniform, so this ain't Norwich Thorpe. But there's been no announcement about changing trains, so we'd best hang on where we are.'

Avril set off at trot for the Ladies, passing a lad of fourteen or fifteen pushing a scantily laden trolley. She waited until she had swapped places with Daisy, then beckoned to the boy. 'What have you got for half a crown? A mug of tea – no, two mugs of tea – would be very welcome.' She eyed the rolls and sandwiches suspiciously, then pointed to two which looked as though they contained lettuce and tomato as well as some sort of cheese. 'I'll have two teas, please, and two cheese salad rolls, if that's what they are.' She fished around in the breast pocket of her tunic. 'What's the damage?'

Miranda spent most of the afternoon in jumpy distraction. She was on ambulance driving, but managed to swap with another girl, hoping that when she drove into the city she would find Avril waiting on Castle Meadow, where all the gharries from all the airfields congregated so that the troops might know precisely where to find them for the return trip.

She had been edgy all afternoon, but as soon as she stopped the gharry on Castle Meadow and went round to remind her passengers that she would be leaving at ten o'clock, she began to feel apprehensive as well. Suppose Avril had missed her train? It was not unlikely, since most trains would be full of troops, heading for whatever part of the coast had been selected as the jump-off point for the planned invasion. On the other hand, Avril would have been told to arrive at RAF Scratby by midnight, so in the event of something's preventing her from getting here before Miranda, and the gharry, left, she would still have two hours before she was liable to get hauled over the coals for tardiness.

Miranda was just deciding that, if the worst came to the worst, she would disable the engine in some way and claim that that was what had held her friend up, when a familiar head appeared in the window of the gharry, flaxen hair flopping over a broad forehead, light blue eyes sparkling with excitement.

Both girls squeaked each other's names and Miranda threw open the gharry door, nearly sending her friend flying, but Avril righted herself and the girls hugged exuberantly, Avril laughing whilst tears ran unchecked down Miranda's cheeks.

Miranda was the first to recover. She rubbed the tears away, then produced a handkerchief and blew her nose before shoving the hanky back in her battledress pocket. 'Oh, Avril, it's just so wonderful to see you,' she gasped. 'I couldn't believe my eyes when your letter came saying you'd re-mustered as a driver and were being posted to RAF Scratby.'

Avril laughed again. 'Then you can imagine how

flabbergasted I was when my posting came through,' she said as Miranda slammed the driver's door shut, locked it and then went round to secure the passenger door. When she re-joined Avril on the pavement she took careful stock of her friend before suggesting that they might go down to the Foundry Bridge, over the river Wensun. 'There's a food outlet, a big van, parked down by the river. All the forces personnel go there, knowing his grub's good and cheap. We can pick up a bottle of pop and a couple of sandwiches and go and sit on the river bank and talk.' She glanced at her wristwatch. 'We've got a couple of hours before I've got to drive the gharry back to the station, so we can sit and watch the boats and catch up. Agreed?'

Avril agreed with enthusiasm, saying that after twelve hours in stuffy railway carriages or on almost equally stuffy station platforms she would appreciate a quiet time in the fresh air. 'I crossed the bridge near the station, and thought the river banks, with the willows leaning over the water, looked really attractive,' she said. 'Another day, perhaps we could take a boat out . . .' But by now they had reached the van, and when they got to the head of the queue Miranda greeted the owner with a cheerful grin and asked what was tonight's special.

'Well, how hungry are you, together?' he asked, in a rich Norfolk accent, eyeing them judiciously. 'I guess you had a cookhouse meal earlier so you won't want a sausage sandwich . . .'

'A sausage sandwich will be fine, Claude,' Miranda said quickly. She knew all too well that if she did not make up her mind at once Claude would run through his entire stock, for he liked to please his customers.

Having made a decision Miranda added a bottle of pop and two paper cups, then handed over her money, and armed with a fat sandwich each the girls hurried towards the river. Presently, settled beneath the branches of a willow, Miranda watched as Avril took a big bite out of her sandwich, grinned, and nodded.

'This sausage tastes pre-war, and the bread's delicious,' she announced. 'Pour me some pop, would you?'

Miranda complied, saying as she did so: 'So you appreciate our Claude's grub, do you? I believe his mother makes the bread, or perhaps it's Claude himself; at any rate he doesn't approve of the national loaf and always serves homemade stuff. And now let me have a proper look at you.'

She scanned her friend from the top of her flaxen head to her well-polished air force issue black shoes. 'You're thinner. Now I wonder why that is? Everyone tells you that the girls on balloons get extra rations because it's such hard work; but of course the work itself might have slimmed you down. And don't think I'm criticising, 'cos you look grand. I expect you'll notice changes in me too, though I don't think I've lost much weight.'

'You look worn out,' Avril said with all the frankness which Miranda remembered. 'I guess driving is pretty tense, what with the blackout an' all.' She hesitated. 'Steve still all right? Do you realise how much we've lost touch over the past three years? Oh, I know we've exchanged scrappy little letters from time to time, and we did meet up once, but to be honest, Miranda, if it hadn't been for this posting I reckon we'd have lost touch altogether. Somehow there was always something more important to do than write letters.'

361

'Steve's okay, or he was last night when I telephoned the Mess,' Miranda said. 'But there's a big offensive coming up . . .' she lowered her voice, 'I expect you've heard all about it, though it's supposed to be top secret. Anyway, bombing raids over Germany are taking place whenever the weather's good, and so far this summer has been brilliant.' She looked shyly at her friend, then waved a finger under Avril's nose. 'That, dear Avril, is an engagement ring. I didn't want to get engaged. I had a silly superstitious fear that if we did something which made both of us so happy we'd be tempting fate to throw a spanner in the works. But in the end I just wanted to do whatever Steve wanted, and that was to get engaged.'

Avril seized her friend's hand and gazed at the pretty little ring on her third finger. 'How on earth did he save up the money for this?' she demanded. 'I don't know much about jewellery prices . . .'

Miranda laughed. 'He didn't buy it. Do you remember Granny Granger? I think you met her once.'

'Yes, I remember; a lovely old lady,' Avril said at once. 'Don't say she's gone for a burton?'

'Good heavens, no,' Miranda said, looking shocked. 'Steve and I had a spot of leave and decided to take it at the same time, and go home to Liverpool. While we were there Steve told Granny Granger that we wanted to get engaged and would do so as soon as he could afford to buy a ring. Whereupon the old lady trotted up to her bedroom and came down again with this dear little ring in a tiny green velvet box. She said it had belonged to her mother, so it's really old, an antique almost, and since she meant to leave it to Steve in her will he might as well have it now, so we got engaged on the spot.'

Avril whistled admiringly. 'Ain't you the lucky one? But shouldn't the ring have gone to Steve's mother rather than to Steve? It seems an odd thing to leave to a feller.'

'Not really. Mrs Mickleborough will get Granny's engagement ring and all the rest of her jewellery, which isn't saying much. Of course she gave this to Steve on impulse really, but we both took it as a sign that she thought getting engaged was a good idea, and I have to say we've never regretted it. It's – it's kind of nice to belong to someone else, to look towards a shared future . . . oh, I don't know, I'm not putting it very well, but I guess you understand.' She hesitated as a large rowboat full of RAF personnel splashed its way past, then spoke diffidently. 'Have you got a boyfriend, queen? You never mentioned one in your letters, but then you didn't write often, or at much length . . .'

Avril cut across the sentence, the colour rising in her cheeks. 'No, I've not got a boyfriend, though of course I've been out with several people over the last three years. After Gary was killed I could see all too clearly that having a boyfriend in wartime is nowt but a ticket to pain. It's why you look so worn and weary. I'll bet you spend ninety per cent of your time worrying that something bad will happen to Steve. Well, I can do without that. Maybe I'm selfish – a great many men have told me I'm hard – but I don't mean to hand over my heart for breaking twice in one lifetime.'

Miranda nodded. 'I know what you mean, because I suppose it was the reason why I didn't want to get engaged,' she admitted. 'But you're not just shutting the door on the possibility of being hurt, queen, you're shutting it on the chance of happiness. And it takes two to

363

tango, as they say. What about the feller? Isn't he allowed a voice in this decision? And don't tell me there isn't a feller. What about Julian; what about Pete? I know you write to them both and I bet there are lots of others chasing you, because with that blonde mop you always had chaps in tow when we were living in Russell Street and I can't believe it's any different now.'

'Oh, them!' Avril said contemptuously. 'They're just pals, as you used to be so fond of remarking. As for new blokes, you obviously don't know balloon sites. They are – were, I should say – all staffed by women except the sergeant in charge who was usually a man, so us balloon ops didn't have the same opportunities that you get as an MT driver. Of course we went to RAF stations for dances and social events, but I never got close to anyone, not really close. And looking at the strain on your face, I can only say I'm grateful I never got involved.'

Miranda was in the middle of admitting that she did worry about Steve most of the time when she heard a clock begin to strike and jumped to her feet, knocking over the bottle of pop and casting crumbs to the four winds. 'Heavens, I'm supposed to be back at the gharry, loading the fellers up,' she said, beginning to scramble up the bank, with Avril in hot pursuit. 'Oh, damn, we're going to have to run. I dare not be late, because everyone in my hut knows you're arriving today and will assume I'm risking their passes because my friend missed her connection.'

Miranda had always had friends amongst the other MT drivers and mechanics who shared the care and maintenance of all the vehicles on the station, but none had suited her as well as Avril. Perhaps it was their shared background, or the fact that they were the only two Liverpudlians in their group, but whatever the reason the two girls, who had been close when they shared the flat, grew closer still. A couple of times Steve suggested that Avril might like to make up a foursome with a member of his crew, but in the end Miranda seized the opportunity, when she and Steve both got a forty-eight, to suggest that they should spend it alone together. 'I'll explain to Avril, and we can enjoy ourselves with a clear conscience,' she told Steve when she telephoned him at his Mess. 'I'm not suggesting we should share anything other than a meal and a dance at the Samson and Hercules though, so don't you go getting ideas.'

Steve said virtuously that of course he would expect nothing but friendship from a fiancée so high-minded. Chuckling, Miranda told him not to be so cheeky and replaced the receiver before he could reply.

She told Avril that she and Steve meant to spend their forty-eight together, since the weather was still blissfully fine. Indeed, it had been blissfully fine throughout Operation Overlord, as the invasion became known, and the thousands of Allied soldiers now pushing their way across German-occupied France must be grateful to have the weather on their side. All leave had been cancelled, but Steve's Lancaster, overflying occupied France in order to bomb Germany, had limped home after sustaining a good deal of damage, and this enabled the crew to ask permission to take a forty-eight whilst their Lancaster, which they had named Lindy Lou, had her many injuries repaired.

Leave usually started after work so that one might

catch the gharry either to the nearest railway station or into the city, and on this occasion Steve and Miranda met on Castle Meadow, each with a kitbag slung over one shoulder, and Steve, at least, with an anticipatory gleam in his eyes. Kissing was forbidden whilst in uniform, and one was always in uniform, but Steve had already planned what they would do. 'We'll catch a bus out of the city heading for Ringland Hills,' he said, starting to walk towards the bus station. 'There's a nice little pub in the village which will do us supper and only charge us five shillings, or ten bob for bed and breakfast,' he said, taking her arm in a proprietorial manner. 'You'll love it; all the chaps say the food's prime, the beds soft and the landlady discreet.'

Miranda, giggling, gave Steve a shove. 'Enough of that,' she said severely. 'It all sounds fine apart from the landlady. She can keep her discretion to herself.'

They reached Surrey Street and found the bus they wanted waiting, and very soon they were in the cosy little pub with a remarkably good meal on the table before them while Steve, having reluctantly booked two rooms, spent a good deal of energy trying to persuade Miranda that sharing would be much more fun than going off to their own beds after supper.

When they had first entered the pub the bar had been empty, but now it was beginning to fill up, and Steve hushed his companion when she began to argue. 'I was only teasing,' he said in an undertone. 'Of course there isn't a law against not sharing a room if you're engaged.' Then his voice sharpened. 'Oh, hell; there's a face I recognise! She's not in uniform – a bit old for that probably – but I'm sure I know her from somewhere. Oh, heck, she's coming over. I do hate it when somebody whose name I can't recall expects to be recognised and made welcome, and all you can do is wonder who the devil it is.'

Miranda was beginning to say that it was his imagination, that the woman was not really heading for them but had spotted a vacant place on the bench beside her, when she broke off short. 'Lynette!' she squeaked excitedly. 'What on earth are you doing here?'

The former member of the Madison Players approached, beaming, and Miranda jumped to her feet to give her a hearty kiss. 'I were just about to ask you the same, kiddo,' Lynette Rich said cheerily. 'It's the last place I should have expected to meet someone I know.' She dug a plump elbow into Miranda's ribs. 'We come here, me and my American feller, to have a quiet weekend away from all the fuss and botheration, and who's the first person I set me eyes on? It's little Miranda Lovage, though she ain't so little now. They say it's bad manners to ask a woman her age, but when I last seen you you were just a child, and now I suppose you must be nineteen or twenty.' She turned to stare piercingly into Steve's face. 'Do I reckernise you, young feller? I hopes as you haven't brought my little friend here with the intention of misbehavin'.'

Steve grinned. 'We've seen each other before, when Miranda took me round to the theatre a couple of times whilst she was searching for her mother,' he said. 'You're a dancer, aren't you?'

The plump, smiling lady nodded her peroxided curls vigorously. That's me; or that *was* me rather. I'm with ENSA; we entertain the troops . . . well, you know all that, and this was to be a bit of a treat between shows because once it's safe to do so they'll send us across to the jolly old Continong to entertain the troops over there. It'll be a change from . . .'

She stopped speaking as a voice hailed her, and a heavily built, middle-aged American with so many stripes on his sleeve and medals on his chest that Miranda guessed he was someone high up in the USAF crossed the room and put a hand on his companion's arm. 'Gee, honey, you find friends everywhere,' he said admiringly. 'But we're in a bit of a fix, sweetie; the landlady says they've not got a room.' He pointed an accusing finger at Steve. 'This young guy has took 'em both, so unless I can persuade your pals to give one up . . .'

After that there was much talk and much persuasion on the part of Lynette and her friend, though Steve was far too sensible to join in. He stood back, well aware that Miranda would presently bow to the inevitable, as indeed she did, though it must have been almost midnight when the two couples climbed the winding wooden stair, exchanged goodnights and disappeared into their respective rooms. Once there, Miranda allowed her annoyance to show, actually accusing Steve of having planned the whole business, though she knew very well that he had done no such thing. However, they managed to undress discreetly and climbed into bed, pulling the bolster down between them. 'A bit of a cuddle wouldn't hurt,' Steve said hopefully when they had blown out the candle and rolled up the blackout blind and were lying in the friendly summer dark. 'I won't do anything you wouldn't like, honest to God, Miranda.'

'Go to sleep!' Miranda replied smartly. 'Go straight to sleep; do not pass Go, do not collect two hundred pounds.

And just remember, all Waafs have a scream like a train whistle, so if you put so much as one finger across that bolster . . .'

'I wasn't considering a finger . . .' Steve said plaintively, and received a quick smack round the ear. 'Oh, very well. I'm tired too, so we'd best get some shut-eye, or it'll be morning and that damned Yankee will have ate up all the bacon and eggs.'

Miranda and Steve, despite the best of intentions, woke late, and by the time they took their places opposite one another at the small table in the bar the American was paying the bill and thanking the landlady for a delightful visit. He hefted a large suitcase out to the waiting taxi and Lynette, with a cheery wave, was about to follow him when something seemed to occur to her and she turned back. 'I take it you've seen your mam?' she bawled across the room. 'You could ha' knocked me down with a feather when I walked slap bang into her on Lime Street. I could see she didn't remember me – well, I weren't always blonde and I've put on a bit more weight than I should over the past two or three years. She said she were with a concert party, come over from the States to entertain the doughboys, but before I could tell her how worried we'd all been someone shouted and she gave me a big smile, said "Excuse me, but I'm wanted" and disappeared into the crowd. You knew she were back, of course?'

Sheer astonishment had caused Miranda's throat to close up, making speech impossible, but Steve seized Lynette's arm, digging his fingers into the soft flesh until she squeaked. 'Miranda don't know anything about her mother, except that she might have been living in America. She's not seen her since the day she disappeared,' he said urgently. 'Are you sure it was Arabella? Did the person who shouted use the name Arabella? Oh, Lynette, you can't just walk away, having told only half the story.'

But Lynette was shaking her head. 'I dunno. I called her Arabella but she just looked straight through me as if I didn't exist. It were only when I grabbed her arm that she looked at me. At the time I would have sworn it was Arabella, but afterwards . . . oh, I don't know, I suppose it could have been one of them lookalikes. Which twin has the Toni, sort of thing. Still, it might be worth you havin' a word with whoever runs the Yankee ENSA; see if you can trace her through them.' A bellow from the yard outside made her turn hastily away from them. 'I've gotta go,' she shouted over her shoulder. 'See you again. Sorry I can't stay . . .'

Miranda jumped to her feet just as the landlady appeared with two plates full of bacon, eggs, fried bread and sausages. She would have run out of the room but Steve caught her arm and made her sit down. 'The car went off the moment she climbed into the passenger seat,' he said cheerfully. 'And anyway there was no point in asking any more questions, because she'd already told us everything she knew. But she's given you a very good clue, queen, the best you've had so far. Now I wonder whether anyone else in Liverpool recognised her?'

'I've got to get back to Liverpool!' Miranda cried wildly, ignoring Steve's words. 'I've simply got to find her. If she's lost her memory and doesn't know who she really is, then I can tell her she's my mother, say how sorry I

370

am that I wasn't a better daughter. And there's other things: she won't know she was kidnapped, or by whom. She won't know what happened to her in that storm, how she escaped drowning, I mean. Oh, once I've helped her to unlock her memory it will all come flooding back. I must go up to Liverpool at once!'

Steve, however, was shaking his head. 'No you mustn't. You're a member of His Majesty's forces, and you can't possibly get up to Liverpool and back in the course of a forty-eight. Besides, Lynette never said *when* she bumped into Arabella. The Yanks have been in the war now for over two years; it could have happened way back. I'm afraid you're going to have to keep on being patient and sensible, because rushing your fences will only lead to a fall. And now, darling Miranda, do let's get on with what's left of our little holiday. Going AWOL will only get you court martialled and that won't help to find your mother. I'll tell you what, though: write to Lynette, care of ENSA, and ask all the questions which you didn't have time for just now. She might remember a bit more if you give her a few days.' He dug his fork into the egg yolk. 'Aren't we lucky? This egg is cooked just as I like it with the yolk runny and the white firm. Oh, come on, Miranda, cheer up. You're on holiday and you've had a clue to your mother's whereabouts at last!'

Chapter Thirteen

Avril had waved Miranda off, gone to the NAAFI for a cup of tea and a natter, and then repaired to their hut. She undressed slowly and climbed into bed, expecting to sleep at once for she had had a tiring day, but in fact she lay wakeful, suddenly aware that she was missing the younger girl. Avril wondered how she and Steve were getting on, and cast off her blankets, for it was a hot night. She hoped they were making the most of their leave and turned and twisted, trying to find a cool spot, but finally decided to stop courting sleep and instead think back over her time at RAF Scratby.

Miranda had made it easy for her, she thought now. There had been a great many girls to meet as well as a good few young men, for, one way or another, Miranda knew practically all the personnel on the airfield and introduced Avril to each one. Everyone was friendly, the men intrigued by the combination of her Liverpool accent and Nordic good looks and the girls fascinated to learn that she had spent the last few years on a balloon site and eager for details.

But now Avril let her mind go right back to the time when she had joined the air force to get away from the streets where she and Gary had once been happy . . . she had joined in fact to forget the pain which losing him had caused her. Before she had met Gary she had never known what it was to love someone, for though she supposed she must have loved her parents she could scarcely remember them. Along with most of the children in the home, she had hated the place, the staff and a good few of the other occupants. When she had met Miranda she had been living in a hostel, working as hard as she could at her job and scarcely believing that she could ever escape from the treadmill of trying to earn enough money to be independent. Then Gary had entered her life.

Before then, Avril had had several boyfriends but had never taken them seriously. They had families – mums and dads, brothers and sisters – and whenever she was taken to a young man's home she felt panicked, like someone thrown into deep water before learning to swim. She floundered, unable to find the right attitude, always aware that she was different.

Knowing Miranda had helped, because Miranda, too, had no cosy home background. She had talked of her loving mother, but Avril secretly thought a good deal of what her friend said was wishful thinking. If Miranda's mother had truly loved her, why had she gone away and not come back? So, gradually, almost imperceptibly, Avril began to relax. And when she met Gary, and discovered that he, too, had been brought up in a children's home, she had begun to talk of her past, and to her delight had found Gary understood.

Very soon she realised she was deeply in love with him, so that the shock of his death had been almost unbearable. Running away, determined to make a career for herself in the air force, she had accepted the position of kitchen worker on an airfield in Lincolnshire, lowly and disgusting though this was to her way of thinking, because she was determined to do well, to be the best C and B the air force had ever known.

She had reckoned without Corporal Greesby, of course. She had no idea whence his dislike had sprung, but she soon discovered that it was in his power to make or break her and that the best way to escape his malevolence was to keep her head down and do as she was told. 'Never explain, never complain' was an old army saying, but apparently it also applied to the air force, and Avril and one or two other girls for whom Corporal Greesby had developed a dislike soon learned to follow its advice. So when the notice had appeared on the bulletin board in the Mess, asking for women volunteers who were strong, fit and healthy to take over from the men on balloon sites, Avril had been the first to put her name forward, and had been immediately accepted. She had been given a rail pass to Cardington, where she would be trained, along with several other girls from her hut, to fly the great unwieldy barrage balloons.

If the Royal Air Force wondered why so many girls from Corporal Greesby's kitchen applied for the balloon corps they didn't ask, and Avril suspected they didn't care, though she got a good deal of pleasure from a small revenge which she personally carried out upon the corporal, spiking his usual enormous helping of chocolate pudding with a bar of Ex-lax chocolate crumbled over the top. Grinning evilly, she told one of the other girls that the corporal would be spending the next few hours glued to the bog, and shouldered her kitbag with the feeling that honour had been satisfied.

Number One balloon training unit at Cardington was

like a breath of fresh air after the horrors of Corporal Greesby's kitchen. The course lasted ten weeks, during which Avril learned skills of which she had never previously heard. The sergeant who taught them to splice rope and wire, inflate the balloons with hydrogen and drive the winches which operated the winding gear was a sensible man in his forties, who had been a teacher in civvy street and knew exactly how to deal with his recruits. By the end of the course they appreciated not only his skills but also his kindness, and in Avril's eyes he had rescued the reputation of the air force.

After their initial training the girls spent a week at an old aerodrome actually working with a balloon. They were divided into teams of twelve Waafs and a flight sergeant, and, to their relief, when they got their posting at the end of the course they stayed with their team, though the flight sergeant would be allocated when they actually reached their balloon site.

From that moment on Avril was in her element. The work was hard, heavy and frequently dangerous, but she loved it. Most of the sites were on the outskirts of big cities or built-up areas which needed extra protection from the Luftwaffe raids. At first it was difficult to see what extra protection the balloons offered, but the girls had a talk from a flying officer who assured them that the blimps were best avoided, both by the enemy and by their own aircraft. 'The Luftwaffe fly high when they come in for a bombing raid, and do their best to keep well clear of the balloons,' he assured them. 'No doubt you've been taught that a plane which flies too near a balloon can be caught up in the cable, which moves with a sawing motion and can cut through wings, tail, even fuselage. So never think your work isn't important, because it has saved countless lives.'

By the time the order came that Waafs were to leave the balloon sites Avril viewed the prospect of re-mustering with dismay. Only when she learned that, because she had volunteered for balloons, she might choose her new trade did she begin to see that this, in fact, might not be a bad thing. Balloons were all very well, but they weren't exactly a career move; if she re-mustered as, for instance, an MT driver, then they would teach her, not only to drive, but also to repair and maintain all the many and various vehicles used by the air force, and this would still be a useful skill even when the war was over. So off she went to Wheaton, and because she was bright and hard-working she emerged at the end of the training period a fully fledged MT driver.

Naturally enough she watched the bulletin board anxiously, hoping to get a posting soon, and was almost unbelieving when she learned that she was to go to RAF Scratby, the very airfield, had she been given the choice, which she would have chosen.

And now here she was actually lying on her hard little bed feeling a fresh breeze blowing in through the window with a touch of salt on its breath, for the airfield was only a couple of miles from the sea. I wonder whether the beach is mined, Avril found herself thinking sleepily. I know most of the beaches are, particularly along the south and east coasts, but I've read in the newspapers that they have to leave an area clear of mines so that lifeboats can be launched. Oh well, I expect we'd get court martialled if we tried to so much as paddle, and there are lots of other things to do when you're on a proper RAF station. She snuggled her face into the pillow, remembering the meal they had been served that evening in the Scratby cookhouse, some sort of stew with not very much meat but an awful lot of carrots, and a syrup pudding. Tiddles Tidsworth, watching her, had laughed and asked if the food was up to balloon standards.

Avril had laughed too. On a balloon site one took turns at everything: guard duty, driving the winch, cooking the meals. When it was your turn to cook you were given the ingredients and told to go ahead; there were no such things as menus, or suggestions even. Some girls could cook naturally, others couldn't. Avril remembered Sandra, who didn't understand about boiling potatoes until they were soft, and Janette whose meals were so delicious that at first they had suspected she was buying extra grub from a restaurant somewhere. Avril had assured Tiddles that it was a treat to have food cooked for you and left it at that. No point in putting anyone's back up by saying that the stew could have benefited from some flour to thicken it or even a bit more meat. Smiling at the recollection, she fell asleep at last.

Miranda had spent the day ferrying personnel between airfields, and knew that Avril had been doing the same, so at eight o'clock, when she was free at last, she went straight to the cookhouse, hoping that someone would realise that the MT drivers on duty would not have been fed.

The large room with its many tables and chairs and its long wooden counter was almost empty, but to Miranda's relief those who were in there all seemed to be eating and there was a smell of hot food in the air.

She went over to the counter and a weary little Waaf clad in blue wrapover apron, white cap and leather clogs greeted her with a tired grin. 'Evenin', Lovage; what can I do you for? Cheese on toast, beans on toast, scrambled eggs on toast? Or a mixture of all three?'

Miranda settled for cheese on toast and was turning away with her plate of food when the girl behind the counter spoke again. 'Your mate come in ten minutes ago; she's over there in that corner. She were one of the lucky ones; got in before Corp used the last of the fried spuds. Help yourself to HP Sauce; it's by the bucket of tea.'

Miranda collected a mug, dipped out her tea and went across to where Avril was sitting. She had one of the tables to herself and Miranda was surprised to see that she had, spread out upon it, five or six sheets of cheap airmail paper. She scowled as Miranda's shadow fell across her table, then looked up and smiled as she recognised her friend.

'Wotcher!' she said cheerfully. She pushed one of the chairs towards Miranda. 'Do sit down, only don't drip that tea all over my letters.'

'Letters?' Miranda said. 'Don't you mean letter? Is it going to be an awfully long one? Or are you expecting to make a lot of mistakes?' She sat down as she spoke and eyed the other girl curiously.

'Neither,' Avril said positively. She waved a newly sharpened pencil under her friend's nose. 'I do this every week or so, and it's a real bind, but I know my duty. I quite like getting letters myself, though by the time they've gone through the censor they often look more like those lacy paper things people used to stand cakes on . . . can't remember what they're called . . .'

'Doilies,' Miranda supplied. She took a big bite out of her toasted cheese, then leaned forward so that if she did dribble brown sauce it would fall on her plate rather than on her uniform. 'Who are you writing to anyway?' She half expected Avril to tell her to mind her own business, but though her friend tapped the side of her nose in the well-known gesture she replied readily enough, whilst producing from her gas mask case several crumpled and really rather dirty pages which she smoothed out, ticked off and laid out, parade ground fashion, each one on a separate sheet of the airmail paper.

'I don't mind tellin' you, because you won't know any of them,' Avril said. She pointed. 'That's to Danny, that's to Simon, that's to Frank and that's to Freddy, and then there's one for P— Paul.' She looked challengingly across the table at her friend. 'Satisfied?'

'Yes, I suppose so. Are they all service personnel? Or are you still in touch with any of your old pals from the factory? Come to that, are you still in touch with people from the children's home? I know I ought to drop Aunt Vi and Beth a line from time to time – well, I do – but I warned Beth last time I wrote that if she didn't reply I wouldn't write again.'

'Has she? Replied, I mean,' Avril asked. She wrote *Dear Danny, Lovely to get your letter*, then looked questioningly up at her friend.

'Not yet, but Steve had a letter from his mam – they're back in Jamaica Close – and she says Aunt Vi and Beth are okay though Aunt Vi disapproves of Beth's feller and they're always having rows.' She leaned forward to stare as Avril began to write on the next sheet of paper.

'Whatever are you doing, queen? Don't you finish one letter before you start the next?'

'Course not; that'd be a waste of time,' Avril said impatiently. She pulled the next sheet towards her and proceeded to write. She had large, rather childish handwriting, and Miranda read it upside down from across the table with ease. *Dear Simon, Lovely to get your letter* . . .

Even as Miranda watched, Avril pulled forward the third sheet. *Dear Frank, Lovely to get your letter* . . . 'Aircraftwoman Donovan, what on *earth* do you think you're doing? Surely you aren't going to write exactly the same letter to all those fellers? Next thing you'll have half a dozen pencils all working together so you only have to write the once; the pencils will do the rest.' She was joking, but Avril answered her quite seriously.

'I know what you mean, and I've tried it, but it simply won't work. This method is better, because I can write quite a lot when I don't have to think about what I'm saying. If I wrote to each bloke separately I'd never have a spare moment, so this is the obvious answer.' As she spoke she was finishing off the line of papers, *Dear Frank* being followed by *Dear Freddy* and *Dear Paul*.

Miranda watched, fascinated, as her friend rapidly scrawled identical messages on the first four sheets of paper. 'What's wrong with Paul?' she asked, indicating the last sheet, still blank apart from the salutation. 'Is he special? In fact, is Paul the reason why you won't settle down with one chap, you greedy girl, you?'

'Special? Not particularly,' Avril said, but Miranda saw a flush climb up her friend's neck into her cheeks. 'But they're a long way off and all my letters to them go by sea, so as you must realise, nosy, they don't get all of them by a long chalk. Last time I wrote to Paul he wrote back to say only half my letter had arrived; some idiot in the censorship office had seen fit to tear it in two, or at any rate only half arrived on Paul's notice board. After that it seems only fair to write in a bit more detail, otherwise he's behind the rest of the blokes, if you see what I mean.' She glared across the table. 'Have you any objection? It was you who told me letters were important to fellers a long way from home, if you remember . . .'

'Oh, I don't blame you,' Miranda said quickly. 'It just seems a bit cold-blooded, that's all. I dare say you've given all of them the impression that they're the only bloke in your life, and that after the war . . .'

Avril snorted. 'I can't help what they believe, that's up to them,' she said firmly. 'And if you're going to keep talking I'll get in a muddle and repeat the same sentence twice in one letter, and that would be awful, wouldn't it? I mean, one of them might guess that he's not my only correspondent. And don't you go dribbling brown sauce over my last two sheets of airmail paper, or you can jolly well buy me another pad from the NAAFI.'

'Sorry,' Miranda said hastily, cramming the last piece of toasted cheese into her mouth, and speaking rather thickly through it. 'As I said, it just seems a bit cold-blooded. What happens if Tom, Dick or Harry suddenly stops replying to your form letters?'

This time a real flush turned Avril's pale skin to scarlet. She glared at Miranda and Miranda saw that her friend's lip was trembling. 'You mean when one of them is killed, don't you?' she said, her voice breaking. 'Someone in his flight will go through his mail and let me know. And now you can bloody well gerrout of here and leave me to finish me letters in peace.'

Miranda jumped to her feet and went round the table to give Avril a hug. 'I'm really sorry, queen,' she said gently. 'It was very wrong of me to pry and even more wrong to assume that your letter writing was some sort of game. I can see now that you're making a load of fellers happy and harming no one. Will you forgive me?'

Avril gulped and wiped her eyes with the backs of her hands, causing a couple of large teardrops to splash onto one of her letters, but she turned and gave her friend a rueful grin. 'The thing is, Miranda, I've only got one life. The letters are full of what I've been doing – except I never mention other chaps, of course – so the letters are bound to be nearly identical, even if I went to the trouble of writing on separate days. This way, I'm keeping four or five guys happy without making promises I don't intend to keep.'

'Well, bully for you,' Miranda said. 'I'm dog tired; I've been driving all day. I'll just get myself a slice of spotted dick and then I'm for bed. How long will it take you to finish your – er – letters?' Some imp of mischief made her add: 'How do you sign off? Not SWALK?'

To her relief, Avril laughed. 'Course not. I just say *Thanks again for your letter, can't wait for the next, Avril.* Does that suit your majesty's sense of what's right and wrong? It had better, because I don't intend to change my way of life just to suit you.'

'All right, you've made your point.' Miranda carried her plate across to the counter, swished her irons briefly in the barrel of lukewarm water, dried them on a rag of dishcloth and pushed them into her gas mask case. Then she waved to Avril, busily writing once more, and set off for their hut. Dead tired as she was she still forced herself to go along to the ablutions and have as good a shower as she could in cold water before getting between the blankets. She had been there only what felt like a few minutes when she was awoken by Avril crashing into her own bed. Miranda sat up on her elbow and gazed in the dimness across to where Avril was already snuggling down. 'Finished your letters?' she asked sleepily. 'There was no hot water but I managed to get a shower, though it was cold. How about you?'

'I done 'em, the letters I mean, but I've not been to the 'blutions; too late, too tired,' Avril droned, her voice already sleep-drugged. 'I'll wash in the mornin'. G'night.'

'G'night,' Miranda echoed, and almost immediately fell fast asleep.

Avril lay watching the light gradually strengthen through the small window, and thinking that she had had a narrow escape in the cookhouse the previous evening, when Miranda had come so jauntily across the room to join her at her table. How easily she might have been writing to Pete Huxtable first instead of last, and for some reason, a reason which she could not explain even to herself, she had no wish for either Miranda or anyone else to know that she was writing to Pete. He had had a very varied war so far and oddly, though they had not been particularly close when she had lived in the flat, as time went on she had grown to appreciate him and to prefer him to all her other suitors. Whilst she had been what she now thought of as a kitchen slave, she and Pete had been exchanging letters – fairly short uniformative ones – and when he had suggested a meeting she had jumped at it. She was missing Miranda, her job at the factory and the girls she had known there, and meeting Pete had been a bit like plunging back into her past. They had agreed to meet in Lincoln, since Pete was familiar with the city, being at the time at RAF Waddington, so he had telephoned her with instructions to meet him at the Saracen's Head, a pub on the high street. 'But I'll never find it. Lincoln's a huge city, and I've never been off the station,' Avril had wailed. 'Is there some sort of landmark which will tell me I'm goin' in the right direction?'

Pete had laughed. 'It's on the high street, right next door to what they call the Stonebow, which is a sort of arch under which all the traffic has to pass,' he had told her. 'Honest to God, Avril, every soul in Lincoln knows the Saracen's Head. Be there at seven o'clock and we'll snatch a meal and catch up with each other's news.' He had chuckled. 'I gather you aren't too keen on working in a cookhouse. You can tell me why not over a meal at the Cornhill Hotel.'

Avril had agreed to this and had been astonished by the flood of pleasure which broke over her like a wave at the sight of Pete Huxtable's plain but well-remembered face. They were both in uniform, but had held hands discreetly below the table at the hotel. When Pete had told her that other members of his ground crew spent their forty-eights with their girlfriends at the hotel, she had looked at him suspiciously, thinking he was about to suggest that they should do likewise, but the matter-of-fact way he spoke and his usual friendliness soon assured her that he was not going to try anything on.

He was doing an important job, servicing the engines of great bombers, and proud of his ability, but he was still the rather shy young man she had known from their Liverpool days.

They had remained friends throughout their time in Lincolnshire, always trying to time their trips to the city to coincide, and thinking about it now Avril realised that her desperation to be free of Corporal Greesby and the cookhouse had really only come to a head when Pete was posted to Malaya. She knew he would have a long and dangerous sea voyage and at their last meeting she had been prepared, if he demanded it, for them to spend their forty-eight as guests at the Cornhill Hotel. Pete, however, had merely said that he could only bear his posting if she would both promise to write and also look kindly upon him when the war was over and he was free to ask her to wed him.

At the time this had caused Avril considerable hilarity, for, as she told him, she did not intend to marry anyone, not even someone as nice as he. 'I'm goin' to have a career. Oh, I might marry when I'm really old, say thirty-five, but until then I'm goin' to earn lots of money and have lots of fun,' she told him airily. 'So don't you try and tie me down, Pete Huxtable.'

Pete had agreed meekly that he would do no such thing and said he applauded her decision to have a career. 'Though I can't think that cooking for forty and peeling potatoes far into the night is going to help your future much,' he had said, keeping his voice serious though his eyes had twinkled. 'In fact the only thing it will prepare you for is marriage – if you intend to have a great many children, that is.'

With thoughts of the children's home in mind, for the food provided there had been very similar to that which was slopped on to plates daily by the cookhouse staff, she had shuddered and assured him that she would apply for a posting as soon as she had suffered Corporal Greesby and the cookhouse for the obligatory six months, but then Pete had been posted and her whole attitude had changed. Losing her pal Miranda, and then Pete, and doing work she hated under a man she disliked, had caused her to watch the bulletin board closely, and when the request for girls to apply to become balloon operatives appeared on the board she was first in the queue. She had told no one that Pete meant more to her than any of her other correspondents, so now, chuckling to herself over her narrow escape from Miranda's curiosity, she fell abruptly asleep and was only woken when the tannoy began to shout. She had been late to bed, thanks to writing all her letters, but nevertheless grabbed her clothes, towel and soap and tore out of the hut, covering the short distance between her bed and the ablutions at greyhound speed. She bolted into the hut, which possessed three curtained-off showers, half a dozen curtained-off lavatories and a great many wash basins. For Avril, who for two years had known nothing but the primitive arrangements which balloon sites offered, the mere thought of a shower either hot or cold was always welcome, and since two were already occupied she went happily into the third, hanging her pyjamas on the hook and plunging under the water. Soon, clean and fully dressed apart from shoes and cap, she returned to their hut and there was Miranda, ready for the off. The two girls grinned at one another and set off for the cookhouse, for their day's work would begin at eight. Miranda would be driving yet more airmen to some unspecified destination and Avril was on ambulance duty, which she hoped sincerely would prove to be a sinecure that day. The British airmen only flew at night – unlike the Americans who, she knew, did daylight raids – so though the ambulance was always manned and ready, its chief work came after dark. That meant she would be free until noon and on call from six or seven o'clock, which should give her plenty of time to write to Pete, for she had not liked to do so the previous evening with Miranda's too knowing eyes upon her.

In fact, however, she had no opportunity to write letters, for she was called to the small bay to service the engine of a car which the driver was having trouble starting, and by the time she finished she was ready for a meal, so she searched out Miranda and the two joined the cookhouse queue together. They reached the counter and had just had corned beef hash, cabbage and gravy slapped on to their plates when Miranda turned to her friend. 'I forgot to ask if you ever write to Pete Huxtable?' she said airily. 'Steve says he's out in Malaya now; but I guess you know that, don't you?'

Despite her best efforts, Avril's mouth hung open for quite ten seconds before she pulled herself together. 'What makes you think that?' she asked belligerently. A sudden thought struck her. 'You looked at the letters on the board and saw the one I got from him! Miranda Lovage, you are a thoroughly sneaky person! And why shouldn't I write to Pete, anyway? He were real nice to me after Gary and Timmy died. Besides, what are you trying to make of it? I've gorra grosh of fellers what I write to and I dare say there's chaps here what'll want me to go to the flicks or to a dance with them. What's wrong wi' that?'

Miranda laughed. 'Nothing, you fool,' she said, 'so why be so secretive? Why not admit you write to Pete and actually rather like him? As you'd be the first to point out, liking someone is no sin.' As she spoke they had managed to find an unoccupied table and put their plates on it, so now they pulled up two chairs and sat down.

Avril shrugged. 'I dunno; I guess I just wanted to keep it to myself. That Pete and I are going to go steady when he comes home, I mean,' she said sulkily. 'I always swore I wouldn't get involved because it was just a pathway to pain, and so it is. I worry about Pete all the time, but I tell myself he means no more to me than the other fellers. You see, while I pretend he's not important . . . oh, I don't know, I can't explain. It's got something to do with the fact that I knew him before either of us had joined the RAF. I'm afraid I can't explain better than that, because I don't understand it myself. Only on my last balloon site we had this lovely flight sergeant. Gosh, she was beautiful, and tremendously efficient too. She'd been in the WAAF from the very beginning and a couple of months after she joined she got married to a tail gunner. He was killed six weeks after their wedding; she was devastated, but went on with the job. Her dead husband's best pal began to take her about. He was a fighter pilot trying to defend the troops when the Dunkirk evacuation began. He ditched and was presumed dead. After that she kept herself to herself for a couple of years, but then she had an affair with the boy next door who was a bomb aimer. He was killed over Cologne. Fellers started looking at her funny, and no one would take her out, though she was so beautiful! They thought she were a jinx, you see. Nothing's ever happened to none of my fellers, and I reckon that was because I didn't really love any of 'em. Only – only Pete is a bit different, so I won't risk him. He's no beauty – plain as a boot, in fact – but he means a lot to me. So he's stayin' under hatches until the war's over, understand?'

'Oh, poor Avril,' Miranda said softly. 'But I do understand, in a way. You thought you lost everything when Gary died and you're afraid of losing everything again. And I think I can imagine how that feels – even though my Steve is in England and I know he doesn't mean to worry me, some of the things he says keep me awake at nights. So don't think I don't sympathise, because I do.' She pushed her empty plate to one side as she spoke and stood up, fastened the buttons on her tunic and slapped her cap on her head. 'Are you coming to the NAAFI? And just think – there's one good thing about having your feller abroad: you don't have to join the queue for the telephone, which seems to get longer with every passing day!'

Chapter Fourteen

Miranda had become Group Captain Llewellyn's personal driver whenever he needed to be taken on a long journey, and these were happening rather frequently now, because Operation Overlord, which had started the previous June, meant a great many meetings of the top brass. Avril, on the other hand, drove whatever she was given – the blood wagon, the liberty truck, convoys carrying heavy weapons from one place to another – just about anything. Which was why, when the letter arrived, she was called in from her post as ambulance driver for the day to receive it.

Avril's forehead wrinkled into a frown. What had she done to receive an official letter? But the Waaf who had come to fetch her scowled up at her and jerked an impatient thumb. 'Come along, Donovan, you're wanted in Flight's office,' she said impatiently. 'Letters ain't always bad news . . . maybe it's a perishin' postin', or you're bein' made up to corporal, ha ha!'

But at the mere mention of a posting Avril jumped down from her seat in the ambulance and hared off across the grass to their flight officer's small room. She shot through the doorway, her heart hammering in her throat, but at a glance from the officer's chilly blue eyes she pulled herself together. She came stiffly to attention and saluted with such force that her right temple tingled.

Then she said, as coolly as she could, 'LACW Donovan reporting, ma'am.'

'Official letter, Donovan,' the flight officer said, and she must have seen the shock which Avril was trying so hard to hide, for she unbent a little. She handed it over, advising, as Avril's hand closed on the flimsy paper, 'Take it to your hut and read it in there. They won't miss you on the blood wagon for several hours yet. It passes my comprehension why we have to man the ambulance all through the day when our planes only attack by night.'

Avril could have told her; enemy planes did not work by the same rules as the British ones, which meant that the airfield could be attacked at any hour of day or night, but she realised that Flight Officer Adams was only making conversation to give her support, for she must have already guessed what the letter contained. So Avril answered accordingly. 'It's something we all query, ma'am,' she said, hoping her voice was not wobbling. She threw off another smart salute, turned with a click of her heels and strode out of the room.

She pushed open the door of their hut, glad to find it empty, and went over to her bed, slumping on to it and unfolding the sheet of paper. She found she was trembling so much that the words on the page blurred. For a moment she simply sat there, staring at the paper before her, then she took a deep breath and held it for a count of ten, releasing it slowly in a low whistle. She did this twice and then the words on the page were clear, could be calmly read.

Her eyes went first to the signature: a known name, occasionally mentioned in Pete's letters, and of course it said what she dreaded to hear, that Corporal Peter

Huxtable had not returned from a raid and was accordingly posted as missing. Since Corporal Huxtable had given her name as his next of kin it was his duty to inform her that Lancaster BT 308 had been shot down, but that the pilot of the aircraft following it in the formation had seen several parachutes open and thought that some of these had reached the ground safely.

Avril took another deep breath and expelled it even more slowly than she had the first. She thought of the dangers which Pete must face even if he had managed to get out of the plane; landing behind enemy lines in an area his aircraft had recently been bombing could mean that a trigger-happy air raid warden – if they had such things in Malaya – might blast off a round of deadly bullets without a moment's consideration. But on the other hand, there was that thing called the third Geneva convention . . .

The hut door burst open, stopping Avril's thoughts in mid-flow. The little Waaf who had instructed her to go to the flight officer came into the hut. Her face was pink, concerned, but Avril met her gaze blandly. 'In a hurry, Ellis? If you've come to find out what was in my letter . . .'

The other girl's face turned from pink to crimson and her eyes sparkled indignantly. 'Flight told me to make sure you were all right,' she said stiffly. 'But I can see there was no need for concern. God, you're a hard nut, Donovan; don't nothin' crack your shell?'

Avril made a great play of putting her letter away in her locker, so that the other girl could not see her face. When she was in full command once more, she swung round and spoke, her voice even and unemotional. 'Not while I've got nothing to moan about,' she said quietly. 'My feller's missing, but the aircraft behind his in the formation saw 'chutes opening. My feller will come out of it all right; he's like a cat, always lands on his feet.' She hesitated, then gave her fellow Waaf a tight little grin. 'But thanks for coming over, Mary; it were real good of you.'

Together the two girls left the hut and Avril began to chat of other things, the work in which she was engaged, the meal they would presently eat in the cookhouse and how she missed her best friend Lovage, who was now seldom on the airfield, but taking the top brass wherever it wanted to go. She missed her, of course she did, but Miranda would be back, probably before dark . . . The two girls chatted on, as though neither had a worry in the world.

Miranda had a perfectly dreadful day. Some senior officers were a positive joy to transport from one place to another, but Air Commodore Bailey was not one of them. He made no secret of the fact that he did not like women, did not trust women drivers and had no intention of placing his valuable life in the hands of someone he described as 'a chit of a girl'. In normal circumstances, therefore, Miranda would never have been told to drive the commodore, in his beautifully polished staff car, from the station he had been inspecting the previous day to what was described as an unknown destination in the north of England. But when the orderly officer went to wake the commodore's driver he found him writhing in his bed, sweat standing out on his forehead, obviously burning up with fever. The man had to be hospitalised at once, and within the hour was on the operating table having a burst appendix removed, and poor Miranda, looking forward to a quiet day for once, was given her new orders, reminded of the air commodore's feelings regarding women drivers and sent round to the Commodore's quarters to be given details of her destination.

Dismayed, for everyone knew Air Commodore Bailey, Miranda begged to be excused, suggesting that almost any man in the MT section might take her place. But men were at a premium and the officer who had given her her instructions raised a quizzical eyebrow. 'What do you mean, Lovage? Oh, I dare say he can be a bit difficult, and women don't like that, but I'm sure you'll charm the pants off him, if you'll forgive the expression. Just do your best and don't get lost, and we'll see you back here before dark.'

Not at this point knowing her eventual destination, Miranda could only assure the orderly officer that she would do her best, but when she read her instructions and realised she was going up to Northumberland she gave a soft whistle of dismay. She thought it extremely unlikely that she would be back at the airfield before dark, for the days were getting shorter and, though the main roads would probably be quite clear, if one came across a convoy heading in the same direction it could add hours to any journey.

However, orders were orders and Miranda nipped into the ablutions to damp her curly hair into submission, though it was cut short and little could be seen beneath her cap. Then she checked her appearance, which was as immaculate as a clothes brush and Brasso could make it, and she drove to the meeting point, where she had her first unpleasant experience of the day. The air commodore, deep in conversation with the group captain, crossed the concrete apron and paused to allow his driver to wriggle out from behind the wheel and come round to open the rear passenger door for him. He began to thank her, but then the words seemed to shrivel in his throat. 'What – what – what?' he barked. 'Where's Jones?' He put a hand out to rest on the roof of the car, but made no attempt to climb inside. Instead he swung round to face the group captain. 'I remember you telling me Jones had been carted off with a pain in his innards, but you never said . . .'

The group captain hastily cut across what he must have guessed would be an offensive sentence. 'LACW Lovage is one of the best drivers we have, so you'll be in good hands,' he said soothingly. 'She has her instructions and understands that you must reach Northumberland before the weapons trials can begin.' He turned to Miranda, still holding the passenger door open. 'You can get the air commodore to his destination without trouble, can't you, Aircraftwoman?'

'I'll do my best, sir,' Miranda said. 'So long as we don't find ourselves held up by a convoy or by closed roads . . . but I've got a map which the orderly officer assured me is up to date, so we'll hope for the best.'

The air commodore, a large man who probably weighed in at over fifteen stone, had climbed into the car and leaned back against the leather, but at her words he jerked forward, waving a sausage-like forefinger almost in her face. 'Hoping for the best is not good enough, young woman,' he growled. 'If one route is closed to us by heavy traffic or convoys we must find an alternative one.' He might have gone on at some length but Miranda closed the door smartly and got back behind the wheel. Giving her a wink, the groupie stood back and saluted smartly as Miranda put the big car into gear and drove forward, trying to take no notice of the muttered imprecations coming from the rear seat.

She had hoped that the air commodore might unbend when he realised the quality of her driving, but she hoped in vain. He criticised constantly, accused her of taking wrong turnings, complained if she drove too fast but disliked it even more when she had to slow to a crawl. He refused to leave the road for so much as a cup of coffee or what the troops called a 'comfort break', and by the time they reached the airfield where the trials were taking place Miranda was as tired as though she had driven to Scotland and back. However, she did not mean to let it show, and when the guards at the gate of their destination waved her down and examined her papers and those of her illustrious passenger she put a brave face on it. The guards told her where to go and said a trifle reproachfully that she was early, so the commodore would have to kill half an hour before a meal was served in the officers' Mess. Miranda could not help shooting a triumphant glance at her reluctant passenger as she drew to a halt and got out to open the rear door. 'There you are, sir, with thirty whole minutes in hand,' she said chirpily. 'I've been told to go to the Mess and await further instructions from you, but first I have to go to the cookhouse. I'm sure they'll find me bangers and mash, or a plateful of . . .' She stopped speaking as her passenger, ignoring her completely, marched stiff-backed into the officers' mess, slamming the door behind him with enough force to take it off its hinges.

'What a mean pig,' Miranda muttered. But some men were like that; if you proved you were as good at your job as a man, they resented you all the more. And this elderly air commodore was probably bursting for a pee – she was herself – and so had not dared to stop and throw even a word of thanks to the driver who had managed to get him to his destination with thirty minutes to spare.

Despite her hopes and everyone's expectations, however, the trials took longer than expected and it was full dark when the big car eased out of the tall gates once more and headed for the main road south. Miranda had managed to grab a second meal of sorts at the cookhouse as soon as she realised that they would not be leaving until much later than planned, and she supposed that someone must have fed her officer, so when he climbed into the car, smelling faintly of both food and alcohol, she hoped that his temper would be much improved. In her experience a man who has been well fed and watered was usually either chattier or more comatose as a result. After a mere couple of miles, a peep in the rear view mirror showed the air commodore comfortably settled in one corner of the long leather seat, eyes tightly closed, little bubbles of saliva coming from the corners of his mouth. Miranda could not help a little chuckle of pleasure escaping her. Thank God! If only he would sleep all the way to his quarters, how happy she would be. In order not to wake him she took extra care, and of course care was necessary due to the blackout, but even so she only took forty minutes longer on the return journey than she had going north.

As she drew up beside the administrative offices, she wondered for the first time how she should wake her passenger. She could imagine his rage if he realised she had known he was sleeping, had seen him dribbling – disgusting old man – on to the leather upholstery of the beautiful car. But the orderly officer, who had no doubt arranged the trip with considerable trepidation, must have been keeping a lookout for them, because he popped out of the offices like a jack-in-the-box, and when she tried to get out of her seat and go round to open the rear door he shook his head and put a finger to his lips. 'I'll wake him gently, but don't expect any thanks for your good driving,' he whispered. 'And as soon as he's awake and on his feet you'd best get rid of the car and see if the cookhouse can dream you up char and a wad, late though it is.' He patted her shoulder and even in the pale light she saw the flash of his teeth, white against tanned skin. 'Many thanks, LACW Lovage; I take it all went according to plan?'

Miranda nodded. 'Yes sir. We arrived early and left late,' she said cheerfully. She lowered her voice. 'I don't envy Corporal Jones, sir.' The orderly officer chuckled, but just at that moment there was a heaving and a muttering from the figure slumped on the rear seat and Miranda, quick to see the good sense of a speedy disappearance, only waited until her passenger was out of the car before making off without a backward glance.

She decided to see if Avril would accompany her to the cookhouse, for there are few things worse than sitting down to a plate full of lukewarm food, the only person in a great echoing room set with dozens of tables and chairs, all of them empty except one's own. Upon investigation, however, she discovered that there were only two girls in their hut, neither of them Avril. She emerged from the hut, closing the door softly behind her, and almost immediately came face to face with another Waaf. 'Hiya, Lovage,' the girl said cheerfully. 'Lookin' for your pal? She's gone to the NAAFI; said she'd wait up for you when you weren't in for a meal earlier.'

'Thanks. I hate eating alone in the cookhouse, so I'll get Avril to keep me company,' Miranda said. When she got to the NAAFI, however, expecting to find Avril the centre of a group, she saw her friend sitting alone at a small table, industriously scribbling. She had a mug of coffee before her but when Miranda got near enough she could see that the drink was cold by the skin on it, and the way Avril was hunched over the page upon which she was writing warned Miranda that something was up. She slid into the seat opposite and tapped the other girl's mug. 'You've let your drink go cold,' she said disapprovingly. 'What's happened?'

Avril said nothing but fished in her tunic pocket and handed the letter to Miranda, who read it at a glance and then whistled softly beneath her breath.

'Oh, Avril, poor old Pete! But missing doesn't necessarily mean . . .'

'I know, I know,' Avril said impatiently, 'I'm being sensible and telling myself it just means more waiting. He – he gave me as his next of kin, otherwise I really would be waiting, and wondering, too. But since his squadron leader says they saw chutes open, at least there's hope. Oh, Miranda, I wish I'd been more generous! To pretend he meant no more to me than the other fellers I'd gone with was just plain stupid, and now I'm payin' for it.' She gave her friend a watery grin. 'I'm writin' a letter to him now. I'm going to add a page or two each day and then, when he comes home – I suppose I should say *if* he comes home – he'll get a whole batch of news in one go. And I've started the letter by sayin' I won't go out with anyone else because he's the only feller that matters to me and always will be. Do you think I'm doin' the right thing?'

'Yes, of course you are,' Miranda said, keeping her inevitable reflections to herself. Avril loved dancing, the cinema and the company of young men. Miranda could appreciate her feelings, but doubted whether Avril would be able to stick to a nun-like existence. However, only time would tell, and right now her friend was undoubtedly sincere.

It was four whole months after the squadron leader's first letter telling her that Pete was missing before Avril got another letter, this time with Pete's familiar handwriting on the envelope. On their way to breakfast they had stopped off at the bulletin board in the Mess and Avril had taken down the letter, her heart hammering in her throat. Seeing Miranda's interest, she shook her head. 'It's probably been in the post for months, or stuck in the wrong pigeon hole, so I don't mean to get all excited,' she said. 'I won't wait till we reach the cookhouse, I'll read it now.'

She slit open the envelope with clumsy fingers and pulled out the printed sheet it contained. 'I told you it would be nothin',' she said bitterly. 'It's one of them forms . . . oh, my God, my God, my God!' And Avril, who never showed emotion, who had not cried even when Gary had been killed, or not publicly anyway, burst into tears.

'What is it? What is it?' Miranda asked agitatedly. 'Oh, Avril, I'm so sorry . . .'

Avril raised a tear-drenched face, her mouth beginning to form into a watery smile. 'He's a prisoner of war,' she said huskily. 'It's one of them standard letters giving his address and saying he has been in hospital but is out of it now, and he's scrawled on the bottom *Love you, Avril. Pete.*' Miranda was in the middle of telling her friend how happy she was when Avril gave a whoop and bounced across the Mess. 'I'm goin' to get that letter, the one I'd been writin' for the past four months,' she said jubilantly. 'It'll take him a month of Sundays to read it, but I'm sure he won't mind that. And I promised him that we'll get together just as soon as he's back in Britain.' She gave Miranda a defiant look. 'That means as Mr and Mrs Huxtable, even if we can't marry straight away, because I was a fool, and wasted the time we could have spent together.'

'Oh, Avril, I'm so happy for you, and I'm sure it won't be long before the war's over and Pete can come home,' Miranda said. She grinned wickedly at her friend. 'Does this mean you'll come to dances and start flirting again, the way you did before Pete went missing?'

Avril laughed with her but shook her head. 'No point,' she said. 'I'm a one man girl now, and it means just that. And now let's get to the cookhouse because I'm absolutely starving; no matter what rubbish they're handing out I'll eat every scrap.'

'How do I look?'

The war had been over for several months and Miranda

and Steve were alone in the living room of the small flat into which Avril and she had moved only the previous week, because despite Avril's brave words Pete had said that he would prefer to start their married life after the wedding rather than before it. This had made Avril go scarlet to the roots of her hair, whilst Miranda, who had been present at the time, had had to stifle a laugh.

Pete had returned from the POW camp thinner and sporting a black beard streaked with grey, and looking, for a moment, a dozen years older than the Pete she had known. Avril would have walked straight past him, and when he had grabbed her, accusing her of forgetting him, Avril, once so proud of never showing emotion, had wept bitterly. But the weeping had been of short duration, and the kissing and cuddling that followed had been quite sufficient to prove to Pete that, beard or no beard, he really was her dearest love.

Now, however, Miranda twirled until the skirt of her new-second-hand dress flew out, showing her petticoat, and Steve got up from the creaking sofa to grab her and give her a kiss whilst assuring her that she looked gorgeous; so pretty, in fact, that she would outshine the bride. Miranda smiled. She had seen Avril's dress and knew that though her own blue cotton was both fresh and attractive, it would be totally eclipsed by Avril's long white gown, borrowed from a theatrical costumiers for this special occasion.

She and Avril had decided that they would like a double wedding but this had been impossible since Pete's first action on arriving in Liverpool was to buy a special licence, something which neither Steve nor Miranda had even heard of before; they themselves would be married conventionally after the banns had been read three times in their local church, and they had arranged with Mrs Mickleborough to have a small reception at her home. It had never occurred to either Miranda or Avril that Pete owned other premises, as well as his cycle shop, in the city. They both knew of course that Pete was ten years older than Steve, and had not wasted those ten years. He had been not a spender but a saver, and before the war had gone in for property, so that now he had a comfortable sum in the bank just waiting, he told them, to be spent on a home for his wife to be.

Realising that a double wedding was out of the question, Miranda had thrown herself wholeheartedly into the preparations for her friend's great day. She had agreed to be a bridesmaid and had found a pretty dress on Paddy's Market, and she and Steve had put their gratuities together to buy a small kitchen table and two stools for the newly-weds, which had just about cleaned them out financially.

As soon as the wedding was over, Pete would move into the flat in which Miranda and Steve now waited, and the lack of somewhere of their own was the main reason why Miranda and Steve had still not settled on the wedding date. Because of the bombing every single room in Liverpool was bulging with occupants and as soon as a property came up for rent it was grabbed. When Miranda moved out of this flat she would have no option but to go back either to share with Aunt Vi or to accept a put-you-up in the Mickleboroughs' front parlour. She told herself it was unfair on Steve's mum to add yet another person to a house already bursting at the seams, but Steve assured her that his mother would take an extra non-paying lodger in her stride, especially if that person was willing to help in the house and even do a bit of cooking.

The door opening put an end to Miranda's thoughts and she beamed as Avril bounced into the room. She had always been a big, tall girl, but dressed in dazzling white satin with a wreath of lilies of the valley crowning her smooth flaxen head she looked like a princess, Miranda thought. Steve wolf-whistled, his eyes rounding. 'Avril Donovan, you look fantastic!' he breathed. 'Wait till Pete sees you; he'll be over the moon to think you're his and his alone. Can I kiss the bride? 'Cos I am acting father of the bride, after all.'

Avril curtsied. 'Ta very much; I thought I looked good, but now I'm sure of it,' she said. 'You ain't one to pay compliments you don't mean, old Steve. But just remember this 'ere bridal gown is the very same one what Miranda will be wearing in a few weeks, so just you keep your kisses for her, young feller.'

Miranda was about to make a joking remark when something occurred to her and she clapped a hand to her mouth. 'The bridegroom isn't supposed to see the bride before the wedding, because he won't be so astonished at how lovely she looks in the dress,' she said. 'Oh, hell, does that mean, if I wear that dress, we'll have bad luck?'

'No, of course not . . .' Steve began, but Avril interrupted.

'You're mad, you. It ain't the dress, it's the woman,' she explained. 'It's something to do with ancient times, when they rigged some girl up in wedding finery with a real thick veil in front of her face, and passed her off as the bride, or so I've heard tell. So you needn't worry, Steve – oh, heavens, where's me perishin' veil? Miranda Lovage, you're supposed to be helping me to get ready, and you never even noticed I'd not got me veil on yet.'

Miranda shot out of the room, fetched the veil and draped it elegantly over her friend's coronet of the tiny sweet-smelling flowers. She stepped back to admire the effect just as a taxi drew up in the street below, and sounded a toot-toot-ti-toot-toot on his horn.

Both girls squeaked and headed for the stairs whilst Steve, following, told them that they had plenty of time and reminded Avril that if she didn't pick up her skirts she would soil them on the piles of wet snow left over from the storm a week before.

The three of them bundled into the taxi and Avril grabbed Miranda's hand. 'I hope I'm doin' the right thing,' she muttered. 'I hope Pete is, for that matter. We've been apart for so long that sometimes he seems like a stranger. Partly it's the beard, but I can't expect him to shave it off just because it makes him look so different. Besides, I know he's rather proud of it.'

Miranda patted the hand which clutched her own. 'You're both doing the right thing,' she said gently. 'It's the same thing that Steve and I will be doing in a few weeks, and we have no doubts, do we, Steve?'

Steve pretended to frown and consider, but just then the taxi drew up outside the church and in his role as surrogate father of the bride he had to be first out so that he could accompany Avril to where Pete awaited her at the top of the church.

Avril tucked her hand into Steve's arm as they reached

405

the porch, and glanced behind her as her friend adjusted her train. Her veil was down but it was a frail and beautiful affair through which she could see quite easily. She smiled her thanks, and then the organ music swelled and they began to process up the aisle. She was clutching Steve's arm so hard that she saw him wince, but then he was pushing her gently towards her waiting bridegroom, and the three of them stood, shoulder to shoulder, as the priest began the wedding service.

Avril clutched her bouquet nervously. The sonorous words rang out. 'Dearly beloved, we are gathered together here in the sight of God, and in the face of this congregation, to join together this man and this woman in holy matrimony; which is an honourable estate . . .'

Avril had been staring straight ahead of her, waiting for her heart to stop beating so fast, knowing that the time was about to come when she would have to speak, and speak calmly what was more. For the first time, she risked a glance at Pete, standing so still and straight beside her, and a squeak of surprise emerged from her lips, just as the priest said, 'First, it was ordained for the procreation of children, to be brought up in the fear and nurture of the Lord . . .' He paused, but when Avril said nothing more he continued with the service whilst Avril caught Pete's hand and squeezed it convulsively. The black beard, of which she knew Pete was secretly proud, had disappeared, and above the clean lines of jaw and chin she saw the love in the eyes he fixed upon her. Avril smiled at him; her heart was dancing with joy. At that moment she knew without any doubt that she and Pete were about to set out on a journey together, and that, whatever might befall them, their happiness was assured.

Chapter Fifteen

Miranda woke early, because her feet were cold. For a moment she just lay there, staring at the ceiling above her head and wondering where on earth she was. Not in the Nissen hut with fellow Waafs all around her; not in the Mickleboroughs' crowded, happy house in Jamaica Close . . .

Then someone sighed gustily almost in her ear, a warm hand stole across her waist, and memory returned with a rush. She was in the Elms private hotel, the wandering hand belonged to Steve, her brand new husband, and the pair of them were having the only honeymoon they could afford before moving into the little rooms above the village butcher's shop.

Turning her head very carefully on the pillow, Miranda stared intently but lovingly at Steve's unconscious face. He wasn't handsome, but there was something sweet in the curve of his lips, and today, she remembered, something very exciting was going to happen, or so she and Steve hoped. Her very best chance of finding her mother would be between nine and ten o'clock at the Pier Head and she meant to be there in good time, come hell or high water.

She and Steve had learned about it by chance, when Steve had met an old pal from the air force, who had been rear gunner in his Lancaster. Miranda had been at work, for the solicitors had been happy to give her her old job back, so Steve and Tony had gone into the nearest pub to tell each other how the peace was treating them.

Now, Miranda imagined the scene about which Steve had told her when he met her out of the office. He had told his pal, a journalist with the *Echo* once more, how he and Miranda had married only the previous day, and in describing his wife he had added the information that Miranda was the daughter of the missing actress from the Madison Players. Tony, who had covered the original story for his newspaper, had been very interested, especially when Steve mentioned the newsreel in which Miranda had been certain her mother had appeared, and the fact that Lynette Rich, also a former Madison Player, had told them that Arabella had taken part in a revue put on for the Americans by actors and actresses from the USA.

'Well now, it's lucky you met me,' Tony had said, producing a card from his raincoat pocket. 'The Yanks who've been entertaining their troops are leaving the country in a couple of days and congregating at the Pier Head first for what they describe as a farewell photo shoot.' He pressed the card into Steve's hand. 'Tell your wife to hang on to your arm and show this to anyone who tries to stop you getting near the performers. It's my press card, but I shan't be covering that particular event, and if your wife spots her mother she'll be able to approach her.' He had looked doubtfully at Steve. 'Or do you think it's best to let sleeping dogs lie? After all, it's been a long time since Arabella Lovage disappeared. It just doesn't seem possible that she wouldn't contact her daughter . . . but I leave it up to you. Tell her and risk disappointment or keep it to yourself. The choice is yours.'

Lying now, almost nose to nose with Steve in the creaky old double bed, Miranda was devoutly thankful that Steve had decided to tell her everything, though he had warned her that her hopes would probably be dashed. 'Tony pointed out that if Arabella is alive she would surely have made some effort to get in touch,' he had said. 'But now I've told you, and as Tony said the choice is yours. Go down to the Pier Head and see if you recognise anyone, or forget all about it.'

And I made my choice without a second's hesitation, Miranda remembered. As it said in the marriage service, *for better for worse, for richer for poorer, in sickness and in health.* She would never forget Arabella, and to pass up the chance of flying into her mother's arms and hearing her story would be to forego everything she'd ever dreamed of.

So when Steve had suggested spending a couple of nights at a small hotel in the city centre before moving into the flat she had agreed eagerly. It might not be much of a honeymoon but it was all they could afford and the Elms was only a short walk from the Pier Head.

Miranda dangled one foot out of bed until it got quite cold, then pulled it back in and planted it squarely on Steve's warm body. He groaned, then turned and seized her, proving, Miranda thought, that he had been awake all along. 'Morning, beautiful!' he said, whispering straight into her ear because it seemed no one but themselves was yet stirring. 'Ready for your great day? I've booked us in for eight o'clock breakfast; what's the time now?'

Miranda reached out a lazy hand and picked up her wrist watch, lying on the bedside table. 'Ten to seven,' she announced. 'There's no point in getting up yet; the staff won't even have started their own breakfast, let alone ours.'

She snuggled down again as she spoke, trying to pull Steve down with her, but he resisted, capturing her wrists and holding them firmly. 'If we get up now we'll be first in the bathroom,' he said. 'There was a rush for it yesterday, because most of the people staying here are sales reps or office workers, and they want to be up and away by nine o'clock.'

As he spoke he scrambled out of bed, accidentally kneeling on Miranda's toes and causing her to exclaim: 'Ouch! I'll get you for that, Steve Mickleborough!' She aimed a punch at him, but he dodged, then crossed the room and reached out to where their dressing gowns hung on the back of the door.

'Better put 'em on in case the old feller in the room next door is on the prowl,' he observed. 'Go quietly, or that chap with the huge moustache will complain that he wants his room moved again, because we make more noise than all the trains arriving and departing at Lime Street Station.'

'If he does, I'll tell him that it's my husband who whistles and sings the minute the bathroom door is locked,' Miranda said. 'Oh, Steve, I can't wait till we're in our own little place, with no one listening to our every move. But even here, even on your mam's living room couch, being married is the best thing that ever happened to me. I wish we'd done it sooner.' She had been whispering as they glided softly up the corridor and let themselves into the bathroom. She looked around for the box of matches, pounced on them, and as Steve turned the gas tap on the geyser held the flame through the small aperture and blew out her cheeks in a breath of relief as it caught. 'First go off,' she said triumphantly. 'Naturally I learn how to do it properly on our last day! Fill the jug, there's a dear. That woman made it pretty plain that baths were only allowed between six and ten in the evening, so a good wash will have to suffice.'

Presently, washed, brushed and with their shared sponge bag clutched in Miranda's hand, Miranda and Steve left the bathroom. They mumbled an awkward 'Good morning' to the short queue of would-be occupants standing patiently in the corridor, and received various grunts in reply. In their own room once more, Steve consulted his watch and then put both arms around Miranda as she shed her dressing gown and reached for her clothes. 'God, you're gorgeous,' he mumbled. 'It won't be breakfast time for ages, so how about a bit of smooching? There's time, honest to God there is.'

'No there isn't, because I mean to look my best so that if we do meet Arabella she'll be proud of me,' Miranda said. 'And unlike my mother I'm not a star of the stage, so it will take me quite a while to get ready.'

Steve laughed and gave her a quick kiss on the cheek, then turned to his neatly piled clothing and began to dress. 'Don't forget we've got to put our suitcases in the left luggage at the bus depot,' he reminded her. 'And before that there's breakfast and paying our bill, and afterwards we have to walk down to the Pier Head.'

Miranda pouted. 'All right, all right, I'm doing my

411

best,' she said. 'Shall I wear the blue blouse or the pink one? Only I've already packed the blue one . . .'

'Shut up and get a move on,' Steve said severely. 'Are you ready? Then let's go and get breakfast eaten, and mind you eat lots because you won't get anything else until later on this evening, when we go to Mam's for our share of the big pan of scouse she's preparing.'

Miranda promised to eat up, but in fact most things were still on ration or unobtainable, and though the recently introduced bread ration was quite generous Mrs Ada of the Elms was not. She watched her guests with an eagle eye, and though more than one cup of tea was allowed it grew weaker and weaker with every cup, and Steve had made Miranda laugh the previous day by declaring that the old skinflint dried out the tea leaves given to her guests on a Monday and made tea – or something vaguely resembling tea – with those same leaves on a Tuesday.

Accordingly, breakfast was not a lengthy meal and by half past eight they had handed over the key to their room, paid their bill – checking it carefully first – and set off for the bus depot, where they left their suitcases and accepted in their place two green tickets so that they might reclaim their property later.

Despite the fact that it was sunny there was a distinct nip in the air and Miranda was glad of her old winter coat, particularly as the breeze always seemed to get stronger when one neared the docks. But today the blue sky gave an illusion of summer, and the faces of folk going about their business, though pale and war-weary, were smiling as if in anticipation of the good weather to come.

They reached the Pier Head and Miranda clutched Steve's arm tightly. She was dressed in her best and even though her green suit and pink blouse had both come from Paddy's Market she thought she looked both neat and smart. Despite the cold wind she had cast off her overcoat, which was old and patched, and Steve held it over his arm while she turned an anxious face to his. 'Is my hat on straight?' she asked. 'Is my hair tidy? Oh, I'm sure my nose must be blue with the cold. Will Arabella recognise me, do you suppose? If she does, should I run up to her and give her a big hug? But what if she doesn't? What if I run towards her and she just stands there, staring; what do I do then? Oh, darling Steve, I'm scared stiff; I almost wish I'd never come.' She tugged at his arm, and began to turn away just as a large cream-coloured coach drew up in front of them, closely followed by another. Even as they watched the doors of both coaches opened, and a great many beautiful, excited people poured out and began to take up their positions at the foot of the gangway belonging to the ship upon which they were about to embark.

Miranda and Steve both watched, fascinated, as a tall, handsome man in his forties began to try to calm the excited babble, and to arrange both the actors and actresses themselves and those members of the press wielding cameras into some sort of order.

Miranda stared. There was no thought, now, of turning to flee. As the cameras clicked and whirred her gaze went from face to face, trying to find the one she remembered from long ago. If only her mother had had some clearly visible imperfection, but Arabella's skin had always been pale and flawless, and anyway without exception all the

413

women who had got off the coach were heavily made up.

Miranda was still scanning every fair-haired woman when Steve bent and whispered in her ear. 'See anyone you know, queen? I can't help you much, 'cos all I really know is that your mam was beautiful and very very blonde. There are one or two brunettes amongst the line-up but mostly they're blondes.'

Miranda snorted. 'Bottle blondes, that's what they are,' she said scornfully. 'Arabella despised bottle blondes. But oh, Steve, if only they wouldn't keep moving about! I no sooner begin to examine one face than its owner flicks round and turns her back on me. I wish someone would tell them . . .'

As though on cue the tall man took off his dark glasses and pinched the bridge of his nose before beginning to speak. 'Settle down, people; give the good gentlemen of the press a chance to see how us Yankees can behave ourselves. We'll have small girls in the front in a crescent and the rest of you fall in behind, whilst I fetch the star of the show from . . . ah, here she comes.'

All eyes turned to the last coach. A tall and very beautiful woman in a cream dress which clung to every curve of her slender body descended from the vehicle and appeared to drift across to where the man awaited her. She murmured something to him then turned to face the battery of cameras, and even as she gave her audience the benefit of a dazzling smile the wind tore off the tiny hat perched on her head and sent it flying towards the Mersey, whilst the great mass of her hair, released from its many pins, descended in a whirling cloud of primrose around her shoulders. The cameramen moved forward eagerly as the woman turned, pointing desperately to the neat little hat, but though there was not a man present who would not have dived into the Mersey had it been possible to catch it there was not a hope in hell of doing so, Miranda saw. The hat was gone, the lady was laughing and protesting, Miranda presumed she was saying words to the effect that she had other hats, and the tall man was putting his arm round her, drawing her close, kissing the top of that glorious primrose head.

'Is it her?' Steve was saying anxiously. 'Is it your mam, sweetheart? Don't tell me *she's* a bottle blonde, because I wouldn't believe you. Oh, damn, they're going for another photo shoot. But it'll be over in a few minutes; the captain has come to the top of the gangway to welcome his passengers aboard. Then you can nab her . . .'

But his voice was almost drowned by the eager shouts of cameramen and journalists. 'Show a leg, ladies! Do a bit of a dance for us! That's right, lass, hold out your arms as though you wanted to embrace the whole of Liverpool . . .' Someone else shouted: 'The whole of England, you mean,' and there was laughter and much bustling to and fro as the cine cameras – there were two of them – trundled across the uneven paving to snatch views of the Americans leaving Britain which would appear, Miranda guessed, in newsreels all over the world.

Then the cameramen moved back, allowing the journalists their turn, and men with notebooks began to converge on the company. The biggest crowd was around that wonderful primrose hair, and Steve took his wife's hand. 'We've got our press pass, remember,' he whispered. 'You can ask her anything you like, only it will

415

have to be you, because she's your mother, or you think she is. Is that right?' The crowd was beginning to thin as the men and women from the concert parties headed for the gangway. But still the man in dark glasses and the woman within the circle of his arm remained. Clearly they were the most important members of the group, and intended to shepherd their flock aboard before embarking themselves. Steve tugged on Miranda's hand, meaning to lead her up to the man and woman now standing at the foot of the gangway, but Miranda shook herself free.

'You stay here please, Steve,' she whispered. 'This is something I've got to do alone.'

Steve watched the small, straight-backed figure in the green suit and the perky little hat approach the couple, who smiled graciously. Then the woman turned to her companion and he handed her something which looked like a notepad, and a pencil. She scribbled something and gave the sheet of paper to Miranda, who promptly turned round and re-joined Steve. She was very pink, and there were tears in her eyes, but when Steve asked her what had happened she would only shake her head.

When the couple had climbed the gangway they leaned on the rail, watching as preparations for departure were carried out by smartly uniformed sailors. Steve put his arm round Miranda, bent his head and kissed the side of her neck. 'Want to leave?' he asked, but she shook her head. So they stood there, almost alone on the quayside now, and Miranda gave a little wave just as the couple on board the liner turned away, and watched in silence until the ship was out of sight.

'Are you disappointed, darling?' Steve asked anxiously,

as he and Miranda began to walk slowly back the way they had come. 'I really thought it must be your mother, because of her wonderful hair. What did she give you, by the way? I saw her hand you something that looked like a piece of paper . . .'

'It was; she thought I wanted her autograph,' Miranda said bitterly. 'Oh, Steve, when my eyes met hers, when she looked at me as though she had never seen me in her life before, I could have wept. She's married to that man, you know, the one wearing dark glasses. I heard one of the chorus telling a reporter that she was Mrs Salvatore, though that isn't her stage name. He's an – an impresario and they're very wealthy and extremely happy. She's the leading lady in all his productions . . .'

'But *not* your mother,' Steve said with a chuckle. 'Oh, sweetheart, I'm so very sorry to have raised your hopes for nothing. But it was worth a try, wouldn't you say? If you'd not had the chance to discover for yourself . . .'

Miranda pulled him to a halt and turned to gaze at him, round-eyed. 'Are you mad, Steve Mickleborough?' she said. 'Of course she was my mother! We've wondered many times if she might have lost her memory, and now I'm sure that must be what happened. She looked at me so coolly, with not a trace of interest. And if I'd told her who I was – and who she was – I'd also have had to tell her that she was once a second-rate actress in a second-rate rep company, about to marry a man she didn't love just to settle all her debts and keep her head above water. Oh, Steve, it would've been the wickedest, cruellest thing! As Mrs Salvatore and her husband's leading lady she has a wonderful life, and that, after all, was what I wanted to find out. I always said that if I could know she was alive and happy I'd be content.' She looked up at Steve and saw his face wreathed in a grin, and hid the tiny stab of pain in her own heart. 'So I'm afraid you can't claim to have married the daughter of a star after all, just plain little Miranda Lovage . . .'

'. . . who is now Miranda Mickleborough,' Steve said contentedly. 'And you've done the right thing. You must know, queen, that you're quite old enough to manage very well without a mother. Most girls have left home and family by the time they're twenty-one. In fact you should be more interested in having a daughter of your own, and I'll help you do just that. So let's go and collect our suitcases and go back to the village to claim our rooms.' They were beginning to walk back towards the main road once more when Steve suddenly remembered something. 'Did you ask her for her autograph . . . no, of course you didn't, she just gave it to you. I wonder if she signed Salvatore or her stage name? Let's have a look.' Miranda delved into her pocket and produced the sheet of paper. Scrawled across it was one word.

Steve stared. 'Miranda; she signed it Miranda,' he said in an awed voice. 'Did you tell her your name, queen?'

Miranda shook her head. 'I didn't say a word, but of course it's not really odd,' she said in a low voice. 'She called me Miranda because she had always loved the name, she told me so many times.' She heaved a sigh, then took the paper from Steve and was about to push it back into her pocket when she changed her mind. Very slowly and deliberately she tore the page into tiny fragments, then opened her hand and let the wind take them. Like a cloud of confetti the tiny pieces were caught in the breeze and carried in the wake of the great liner, already, no doubt, settling into its voyage towards America, and suddenly it seemed like a message, a portent almost, to Miranda. She watched the 'confetti', blue as her mother's forget-me-not eyes, as it curtsied and cavorted higher and higher in the blue sky, and suddenly she knew she had done the right thing. It was important, she reminded herself, to let go, and unwise to cling, whether to your grown-up child or your mother. Furthermore, if at any time in the future she decided she should contact Arabella, she now had her married name, and her stage name, too.

Hand in hand, the young couple watched until the last scrap of paper disappeared, then turned and began to walk up the slope once more. We're leaving the past behind us and doing the right thing, the kind thing, Miranda told herself contentedly. After all, she had had her mother's love for the most important years of her growing up, and now, bless him, she had Steve's. She squeezed his hand and began to sing beneath her breath, so that only Steve could hear.

For this time it isn't fascination,
Or a dream that will fade and fall apart,
It's love, this time it's love, my foolish heart.

Steve returned the pressure of her hand and she saw that his eyes were wet, but he grinned at her and gave her a little push. 'Race you to the main road,' he said. 'Oh, darling Miranda, I love you, too!'

A Sixpenny Christmas

Katie Flynn

As the worst storm of the century sweeps through the mountains of Snowdonia and across the Mersey, two women, Molly and Ellen, give birth to girls in a Liverpool maternity hospital.

Molly and Rhys Roberts farm sheep in Snowdonia and Ellen is married to a docker, Sam O'Mara, but despite their different backgrounds the two young women become firm friends, though Molly has a secret she can share with no one.

But despite promises Ellen's husband continues to be violent, so she throws him out and years later, when Molly is taken to hospital after an accident, Ellen and her daughter Lana are free to help out. They approach this new life with enthusiasm, unaware that they are being watched, but on the very day of Molly's release from hospital there is another terrible thunderstorm and the hidden watcher makes his move at last . . .

arrow books

ALSO AVAILABLE IN ARROW

The Runaway

Katie Flynn

When Dana and Caitlin meet by chance on the ferry from Ireland, they tell each other that they are simply going to search for work, but they soon realise they have more than that in common. They are both in search of new lives in Liverpool, leaving their secrets behind in Ireland. But Dana is ambitious and resourceful, and when the opportunity comes to own their own tearoom she persuades her friend to join her.

No one is willing to rent property to a couple of girls, however, especially during the Depression. So when Caitlin's new man friend says he'll back them, they are delighted and soon the tearoom is thriving.

Then fate intervenes, and soon the girls find themselves fighting to survive in a world on the brink of war.

arrow books

ALSO AVAILABLE IN ARROW

The Lost Days of Summer

Katie Flynn

Nell Whitaker is fifteen when war breaks out and, despite her protests, her mother sends her to live with her Auntie Kath on a remote farm in Anglesey. Life on the farm is hard, and Nell is lonely after living in the busy heart of Liverpool all her life. Only her friendship with young farmhand Bryn makes life bearable. But when he leaves to join the merchant navy, Nell is alone again, with only the promise of his return to keep her spirits up.

But Bryn's ship is sunk, and Bryn is reported drowned, leaving Nell heartbroken. Determined to bury her grief in hard work, Nell finds herself growing closer to Auntie Kath, whose harsh attitude hides a kind heart. Despite their new closeness, however, she dare not question her aunt about the mysterious photograph of a young soldier she discovers in the attic.

As time passes, the women learn to help each other through the rigours of war. And when Nell meets Bryn's friend Hywel, she begins to believe that she, too, may find love . . .

arrow books